D0985743

Praise for the Zoe Chambers Mystery Series

"I loved *Bridges Burned*. The action starts off with a bang and never lets up. Zoe's on the case, and she's a heroine you'll root for through the mystery's twists and turns—strong and bold, but vulnerable and relatable. I adore her, and you will, too."

– Lisa Scottoline,
New York Times Bestselling Author of *Betrayed*

"New York has McBain, Boston has Parker, now Vance Township, PA ("pop. 5000. Please Drive Carefully.") has Annette Dashofy, and her rural world is just as vivid and compelling as their city noir."

– John Lawton,
Author of the Inspector Troy Series

"I've been awestruck by Annette Dashofy's storytelling for years. Look out world, you're going to love Zoe Chambers."

– Donnell Ann Bell,
Bestselling Author of *Deadly Recall*

"An easy, intriguing read, partially because the townfolks' lives are so scandalously intertwined, but also because author Dashofy has taken pains to create a palette of unforgettable characters."

– *Mystery Scene Magazine*

"Dashofy has done it again. *Bridges Burned* opens with a home erupting in flames. The explosion inflames simmering animosities and ignites a smoldering love that has been held in check too long. A thoroughly engaging read that will take you away."

– Deborah Coonts,
Author of *Lucky Catch*

"Dashofy takes small town politics and long simmering feuds, adds colorful characters, and brings it to a boil in a welcome new series."

– Hallie Ephron,

MONROEVILLE PUBLIC LIBRARY Author of *There Was an Old Woman*
4000 Gateway Campus Blvd.
Monroeville, PA 15146-3381

"A vivid country setting, characters so real you'd know them if they walked through your door, and a long-buried secret that bursts from its grave to wreak havoc in a small community—*Lost Legacy* has it all."

— Sandra Parshall,
Author of the Agatha Award-Winning Rachel Goddard Mysteries

"A big-time talent spins a wonderful small-town mystery! Annette Dashofy skillfully weaves secrets from the past into a surprising, engaging, and entertaining page turner."

— Hank Phillippi Ryan,
Mary Higgins Clark, Agatha and Anthony Award-Winning Author

"Discerning mystery readers will appreciate Dashofy's expert details and gripping storytelling. Zoe Chambers is an authentic character who will entertain us for a long time."

— Nancy Martin,
Author of the Blackbird Sister Mysteries

"A terrific first mystery, with just the right blend of action, emotion and edge. I couldn't put it down. The characters are well drawn and believable...It's all great news for readers.

— Mary Jane Maffini,
Author of *The Dead Don't Get Out Much*

"Intriguing, with as many twists and turns as the Pennsylvania countryside it's set in."

— CJ Lyons,
New York Times Bestselling Author of *Last Light*

"Dashofy has created a charmer of a protagonist in Zoe Cambers. She's smart, she's sexy, she's vulnerably romantic, and she's one hell of a paramedic on the job."

— Kathleen George,
Edgar-Nominated Author of the Richard Christie Series

UNEASY PREY

**Books in the Zoe Chambers Mystery Series
by Annette Dashofy**

UNEASY PREY

A ZOE CHAMBERS MYSTERY

ANNETTE DASHOFY

HENERY PRESS

LIBRARY

MAY 17 2018

MONROEVILLE, PA

Copyright

UNEASY PREY
A Zoe Chambers Mystery
Part of the Henery Press Mystery Collection

First Edition | March 2018

Henery Press
www.henerypress.com

All rights reserved. No part of this book may be used or reproduced
in any manner whatsoever, including Internet usage, without
written permission from Henery Press, except in the case of brief
quotations embodied in critical articles and reviews.

Copyright © 2018 by Annette Dashofy
Cover art by Stephanie Savage

This is a work of fiction. Any references to historical events, real
people, or real locales are used fictitiously. Other names,
characters, places, and incidents are the product of the author's
imagination, and any resemblance to actual events or locales or
persons, living or dead, is entirely coincidental.

Trade Paperback ISBN-13: 978-1-63511-320-4
Digital epub ISBN-13: 978-1-63511-321-1
Kindle ISBN-13: 978-1-63511-322-8
Hardcover Paperback ISBN-13: 978-1-63511-323-5

Printed in the United States of America

In loving memory of my mom, Helen Riggle
04/10/1920 – 01/04/2017

ACKNOWLEDGMENTS

Uneasy Prey was a challenging book to write. My mother's health began to fail and she passed away when I was in the middle of the first draft. I'm ever so grateful to my family at Henery Press for their patience and deadline extensions during that horrible time.

Much of the story was sparked from something that happened with Mom years ago when she'd let some con men pretending to be with the water company into her home (and I thought I'd trained her better than that). Thankfully, they didn't harm or rob her, but the incident provided fodder for this tale.

As always, I had a lot of help with this book and I fear I may leave someone out, but here goes.

Thanks to Kevin Burns for patiently and thoroughly answering my questions about police procedure, to Lee Lofland and the Writer's Police Academy for letting me experience some of what law enforcement faces every day, and to Chris Herndon for helping me with questions about the coroner's office. Mistakes within these pages regarding the police, coroner, or EMS are mine and mine alone.

Much thanks to Summer Wallace, who has interviewed me numerous times for our local newspapers and who guided my creation of the reporter who plays a key role in this story. Summer, we need to meet for lunch again soon!

I can't imagine trying to write a coherent mystery without my critique group. Jeff Boarts, Tamara Girardi, and Mary "Liz Milliron" Sutton, you guys are the absolute best!

My heartfelt thanks to Art Molinares, Kendel Lynn and everyone behind the scenes at Henery Press; my editors Erin George and

Rachel Jackson; and my incredible cover artist Stephanie Savage. I love you all.

And for providing eagle-eyed proofreading services, thank you, Anne Tiller Slates, Wanda Anglin, and Edie Peterson. I can't believe how many little flubs slip past me. I'm grateful you ladies pick them up.

There aren't words enough to express my gratitude to Pennwriters and to my Pittsburgh chapter of Sisters in Crime. You are my tribe.

Thanks to Ramona Long and her morning "sprint" club on Facebook. The simple act of signing in every morning and promising to devote one hour to nothing but writing got me through my mom's illness and kept me moving forward on this book.

A shout of thanks to Tami McClain, Leta Burns, and all the gang that is the Zoe Chambers Mysteries and Friends Facebook group. You guys and gals are the reason I keep doing what I'm doing. You "get" me and I thank heavens for the fun and laughter you provide as well as the promotional support. (If you're on Facebook, search for us and join!)

A word about my fictional Golden Oaks Assisted Living. Over the years, I've dealt with several senior living facilities. Golden Oaks is none of them and all of them. I've borrowed and merged and relocated bits and pieces from various places to create what I hope is a bit of reality in fiction. The people who cared for my mom over the last two years of her life are angels on earth. I can't express how grateful I am for the safe and comfortable life for Mom that you all provided.

Lastly, I want to thank my husband. He keeps my feet on the ground when I soar too high and he raises my spirits when I get too low. Ray, you are my safe place to fall and I love you forever.

ONE

Tony DeLuca snapped a note in her direction. "Welcome back. You're up. Ninety-two-year-old female. Unresponsive."

Not the greeting Zoe Chambers had hoped for from her crew chief on her first day back at work after eight weeks of medical leave for torn ligaments in her knee. So much for easing back into the "routine," if there was such a thing on an ambulance service. Especially in the middle of January.

Tony swiveled in the office chair and bellowed toward the door to the crew lounge. "Earl!"

Zoe accepted the note and took two steps toward the garage before noticing the address.

Less than a minute later, Zoe perched on the passenger seat of Medic Two. Her long-time partner, Earl Kolter, wheeled the ambulance out of the bay and flipped on the emergency lights and siren. Just like old times.

While he drove, Zoe clamped a new run report to the aluminum clipboard in her lap and began filling it out. "This is Oriole Andrews' address, you know."

"Yep. And 'unresponsive.'" Earl echoed the information Zoe had read to him from Tony's note. "That's a new one for her."

Like most small-town ambulance services, Monongahela County EMS in southwestern Pennsylvania had its share of patients who racked up the frequent flyer miles. Oriole Andrews was one of them. Last spring she'd fallen outside while washing windows and couldn't get up. In late July, she'd stayed out in her garden too long and suffered heat exhaustion. Zoe and Earl had been on that one, and before Oriole would allow them to transport her to the hospital, she'd insisted they each accept a bag of fresh picked green beans, tomatoes, and zucchini. The woman wouldn't take no for an answer. Especially when doctors advised her to take it easy.

Zoe scribbled what information she had on the report. "I hope she wasn't out shoveling snow."

Earl snorted. "There's barely an inch on the ground. She'd wait until there was at least a foot."

Still, "unresponsive" could mean a lot of things. Had she gone out of the house on this bitter January afternoon and fallen? Hypothermia would set in quickly. Heart attack? Stroke? The woman gave the appearance of being indestructible, but at her age, anything could go wrong at a moment's notice.

Sirens whooping, they careened into the former coal mining town of Dillard, past the Vance Township Volunteer Fire Department and the police station, its parking lot empty. Earl braked as they rounded the bend at the far end of town and made the hard left turn onto Andrews Lane, named for Oriole's family. A spattering of early twentieth-century residences dotted the road. Near the top of the hill, Oriole's world-weary farmhouse predated them all. Earl cut the siren and parked at the edge of the road, next to the winter's worth of grimy snow piled knee deep by the township's plow.

Zoe stepped from Medic Two's cab into the biting chill. The dilapidated house's weathered wood siding blended with the gunmetal sky, as did the dented gray Ford Focus in the driveway. Lights blazed from the first-story windows.

As Zoe grabbed the heart monitor/defibrillator, she spotted Janie Baker, Oriole's granddaughter, stepping out onto the sloping porch, clutching a bulky cardigan at her throat. "Hurry, please," she wailed.

Earl came around from the rear of the ambulance, snatched the jump kit and portable oxygen tank, and trudged toward the house. Zoe trailed behind, picking her way around patches of ice. The last thing she needed was to slip and reinjure her newly mended knee.

Janie held the door for them, her eyes frantic. "Gram's in the basement. She must've fallen down the stairs. I can't wake her up."

Earl urged Janie to lead the way.

They followed her down a narrow hall to an open doorway. She gestured toward it. "Down there."

Earl stopped on the top step and swore so softly Zoe almost didn't hear. She craned her neck to see past her partner as they thudded down the stairs, but she didn't get a good view of the patient until they reached the bottom.

Oriole Andrews lay in a heap. One leg was twisted at an unnatural angle. An arm was pinned beneath her, either broken or dislocated. Zoe winced. The elderly woman faced a long painful recovery.

Provided she survived the fall.

Earl set the equipment down and dropped to his knees beside her. "She's breathing."

Zoe moved around her partner to kneel across from him. "Mrs. Andrews?" She patted the old woman's pale cheeks. "Oriole? Can you hear me?"

No reaction.

Earl opened the jump kit and tugged out the blood-pressure cuff. "I'll get the vitals."

Zoe started setting up the heart monitor. She glanced up at Janie, who remained at the top of the stairs, a hand pressed to her mouth. "Any idea how long she's been here?"

Janie didn't respond.

"Janie?" Zoe said, louder this time.

Hearing her name jarred her out of her stupor. "I'm sorry. What?"

Zoe repeated the question.

Janie gave a spastic shake of her head. "No. I stopped by to make sure Gram had something for supper, and if not, I was gonna cook for her. She didn't answer the door, so I let myself in. I couldn't find her anywhere. Until I looked down here. I kept telling her she didn't need to go to the basement. I could get anything she needed from down there. But she never listened to me. I've been afraid something like this would happen."

Earl released the rest of the air from the cuff and removed the stethoscope from his ears. "One-thirty-two over eighty-six."

Pretty good for a woman her age. Zoe had a feeling Janie's BP was considerably higher. They needed to do something to distract her before they ended up with two patients. "Janie, can you do us a favor? Gather all of her medications into a bag so we can take them with us to the hospital."

"Okay." She spun and disappeared from sight.

Zoe gingerly unbuttoned Oriole's flannel pajama top and began peeling and sticking the cardiac electrodes to her chest.

"Respiration's ten, pulse is thready. Pupils equal and reactive." Earl connected tubing to the oxygen tank and positioned a mask over Oriole's nose and mouth.

Oxygen in place and flowing, Earl started doing a physical assessment, palpating the woman's skull with a gentle touch. He made a humming sound in his throat. "Feels like a hematoma here. What my mom would call a nice goose egg."

"At least these stairs are carpeted."

"We probably wouldn't have any work to do if they weren't. Well, I wouldn't."

Zoe ignored her partner's reference to her secondary gig as deputy coroner. With the leads connected, she watched the rhythmic pattern dancing across the monitor. Oriole's heart rate was fast, but regular.

Voices filtered down from upstairs—Janie's and a more masculine one. The thud of footsteps approached the top of the steps.

"You guys need any help?"

Zoe glanced up at Vance Township Officer Seth Metzger. "We will when it's time to move our patient."

Janie appeared next to the young cop. "I have Gram's prescriptions." She clutched a small clear zippered plastic bag to her chest.

Earl extended a hand upward toward the granddaughter, but Zoe reached over and touched his arm, stopping him from asking Janie to bring them downstairs. If the young woman was as unsteady as her voice, she might tumble down on top of them.

"I'll get it," Zoe said. "And I'll have Seth help me bring some splints and the cot back too."

Earl eyed the stairs and then glanced around the dark basement. "Is there a better way to get her outta here?"

"I'll ask." Zoe climbed to her feet and padded up the steps.

Seth and Janie backed away from the landing to allow Zoe through the doorway into the hall.

The three prescription bottles contained routine heart and blood-pressure meds. "Your grandmother has a history of high BP?"

"Yeah." Janie pressed her fingers to her upper lip and spoke through them. "She had some atrial fibrillation too. That's an irregular heartbeat."

Zoe didn't mention that she knew what A-fib was and tried to remember if Oriole had been on the same drugs last summer. "When did they diagnosis it?"

"A couple months ago, I think. Yeah. Right before Thanksgiving."

"And the meds control it?"

"Seemed to." Janie shot a worried glance at the stairs. "At least I thought they did."

"Does she have any other health issues? Anything new?"

Janie did the spastic headshake thing again. "No. Is she...is she alive?"

Zoe gave her a comforting smile. "Very much so."

Tears brimmed in the granddaughter's eyes. "I was afraid..." She swallowed. "Is she awake?"

"Not yet." Zoe wasn't about to discuss the various closed-head injuries that could be at play. "Janie, is there an outside entrance to the basement? Some way we could bring your grandma out other than up these stairs?"

The question seemed to take Janie by surprise. She blinked. "Oh. Yeah. Around the back."

Zoe slapped Seth's arm. "Give me a hand?"

"You bet."

It took another fifteen minutes or so to ready Oriole for extrication from the basement. With the broken or dislocated shoulder immobilized, the leg velcroed into a splint, a cervical collar firmly in place, and Oriole secured to a backboard, Zoe, Earl, and Seth carried their patient and their equipment up five steps and through the exterior bulkhead to the waiting stretcher.

Janie stood to one side, her gloved hands folded and pressed to her mouth. Zoe wasn't sure if she was blowing on them to keep warm or praying. Or both.

Zoe quickly bundled the old woman against the biting cold as Earl buckled the straps.

Seth flipped his collar up. "Be careful. I did a quick job of clearing this sidewalk, but it's still slick. And kinda uneven in places."

Not to mention the two exterior lights on the house—one on the front porch and one above the bulkhead doors—didn't cast much illumination on the side of the house.

Seth and Earl flanked the head of the stretcher while Zoe guided from the foot of it. "Let's go," she said.

Moving slowly, the processional made it to the rear of the ambulance with Janie shadowing them. They were about to roll Oriole into the patient compartment when a voice carried to them from farther up the hill.

"Hey! Wait. What's going on?" A streetlight revealed a shadowy figure picking his way toward them, waving one arm.

"Oh, no." Janie started toward him. She paused to gesture to Zoe. "Go on. Take care of Gram. I'll deal with him."

The older gentleman had made it to the edge of the yard before Janie reached him. His voice sliced through the cold. "What's wrong with Oriole?"

"Go home, Trout," Janie said. "This doesn't concern you."

"Is she all right?"

"No, she's not all right. If she was, she wouldn't need an ambulance."

Zoe and Earl pushed the stretcher into the ambulance and locked it in place. "I'll drive," Earl said.

"You guys okay?" Seth asked. "I'm gonna go see what's going on with Mr. Troutman."

"Go," Zoe said. "And thanks for the help." She climbed in beside Oriole as the officer jogged away and Earl slammed the door.

Once the ambulance reached the bottom of the hill and made the turn onto Route 15, the ride smoothed out enough for Zoe to take another set of vitals. The heart monitor still revealed a steady rhythm, but the rate was slightly faster than it had been at the house. She checked Oriole's blood pressure. One-twenty over seventy. Zoe wished all her patients had a BP like that. Once again, Zoe patted the elderly woman's cheeks. "Oriole? Oriole? Can you hear me?"

Still nothing.

The trip to Brunswick Hospital usually took a half hour. At least the roads were dry.

About fifteen uneventful minutes passed with Zoe keeping an eye on the zigzagging lines dancing across the heart monitor's screen.

Every sway of the ambulance, every pothole added a squiggle; however, she could at least tell Oriole's pulse was regular.

But it was slowing. Gradually. At first, the decreased heart rate hadn't alarmed Zoe. She'd expected it to level out.

It wasn't.

She plugged the stethoscope into her ears, pressed the diaphragm to the inside of Oriole's elbow. Pumped up the cuff. Released the valve slowly. Listened. And watched the gauge.

One-oh-six over sixty-four.

Zoe didn't like it. At all. She removed the stethoscope from her ears and reached for the radio. Time to confer with the ER doc at Brunswick. Before Zoe could punch in the hospital's frequency, Oriole moaned.

Zoe set down the mic and leaned over so she was directly in the older woman's line of sight. "Oriole? Can you hear me?"

She moaned again. "Yeah." Her eyelids fluttered. Opened. Her eyes shifted as if trying to find something. Then they settled on Zoe. "What—where am I?"

"You're in an ambulance on the way to the hospital. I'm Zoe Chambers. How are you feeling?"

Another moan. "Been better."

"Well, we're taking good care of you. You just rest. You're gonna be fine."

Oriole closed her eyes for a moment, wincing in pain. When she opened them again, she fixed Zoe with a confused stare. "I remember you." Her face relaxed. "You're one of Janie's friends. And you helped me before."

Zoe gave her a smile. "Yes, I did."

"I gave you some vegetables. From my garden. You and that young man with you."

"That's right." Nothing wrong with Oriole's memory.

The woman's gaze shifted again, inspecting as much of the ambulance interior as she could with her head and neck immobilized. "What happened?"

Zoe rested a hand on Oriole's wrist. A comforting gesture. But also a chance to check her pulse. "You fell down your basement steps."

"I fell?" Oriole puzzled over the news.

Her heart rate was definitely elevated, and harder to palpate. Zoe stuck the stethoscope into her ears just as Oriole said something. Zoe removed the earpieces. "I'm sorry. What?"

The woman's face had paled even more. "I said I didn't fall."

Zoe sighed. The elderly often hated to admit to their frailty. And arguing would only upset the woman.

"Didn't fall," Oriole repeated. "I was pushed."

"Pushed? What do you mean?"

But Oriole's eyes rolled back in her head and her eyelids fluttered shut.

"Oriole? Oriole?"

Even with all the extraneous tracings from movement, Zoe could see the irregularities of her patient's heart rhythm. She jammed the stethoscope into her ears and took another reading.

Eighty over fifty-two.

Zoe slid across the bench and slammed open the sliding door between the patient and driver compartments. "Earl," she called. "Move it. She's crashing!"

TWO

Freshly showered, attired in his favorite jeans and sweatshirt, and starving for supper, Pete Adams flipped on the kitchen light. One of Zoe's orange tabbies blinked at him from the counter.

"What are you doing there?" Pete asked the cat. Then he realized he was talking to an animal. When had he started doing that? He scooped up the feline and deposited it on the floor by its half-full food bowl.

Zoe could tell the two apart. He couldn't. All he knew was one had some white on it. The other didn't. And one was female, the other male. Pete didn't care enough to check. He just called them both "Cat."

This one looked up at him with accusatory green eyes and meowed.

"You have food." Pete, however, did not.

In the eight weeks since Zoe had moved in with him, this was the first evening he had to fend for himself in the supper department. He had to admit, it was nice coming home from a day on duty as police chief in Vance Township to a hot meal. Zoe wasn't exactly a gourmet chef, but she made a mean roasted chicken. Tonight, though, she was back on her regular EMS shift, and the house felt empty.

The tabby meowed again.

Empty except for the cats.

Pete opened the refrigerator and stared at the contents. A six-pack of beer, some pizza in a zipper storage bag, and a couple of microwave bowls with lids stared back. He pulled out one of the mystery bowls and was about to thumb the lid open when someone knocked on his door.

He stuck the bowl back in the fridge. Who the hell was on his porch at seven o'clock at night? Not a resident in need of police help, or one of his officers would have phoned. Even Sylvia Bassi down the street wouldn't simply drop in after dark.

He hit the switch for the outside light and opened the door. "Nadine?"

The presence of his sister was a red flag on its own. The strained expression on her face dropped a lead weight on Pete's heart.

He held the storm door for her and moved out of her way. "Is Pop okay?"

"No, he's not okay. He's got Alzheimer's. He's never okay."

Pete closed the door on the biting cold that had escorted Nadine inside. Pointing out that their father's dementia was nothing new didn't seem like the right way to calm down his drama-queen sibling. "Is that why you're here?"

She shed her winter coat and slung it over one of the kitchen chairs. "You got a cat?" She sounded astonished.

"Two, actually."

Nadine wandered toward the tabby. It looked up at her and meowed. She scanned the counters, the stovetop, the sink, and the dishes stacked in the drainer before swinging around to look at Pete. "You have a woman living here." It was a statement of fact. Not a question.

"What makes you think that?"

"No dirty pots or plates piled everywhere. And you never had a cat in your life." Nadine arched an eyebrow. "Zoe?"

Pete didn't exactly care to go into the details of his personal life. "Why are you here, Sis? What's wrong with Pop? Besides the Alzheimer's, I mean."

Nadine picked up the cat and stroked its head. "Can't I just drop in for a visit?"

"You never drop in for a visit. The last time you showed up unannounced, you brought Pop along and left him with me." Pete's own words gave him a momentary jolt of panic. "He's not out in the car, is he?"

She rolled her eyes at him. "Of course not. It's twelve degrees out there."

"Then what are you doing here?"

Nadine held the cat closer, letting it snuggle under her chin. "I am here about Dad. He's getting harder and harder for me to handle. My blood pressure is through the roof. I'm not sleeping because he wanders all night." She swallowed. "I've made a decision. I'm putting him in an assisted-living facility."

"A nursing home?"

She cringed. "Not a 'nursing' home. It's a nice place. Or it looks nice from their website."

Pete opened his mouth, ready to chastise her for wanting to dump their father in a home. And for picking one from pictures on the computer. But he stopped and took a long look at his sister. The dark circles under her eyes. The sag of her shoulders. And when had she let her hair go gray? Pete softened his stance. "You should check it out, you know. Don't rely on what you see on their website."

"That's really why I'm here." Nadine lowered the cat to the floor and stood a little taller. "I have an appointment to tour the place tomorrow morning. I want to take Dad. And I want you to come along too."

"Me?" Pete squirmed inside. "You know I'm on duty. I might be able to come into Pittsburgh tomorrow night."

"Nighttime won't work. Pop's sundowning is getting worse. And your work shouldn't be a big issue. The place I have in mind is in Brunswick."

"Why Brunswick? I thought you'd want to at least have him close to you."

"I've had him close to me for a couple of years now. To be honest, I need some distance. And this way he'll be a lot closer to you."

Pete wondered if he was imagining the accusatory tone in her voice. *You get to take over caring for Pop. You won't be able to make excuses for not spending time with him anymore.* Pete didn't need Nadine's criticism. His own guilt cut deeper than anything his sister could say. "What's the name of the place?"

"Golden Oaks Assisted Living." She stepped around the cat, dug a business card from her jeans pocket, and set it on the kitchen table. "The street address and website is on there. Our tour is scheduled for ten o'clock." The look she gave him said *don't be late.* "I'd suggest you check it out online before we get there."

Pete fingered the card without picking it up. "What's Pop think about this?"

"You're kidding, right?"

"Not really. You aren't planning to just dump him there without him knowing what's going on, are you?"

A flash of anger sparked in her pale blue eyes. "I'm not *dumping* him anywhere. Of all the—"

Pete held up both hands. "Bad choice of words. I'm sorry. But I can't believe he's okay with this."

"He will be. He has to be." The anger faded to something else. Something Pete recognized. Guilt. The same as he felt when he didn't spend as much time with their father as he should.

"I'll be there. If something comes up, I'll call you."

She shook a finger at him. "Nothing better come up."

As if on cue, Pete's cell phone rang.

Nadine raised her voice. "And if it does, you're the police chief, for crying out loud. Have one of your officers handle it."

Zoe's photo flashed on the phone's screen. Pete turned his back to his sister and thumbed the green button. "How's your first night back at work?"

"Not so great." Zoe's voice sounded strained. "I think I need to report an assault."

Seth was already waiting at Oriole Andrews' front door when Pete arrived. "Have you gone back inside yet?"

"No, sir. I locked up for Mrs. Andrews' granddaughter once the ambulance left." Seth held up a key ring. "She told me I should hold onto this since it's a spare."

"Any sign of forced entry?"

"None. I walked the perimeter of the house. The doors are all locked and appear undisturbed."

Pete looked at the uneven pavement leading from the street to the porch. "Someone cleared the snow, so we can't tell about footprints."

Seth made a face. "That was me, Chief. Sorry. I didn't want the ambulance crew to stumble when they were bringing Mrs. Andrews out."

"Were there many tracks before you cleared it?"

"Kinda. I didn't know I was dealing with a crime scene." Seth lowered his head. "I screwed up."

"Don't worry about it." Pete might have done the same thing. He noted the letter box next to the door. The mail carrier would have come and gone. Zoe and Earl. The granddaughter. And Seth. But who else?

"Are you thinking what I'm thinking?" the young officer asked, his voice tense. "Those con men?"

"Yeah."

Two weeks ago, Janie Baker had called Pete to this very house. She'd been exasperated with her grandmother—and terrified for her at the same time. A generic white van had stopped when Oriole was home alone, and a man from the van came to the door claiming to be with the water company. She let him in and took him to the basement at his request, supposedly to check the pressure.

"I've told her and told her to never let a stranger in the house." Janie shook her head in frustration.

Oriole shrugged. "He was polite."

Apparently nothing had been stolen. Pete impressed upon the elderly woman the importance of being wary of strangers. "Don't answer the door," he told her. "Call 911 if anyone knocks. We don't mind checking things out. It's our job."

Oriole had grinned. Pete didn't believe for a minute she'd pay one bit of attention to his warnings. And now he feared these fake water-company employees may have returned. With devastating results.

Pete dug the camera from his evidence-collection kit and photographed the door, zooming in on the unmarred lock. "Open it," he told Seth.

Careful not to smudge any fingerprints, Pete hit the light switch with a gloved hand. The old house smelled dank, as if the windows hadn't been opened in a decade. A fine layer of dust coated everything from the side tables to the upholstered furniture.

"What do you want me to do, Chief?" Seth asked.

"Run tape around the yard. The county crime investigators are on their way. I'm going to photograph the interior." And keep his eyes open for anything that looked out of place.

Seth jogged off to get the crime-scene tape from his car. Alone in the house, Pete snapped pictures. Large-scale shots of the living room, dining room, and kitchen as well as tight shots of the ancient television, the marred dining table, and the ancient gas stove. Calling any of it vintage would be kind. Dilapidated was more accurate.

Nothing set off his infamous gut.

He made his way to the hallway leading to the basement door. At the end of it sat an antique-looking dresser, its drawers slightly askew, as if someone had closed them in a hurry. Had Oriole interrupted the thieves going through it?

Behind Pete a floorboard creaked. Seth or the county guys would have made their presence known upon entering. Pete straightened. Holding the camera in his left hand and keeping the right one on his sidearm, he spun.

"Holy shit," the old man at the far end of the hall yelped, clutching his chest. "I didn't know anyone was in here."

Pete relaxed. Slightly. "I could say the same thing. Mr. Troutman, isn't it?"

"Alfred Troutman. Yes, sir." He gave a nervous chuckle. "I don't know if it's a good thing or bad that the chief of police knows my name."

"What are you doing in here, Mr. Troutman?" And where was Seth, who should have stopped him outside?

"Trout, please. Everyone just calls me Trout."

Pete fixed him with a stern gaze but didn't repeat the question.

"Oh, uh. I didn't realize you were in here."

"You said that already. Why are you in here?"

Trout worked his hands as if washing them with invisible soap and water. "I saw the lights. Thought maybe Oriole had come home from the hospital." He glanced around. "Is she here?"

"No. She's still in the hospital."

"Oh. Is she okay?"

Pete studied the man. The confused eyes. The twitching of his mouth. "She's in good hands."

Trout nodded.

Pete approached the older man and put a hand on his shoulder. "If I hear anything, I'll be sure and let you know."

"Thank you. I don't think Janie would bother to tell me anything."

"Right now, though, I need you to step out of the house with me.

Okay?"

"Can't I stay here?"

"No, I'm sorry." Pete didn't want to upset the man further by telling him the house was a crime scene and therefore off limits. He guided Trout to the front entryway and was reaching for the knob when the door swung inward.

Seth recoiled. "Oh. Sorry." His eyes widened at the sight of the old man. "Where'd he come from?"

Trout squinted at him. "You know I live up the hill a ways."

"I'm aware of that." Seth shifted his gaze to Pete. "He showed up as the ambulance was leaving with Mrs. Andrews. I sent him home." Seth turned again to Trout. "What I want to know is how'd you get inside?"

He seemed puzzled by the question. "I walked. How else?"

Seth looked from Trout to Pete and made a face. "He must have slipped in when I was around back."

"It's okay. Take Mr. Troutman out to your car and take a statement from him. I get the impression he tries to keep watch over Mrs. Andrews."

Trout nodded vigorously. "I do."

"He might have seen something," Pete said to Seth. "Get any information you can from him and then make sure he gets home safely. We don't want him falling on the ice in the dark."

The officer smiled, apparently relieved that Pete wasn't going to bust his chops for allowing someone to cross a police line. "On it, Chief. And the reason I came back inside...the county guys just pulled up."

As Seth escorted Trout down the sidewalk to his patrol car, Pete watched a trio of crime-scene techs gather their gear from the county CSU truck. A figure stepped out of a dark sedan behind it, and Pete recognized the man even in the shadows cast by the streetlight.

Monongahela County Detective Wayne Baronick wore a long dark wool coat, the collar turned up against the wind. He strode toward Pete and the house. "We have to stop meeting like this," Baronick said with his trademark smile.

"Suits me. This is a big county. How do you always manage to get assigned to cases in my township?"

"I know how much you love working with me, so I have a

permanent request in to take all calls out this way."

Pete grunted. Not that he'd ever let the young detective know it, but he was glad to see him. Baronick might be overly cocky, bordering on arrogant, but he was a helluva good cop.

"What have we got?" he asked, his smile fading.

Pete updated him on Oriole Andrews' fall down the basement steps and Zoe's report that the woman had regained consciousness long enough to say she'd been pushed rather than fell. And he told Baronick about the so-called water-company employees' earlier visit.

The detective swore. "We've had a rash of those all over the county. You say nothing was stolen?"

"Not that Mrs. Andrews or her granddaughter could tell."

"These guys usually case a house on their first visit. Then they come back a day or two later to rob the place."

Pete looked around at the old woman's battered furniture and meager belongings. "I can't imagine what they planned to steal. She doesn't own a computer. Her TV has to be twenty years old. No DVD player. Hell, she still uses an old rotary phone."

"Does she keep money in the house?"

"I don't know. Possibly."

"Doesn't matter. If they believed she did, they may have roughed her up, demanding to know where she kept it hidden." Baronick shook his head. "Pisses me off. If anyone tried that with my grandparents, you can bet I'd be guilty of police brutality."

The trio of crime-scene techs approached, lugging their bags with them.

Pete held up his camera. "I already photographed the front rooms. I got interrupted at the hallway." He gestured over his shoulder. "There's a dresser back there that looks like it might have been searched."

"We'll check it out," one of the techs said.

After the team headed inside, Pete nodded toward Seth's patrol car. The interior lights were on, revealing the officer and Trout sitting inside. "Neighbor guy slipped past my officer while I was in the house. Name's Alfred Troutman. I bet he doesn't miss much on this street."

"Think maybe he saw the assailants?"

"Maybe. Seth's interviewing him now."

Baronick gazed toward the Vance Township vehicle. "It would be nice to get a license number. Something to help us nail these bastards who prey on old folks."

Pete's thoughts flashed to his father. Confused. Increasingly frail. And like Oriole Andrews or Trout, an easy victim. "We'll nail them," Pete said as much to himself as to Baronick. "No one's going to get away with brutalizing the elderly. Not on my watch."

THREE

The Emergency Department at Brunswick Hospital was quiet. The bitter cold of a January night must be keeping folks inside and out of trouble. For the most part.

Zoe replaced the linens on the cot, while keeping an eye on the cubicle down the hall where they'd left Oriole. Behind the closed privacy curtain, doctors, nurses, and assorted techs worked frantically on their patient. Chimes and beeps emanated from the room, but Zoe was too far away to make out the voices.

She had a bad feeling about the old woman's prognosis. She'd managed to keep her patient alive during the trip, but she was glad the hospital hadn't been even five miles farther away.

"Any word?" Earl appeared from around the corner, a couple bags of IV fluids in his hands to replace those they'd used.

"Nothing yet."

"Did you tell Janie what her grandmother said?"

"About being pushed? No. I figure Janie has enough to handle right now. And who knows. Oriole had a nasty blow to the head. She might not have been thinking straight."

"Uh-huh." Earl didn't sound convinced.

Zoe wasn't either. Oriole had seemed quite clear about that little detail.

From the opposite end of the hallway, Janie Baker headed toward them, clutching a cup of coffee. A young teen in oversized clothes plodded along behind her, his head lowered, a phone clutched in his hands. Marcus Baker, Janie's son. She must have collected him from home before driving to the hospital.

The strain of the evening etched deep lines in Janie's forehead and around her dark-circled eyes. She'd only been a year behind Zoe in school, but looked like she was well into her fifties instead of her mid-thirties.

"Has anyone said anything?" Janie asked.

"Afraid not," Zoe said. The nurses' station behind them was nearly deserted, with the only staff member on the phone. "Everyone's doing all they can for her."

"I know." Janie stared at the cup in her hand. "I can't believe this is happening. I always figured I'd just go over one morning and find Gram dead in her bed. I never expected..." She closed her eyes, but uncontained tears dampened her lashes. "I told her at least a dozen times not to go down those stairs. I did her laundry. There was no reason..."

Zoe moved around the stretcher to give Janie a quick hug. She searched for some words of comfort, but nothing sounded right inside her head. As a paramedic and deputy coroner, Zoe saw a lot of illness and injury. And death.

Stepping back, she turned to the boy, who still hadn't looked up from his phone. "Hey, Marcus."

He grunted an acknowledgement.

"I'm glad you're here to help your mom."

He lifted his eyes and shot a glance toward his great-grandmother's cubicle before focusing again on his phone. In that fleeting moment Zoe caught a trace of emotion in his otherwise vacant stare. But she wasn't sure which emotion. Fear. Worry. Both.

Or something else entirely.

A woman in cartoon-print scrubs rushed from the room and passed them.

"Excuse me." Janie reached out to grab at the woman's arm. "Can I go in and see my grandmother yet?"

The woman paused. Gave Janie what Zoe assumed was supposed to be a comforting smile—but wasn't. "I'm afraid not. We're still working on Mrs. Andrews, and there isn't that much room in there. Why don't you go out to the waiting area? We'll call as soon as we know anything." The nurse patted Janie's arm and then whisked away.

"They told me that before too." Janie held up the cup of coffee. "I got this and intended to sit down out there with it. But I couldn't. I want to be here. To see Gram as soon as they'll let me."

"I know, but the nurse has a point," Zoe said. "You don't want to be in the way and hamper their efforts. They'll be taking your grandma for x-rays and a CT scan. Possibly even surgery. It's gonna be a long night. You might as well rest while you can."

Janie's gaze shifted to the room where all the action was taking place. "I guess you're right. I'm just...scared." She looked at Zoe. "You said she regained consciousness in the ambulance. That has to be a good sign, right?"

Zoe forced an encouraging smile. "Sure. Regaining consciousness is always a good thing." Except when the patient's BP tanks and she immediately loses consciousness again. But Janie needed to cling to whatever hope she could find. Zoe wasn't about to snatch it away.

Another round of warning beeps and whistles went off inside Oriole's room. From over the PA, a calm yet urgent voice announced, "Code blue in room twelve. Code blue in room twelve." The woman who had passed by only a minute earlier rushed back into the cubicle. Two other nurses hurried into Oriole's room too.

Marcus kept his head lowered, but his eyes shifted toward the activity.

Janie's hand holding the coffee trembled. "What's going on?"

Zoe caught Earl's knowing glance. She slipped her arm around Janie's shoulders. "Come on. I'll walk with you and Marcus out to the waiting room."

"No. Not until you tell me what's going on."

How could Zoe tell her that her grandmother had gone into cardiac arrest? She couldn't. Not with Janie as fragile as she was. "They're having some complications they need to deal with. I know you want to stay close, but they can't help your gram if they're tripping over you in the hall."

The forlorn look Janie cast at room twelve told Zoe she wasn't fooling anyone. But Janie drew a sobbing breath and nodded.

Pete had gotten the call from Zoe as the county crime techs started processing the basement. Oriole hadn't made it. The news dropped a solemn blanket over the crew.

By eight a.m., Pete headed home to get a shower and wash the smell of dust and mildew from his skin. Getting it out of his nostrils would take more than that. Then again, he planned to attend Oriole's autopsy. Mold wasn't the worst smell he would encounter today.

By the time he'd dried off and put on a clean uniform, he heard the lock on his kitchen door click. Zoe let herself in. She dropped her handbag on the floor and sunk into the nearest chair, lifting one of the tabbies into her lap. Her exhausted blue eyes met his. "Hi."

"Hi, yourself." He crossed to her, leaned down, and planted a kiss on top of her blonde head. "Rough night?"

Her short laugh sounded a lot like a sob. "Yeah. For you too, I guess."

"I've had better."

She gave the cat one more stroke and let it slide to the floor with a soft thud and meow before she stood and surrendered into his arms. "Did you find any evidence of foul play or do you think it might have been an accident?"

"Accident? You're the one who called to tell me Oriole said she'd been pushed."

"I know. But she had a head injury. I've been hoping she was imagining things. I just can't imagine who would push Oriole down the basement stairs."

"I can." Pete told Zoe about the con men posing as water-company employees.

"And you think they came back?"

"I think it's very likely. This may be the first incident we've had here in Vance Township, but Baronick told me these punks gain access when the resident is there to let them in and then go back when they're less likely to be caught."

Zoe's expression darkened. "I'd like to get my hands on them."

Pete had seen what Zoe was capable of when cornered. He smiled. "Anyway, the autopsy's this morning. We should know more afterwards."

"You going?"

"Yep."

"Me too. But I need to stop at the barn first to feed and turn out the horses. I'll meet you there."

Which reminded Pete of his other morning task. "I have a favor to ask you."

Zoe tipped her head and gave him a provocative grin. "Again?"

A rush of heat not caused by the house's furnace surged through him. "Later," he said, keeping his voice low. "No, this isn't that kind of favor. Nadine stopped here last evening. Pop's getting to be too much for her—"

"She wants to leave Harry here for a while?"

"No. She's decided to place him in an assisted-living facility." Pete enunciated the words clearly. Not a nursing home as he'd called it and been corrected. An assisted-living facility. "The place she picked is in Brunswick so he can be closer to me. She's bringing Pop out to tour it this morning at ten and wants me there."

Zoe gave him the same look Pete's mother used to fix him with when he wasn't exactly telling the whole truth. "And the favor is...?"

"I thought about asking you to go in my place." He was only half kidding. Even though he knew better, he still hoped she might say, "Oh, sure. No problem."

Instead, she said, "You need to do this."

Damn. "Yeah, I know. But would you at least go with me? Pop really likes you even if he doesn't remember your name. And you're good with him."

"You don't have to sell me on it. Of course I'll go with you. What's the name of the place?"

What was the name of the place? Pete held up one finger and moved to the kitchen table where Nadine had left the card. "Golden Oaks Assisted Living."

"I know where that is."

He was afraid to ask. "Is it...nice?"

"I've never been inside. But I've driven past it. Looks okay from the outside."

Great. Except Harry Adams wasn't going to be living on the outside.

The stop at the Krolls' barn took longer than Zoe had planned. She wished her cousin Patsy would come home from Florida and stay a while. Patsy Greene kept her horse at the barn Zoe managed and had always been a huge help with the chores when Zoe was on duty. However, since Patsy had discovered their familial connection, including the part about having a cousin—Zoe's mother—in Florida, she'd taken full advantage of the open invitation to visit the Sunshine State any time she wanted.

It was an invitation that did not extend to Zoe. And that suited her just fine.

This morning, the horses had been exceptionally frisky, racing loops around the indoor arena and kicking up their heels rather than heading straight out to the pasture when she opened their stall doors. By the time she made it to Brunswick and the morgue, the autopsy was well underway. Rather than suit up, she took a seat in the office and watched through the observation window.

Pete stood inside the autopsy suite with his back to her. County Coroner Franklin Marshall, Forensic Pathologist "Doc" Abercrombie, and a young female assistant hovered around the body on the table. Zoe couldn't hear the conversation or see facial expressions, but Franklin's body language told her he was not pleased.

The door swung open and Wayne Baronick stopped midstride. "Zoe. I didn't expect to see you here."

"Why not? I was at the scene last night. I'm a deputy coroner. Why wouldn't I be here?"

He smiled and stepped the rest of the way into the office. "I meant out here." He gestured at the room. "As opposed to in there." He thumbed at the window to the autopsy suite. "The smell still get to you?"

She'd never live down her history of bolting for the restroom during her first dozen or so autopsies. "Yeah, but I can handle it now." Mostly. "No, I was late and decided not to barge in halfway through the procedure."

"Uh-huh." He wasn't buying it. "So do we know anything yet?"

Before Zoe could tell him she'd arrived only a few minutes earlier, Franklin turned away from the table and headed toward Pete. The coroner spotted her at the window and raised a hand in acknowledgment. "No," she said to Wayne. "But we're about to."

Franklin stripped out of his protective gear and a moment later joined them in the office. He glared at her. "You're late."

"I know. Sorry," she said as Pete trailed in behind Franklin and closed the door. She'd been late so often and used all of her excuses so many times, she decided to leave it at that.

"Find anything interesting?" Wayne asked.

Franklin took a seat at the desk. "The deceased had fractures of the right tibia and fibula, the left clavicle, and two ribs. She suffered a blow to the left parietal region," he said, touching the side of his own head, "resulting in a subdural hematoma. All consistent with a fall down a flight of stairs. The head injury caused her to lose consciousness. It did not, however, cause her death."

Wayne crossed his arms. "What was COD then?"

"Exsanguination. She bled out due to a tear in her aorta. Basically, during the fall her heart was partly torn away from the aorta, causing her chest cavity to fill up. If it weren't for the concussion, she might very well have been up and walking around following the fall. At least until the blood loss became significant. At that point she would've crashed."

Which was what happened in the ambulance. "But you can't tell whether she fell on her own or was pushed," Zoe said.

"On the contrary. In addition to the more obvious injuries, we discovered some fresh perimortem bruising on her upper arms."

"What kind of bruising?" Wayne asked.

Franklin exchanged a look with Pete, who, from his scowl, appeared to already know the answer. Franklin mimed two claw hands gripping air. "Someone grabbed Mrs. Andrews by the arms with considerable force. I think it's a valid assumption that there was a struggle, at which time she was either pushed or fell down the stairs as a result."

The room fell silent. Zoe imagined the scene. An intruder demanding money. Oriole, scared and alone, probably gave him whatever she could. He wanted more. Grabbed her. Shook her. Terrorized the old woman. And ultimately shoved her. The fall. The pain. The screams.

Zoe suspected Pete, Franklin, and Wayne were visualizing variations of the same thing. "We have to nail these guys," she said.

Pete's eyes glinted. "We will."

Zoe's phone put a halt to further comment. The Krolls' number came up on her screen. The owners of the farm where she kept her horse. She excused herself and ducked out into the hallway to take the call.

"Zoe?" Mrs. Kroll sounded odd. "I hope I'm not interrupting anything."

"Of course not. What's wrong?"

"Oh, nothing really." The tension in her voice said the opposite. "It's just...well, I think I've done something bad. Can you come over?"

Zoe thought of her promise to accompany Pete to Golden Oaks. "What did you do that was bad?"

"I'd rather not say over the phone."

"Are you okay? Did you fall?"

"No, no. Nothing like that. If you're busy, don't worry about it."

Zoe still didn't like Mrs. Kroll's tone. She knew the older woman was alone at the farm since Mr. Kroll had been admitted to the hospital late last week for chest pains. "I'm in Brunswick right now. I can stop on my way home."

"Wonderful. That will be fine. I'll see you soon."

"Is everything all right?" Pete asked as he joined her in the hall outside the morgue.

Zoe pocketed her phone. "I don't know. Mrs. Kroll asked me to stop on my way home."

"Did she say why?"

"No. She sounded...I don't know...embarrassed. Said she didn't want to tell me over the phone."

He reached over and ran a hand up and down her back. "If you want to skip touring the nursing home, I understand."

She looked up at him and noticed the uncharacteristic nervous tension in his ice-blue eyes. "No way. I haven't gone with you to see Harry in a couple of weeks. I'll take the tour with you, but I'll skip out when you start to talk business."

"Business?"

"Yeah. You know. Money. Levels of care. All that fun stuff."

"Great," Pete mumbled. He checked his watch. "I guess we'd better go."

"I need to talk to Franklin a minute. I'll meet you over there."

Once he left, Zoe slipped back into the morgue and found the county coroner and Wayne going over some paperwork. "Franklin? Do you have a minute?"

He glanced at Wayne. "I'm done here," the detective said. "Send me your preliminary report as soon as it's ready."

"Of course."

Wayne paused at the door and turned to wink at Zoe. "When you get bored with that small potatoes police chief, call me. I'll take you out for dinner and dancing."

She grinned at him. Wayne's flirtation had become a game between them, although he usually made a point of hitting on her in Pete's presence. "When I get bored, you'll hear from me," she said, knowing it would never happen.

He winked again and was gone.

Franklin faced her, crossing his arms. "You want to ask me about the case?"

"Actually, this has nothing to do with Oriole. Do you know anything about Golden Oaks Assisted Living?"

The question seemed to startle him. "Why?"

If Pete hadn't told him about his dad, Zoe wasn't about to. "Just checking for a friend."

"I've been to the facility a number of times, but in my funeral-home-director capacity. Not as coroner, if that's what you mean. And I've never been called upon to investigate them or anyone who's died there."

"That's exactly what I mean. Thanks."

FOUR

Pete helped his father out of the backseat of Nadine's sedan in front of the double doors of Golden Oaks. The sidewalk and driveway were dry, with a smattering of salt crystals providing evidence that the maintenance crew was doing their job.

Nadine sped off to find a place to park, leaving Pete with Harry staring at the entrance. A security keypad was mounted to the wall next to the doors, along with a button, an intercom, and a sign stating late-hours visitors should buzz for admittance.

Pete looked down at his father. Harry Adams had definitely declined in recent months. Getting shot last summer hadn't helped. Now his frail frame seemed lost inside the winter coat that used to fit like it was custom made. He clutched a cane in one thin hand, Pete's arm with the other. Pete knew he needed to get Harry inside and out of the cold, but the thought of crossing that threshold—into that world—rooted his feet to the ground.

Harry didn't seem especially keen on the idea either. He eyed the varnished oak doors with their polished brass fixtures. "Looks fancy."

"Yes, it does, Pop."

"I don't need any of that...what do you call it? Filet mignon? Just take me someplace I can get a good burger. And a milkshake."

Harry thought they were going out for dinner and this was a restaurant. "We'll get a milkshake later," Pete told him. "Hey, Pop, did you know Zoe's going to meet us here?"

"Zoe? That's nice."

But Pete could tell his father had no clue who Zoe was.

Nadine hurried toward them, her boots crunching on the heavily salted walk. "Okay, let's go in."

Pete glanced toward the street. "Zoe'll be here in a few minutes."

"She can find us inside. It's too cold to wait out here."

They stepped through the double doors into a spacious entryway decorated with antiques. Or faux antiques. Floral and lace draperies hung in the windows. Forties big-band music drifted through the air along with the smell of potpourri. To their right was a sitting area done up like a formal living room complete with an upright piano. To the left, a currently unoccupied dining room. In front of them, a woman sat behind a desk next to a sweeping staircase.

Not at all what Pete had imagined.

The woman at the desk smiled at them. "May I help you?"

Nadine stepped forward. "We have a ten o'clock appointment for a tour."

"Wonderful." The woman gestured toward the living room. "Please have a seat. I'll let Connie know you're here."

No sooner had they gotten Harry settled in a sturdy but comfortable-looking chair than Zoe breezed in, paused to look around, and headed over to them.

"Sorry I'm late." She smiled at Pete and then at his sister. "Hi, Nadine."

The two exchanged a quick hug before Zoe stepped over to Harry. "Well, hello, handsome."

He beamed at her. "Hello, sunshine." She bent down, wrapped him in an embrace, and kissed his cheek. "Pete told me you were coming."

So he did remember her. Or he did a helluva job of faking it. Pete wasn't sure which.

"We're waiting to be seated," Harry added.

Pete whispered in Zoe's ear, "He thinks we're here for dinner."

To Harry, Zoe said, "I hope we get served soon. I'm starved."

A thin woman with short gray hair bustled toward them, extended a hand, and introduced herself as Connie Smith. After making a fuss over Harry, she directed them to follow her.

The tour took maybe ten minutes as Connie showed them the different style of rooms available as well as the nurses' stations, activities room, and the dining room. Pete trailed behind the others. Nadine and Harry, arm in arm, stayed with Connie, the two women discussing details, Harry looking around in a daze. Zoe kept veering off to chat with residents, some in wheelchairs, others in easy chairs. Pete felt their eyes on him, scrutinizing the man in the uniform.

Why hadn't he worn his civvies?

Because, technically, he was on duty.

When the tour concluded, Nadine directed Pete to take Harry back out to the living room while she conducted business with Connie. From the satisfied expression on his sister's face, Pete surmised the decision had been made, with or without his approval.

He sat with his father on a sofa. Zoe perched on an ottoman facing them and took one of Harry's hands in hers. "This place is pretty swanky, don't you think?"

He didn't answer. Instead he continued to scan the room with a perplexed scowl.

She turned her gaze to Pete. "What about you?"

"Better than I expected."

She tapped Harry on the knee to get his attention. "I wouldn't mind moving in here."

He brightened. "Are you and Pete going to live here after you get married?"

Pete wasn't sure if Zoe laughed or choked.

"I already have a house, Pop," he said a little too quickly. But at least his father seemed to realize it wasn't a restaurant.

Zoe regained her composure and checked her watch. "I should be going. I promised Mrs. Kroll I'd stop and find out what she did that was so awful."

Pete stood with her, but she motioned for him to sit back down. "I know my way out. You stay with Harry." She bent down to give him another kiss on the cheek. "Good seeing you again."

"Behave yourself, sunshine," he told her with a wink. "Take care of that son of mine."

"Will do." She grinned at Pete. "I'll see you at home later."

"You bet."

He watched her go, wishing her thigh-length winter jacket was just a bit shorter.

"She's a good girl," Harry said once Pete was seated again.

"Yes, she is."

"You ever gonna marry her?"

"One of these days. If she'll have me."

Harry nudged him with an elbow. "She will." He grew somber, looking around the room, his gaze settling on a white-haired gent pushing an equally white-haired woman toward the dining room in a wheelchair. "This is a really nice place."

Pete relaxed. Maybe the transition wouldn't be as rocky as he'd feared.

"Really nice," Harry repeated. He nodded and then added, "But I sure as hell never want to end up in a place like this."

"Thank goodness," Mrs. Kroll said as she opened the sliding-glass door for Zoe. "I'm so glad you're here."

The modular home sat on part of the footprint of what had been a circa-1850s farmhouse—a venerable old structure the Krolls had shared with Zoe. And one she still missed as if it were a member of her family.

Zoe stomped a skiff of snow from her boots, stepped into the overly warm house, and slipped out of her jacket. "I came as soon as I could. What's wrong?"

Mrs. Kroll pulled out a dining-room chair and motioned for Zoe to sit in it. "I have coffee made. Do you want some?"

She ignored the chair. "You sit down and let me get it."

Mrs. Kroll waved off the offer and shuffled into the kitchen.

Rather than stand there and argue, Zoe followed her and leaned back against the counter as the older woman filled two waiting cups. "What is it you did that was so bad?"

Mrs. Kroll handed her a steaming mug and made a pained face. "This nice young man came to my door this morning. Told me he was from the water company and needed to come in and check my pipes."

A chill icier than the January winter pierced Zoe's brain. "Mrs. Kroll, you don't have city water."

"I know. And I told him that. But he said they were going to run lines out here next week and were testing residents' pipes to make sure they could handle the increased pressure." She grinned sheepishly. "He was so nice and polite."

And, if Oriole was any evidence, deadly. "You didn't let him in, did you?"

"Well, yes. He seemed so..."

"Nice." Zoe's jaw ached at the word.

"Yes," Mrs. Kroll said brightly, pleased that Zoe understood. "He wanted me to take him down into the basement, but of course this new house is on a slab."

Thank heavens. Oriole hadn't fared so well with the basement stairs.

"So he had me take him back into the bathroom and flush the toilet."

Zoe eased around the corner to glance into the living room. The TV and DVR were still there. And the Krolls didn't own a computer to steal. "Where's your purse?"

"In my bedroom."

Which they would've had to pass through to get to the bathroom. "Did you check it to make sure your money's still in there?"

"No." Mrs. Kroll dragged the word out.

"You should do that now. And check any other money you might have stashed around here." Zoe dug her phone from her pocket. "I'm gonna call Pete."

Mrs. Kroll fluttered a hand at her. "Oh, you needn't bother him."

"Yeah, I do. What kind of car was this guy driving?"

"A white van. It looked very businesslike."

"Did it have a logo or emblem on the side?"

"No." That same doubtful tone. "There was a second person who stayed in the van. He looked like he was texting on his phone."

"Did the guy who was in here have his phone out?"

"No. He had one of those bigger gizmos. What d'ya call them?"

"A tablet?"

"Yeah. He was making notes on one of those."

Probably communicating with his partner outside. Sending him a list of what they might come back for.

"He might have been telling the truth. Maybe we are gonna get city water out this way."

If they were, Zoe would've heard about it. "Afraid not. Go make sure your cash is still where you kept it. I'm calling Pete."

*   *   *

It was almost noon by the time Pete returned to Dillard and the Vance Township Police Station. His sister had signed the papers and written a check to Golden Oaks after the Connie woman assured them a room would be available later in the week. Just as soon as it had received a fresh coat of paint and the carpeting had been cleaned. The staff all appeared genuinely caring and skilled. The home seemed more like a bed and breakfast than a hospital or rehab facility. But he still couldn't shake the heartache of Harry's comment.

I sure never want to end up in a place like this.

A gray Chevy sedan sat in front of the station with a woman behind the wheel. Pete parked the Explorer in his usual spot and headed inside.

Nancy, his secretary, had the phone wedged between her ear and her shoulder and held up one finger to stop him outside her door. "He just walked in. I'll give him the message." She hung up and glared at him. "It's about time you got here."

"I was at the morgue."

The glare didn't waver. She held out a handful of pink message slips. "Most of these are reporters wanting a quote. Lucky for you they've already talked to Detective Baronick or they'd have been camped out front."

He took the stack and thumbed through them. Baronick and his veneered smile were good for something.

"One of those is from Janie Baker. She wants to know when she can get back in her grandmother's house to get some things."

"Once the crime-scene team is done," Pete said more to himself than to Nancy. "I'll call and talk to her."

"And there have been several calls from some of our older residents or their families. They're worried something like this might happen to them or their loved ones."

"Not if I can help it."

"One more thing," Nancy said just as the front door swung open, setting the attached bells to jingling. The woman from the gray Chevy stepped inside with a leather satchel slung over her shoulder. Nancy tipped her pen at the woman. "This lady is here to talk to you."

The woman gave him an appraising look before offering him a hand and a smile. "Lauren Sanders. I'm a reporter with *The Phillipsburg Enterprise.*"

Pete studied the woman as he shook her hand. "I'm sorry, but the last I heard, Phillipsburg doesn't have a newspaper. Hasn't since before I moved here."

"Which was eight years ago. *The Phillipsburg Gazette* went out of business ten years ago when their parent company downsized."

"You've done your homework. But that doesn't change the fact that—"

"*The Enterprise* is a new weekly edition being put out by the same publisher who owns several other papers in the tri-state region." She held out a business card, which confirmed in print what she'd just told him. "I'm new to the area, but you're right. I've done my homework. Right now I'm working on a story about the series of home invasions involving senior citizens taking place around Monongahela County. I was hoping you'd grant me an interview about last night's homicide."

Something about the glint in the woman's eyes made Pete think he was dealing with a human pit bull. This wasn't some eager kid, but rather a newshound determined to make a name for herself. Or at least a byline. "County Detective Wayne Baronick is handling the media on this case. You should check with him."

"I already have. He's very good at talking a lot without saying much."

Pete struggled against smiling. "And you think I would tell you more?"

"If I ask the right questions, yes."

"Sorry. I have no comment at this time." He pinched her business card between his index and middle fingers and aimed it back at her.

She refused to take it. "Can you at least confirm a few specifics? I understand two men in a white van claiming to be utility workers forced their way into the victim's home several days prior to her death?"

"Forced" wasn't quite the right word. Oriole had invited them in. Pete suspected the reporter was baiting him into a response, and he wasn't about to be drawn into her trap. "No comment."

"Oh, come on, Chief. Detective Baronick already told me that much."

"Then quote him. Not me." Pete's cell phone rang.

"Shouldn't you issue a warning to older residents to use caution and not open their doors to utility workers unless they show proper credentials?"

Zoe's name and photo appeared on screen. Pete set the reporter's business card down on the counter. "Excuse me. I have to take this."

He turned and headed down the hall. The reporter's voice trailed after him, but he answered the call and plugged his other ear so he couldn't make out what she said.

"Hey, Zoe. I'm glad you called."

"Really?"

"Yeah." He ducked into his office. "Your timing is perfect."

"You may not think so after I tell you why."

He froze. "Oh?"

"I need you to come out to the farm. I think the same guys who attacked Oriole Andrews stopped here this morning. And Mrs. Kroll let one of them into the house."

FIVE

Mrs. Kroll sat at her dining-room table, a sheepish grin on her face, when Pete arrived. "I wish Zoe hadn't called you."

Zoe leaned in the doorway to the kitchen, arms crossed, giving Pete a wide-eyed look of exasperation.

"I'm glad she did," he told the older woman. "This is serious."

"I know." Mrs. Kroll may have been in her late seventies, but she sounded like a belligerent teenager.

In a whispered exchange, as Zoe let him into the house, he'd learned Mrs. Kroll didn't yet know about Oriole Andrews. Zoe had been afraid to break the news to her alone. Right now, Pete preferred getting as many answers from the older woman as possible before sending her into a panic. "Tell me what happened."

Mrs. Kroll glanced at Zoe. "Ask her."

"I'd rather hear it from you."

With a sigh, Mrs. Kroll launched into her tale of the nice young man from the water company who came to her door and was so polite.

"Did the second man come inside at all?"

"No. He never got out of the van."

That she was aware of. Pete wondered what that second person had done while the first one kept Mrs. Kroll occupied with toilet flushing. He glanced at Zoe. "Is anything missing?"

"I had her check her cash. Nothing seems to have been taken."

The unspoken word "yet" hung between them.

"And while we were waiting for you, I went outside and checked for footprints in the snow. The second guy didn't leave the van."

Pete looked at Mrs. Kroll. "Did you happen to get a license number?"

"No. I never thought anything about it until after they left. Then I got to wondering if maybe I'd done something I shouldn't. That's when I called Zoe."

"You're here alone?"

"Marvin's in the hospital again. He's supposed to be released tomorrow morning."

Not that an elderly man in the house would be any help against a young killer. "Can you give me a description of the men?"

"I didn't really see the one in the van."

"What about the one who came in the house?"

"He was young."

"How young?"

"Oh, I don't know. Like you and Zoe."

Pete was forty-six. Zoe, ten years younger. "Are you sure?"

"Not really. All you kids look young to me. I could swear my doctor can't be more than twelve."

"What about his hair? His eyes?"

"Brown hair, brown eyes."

"Did you notice anything about the way he spoke?"

Mrs. Kroll gave this one some thought, but answered, "No. He sounded like anyone else. Just more polite than most."

Perfect. They were looking for a well-mannered male under the age of fifty—maybe—with dark hair and eyes. "Was there anything at all about him that struck you as unusual? Or noticeable? A birthmark? A tattoo?"

"No."

"How about jewelry? Did he wear any rings? Or have any piercings?"

"Not that I saw." Mrs. Kroll scowled. "Is all this really necessary? I promise not to open the door to strangers ever again. Can't we leave it at that?"

Pete met Zoe's gaze and knew she was thinking about another elderly woman. He came back to Mrs. Kroll. "I'm afraid we can't." He stuffed his notebook back in his pocket and knelt, taking her bony hand in his. "Listen. If anyone ever comes to your door that you don't know, I want you to call 911 and tell them. I'll come out, or one of my men will."

"I don't want to bother you."

He'd had this same conversation with Oriole the day Janie had called him. "It's not a bother. It's our job. Any utility with a legitimate crew out or anyone who's legally going door to door...we'll know about them."

"I don't see the need to trouble you." She fidgeted. "Okay, I promise to call. But it really isn't a big deal. He didn't do anything or steal anything."

Pete exchanged another glance with Zoe before meeting and holding Mrs. Kroll's gaze. "I assume you haven't heard the news today."

For the first time, a look of trepidation crossed the older woman's face. "I don't usually turn the TV on when Marvin isn't here. And it's been too cold to go down to the box for the paper."

"Do you know Oriole Andrews?"

"Yes, of course. We've been on a number of committees together. Oh, not in recent years, but..." Mrs. Kroll's voice trailed off and tears of apprehension welled in her rheumy eyes. "Why?"

Zoe joined Pete at Mrs. Kroll's side as he broke the news about Oriole's death.

"You think the men who were here this morning," Mrs. Kroll said, her voice damp and choked, "killed Oriole last night?"

"We think it's a good possibility."

"Oh dear lord." Mrs. Kroll pulled her hand free from Pete's and rummaged through her pockets, coming up with a tissue. "Do you—do you think they might come back here?"

"They may. Can you go stay with your son for a few days? Or can he come here?"

"No, no, no." Her voice was muffled through the tissue. "I'm not leaving my home so some hoodlum could come and do as he pleases. And Alexander has a job and family to deal with."

Zoe cleared her throat. "I'll stay with her."

Mrs. Kroll turned to her, straightening in her chair. "Oh, Zoe dear. Would you? That would be wonderful."

Pete hadn't anticipated this turn of events. "No."

Mrs. Kroll looked at him, pleading. "Oh, please. It would be like old times. Zoe's shared my home before and we get along splendidly."

How the two women got along wasn't the issue. He stood, fixed Zoe with a stern gaze, and tipped his head toward the living room.

She excused herself from Mrs. Kroll and joined him. "She's right. We get along well. And she'll be more comfortable with me staying here than if she had to move out."

"That's not the point, and you know it."

"It'll just be temporary. Until you catch these guys. Then I'll be back."

"That's not the point either." Although he couldn't help but think how hard he'd lobbied to get her to move in with him in the first place.

She gave him that flirtatious grin that drove him crazy. "I'll leave my cats with you as collateral."

"That isn't the point," he repeated through clenched teeth. "What's going to stop these guys from doing to you what they did to Oriole?"

Zoe planted her hands on her hips. "Because they're cowards. They only prey on the elderly and the weak. You don't see them targeting any capable adults, do you?"

"What makes you think you're so intimidating that you'd scare them away?"

Any hint of that sexy grin was gone. "Hey. I ride horses. I sling hay bales. I handle pitchforks. If I can get kicked by a thousand-pound animal and come back yelling loud enough to put him in his place, I can handle some young punk who gets his jollies bullying little old ladies."

Pete had seen her kick some serious bad-guy ass in the past. But he'd also seen her nearly die at this very spot. "You're not as tough as you think. I won't have you and Mrs. Kroll becoming their next two victims."

Zoe's face clouded at the suggestion that he doubted her ability to take care of herself. "She's not going to leave her home. And I'm not leaving her alone."

Before the discussion could escalate into a full-fledged screaming match, Pete's cell phone rang. Caller ID revealed the station's number. "What?" he snapped.

Nancy's voice was understandably icy. "One of the crime-scene techs up at the Andrews' house just called and asked you to respond. There's some sort of trouble with the family." After a pause, she added, "And you could use some work on your phone manners."

*   *   *

Pete knew he hadn't dissuaded Zoe of her bone-headed delusions. Part two of that debate would have to wait until after he dealt with Oriole's family.

He was better acquainted with Marcus Baker than with Janie. At only thirteen, the kid had already tiptoed the fine line between innocent pranks and delinquent behavior, tumbling more than once to the side requiring a visit—and a stern lecture—from Pete.

In his few encounters with Janie Baker, she'd struck him as timid. Mousey. Not homely by any means, and perhaps she might even be pretty if she made half an effort. But she tended to slouch, walking with her head down, rarely smiling. Her drab winter coat appeared decades out of style and several sizes too large, probably purchased from a secondhand store.

When Pete arrived at Oriole's house that afternoon, Janie behaved like the old Mad Mouse rollercoaster he remembered as a kid. As he pulled up, he caught a glimpse of her pacing outside the yellow crime-scene tape.

The moment she spotted him, she scurried to his car. "You didn't return my calls."

"You're right. I didn't. And I'm sorry."

Dark circles framed her bloodshot eyes. "They won't let me back in Gram's house."

"They will. As soon as they're done." He hesitated to use the term *processing the crime scene.*

Janie half turned, gazing at the old house with a look of forlorn desperation in her moist eyes. "Done?" She spun back to Pete. "They've been at it for hours. Gram was in the basement. I just want to go upstairs to her room to pick out—" Her voice caught and she lowered her face from his view for a moment. Once again lifting her chin, she said, "I need to choose an outfit for Gram to be buried in."

He patted Janie's sloped shoulder. "Let me find out how much longer they'll be."

"Thank you, Chief. I'd appreciate that."

She refused his offer to sit in the heated SUV, so he left her standing next to the vehicle while he ducked under the police tape and approached the house.

Before he reached the front porch, the door opened and one of the techs stepped out carrying a brown paper bag. Instead of moving aside, the tech blocked Pete's way. "Chief Adams, I'm glad to see you." The tech glanced past Pete and made a face. "That woman out there has been driving us nuts."

"She's the victim's granddaughter. More than that, she's been the victim's caregiver for as long as I've known them. Cut her some slack, okay?"

The tech bristled. "You can't mean let her inside before we're finished processing."

"Of course not."

"Okay. Because that seems to be what she wants."

"I'm sure she's overwhelmed with final arrangements and isn't thinking about what we, as law enforcement, have to do." Pete offered the young tech a knowing smile. "We need to have some compassion for the living while seeking justice for the deceased."

The tech's hard scowl softened. "You're right. But I still can't let her contaminate my crime scene."

"I agree. Just remember, our crime scene was her home. How much longer until you finish up?"

"We're almost done. Shouldn't be more than another twenty or thirty minutes."

"I'll let her know. By the way, did you find anything?"

"Nothing that jumps out at us. No signs of forced entry. Possible evidence of a struggle in the one bedroom where the old lady slept."

Pete winced at "old lady." This kid needed people skills if he ever hoped to work with the public. "A struggle in the bedroom?"

"Or maybe she just fell out of bed. It's hard to judge at this point."

Pete thanked the tech and returned to Janie, who was holding her collar up to her ears against the breeze.

"They'll be another twenty or thirty minutes."

Her pained expression told of her displeasure.

"I need you to do something for me."

The distraction worked. She blinked and her face softened. "What?"

"Go through the house as soon as you get a chance and let me know if anything's missing."

"You think whoever pushed Gram down the stairs robbed her too?"

"It's very possible."

"She didn't have much worth stealing." Janie gazed wistfully at the old house. "But I'll do my best."

Pete touched her shoulder. "Good girl. Now why don't you go home and warm up until they finish."

She watched the young tech with the brown bag cross the yard to their van. "Thank you, Chief. But I'll wait here." She looked up and met Pete's gaze. "Gram may be gone, but this is still her house. And her stuff. You know?"

Pete found himself thinking of Harry being moved from their family home into Nadine's house and now to an assisted-living facility, leaving his stuff—and what memories he had left—behind. If only he'd been as fortunate as Oriole, living and eventually dying at home. "Yeah," Pete said. "I know."

Zoe parked her battered Chevy pickup—the one Pete had been trying for months to get her to sell—in her old spot on the hillside above the Kroll house. She slid down, dragged the laundry basket full of her things across from the passenger side, and braced it against one hip while she slammed the door. Pete would be furious when he learned she'd gone home, packed, and moved in with Mrs. Kroll against his wishes, but he'd have to get over it.

Gazing at the modular home, Zoe remembered a very different structure. The massive farmhouse in which she'd once lived. She looked down at the basket containing some jeans and sweatshirts, a uniform for her next shift, and her toiletries. She'd left here last summer with nothing but the sooty clothes on her back. And the cats.

The throaty rumble of an engine drew her out of her memories. A white Toyota Tundra crawled up the slippery farm lane from Route 15. Zoe lugged her laundry basket to the rear of her pickup and waited. The Toyota swung off the lane and stopped.

The driver's window powered down, revealing a smiling, suntanned Patsy Greene. "What's going on? You moving back in?" Her tone was joking.

"As a matter of fact, I am."

Patsy's smile turned to shock. "Why? Oh, don't tell me you and Pete—?"

"We're fine." Better than fine most days, but Zoe didn't care to discuss their current disagreement with Patsy. "I'm just going to stay with Mrs. Kroll a few days."

"Is she okay?"

"She's good. When did you get back from Florida?"

"Late yesterday. This is the first time I've been able to get over here. Are the horses all right?" Patsy's cautious tone told Zoe she was still seeking the rationale for the move back to the farm.

Zoe assured her all was well. "Have you heard the news? About Oriole Andrews?"

"Yeah. Horrible. That poor woman."

"Then you know they suspect a home invasion."

"By con artists pretending to be water-company employees. Yeah."

Zoe explained how the same guys paid a visit to Mrs. Kroll that morning.

"You're kidding me."

Zoe shook her head. "Wish I was."

"That's why you're moving back in with her." Patsy reached down to tinker with something on her instrument panel. "By the way, have you heard from Kimberly?"

Zoe shifted the laundry basket to her other hip. "No. Why would I hear from my mother?"

"I'm surprised. I'd have thought she would have called you by now."

"I don't know why you're surprised." Zoe and her mother had never been on good terms, but they hadn't spoken at all since last June. While Zoe didn't really miss the contact with Kimberly, she ached over the lost connection with her stepdad.

Patsy gave up on whatever setting she was trying to adjust. "We had a long talk about you. In fact, several."

The revelation that her mother gave Zoe more than a passing thought boggled her mind. "Should I hire an attorney?" She was only half joking.

"What? No. Seriously. Your mother wants to reach out to you. To make amends."

"Okay." Zoe dragged the word out. Kimberly? Making amends? Not likely. "Whatever you say."

Patsy gave her a sour face. "Just wait and see. I'm heading out to check on the horses. You need me to do anything?"

"Just keep an eye out for unmarked white vans."

"Will do." Patsy waved and powered the window back up.

Zoe watched the Toyota maneuver back onto the lane, up the hill, and over the crest toward the barn. She turned toward the house, but paused. Kimberly intended to reach out to her?

Right.

SIX

The next morning, Zoe ambled along the same path she'd once traveled multiple times a day to return from the barn to the Krolls' house. This was the first time she'd walked it since fire destroyed the old farmhouse she'd shared with the elderly couple. The air was cold, but less biting than the previous few days. However, if the forecast and the leaden gray clouds overhead were any indication, snow was on its way.

She unlaced her boots and tugged them off before carrying them inside. The aroma of brewing coffee and smoked pork filled the house and started her mouth watering.

Mrs. Kroll brought a plate heaping with scrambled eggs and bacon from the kitchen and set it on the table. "Sit down. Have some breakfast."

Zoe deposited her boots on the rug next to the door. "You're going to spoil me if I stay too long."

"Nonsense." Mrs. Kroll headed back to the kitchen. "I'm thrilled to have you here. I slept like a lamb knowing you were in the house."

Zoe followed her and poured a cup of coffee. "Did you eat already?"

"I just had some wheat toast. I'm fine." Mrs. Kroll pointed toward the table. "Eat before it gets cold."

Zoe eyed the pound of bacon and the carton of eggs sitting next to the stove. "I hope you aren't expecting to cook all that for me."

Mrs. Kroll nudged her toward the table. "Alexander called while you were in the barn. Marvin's doctor signed his discharge papers, and they're on their way home. I have two hungry men to feed."

Zoe hadn't finished even half her breakfast when the rumble of an engine grew louder, and a small SUV pulled up to the back deck.

"They're here," Mrs. Kroll announced, pushing up from her chair and hurrying to the glass doors.

Alexander Kroll helped his father from the car, but the older man pulled away from the attempt to steady him.

"I'm so glad you're home," Mrs. Kroll said as her husband stepped inside.

"So am I. If I never see the inside of a hospital again, it'll be too soon." He looked around the house as if refreshing his memory of the place. "Zoe, I didn't expect to see you here."

She shot a glance at Mrs. Kroll, unsure of how much she wanted to reveal to her husband.

But he didn't seem interested in the reason for Zoe's presence anyway. "I need to change out of these clothes. They probably have germs on them. Blasted hospitals are full of sick people." He trudged off to the bedroom.

Alexander stepped inside, carrying a small duffle and several sheets of paper, which he held out to his mother. "They said to make a follow-up appointment with his doctor within a week."

Mrs. Kroll gave her son a peck on the cheek. "He already has an appointment for Friday, I think. You can check the calendar to make sure."

"Good."

She took the bag from him. "You'll stay for some breakfast?"

"Sure, Mom."

Zoe climbed to her feet. "I'll get it started."

"Thank you, dear." Mrs. Kroll trailed after her husband.

Zoe heated the skillet and started cracking eggs. "I hope you like scrambled. That's how mine always end up even if I start out trying for over easy."

Alexander chuckled as he joined her in the kitchen. "That's fine. So what's going on? I mean, I'm happy to see you, but why are you here?"

She told him about his mother and the man she'd let into the house yesterday morning.

Alexander paled. "I heard the news about Mrs. Andrews. Do you think these were the same guys?"

"I'm afraid so."

"Good lord." He ran his fingers through his thinning hair.

"Your mother refuses to leave, so I moved in until they're caught."

"Thank you. It means a lot to me knowing you're living here again."

"Only temporarily."

He smiled. "Of course. But still. It eases my mind."

Zoe used a two-pronged fork to settle a strip of bacon into the hot skillet. It crackled and spit, and she bit back a yelp as a bead of hot grease seared the back of her hand. "That's kind of you to say. But my being here didn't help much the last time."

"You saved Mom's life."

Zoe's shoulders tensed at the memory. "It was my fault that she was in danger in the first place." She added more bacon to cover the bottom of the sizzling skillet. The sweet and smoky aroma wafted upward to fill the kitchen.

"I've never blamed you." Alexander rested a hand on her arm. "None of us have."

They didn't have to. Zoe blamed herself enough for all of them. "There's a problem for tonight, though. I'm on duty."

"I didn't realize you were back to work. That's wonderful. And no problem. I was planning to stay tonight anyway to make sure Dad's okay."

"Dad is fine," Mr. Kroll growled as he shambled across the living room, Mrs. Kroll at his arm. "You should be with your wife and my grandkids."

"They're not going to be home either," Alexander said. "Margie's taking them to her folks' house for a couple of days, so I'm batching it." He gave Zoe a conspiratorial wink. "You'd be doing me a favor."

Mrs. Kroll came around the corner. "You know your father's kidding. Of course we'd love to have you stay." She edged between her son and Zoe and lowered her voice. "Did you tell Alexander about...you know?"

"Yes, she did," he said.

Mrs. Kroll shushed him. "I didn't tell Marvin and would rather you didn't either. I don't want him upset."

Zoe met Alexander's gaze and raised a questioning eyebrow. He shrugged and nodded at her. "As long as one of us is around in case these guys come back," he said.

"What are the three of you whispering about?" Mr. Kroll called from the dining room.

"Nothing, dear." Mrs. Kroll nudged Zoe away from the stove and took the fork from her. "Now get out of my kitchen. Both of you."

They moved to the dining room where Zoe realized her half-eaten breakfast had gotten cold.

"Bernice, did you tell her yet?" Mr. Kroll asked.

Zoe picked up her plate and headed to the microwave. "Tell me what?"

"No." Mrs. Kroll dragged the word out. "I haven't."

Zoe didn't like the ring of guilt in the older woman's voice. "Tell me what?" she repeated.

Mr. Kroll buried his hands deep in his cardigan's pockets. "I'm afraid I have some news you aren't gonna like."

Neither the police academy nor his years with the Pittsburgh Bureau of Police had trained Pete for some of the tasks he encountered in Vance Township. Such as dealing with a dozen or so escapee beef cows.

He spent a good portion of his morning directing traffic while a local farmer attempted to round up the wayward herd. The break in the fence was plainly visible to Pete and the farmer. Not so much to the cattle, who seemed to prefer congregating in the middle of Route 15. Maybe they'd had enough of winter and were looking for the road south. Finally a couple of neighbors showed up to help coax the Herefords back into their snowy pasture.

Leaving the farmer to patch his fence, Pete returned to the warmth of his station—which was a helluva lot warmer than his bed had been last night. Zoe had left a note for him, but ignored his calls and texts. Okay, maybe his messages had carried more than an undercurrent of his displeasure with the situation. Calling her a stubborn jackass had likely been too much.

Nancy was on the phone and flagged him down before he could slip past the front office. "He just got in. I'll let him know," she said and hung up.

"Let me know what?"

"Detective Baronick will be here in about five minutes with the lab reports."

"He could just email them."

Nancy shrugged. "You can call him back yourself and tell him."

Pete glared at her. At one time, she had been quiet and eager to please. Of course, back then he'd have put money she wouldn't last a month on the job. "You said he's five minutes away. He's not going to turn around and go back to Brunswick." Maybe he'd show up bearing Starbucks. "Is there anything else I need to know?"

Nancy held out a small stack of pink message slips. "Mostly the usual stuff. No reports of the white van or fake utility workers."

"Good."

Pete thumbed through the messages on his way down the hall. Nothing from Zoe. Ordinarily, she'd call his cell phone. But after his jackass comment, he'd be happy with any contact, even a call routed through Nancy.

Lauren Sanders, the reporter from the fledgling newspaper, had called three times. Wonderful. Janie Baker wanted to speak to him. Another slip noted a request from a local woman for Pete or one of his officers to have a chat with her son regarding the hazards of skipping school. Pete knew the kid. Skipping school was the least of the boy's issues. Pete moved the mother's request to the top of the pile.

Another of the pink slips caught his attention. Not a local area code. No message other than "Please call Mrs. Jackson as soon as possible." Mrs. Jackson? The name stirred up a dust storm of unease in the back of his brain.

The bells on the front door interrupted before he could make sense of the note. Nancy's voice drifted back to him. "He's in his office."

A moment later, Baronick strutted in carrying a folder, but sans Starbucks. "Good morning, Chief." He checked his phone. "Is it still morning?"

"Barely." Pete lowered into his chair and gestured at the paperwork in Baronick's hands. "Lab results?"

The detective dropped the folder on the desk and took a seat across from Pete. "Preliminary. They're still working on the trace evidence, but they pretty much finished sorting through the usable fingerprints."

Pete spun the folder to face him and flipped it open.

"As expected, the bulk of the prints belonged to Mrs. Andrews, her granddaughter, and the granddaughter's son," Baronick said while Pete scanned the report.

"The bulk of them. But not all."

"No. There was one other person in the house. Unidentified prints were found in the living room, the kitchen, dining room, bathroom, and bedroom. Our con artist was just about everywhere."

Pete flipped back through the pages and reread the report, slower this time. "Don't you find it odd that he didn't wear gloves while searching the house?"

The detective leaned back, crossing an ankle over his knee. "Not really. If he was playing the part of a utility worker, he wouldn't want to raise the old lady's suspicions."

"It's January. Everyone wears gloves."

"I don't know. Maybe she invited him to sit down and have tea or something."

"Or something," Pete echoed. "Did Janie Baker mention any caregivers coming to the house? Physical therapists? In-home nurses?"

"Nope."

The bells on the front door jingled.

Pete ignored them. "And these fingerprints aren't in the databases?"

"Nothing's turned up yet, but the techs are still working on IDing them." Baronick grinned. "You know it's not like on TV."

"Really?" Pete muttered sarcastically. "Do you have anything else?"

"Not yet. Our con men must be laying low for a while." Baronick uncrossed his legs, shifting forward in the chair. "We've released statements to the press and have posted on our social-media sites for citizens, especially the elderly, to use caution with strangers at the door. You know, check for official identification and look for utility-company emblems on vehicles, et cetera, et cetera. And we're encouraging them to call 911 if they have even the slightest doubt."

"Good." Pete thought of his father. If Harry was living alone, would he bother phoning the police to report a smiling stranger at his door? "The problem is a lot of older folks are too trusting."

"Which is what these sons of bitches count on." Baronick climbed to his feet. "We just have to keep hammering at our senior citizens to keep their doors locked."

"And remind their neighbors to keep an eye out too."

"Yep." The detective headed into the hall. "I'll keep you posted. You do the same."

Pete picked up his empty coffee cup and glanced at the equally empty pot in the corner as voices drifted back from the front of the building. The stack of messages beckoned as did the lack of a message from Zoe. He'd call her, he decided. Apologize. Try to convince her to come home. Then coffee, followed by returning the list of calls. Satisfied with his plan, he reached for the phone.

"Excuse me."

He looked up to find the reporter from the new Phillipsburg paper at his doorway.

"Chief?" She gestured toward the front of the building. "The detective told me to come on back."

Pete made a mental note that he owed Baronick. Payback would be a bitch. And where the hell was his gatekeeper secretary? "Lauren Sanders, right?"

"Yes." She smiled, pleased he'd remembered her name, and took it as an invitation to come in. "I received the statement the county police released this morning and wanted to ask you a few follow-up questions. If you don't mind."

Pete doubted it mattered if he minded or not. "I don't know what I could add."

She claimed the chair Baronick had vacated, deposited her large leather satchel on the floor next to her, and opened a small notebook similar to the one Pete used. "Has there been any progress made on tracking down the van or the men driving it?"

"Every police officer in this end of the state is on the lookout for them."

Sanders looked up at him. "In other words, no."

He held her gaze in silence.

She didn't blink, but her lips slanted in annoyance. "How about Oriole Andrews' homicide? Do you have anything new to share?"

"It's an ongoing investigation." His standard response.

"Come on, Chief Adams. Give me something I can use."

"Sorry. You have the statement. That's all I have for now."

Sanders reached into her satchel and pulled out a single sheet of paper. "This statement..." She held it up in front of Pete. "...contains the exact same precautions I suggested you release yesterday."

If she was looking for a pat on the back, he wasn't giving it to her.

"I'm not the enemy here. We're on the same side, you know."

He could usually read people. This one, though, was tough. Her eyes never wavered. She sat forward in the chair, her posture straight while not rigid, her jaw set but not clenched. Sanders had been in the game long enough to have honed the appearance of integrity.

And he was pretty sure she was assessing him at the same time he was sizing her up.

He leaned back, striking a practiced relaxed pose. "We're on the same side as long as it gets you a story."

Her mouth twitched ever so slightly. "We're on the same side," she said, "as long as it results in no more lives lost." She tilted her head. "Getting the story is the bonus."

Sanders was good. She said the right words. Offered all the right body-language cues. At some point he might even invite her to the Saturday night poker game. For now, he wasn't convinced of her sincerity, but his gut wasn't sending him any warning signals either. He came forward and stood. "I'm afraid I really don't have anything else to add to the statement right now."

"Not even off the record?"

Definitely a pit bull. "Sorry." He wasn't and had no illusions that she believed him.

Sanders took the hint though, closing her notebook and gathering her satchel. She stood and extended a hand to him. "I'd appreciate a call if anything breaks on the case."

Her grip was firmer than that of many men Pete had shaken hands with. "When there's anything to release to the public, I'll call a press conference."

He knew it wasn't the answer she'd hoped for.

Once he heard the bells on the front door signal the reporter's exit, he moved a few papers on his desk to find the business card Sanders had left on her previous visit. He intended to do some investigating into the area's newest newshound.

His intercom beeped, followed by Nancy's strained voice coming through the speaker. "Chief?"

Ah. His missing gatekeeper. He hit the button. "Why did you let that reporter back here without checking with me first?"

There was a momentary pause. "You know, I do sometimes need to use the facilities. I'd told her to wait."

Except Baronick had countermanded her orders. Of course.

"Never mind that." Nancy sounded rattled. "A call just came through county 911. Report of an intruder."

Dammit. Pete bailed from his chair, snagged his coat from the hook, and charged down the hall. He paused at the front counter. "Address?"

Nancy handed over a slip of paper. He recognized the street name and number and knew she did too.

Oriole Andrews' house.

SEVEN

"What news?" Zoe held her plate of rapidly congealing eggs and bacon, her intention to nuke it in Mrs. Kroll's microwave momentarily forgotten.

Mr. Kroll crossed to her and took the plate from her hands, setting it on the counter. Zoe caught the fleeting glance exchanged between Mrs. Kroll and Alexander. Everyone was in on this except her.

"What news?" Zoe repeated.

Mr. Kroll fidgeted. "You know we've been struggling lately. Medical bills for me and for Bernice and all."

Zoe knew.

"We were really counting on the money from leasing our gas rights to get us out of the hole." His shoulders slumped. "And then Federated Petroleum pulled out of the county."

The fiasco of a couple months ago was all too fresh in her memory. "Yeah. I know." Her mind rushed ahead, filling in the blanks. They were going to sell some parcels of land. No, that wouldn't affect her. They were about to raise her board to keep her horse there. Money was tight for her too, but she'd manage. The Krolls had already cut her a deal since she oversaw the barn duties.

Mr. Kroll took her by the shoulders, gazing at her with sad eyes. "We've found a buyer for the farm."

"What?" The farm? The whole farm?

"We were planning to put it on the open market in the spring, but the Realtor we spoke with already had someone looking for property." The words tumbled out of the old man once the news had been revealed. "The guy came out, liked what he saw, and made us an offer. I know it sounds like a cliché, but it really was one we couldn't refuse."

Zoe leaned back on the kitchen counter, grateful Mr. Kroll had

had the foresight to take the stoneware plate away from her. Thoughts continued to bounce around inside her brain. "So..." She dragged the word out. "...the barn will be under new ownership. Do you think he'll want to keep me on as manager?"

Mr. Kroll shot another sorrowful look at his wife. "I'm sorry, dear. He has plans for the property. Plans that don't include livestock."

The reality of the situation sunk in. "Not at all?"

Mr. Kroll shook his head sadly. "You'll need to let the boarders know they'll have to find new homes for their horses."

Including her own.

"I'm sorry."

Zoe had been more-or-less homeless since fire claimed the Krolls' old farmhouse. She'd become comfortable at Pete's. And he didn't object to her cats. Finding new digs for a horse wasn't going to be quite so easy. Plus, she'd long thought of the farm almost as her own. She knew every plank in the barn, every trail, every creek and spring on the acreage. "How long do we have?"

There was that look between the Krolls again. "I should have told you sooner, but it happened so fast and then I ended up back in the hospital." He ran a hand alongside his neck, as if massaging away the tension. "The closing is February first. And the new owner wants to take possession immediately."

Meaning..."He wants us out in two weeks?" she asked incredulously.

Mr. Kroll lowered his head and his hand. "I'm afraid so."

Janie Baker stood, arms crossed, at the base of the hill as Pete swung his SUV onto Andrews Lane. He braked and powered down the passenger window. Her breath fogged in the cold air, veiling her face a moment as she stepped up to the vehicle.

"I tried calling you directly," she said, her voice accusatory, "but when you didn't get back to me, I had to call 911."

The message slip he hadn't gotten to. He started to explain that his number was for non-emergency calls, but stopped. "What's going on?"

She shot a glance up the hill. "I was going to check the house.

With no one living there, I figured I should turn down the heat, shut off the water. That sort of thing. But when I pulled up out front, I saw movement inside."

"What kind of movement?"

"Shadows. Sort of. A figure passing by the front window."

Had the con men come back yet again? "You didn't attempt to go in, did you?"

Her eyes widened. "Heavens no. I didn't even get out of my car. I called you and drove down here to wait."

"Did you see another vehicle near the house?"

"No." Her eyes shifted. "I don't think so. But they could have parked somewhere else, couldn't they?"

Pete scanned the street leading up to the house. Just the usual residents' cars and pickups parked in front of their homes. Nothing out of place. "You wait here. I'll go investigate."

"I want to come with you."

"Janie—"

"I'll wait in the car." Her hands rested on the edge of his passenger door. "Please."

He sighed. "Fine."

She climbed in, clicked the seatbelt, and folded her hands in her lap like an obedient child. Pete powered her window closed and eased the SUV up the hill.

He parked in front of the old house. It always looked in need of a good handyman, but now the place appeared despondent, as if it too mourned Oriole's loss. There were no signs of a white van. Or any other vehicle.

He unclipped his seatbelt. "Stay here."

"Okay."

Pete stepped into the bracing chill and pulled his collar tighter around his neck. With a glance back to confirm Janie was staying put, he approached the house. Somewhere down the valley, a dog barked. The loud pulsing growl of a semi Jake braking as it approached the sharp turn into town carried all the way up to Pete. But no sounds from inside.

He wrapped his gloved fingers around the doorknob, half convinced Janie Baker had grown jumpy and paranoid—and understandably so—until he turned the knob and it clicked open. As jittery as the granddaughter was, she wouldn't have forgotten to lock up. Another glance over his shoulder. She was still in his car, but he could make out her wide eyes fixed on him.

He removed his gloves, stuffing them into his duty belt. With one hand on his sidearm, his finger ready on the holster's release, he pushed the door open, trying to be quiet. The creaky hinges squelched that plan.

"Police," he called.

There was a thud from upstairs. Then slow footsteps above Pete's head.

He drew his Glock and approached the base of the staircase to the second floor. "Come to the top of the stairs and keep your hands where I can see them."

A frantic quivering voice drifted down to him. "Don't shoot."

Pete could track the intruder's movements as the footsteps headed down what Pete knew to be the upstairs hallway. Floorboards creaked. A figure, familiar even in the shadows, appeared, hands raised. "Mr. Troutman?"

The elderly gentleman stood stock still, his hands high over his head. "Yes. Please don't shoot. I'm not armed."

Pete re-holstered his Glock. "I'm not going to shoot. Come on down here."

Trout didn't move. "Can I lower my hands? If I don't hold onto the banister, I'm afraid I'll fall."

"Please." The last thing Pete wanted was another of the township's senior citizens taking a tumble. "Do you mind telling me what you're doing in here?"

Trout shuffled down the stairs, each step deliberate. Cautious.

Or he was buying time before answering. "Mr. Troutman?" Pete said.

At the bottom, Trout looked up at Pete. "Yes?"

Worry lines creased the old man's face. Pete had seen a similar vapid look in his own father's gaze. Similar, but not quite right. Trout was trying to feign confusion. "What," Pete asked, keeping his voice firm, "are you doing in here?"

Trout's expression shifted from faked bewilderment to admitted defeat. "I wasn't stealing anything. Honest." He extended both arms out to his sides. "You can search me. I don't mind."

Behind Pete, the front door swung open. His hand again went to his sidearm as he spun. Janie Baker stood there, taking in the scene.

"Trout?" she said. "What on earth—"

Tension released its grip on Pete's shoulders. In response, he released his grip on his gun. "I told you to stay in the car."

"I know, but I thought you might need help." She shot a fierce look at the elderly man. "How did you get in here?"

It was a fair question and one Pete would have asked had Trout answered the first one.

"I have a key." He defiantly crossed his arms in front of his chest.

"A key?" Janie's voice was a screech. "How'd you get a key?"

"Oriole gave me one."

"She most definitely did not."

Pete raised his hands in a "T." Time-out.

The two fell silent, but glared at each other.

"Yes, she did," Trout whispered.

Janie opened her mouth to reply, but Pete snapped his fingers and held the flat of one palm toward her. "Go back out to the car and stay there."

She pressed her mouth into a rebellious scowl, shot an even darker scowl at Trout, and stomped out of the house, slamming the door as she went.

Pete turned back to a victorious Trout. "Talk."

The old man again attempted the befuddled look. "What?"

A dull headache throbbed inside Pete's forehead. "Look, Mr. Troutman—"

"Trout. Please."

Pete battled the urge to shake the old man. "Trout. You need to tell me what you're doing here."

He held Pete's gaze for a moment before looking down with a conciliatory sigh. "Oriole and I have been friends a long time. I always worried about her being here alone." Trout's eyes glazed as he glanced around the house. "I guess I had good cause to worry. Anyhow, even though she's gone now, I still feel...responsible for her. For her home."

Pete recognized the depth of the grief in the old man's face and in his voice. Trout had been in love with Oriole. Gentler, Pete said, "That doesn't explain what you're doing here. Have you seen anyone trying to break in?"

"No. I don't expect you to understand, but I still feel her presence here." He hugged himself. "I miss her."

Not for the first time, Pete saw his father in Trout's face. "I do understand. But she's gone. You can't just come in and make yourself at home any time you're lonely."

Trout blinked and tears trickled down his pale wrinkled cheeks. "I know. I'm sorry."

Pete gave the old man's frail shoulder a soothing pat before putting his gloves back on. "Go home, Trout."

"All right."

Pete walked him to the door, but stopped him before he could step outside and held out a hand.

Trout looked at it, perplexed.

"The key," Pete said.

The pain in the old man's eyes gnawed a hole in Pete's heart. He almost wished he could let him keep it. But Trout dug in his pocket, pulled out a key ring, and struggled to work one of the keys free. Once he did, he pinched it between his finger and thumb before dropping it into Pete's gloved palm.

Trout shambled across the snowy yard and up the road without a backward glance at Pete's SUV or Janie, who opened the car door and started to climb out.

Pete waved at her to get back in. "I'm going to do a quick check of the house," he called to her. "Make sure nothing's been tampered with."

She swung her feet back inside.

He closed the door, dug a small evidence bag from his coat pocket, and deposited Trout's key into it. Once Pete returned to the station, he'd dust the key for prints. He was pretty sure they'd match the unidentified set the crime scene techs had lifted from the house.

With the bag labeled and tucked safely away, he did a walk-through of the downstairs. Nothing seemed moved or changed from his last visit.

He climbed the stairs.

Four doors greeted him. Three closed. One at the far end of the hallway—the front of the house—stood open. Judging from the footsteps Pete had heard upon announcing his presence, this was the room Trout had been in. To be thorough, Pete paused at each of the closed doors, opened them, and peered inside. The first room appeared to be used as storage. Stacks of dusty boxes. An equally dusty dining table with a set of chairs turned upside-down on top of it. An old treadle sewing machine. Shelves of books. Nothing appeared disturbed.

The second room contained a more modern sewing machine, one of those things in the shape of a female figure that he'd seen dressmakers use as a model, an ironing board and iron, and shelves of fabric.

The third room was a small tidy guest room. A bed with a colorful quilt, a set of bedside stands, and a dresser. A closet door stood open, revealing a rod and a dozen or so empty hangers.

Pete moved on to the final room. He stood in the doorway to what had been Oriole's bedroom. The forensics crew had left fingerprint powder on many of the surfaces. The furniture was the big heavy stuff that fit best in these old houses with their high ceilings. The oak headboard alone would never have fit in his own bedroom. But the set also included a dresser, a chest of drawers, and a mammoth chifforobe. A delicate round table covered with a lace doily sat next to the bed on one side with a reading lamp and a box of tissues perched on it. He rounded the foot of the bed, which had been stripped down to the mattress, and stopped. A second table, the match to the first, lay on its side. A book sprawled open, pages down, on the floor.

The crime-scene tech had mentioned something about a possible struggle in the bedroom. Was this what he'd referred to? Or was the thud Pete had heard earlier the table tipping over?

He pivoted, scanning the rest of the room. At first glance, nothing else appeared out of place.

Except...

Two of the dresser's bottom drawers were askew, much like he'd found the drawers on the dresser by the basement door. These antique pieces didn't have the modern hardware and drawer slides that allowed perfect alignment with ease. Often, they required some fussing and jiggling to get them neatly closed. Pete remembered such a piece in his childhood home. Harry would always say "you have to hold your mouth just right to get it to close."

The other drawers in the set were shut perfectly. He crossed the room to the dresser and opened one of the cockeyed drawers. Inside was a mishmash of undergarments. He wasn't surprised. Even if Oriole had been a compulsive neatnik, the crime-scene guys had gone through her things and didn't make an effort to put them back the same as they'd found them.

Pete slid the drawer closed. As suspected, it jammed on one side. He shifted it a bit, lifted up slightly, and it slipped into place with a thud. "Have to hold your mouth right," he said to the empty room. Something the crime-scene techs wouldn't have bothered to do.

He eyed the top drawers that weren't askew and opened one containing a tidy stack of folded sweaters. Nothing even slightly akimbo. He eased the drawer closed. It jammed, same as the other. After a bit of adjusting, it slid into place.

Pete pulled out his pen and notepad and jotted down his findings. Before leaving the room, he snapped a few photos with his phone.

Janie remained seated in his SUV, right where he'd left her. He climbed behind the wheel.

She stared at him expectantly. "Well?"

"Everything looked fine to me."

She placed a hand on her chest. "Good."

Pete reached for the gearshift but paused. "When's your grandmother's funeral?"

"Friday morning. The viewing is tomorrow afternoon and evening."

"I'll be sure to stop by." He sat up straighter, acting like he'd just remembered something. "By the way. Did you manage to get the clothes you wanted for your grandmother?"

"Yes, I did. Those investigators finished up and let me back in just like you said they would."

"Good. Good. I imagine they left quite a mess for you to clean up."

She shrugged. "It wasn't too bad. I mean, there's a lot of that fingerprint stuff on everything, but they're just doing their job, right?"

"Right. Still, you probably had some tidying up to do."

"Honestly, I don't have the energy to mess with it. I know I'll have to clear Gram's stuff out and clean the place up before I can put it on the market, but I'm in no rush." She smiled weakly. "I stayed up late the other night watching old movies. *Gone with the Wind.* Like Scarlett said, 'After all, tomorrow is another day.'"

Pete reached over and squeezed her hand before shifting the SUV into drive. Janie had just provided a few answers for him.

Even if she didn't realize it.

EIGHT

Zoe rested her forearms on the top of the gate, watching the horses vacuuming up the fresh alfalfa she'd just tossed to them. Beyond the herd, the pasture sloped away from the barn, leveled out and then sloped again, down to the creek glazed with ice. Dried stalks of grass poked up through patches of snow. Stark brown trees rimmed the field in the distance. Lazy snowflakes drifted down, but patches of blue offered hope for a clearing sky as well as the only color in an otherwise monochrome landscape.

She'd taken in this view more times than she could count, but the realization that her time on this piece of land was finite gave her an appreciation for it she'd never had before. Two weeks, possibly less.

"What are you doing here?"

Zoe turned.

Patsy strode across the barn's indoor arena toward her. "Don't you have to work tonight?"

Zoe fumbled with her coat sleeve to check her watch. Almost three o'clock. "Yeah. Time got away from me." At least she only had to walk back to the Krolls' house to change into her uniform.

"I stopped in to give the horses some hay. Guess you beat me to it." Patsy slowed as she grew closer, her smile fading. "What's wrong? You look like you lost your best friend." She froze, and her eyes widened. "My God. Did something happen to Mr. or Mrs. Kroll?"

"No. Not like you mean anyway." Zoe had spent the last three hours rehearsing a dozen different versions of how to break the news to her boarders. None of them sounded right inside her head.

"What then?"

Zoe looked at Patsy. Her friend. Her cousin. Her biggest helper with the work here at the barn. Of all the boarders, Patsy would be the hardest to tell. Zoe looked down at her Muck boots. "They've sold the farm."

Silence greeted the statement. Zoe lifted her gaze. Patsy stood motionless, her lips parted in a small oval, as if the word "Oh" was stuck. Only the condensation hanging in front of her face offered evidence she hadn't stopped breathing.

Zoe told her the rest.

"Two weeks?" Patsy's voice was a squeak.

"Yeah."

She shuffled over to the gate and joined Zoe leaning on it. "What are we gonna do?"

"First, I have to figure out how to tell everyone. I want to be the one to break the news. I don't want some hearing it from me and others hearing it through the grapevine."

Long moments passed with the only sounds being the munch of hay and a snort when one of the horses got dust up its nose. Then Patsy turned to face her. "Email."

Zoe looked at her cousin. "Huh?"

"Send a group email. Some might not read it right away, but that's your best chance to get the word out to everyone at once."

"I was gonna call everyone."

"You can do that, but the ones you call first will freak and call their friends before you can get to them."

"True." Zoe rolled the options around in her head for the umpteenth time. "I'll do both. I'll email first and follow up with calls."

"Good. Now what do we do? Where are you gonna keep Windstar?"

"I have no idea." She'd faced the possibility of needing to move her gelding a couple of times in the last year and hadn't come up with any options then either. This time, it was really happening. "Any thoughts about where you'll board Jazzel?"

Patsy turned, crossed her arms, and leaned back against the gate. "Actually, yes."

"Where?" Maybe they could continue being stable buddies.

Patsy gazed across the arena, a thoughtful smile tugging at her lips. "I think Kimberly might be able to help."

*   *   *

While County handled the bulk of the evidence, Pete maintained the capability to process fingerprints at the Vance Township station. As soon as he returned from the Andrews house, he headed to the small lab in the rear of the building. Donning latex gloves, he removed Trout's key from the evidence bag, broke out the powder and his favorite brush, and soon lifted two reasonably good prints. Thumb and index finger. He didn't bother entering them into the computer. Instead, he pulled up the unidentified set from the crime scene and held the two print cards up for comparison.

Pete had been considered skilled at fingerprint identification back in his days with the Pittsburgh Bureau of Police, but a rank amateur could have made this match.

Their fourth person at the house was Mr. Troutman.

With another mystery solved, Pete returned to his office and his computer and pulled up the photos he and the county crime-scene unit had taken at Oriole's house the previous couple of days.

The bells on the front door jangled. A moment later, Baronick sauntered in with a paper bag reeking of onions and meat in his hand and claimed the seat across from Pete.

"I only called you fifteen minutes ago." Pete sniffed, and his stomach growled. "And I didn't expect you to drive back out here."

The detective opened the bag and pulled out a huge sandwich. "I was just over in Mt. Prospect Township checking on another case." He took a bite. "Hope you don't mind," he mumbled around the mouthful. "I stopped at that new deli up the road. I missed lunch."

"You could've brought two, you know."

Baronick held out the sandwich with the bite taken from it. "You can have mine." He grinned.

"No, thanks." Pete clicked through the photos on his computer until he located the ones he wanted.

The detective chewed and swallowed. "What'd you find?"

Without looking up from the screen, Pete updated Baronick on his encounter with Trout, the key, and the fingerprints.

"So our four sets of prints all match people known to have frequented Oriole Andrews' house." Baronick wiped his mouth with a paper napkin from the deli bag. "Looks like our intruders wore gloves after all. And we're back to square one."

"Maybe." Pete thumbed through the photos he'd taken earlier today on his phone. "Or maybe square one and a half."

Baronick scowled. "What do you mean?"

"Take a look."

The detective deposited the remains of his sandwich on top of the bag on the desk and moved around to gaze over Pete's shoulder at three photos.

"This..." Pete used a pen to tap on the computer screen. "...is a shot of Oriole's bedroom dresser before the crime-scene techs had touched anything." He pointed to the second photo. "This one was taken after they were done." He held up his phone. "And I shot this one this morning after escorting Mr. Troutman out of the house."

Baronick squinted at the photos. "Zoom in on that last one."

Pete smiled. The detective knew where he was going with this. He expanded the phone's screen and repositioned the photo.

Baronick straightened. "Mrs. Andrews kept her dresser drawers nice and neat. The crime-scene guys, not so much."

Pete swiveled in his chair to look up at the detective. "They left every single drawer misaligned. I checked. That dresser is an antique. No fancy slides on the drawers. You have to jiggle them a little to get them to shut properly."

"My grandparents have furniture like that. I can never get the drawers closed. But my grandmother gets it every time, first try. She knows how to do it."

"From years of practice. The crime-scene guys weren't going to take the time to put everything back just so." Pete held up his phone again, showing the picture of the top drawers closed flush with the dresser front and the bottom two out of kilter.

Baronick shrugged. "The granddaughter probably straightened things up."

"No. I asked. She took what she needed in the way of funeral clothes for Oriole, but she said she wasn't going to worry about the rest of it for a while."

The detective met Pete's gaze. "Troutman."

"He was upstairs when I got there." Pete clicked back a few photos on the computer to the before shots. "I heard a thud and thought he'd knocked over the table beside the bed, but the photos show it was like that before the crime-scene guys started. Trout was going through the drawers."

"Why?"

"That's a very good question." And one Pete intended to ask the old man.

Pete's cell phone rang. The photo of Oriole's dresser was replaced with a photo of Nadine. "I have to take this," he told Baronick and slipped past him into the hall. "Hey, sis."

"Golden Oaks called. They'll be ready for Dad to move in tomorrow morning."

Pete rolled her words around in his head. Not a question. A statement. And Nadine was never one to ask his permission. Yet responding with "and why are you telling me this?" seemed inappropriate. Instead, he said, "Okay."

The line was silent, but he knew she hadn't hung up. Apparently his reply wasn't the right one.

"Isn't it?" he asked.

"I want you to help." She didn't tack on "you moron," but from her snippy tone, it was implied.

"I'm on duty."

"You're the chief of police. Order one of your officers to fill in for you for a couple hours."

They'd had this conversation before. It never ended well. "I can't just—"

"He's your father too. I can't handle this alone."

"Can't you wait until tomorrow evening?"

The heat that blew through the cell signal scorched his ear. "First, have you not heard the weather report?"

"Uh. No."

"You should pay attention to these things. They're calling for an Alberta clipper coming through beginning early afternoon tomorrow. And second, their office staff leaves at four, and they need to be there for the paperwork. So no, we can't wait until evening."

He could've argued the value of his being in his office versus Golden Oaks' office staff, but he knew he'd lose. Nor could he disavow the hazards of having Pop out in a January storm. "What time?"

"I was thinking if you came here tonight and filled up your SUV with Dad's stuff, I could get him in the car and drive him there tomorrow. You can just meet us at the facility at...say...nine o'clock?"

"Any chance you can make it eight?"

"Nine would be better."

Of course it would.

"But whatever time you can come tonight is fine."

Nancy appeared in the hallway at the front of the station. "Chief, you have a 911."

"I have to go," he told his sister.

"Wait," she said. "When do you think you'll get here?"

Nancy planted an impatient hand on her hip. "Incident at the high school."

"I'll call you," Pete said to Nadine and hung up, although he could still hear her yammering on the other end. He pocketed the phone and looked at Nancy. "Did they specify what kind of incident?"

"An altercation." She held up the call slip. "And they gave me the name of one of the kids involved. Marcus Baker."

"On my way." Pete poked his head into his office where Baronick sat at the computer, eating his sandwich. "You might want to come along for this."

By the time Pete and Baronick arrived at the high school and were directed to the gymnasium, the altercation had been broken up. One of the coaches stood over a teen slouched on the lowest bleacher seat, nursing a bloody lip and what looked like the start of a nice shiner. Another coach had Marcus, arms folded, backed against a wall. Two fighters sent to their respective corners. In between, the principal had one hand planted on her hip and rubbed her temple with the other.

When she spotted Pete, she strode toward him. "Chief Adams, thank you for coming so quickly."

"What's going on?"

Before the principal could answer, the boy with the bloody lip leapt to his feet, pointing at Marcus. "He's nuts. I wasn't doin' nothin' and he jumped me. Hid under the bleachers and blindsided me."

The principal faced the boy, both fists on her hips this time. "Robert, be quiet. You'll have your chance to tell your story."

"It ain't a story. It's the truth." Pouting, the boy flopped back down.

"Isn't," the principal corrected him under her breath, probably knowing he didn't hear her. Or care. She turned back to Pete. "And I suspect it is the truth," she said, still too low for anyone but Pete to hear. Then she raised her voice to a normal volume. "We found these two going at it in here. Marcus was on top, punching Robert, who didn't fight back. At least not by the time we arrived." She again lowered her voice. "I'm not saying who started it, but Marcus would have finished it if the coach hadn't pulled him off."

"I understand." Pete turned to Baronick, who lurked behind him. "Why don't you take Robert aside and get his story. Excuse me. His 'truth.' I'll speak with young Mr. Baker."

Baronick cast a scowl at Pete, but nodded and headed toward the bleachers. "You." The detective pointed at Robert and then at the far end of the gym. "This way."

Once they were out of earshot, Pete stepped over to Marcus. "Would you give us a minute?" Pete asked the coach, who shot one more menacing look at the kid and moved away to engage the principal in conversation.

Marcus kept his arms crossed and his head lowered, avoiding Pete's gaze.

Pete hooked his thumbs in his duty belt and straightened to his full height, looming over the kid. "Here we are again."

No reply.

"Do you want to tell me your side?"

Marcus' eye twitched, but he didn't speak.

"This is—what? Your third fight in the last two months?"

One shoulder shrugged.

"So what's up? I thought we had an agreement. I didn't bust you for taking a baseball bat to that mailbox, and in return, you were going to stay out of trouble."

"I wasn't the one bashing those mailboxes."

"Ah. He speaks."

Marcus hunched his shoulders. A turtle trying to draw his head into his shell. "Well, I wasn't."

"Maybe not, but you were in the car with the older kids who were bashing them."

Marcus grunted.

"Destroying mailboxes is a federal offense."

"I know."

"Three years in prison. Two-hundred-and-fifty-thousand-dollar fine. You got a quarter mil sitting around somewhere?"

Marcus finally met Pete's gaze, but his expression clearly indicated he thought Pete was an idiot. "I'm only thirteen. They wouldn't charge me as an adult."

"You sure about that?"

Pete was bluffing, but Marcus was buying it. Worry creased his brow.

"Talk to me," Pete said. "Tell me why you've gone from busting mailboxes to busting heads."

Marcus did his best to look disinterested. "'Cause I felt like it, I guess."

"You guess." Pete shook his head. "Marcus..." He moved closer to the boy, intentionally invading his space. "...isn't your mom dealing with enough right now? Do you think you going to juvie is going to be helpful to her?"

Pete's words must have hit a nerve. For a fleeting moment, Marcus' expression softened.

"Did you jump that boy the way he said?"

Marcus glared in Robert's direction. "He had it coming."

"Why? What'd he do?"

The kid seemed to consider the question, but shook his head. "That's between him and me."

"You really want me to haul your ass to jail?"

"You do what you gotta do, man." Marcus lifted his chin, staring Pete in the eye. "And I'll do what I have to do."

Pete held the boy's gaze, waiting for it to waver. To his surprise, it didn't. The kid had cajones. But more than that, the resolve and underlying anger in Marcus' eyes made Pete think there was more going on here than a simple brawl between two testosterone-driven teens with anger-management issues.

NINE

Zoe sat alone in the ambulance service's office, her laptop set up on the desk where she'd cleared a workspace. She stared at the screen and the email she'd composed—and re-composed at least five times—to her boarders. One version sounded heartless and devastating. Another sounded too Pollyannaish. If she'd been typing on paper, the trashcan would be overflowing.

The police scanner on the shelf above the desk squawked a few routine calls between the static. A minor traffic collision on the other side of the county with no injuries. A Phillipsburg officer radioed in, stating the security alert at a local business was a false alarm.

"You still working on that letter?" Earl asked from the doorway leading to the kitchen, the bunkroom, and the crew lounge in the rear of the building.

"I don't know what to tell them. Most of these folks have had their horses at my barn—" She realized what she'd said and winced. "The Krolls' barn," she corrected, "as long or longer than I have. I have no idea what they're gonna do now."

Earl dragged a chair next to the desk and straddled it. "That's not your concern, you know."

Zoe looked at him, surprised. "What do you mean?"

"I realize you want to help everyone, but it's not up to you. You're the barn manager, not a horse-placement agency. It's your job to inform them of the situation. Nothing more."

He was right. She rocked back in the ancient office chair and swiveled it to face him. "But I do have to find a place for Windstar. I figure if I can help relocate some of the others, I might find a new home for my own horse."

Earl picked up a pen and pointed it at her. "Now that is your concern. Any ideas?"

"No." She grinned, remembering a conversation they'd had last summer about his young daughter wanting a pony. "Unless Lilly still wants to keep Windstar in her bedroom."

Earl chuckled. "Olivia put her foot down on that one."

"Your wife's a spoilsport."

"No comment."

Zoe laughed. But a moment's joviality didn't wipe away the problem. Where was she going to stable her horse?

Patsy had mentioned Kimberly, but refused to elaborate, insisting Zoe needed to speak with her mother. What the heck was that all about? The only conclusion Zoe could reach was that Patsy had decided to move to Florida. Kimberly had opened her home and her heart to Patsy as if she were her daughter instead of Zoe. As a result, Patsy had racked up quite a few frequent flyer miles, traveling south to visit Zoe's mother and stepdad.

It made sense. Patsy loved the south. She had no other family, except for a crazy old uncle in prison. That had to be it.

Zoe had already lost her best friend to New Mexico. Now she was losing her second-closest friend—her cousin—to Florida.

Before she could sink deeper into a quagmire of self-pity, the tones went off. She grabbed a pen and closed the laptop.

"Traffic accident with injuries," the dispatcher from the county emergency operations center reported. "Intersection of Main and Veterans in Dillard."

Earl grabbed his coat from the rack by the door. "We're up."

Crew Chief Tony DeLuca charged into the office to take over at the desk. Zoe closed her computer, shoved it out of the way, and snatched her jacket before following her partner into the ambulance bay.

The trip to Dillard only took three minutes, but a fire truck and one of the Vance Township Police cruisers had beaten them there. Not surprising, since the intersection in question was only a block from the fire station and two from the police department.

Earl eased Medic Two around the flares and the stopped traffic. One of the firefighters directed them toward a pickup with its grill wrapped around a phone pole. Zoe jumped out, yanked open the side door to the ambulance's passenger compartment, and grabbed the jump kit before jogging after her partner.

Seth Metzger stood at the pickup's open driver's side door. The man behind the wheel tried to shove the deployed airbags aside. "I'm fine."

"The paramedics are here. Let them examine you just to be sure," the young officer said.

The patient grumbled but didn't argue when Zoe caught his wrist to feel his pulse and Earl leaned over her to check the man's pupils. "Are you having any pain?" she asked.

"Yeah. In my ass. Look at my truck." He flung his hands up in frustration, pulling free from Zoe's grasp and bumping Earl's penlight.

"I understand," she told him. "But we need to make sure you don't have any injuries requiring treatment."

The man growled but surrendered, extending his arm to her again. "Damn airbag popped me in the face. And my shoulder hurts where the seatbelt caught me. But that's about it."

"You'd be a lot worse off if those two things hadn't bruised you."

"I suppose."

"Pulse is a hundred," Zoe said to Earl.

He pocketed his penlight. "Pupils are equal and reactive."

She dug the blood-pressure cuff from the jump kit. "Sir? Can you slip your arm out of your coat?"

While he complied and Earl started checking their patient's head and neck, Seth cleared his throat. "Can you tell me what happened?"

"I was on my way home from work, just cruising along," the man said. "Under the speed limit, mind you. And this van blew through the stop sign on Veterans Street. I swerved to miss him, but he clipped my quarter panel. Threw me completely out of control and *wham*. I hit this pole."

Zoe glanced over her shoulder. There was no second vehicle anywhere around.

"And this van kept going?" Seth asked.

"Didn't even slow down."

"Can you give me a description?" Seth clicked his pen. "Make? Model? Color? License number?"

"It happened too fast. I have no idea about a make or model. And license?" He snorted a laugh. "No friggin' way. But I can tell you it was white. A white transport van. No windows."

Seth swore.

Zoe looked at him. "What's wrong?" But as soon as the words left her mouth, she knew. "You don't think it's them, do you? I mean, there are a gazillion white vans around."

Seth's jaw had tightened. "Yeah, but most of them wouldn't run a stop sign. Or cause a traffic accident and keep going." He gestured at the patient. "How is he?"

"Vitals are all normal. Slightly elevated BP, and his pulse is a little rapid, but that's to be expected under the circumstances."

Earl had completed his exam. "Doesn't seem to have any broken bones. No double vision or headache."

"Can I get out now?" the patient asked.

Earl folded his arms and eyed the man. "I'd still rather immobilize you and take you to the ER just to be sure."

"Do you guys get paid by the customer? I'm fine." He motioned them away and stepped out of the truck. "See? I'm not going to no hospital. I just need to get a tow truck."

"One's on the way," Seth said.

Earl shrugged. "I'll need you to sign a treatment refusal form."

"No problem."

While Earl headed back to the ambulance for the paperwork, Zoe stuffed the blood-pressure cuff and stethoscope back into the jump kit.

Seth looked around, his face tense. "I need to get going." His voice matched his face.

Zoe assumed he wanted to follow up on the van. "It's long gone. You'll never catch it now."

"I know." Seth shook his head. "I was on my way to a call when I came across this." He aimed a thumb at the pickup. "The call I was responding to was a resident reporting a man in a white panel van, alleging to be with the water company, who tried to gain access to her house."

Zoe shivered—and not because of the January night's chill. "Not again."

"Yeah. And the address? 112 Second Street."

The chill turned frigid. "Sylvia Bassi's house."

*   *   *

Sylvia Bassi had at one time been the Vance Township police secretary. Currently she served on the township's board of supervisors. More than that, she was the community grandmother, and her late son had been one of Zoe's dearest friends.

One word neither Zoe nor any other local would use to describe Sylvia was "victim." Yet when she opened her door to Zoe, Seth, and Earl, her round face was paler than usual, and she clutched a cast-iron skillet in her chubby hand.

"I don't need an ambulance," she said as the trio crowded into her kitchen and closed the door behind them.

Zoe took the skillet from her and set it on the stove. "Nobody does. We were up on Main Street at a traffic accident when we heard. The driver refused transport, so we thought we'd tag along."

Sylvia gestured at Zoe's handheld radio. "As long as you're 10-8 instead of 10-7."

They'd abandoned most of the ten codes years ago, but Zoe remembered them better than the Spanish she'd learned in high school. "Yes. Where Control is concerned, we're available."

Seth took Sylvia by the arm and directed her to one of the chairs. "I, however, am here strictly on business." He pulled out his notepad. "Tell me what happened."

Sylvia took a seat and hugged herself. "Damned young punk knocked on my door. Said he was with the water company and they were having some problems on this street. He needed to come inside to test the pressure."

A memory of Oriole Andrews crumpled at the foot of her basement stairs flashed through Zoe's mind. "You didn't let him in, did you?"

"Good heavens, no. I'm not one of these eager-to-please old biddies they prey on." Sylvia rubbed her arms. "I asked for ID. Didn't expect him to have any, but he did."

Seth looked up from his notes. "Really?"

"Fake." Sylvia's nose wrinkled as if she'd gotten a whiff of something foul. "And not a very good one either."

Seth glanced between Zoe and Earl. "That's new."

Zoe tugged off her gloves and unzipped her jacket. "They know word's getting out and one of the warnings you guys have been telling the public is to insist on seeing a company ID."

Earl let out a low growl. "The bad guys are following the news."

"What did you do after he produced identification?" Zoe asked.

"I told him to come back tomorrow after I'd had a chance to call West Penn Water. He wasn't happy about that. He tried to open my door, but I had it locked. When he tried to force it, I grabbed that." Sylvia nodded toward the skillet. "I guess he reconsidered. Told me he'd be back in the morning, and then he skedaddled."

Seth touched his pen to his notepad. "Can you give me a description of the guy?"

"You bet I can. Caucasian. Dark eyes. Dark hair on the long side. Like he was due for a trim. About five ten. I'd guess his weight as one seventy or so."

Seth lifted his head to look at her.

"I was the police secretary and dispatcher for over thirty years." She sat up straighter. "I learned a thing or two along the way. And I can tell you he wasn't from around here."

"How do you know?"

"I didn't recognize him. That's how."

Zoe bit her lip to keep from smiling. Sylvia did indeed know everyone in Vance and the surrounding townships.

"How about the vehicle?"

"White Chevy panel van."

"Are you sure it was a Chevy?"

She glared at him.

"Right." He made a note. "Chevy van. How about year?"

"Fairly new. But I couldn't tell you for sure."

A loud pounding at the door made them all flinch. Sylvia clutched at her chest. "Good lord. They wouldn't be back already, would they?"

Zoe pressed a hand to her own sternum to quell her racing heart. "With a police car and an ambulance sitting out front? Not likely." She moved toward the door to answer it. "Probably a concerned neighbor." A happier thought occurred to her. "Or Pete."

"Pete's in Pittsburgh dealing with his sister and Harry," Sylvia said. Sheepishly she added, "I called him first, before I dialed 911."

Zoe opened the door to a woman bundled in a dark coat with a colorful scarf. She toted a huge leather bag and flashed a determined smile. Rather than open the storm door, Zoe raised her voice. "May I help you?"

The smile dissolved to irritation for a moment, but the woman quickly pasted it back on her face. She produced a business card, which she pressed to the glass. "My name is Lauren Sanders. I'm with *The Phillipsburg Enterprise*. I picked up a call on my scanner about a possible home invasion at this address."

Zoe had to take the woman's word for her name and position. The glass between them had fogged from the cold, obscuring both the writing on the card and the reporter's face.

"Who is it?" Sylvia asked.

"I'm not sure." Zoe zipped her jacket. "But I'll find out." She slipped outside, careful to block the reporter from attempting to push past her.

"I think both of us would be more comfortable in the house," the reporter said.

Zoe stuffed her hands into her pockets and ignored the comment. "What paper did you say you were from?"

"*The Phillipsburg Enterprise.*"

Zoe opened her mouth to say she'd never heard of it, but the reporter must have been told the same thing before.

"It's new." She held the card out to Zoe. "I'm following the story of the rash of home invasions by these con artists claiming to be with the water company. I'd very much like to interview their latest victim."

"Now isn't a good time."

"And you are...?"

Zoe almost said "a friend of the family," but noticed the reporter gazing at the name tag and patches on her jacket. "I'm a paramedic with Monongahela EMS."

"So the victim suffered injuries during the invasion?"

"It wasn't an invasion. She didn't let them in the house."

"Really?" The reporter reached into the leather bag and came up with a notepad and pen. "What else can you tell me? Why was the ambulance called?" She squinted again at Zoe's name badge. "Zoe Chambers, is it?" Except the reporter pronounced it as if her name rhymed with Joe.

"Zo-ee," she replied instinctively.

"And the victim's name?"

Bad enough the reporter had her name. No way was she giving up Sylvia's. "You'll have to get a statement from the police. I'm not at liberty to share details."

"I've been working closely with Chief Pete Adams and County Detective Wayne Baronick on this case." The reporter smiled as she tossed out the names. "I'm sure they wouldn't mind if you gave me some information on this latest development."

Zoe bristled. Working closely with Pete? He hadn't mentioned anything to her. Then again, they hadn't spoken since they'd argued yesterday about her moving in with Mrs. Kroll.

Zoe eyed the reporter, who wasn't wearing makeup, but even in the harsh shadows of the overhead porch light, Zoe could tell the woman was attractive. Very attractive.

And was that big grin when she mentioned Pete's name because she was trying to gain Zoe's trust or because the thought of him brought a smile to her lips?

Stop it.

Zoe shook off the flash of jealousy. "As I said, I'm not at liberty to—"

The storm door behind her crashed open, slamming her in the back. She staggered.

Seth charged through it. "Sorry. Zoe, we need to get your equipment out of the ambulance." He ran past her toward Medic Two.

Ignoring the reporter, Zoe jogged after him. "Why?"

"It's Sylvia. We think she's having a heart attack."

TEN

Pete wheeled his personal vehicle into one of the spots outside the Emergency Department reserved for law enforcement. The Ford Edge was packed to overflowing with a bookshelf, suitcases, novels, photos, and bags of who-knew-what. Stuff that Nadine felt vital to Harry's comfort at the nursing home.

Assisted-living facility. Nadine had already corrected him three times this evening. Pete needed to pound the politically correct term into his brain.

Right now his mind was on Sylvia. Her phone call earlier about those bastards coming to her door had infuriated him—especially when he was forty miles away and couldn't respond. But Zoe's call about Sylvia being taken to the ER had terrified him.

He blew through the automatic doors and paused at security long enough to flash his badge and tell the guy not to have the Edge towed or ticketed. At the registration desk, a tired but cordial woman in pink scrubs directed him to room four and buzzed him into the treatment area.

The sliding glass door to the room was open, as was the privacy curtain. Sylvia, attired in a faded hospital gown, sprouted wires and tubes leading to a heart monitor, oxygen, and an IV pump. Zoe, in her paramedic uniform, stood next to her. Both looked up when he entered.

"What the hell's going on?" he asked, keeping his voice soft and jovial. "I leave the township for one evening and you end up in here."

"I wish I knew." Sylvia's scowl vacillated between annoyance and worry. "They stick me in this glass fishbowl, poke me with needles, paste a bunch of patches on my chest, and then abandon me."

Zoe shrugged. "Hurry up and wait."

Pete glanced at his watch. "You called me more than an hour ago. I thought you'd be back in service by now."

"I was. It's been a busy night. We didn't even make it back to the garage before getting another call." Zoe rested a hand on Sylvia's arm. "I'm checking on my first patient of the night while Earl's restocking supplies."

Sylvia snorted. "Your first patient just wants to get out of here. I was supposed to go over to Bertie's house this evening to play bridge with the girls."

"You're going to be late."

If she made it at all, which Pete doubted.

"I'm already late. Where's that darned doctor?"

As if on cue, a distinguished-looking silver-haired man in a white lab coat breezed into the cubicle. "Hello, Zoe. Mrs. Bassi." He eyed Pete.

"Dr. Fuller, this is Pete Adams," Zoe said. "He's our police chief in Vance Township."

Pete realized he was in his civvies, making the added introduction necessary. They shook hands.

The doctor raised an eyebrow at Sylvia. "Would you prefer we talk in private?"

She waved the hand not bound by IVs, blood-pressure cuffs, and oxygen monitors. "These two are the closest I have to family right now. I'd rather they hear whatever it is directly from you."

"All right." The doctor crossed his arms. "Your blood work shows your LDL, or bad cholesterol, is a little too high and your HDL, or good cholesterol, is a little too low. Otherwise, everything is well within the normal range. Your EKG concerns me though. I don't believe you've had a heart attack, but I do want to admit you overnight and order a stress test for tomorrow morning. If you pass it, you can go home tomorrow afternoon. Maybe even late morning."

"And if I don't pass?"

The doctor shot a glance at Pete and then Zoe before meeting Sylvia's gaze again. "Cardiac catheterization."

She squirmed. "Can't I just go home and promise to eat a lot of salads?"

"Afraid not. I'd rather get to the bottom of this sooner than later."

"You said I didn't have a heart attack."

"I said I didn't believe you had one. But there's something going on in there. Let's find out what and get you treated. Okay?"

Sylvia scoffed. "No, it's not okay. I'll stay for the stress test. But if I flunk it, you'll have to catch me to go sticking any probes inside my heart."

He chuckled. "Mrs. Bassi, if you can outrun our orderlies, you don't need a heart cath." He shook her hand as well as Zoe's and Pete's, promising to get Sylvia admitted in a room upstairs as soon as possible.

Once the doctor had left, Pete caught Zoe's gaze and tipped his head toward the hall. She nodded. He turned to Sylvia. "I need to talk to Zoe for a minute. Don't go anywhere."

"Smart ass."

Zoe scooped her winter jacket off the back of the chair and bid goodnight to Sylvia before stepping out of the treatment room with him.

He hadn't seen her since she'd moved in with Mrs. Kroll, which felt like days. He wanted to order her to get her sexy ass back home—his home.

Their home.

But the busy ER hallway, with Sylvia on the other side of the glass, tethered to IVs and monitors, wasn't the right place for another heated debate over Zoe's ability to take care of herself. One disaster at a time. "I want to know what happened tonight." He kept his voice low. "All of it."

"Have you talked to Seth?"

"Briefly. But I want to hear about it from you."

Zoe fell silent for a moment. Then she said, "It was them again. The guys pretending to be with the water company."

"I know that much. Sylvia called my cell phone as soon as they left. I ordered her to call 911." He tilted his head down toward Zoe. "Did they cause this?"

"They sure didn't help any." She shot a troubled glance over her shoulder. "I mean, I've seen Sylvia upset lots of times, but never like this. She started complaining about chest pains. Her BP and pulse were elevated, and she was having some shortness of breath, so Earl and I talked her into coming here."

Pete rubbed the ache that blossomed behind his forehead. "She's been through a lot in the last year or so. Having these guys at her door after what happened to Oriole was probably enough to push her over the edge."

Pain shone in Zoe's baby blues as she gazed through the glass at Sylvia in the hospital bed. "I know."

"Have you talked to Rose?" Sylvia's daughter-in-law and Zoe's best friend, who had moved to New Mexico a few months ago.

"I called her as soon as we got Sylvia here. I'll call her again and let her know what Dr. Fuller said."

Earl rounded a corner and strode toward them. "Hey, Pete. Zoe, you ready to go?"

She looked at Pete, a silent question in her eyes.

"I'll stay with her until they get her settled in her room."

"Thanks." Zoe's eyes glistened with a flash of tears and she blinked. "We have to get these guys."

He drew her into his arms. "We will. I promise."

She held onto him, her breath warming his neck. After a moment, she pushed away. "I have to get back to work."

He watched her go, slipping into her jacket as she headed for the exit, and then glanced into the treatment room. Ever the mother hen, Sylvia gave him a pleased smile. He held up one finger at her and pulled out his phone, punching in Seth's number. He wanted an update on the search for the sons of bitches in the white van who had paid another visit to his township.

It had been almost midnight before Pete made it home from the hospital. Why the hell did it take so long to get a patient moved into a room? Exhausted, he fed Zoe's cats and fell into bed only to lie there, eyes wide open, staring at the shadows.

He guessed he fell asleep around four. His alarm went off at six. By seven he was at the station to meet with Kevin Piacenza, his third-shift officer, who thankfully had agreed to stay over a few extra hours while Pete helped get Harry moved into the nursing home.

Assisted-living facility.

The area-wide BOLO on the white panel van had been updated to mention damage from last night's collision, and Pete asked Kevin to check out the local body shops.

When Pete arrived at Golden Oaks, he searched the lot for Nadine's car. Apparently he'd arrived first. He parked his Edge at the front door and climbed out. As much as he hated to admit it, his sister had been right about moving Harry this morning. While the usual gray clouds hung overhead, the temperatures had climbed to near forty, balmy by January standards.

By the time Nadine pulled up behind the Edge at nine thirty, Pete and one of the staff members had unloaded Harry's belongings from the back of the SUV and transferred them into the room that would be his father's new digs.

Nadine held the passenger door open and offered Harry a helping hand. "Here we are, Dad."

Harry struggled out of the car, took the cane Nadine held out to him, and stared at the nursing home's façade, a puzzled look on his face. "What's this place?"

"It's Golden Oaks, Dad."

"Kinda early for lunch, isn't it?"

Before Pete could step in and remind his father about their visit here two days ago, Nadine slammed the car door. "I wanted to beat the crowd."

"Must have good food."

"Yep."

As Harry shuffled toward the door, Nadine shot a glance at the Edge and then at Pete. "Where's Dad's stuff?"

"I already moved it into his room."

"You should have waited for me."

"You were supposed to be here a half hour ago."

"Dad wasn't cooperative about getting dressed this morning. I suppose you just dumped everything in the middle of the room."

Damn, she sounded like their mother hounding him to clean his room. "I didn't know where you wanted it."

"Exactly. I intended to put stuff away as you brought it in. Now I'll have to spend all day sorting through everything."

"What difference does it make? And what was I supposed to do while I waited for you? Sit on my hands?"

They'd reached the heavy wooden doors, and Harry stopped and straightened. "Stop bickering, children."

The stern paternal voice stirred a flood of memories. Pete as a boy. Bratty baby sister Nadine jabbing at him in the backseat of the car. Pop behind the wheel. *Stop bickering, children.*

Pete hadn't heard those words or that tone in decades. "Yes, Pop."

Inside, the same thin gray-haired woman who'd shown them around two days ago waited, a warm smile on her face. What was her name?

Nadine and the woman shook hands, and Pete caught a glimpse of her name badge. Connie Smith. That was it. Pete rubbed his forehead. Good God, was he going to be calling everyone Sunshine before too long the same way Harry did?

Pete surveyed the area. A number of residents gathered in the sitting room to his right. To his left, two ladies sat at one of a handful of tables having coffee near a counter containing a large water dispenser and a bowl of fruit. Another woman, well-dressed in a blue sweater and pearls, her hair styled and sprayed in place, stood holding onto her walker near the receptionist's desk. Two young men chatted with her, smiling and gently touching her arm. Grandsons perhaps. One of them kissed her on her cheek.

"Right this way," Connie Smith said, interrupting Pete's thoughts. She directed them toward the elevator, which Pete had become familiar with in the last half hour of lugging his father's possessions inside.

During the ride to the second floor, Nadine and the woman chatted like old friends. Harry scowled at the various notices and activities lists posted on the elevator's walls. As soon as they stepped out, he balked. "What's going on?" he demanded, a quiver to his voice.

With well-practiced joviality, Connie patted his hand. "This is your new home, Mr. Adams. Your apartment's at the end of this hall. I know it's kind of confusing now, but we have lots of aides to show you around until you get used to it."

Harry's expression had transformed from confusion to fear to obstinate as the woman spoke. "No."

Nadine blanched. "What?"

"No. I'm not staying here."

Pete had been afraid of this. When Nadine looked at him, silently pleading for his assistance, Pete gave her a helpless shrug. What did she expect Pete to do? This was a nursing home. Not a jail.

She shot a dark look at him and turned to Harry. "Dad, we discussed this—"

"No." Harry shook his head adamantly.

Connie took his hand. "You'll like it here. We have games and crafts and exercise classes—"

He jerked his hand free. "I don't play games. I don't like crafts. And the only exercise I need is a walk around the park." Having dismissed both women, he fixed his gaze on Pete. "Take me home, son." Harry turned to get back on the elevator, and Pete believed he would have—except the doors closed before he had the chance. "Dammit."

Nadine appeared on the verge of tears, and the Smith woman promised everything would be fine. Watching Harry jab at the down button, Pete wasn't so sure.

He moved closer to his father and whispered in his ear, "Pop, we need to talk about this."

"I'm not talking. You can't make me stay here. I'm going back to my house. Not yours. Not Nadine's. Mine."

Pete's headache ratcheted up a notch. The house—Harry's house, which he'd shared with his late wife for decades—had been sold to a nice young couple years ago when Nadine had taken him in. "Pop…"

The elevator doors swished open. The elderly woman in the pale blue sweater, who had been speaking with her grandsons downstairs, stood inside with her walker, blocking Harry's entrance. But he also blocked her exit. She stared at him, wide-eyed. "Oh. Excuse me." She smiled and Pete couldn't help but think she must have been a knockout in her younger days.

Harry must have been thinking the same thing. "No. Excuse me." He stepped aside with a grand and gentlemanly sweep of his arm, inviting her out.

"Why, thank you." She stepped from the elevator with remarkable grace for a woman on a walker. "You must be new here." She extended her hand. "I'm Barbara."

Harry took the offered hand, and for a moment, Pete damned near thought his old man was going to kiss it.

"Barbara. That's a lovely name for a lovely lady. I'm Harry."

"It's a pleasure to meet you, Harry. What room are you in?"

He looked at Nadine and the Smith woman, both of whom gaped at him. "Well? What room am I in?"

"Uh. Room 224," the Smith woman stuttered.

As if Barbara hadn't been right there to hear, Harry turned to her and repeated, "Room 224."

"How nice. I'm right across the hall. We're neighbors."

"Wonderful. Maybe you can show me around. Until I get to know the place, I mean."

"I would be delighted."

Side by side, Harry and Barbara tottered past Nadine and the Smith woman and down the hall. "Tell me, Barbara, do they sell chocolate milkshakes here?"

"As a matter of fact, they have delicious milkshakes. And they're free."

Nadine braced a hand against the wall. "Well, I'll be damned."

"I told you it would be fine," the Smith woman said, as if she'd planned on playing matchmaker all along.

Pete watched his father and the elegant woman with the pearls stroll away. Nadine and her new best friend trailed after them. He shook his head and smiled. "Pop, you dog you."

ELEVEN

"Thanks for giving me a lift home," Sylvia said.

"I wasn't gonna let you camp in the hospital lobby." Zoe slowed her battle-weary three-quarter-ton Chevy truck as they approached the turn onto Veterans Street in Dillard. The pickup that had crashed last night had been removed, leaving a fractured utility pole splintered and listing, held somewhat upright by its wires. "You really shouldn't stay at your house alone though."

Sylvia huffed. "What else can I do? With the kids out west, I don't have anyone to come stay with me."

Not that Sylvia would have let her daughter-in-law or grandkids babysit her anyway. But the For Sale sign in front of their house just two doors away from Sylvia's provided a painful reminder that help was no longer close at hand.

"Pete and I talked," Zoe said as she parked in the spot the ambulance had occupied last night. "He wants you to pack some things and move into his guest room. I'm staying with Mr. and Mrs. Kroll until we catch these guys, so it's available." She didn't mention the part about Pete's displeasure with her ongoing vigil at the farm.

Sylvia looked at Zoe askance and smirked. "As if you're actually staying in the guest room."

Zoe's cheeks warmed. Her sleeping arrangements at Pete's weren't something she cared to discuss, especially with Sylvia.

"Besides, there's no way in hell I'm letting some punks scare me out of my own home." Sylvia gathered her oversized handbag—the one Zoe was convinced contained rocks—and released the seatbelt.

Zoe jumped out and circled to the passenger door before Sylvia could attempt the large step down from the old pickup.

Sylvia fluttered a dismissive hand at her. "Quit treating me like an old lady."

"I'm not. I'm treating you like anyone who had spent the night in the hospital and had a stress test this morning."

"And passed with flying colors, mind you."

Not quite true. The doctor hadn't liked what he saw and had ordered Sylvia to make an appointment with a cardiologist ASAP. She'd been as dismissive of him as she was trying to be of Zoe.

But Sylvia looked at the ground and hesitated. "It's a long way down there, isn't it?"

"This is a truck. Not your little Escort." Zoe offered a hand.

Sylvia reluctantly took it.

A gust of chilly wind prompted Zoe to flip the hood of her coat over her head. "It's colder here than it was in Brunswick."

They shuffled toward Sylvia's house arm in arm. "The weathermen said falling temperatures later this afternoon. I think their timing might be off."

On the porch, Zoe opened the storm door—and froze. The wooden entry door wasn't completely shut. "I know I locked up as we were leaving last night."

Sylvia clutched her purse to her bosom. "Are you certain?"

Zoe had grabbed Sylvia's keys and double-checked the lock while Earl and Seth had wheeled the stretcher out to the ambulance. But now the door was ajar. Closed enough to keep the cold out, but not latched. Zoe leaned down for a better look. The wood around the latch plate was crushed, evidence of being forced.

Zoe fumbled for her phone. "I'm calling Pete."

"You do that." However, Sylvia shouldered the door open and stormed in.

"Wait. Don't go in there." But Zoe might as well have ordered the northern wind to stay out. With an exasperated growl, she followed.

Sylvia charged through the kitchen to her living room, where she stopped and covered her mouth, letting out a sob. "Dear lord."

Zoe reached Sylvia's side, catching her arm before looking around. The entertainment center her family had given her two years ago for Christmas now boasted a gaping void where the television had been. The DVD player was also missing, a tangle of cords and cables left behind. The doors stood open and the knickknacks and photos on the shelves all appeared out of kilter.

Zoe tugged Sylvia's arm. "We need to get out of here and call Pete."

"Oh, no." She ignored Zoe's plea and moved toward the unit. "Oh. No, no, no." She reached toward an empty spot on a shelf.

Zoe caught her hand. "Don't tamper with the crime scene."

Sylvia didn't resist, but kept her hand there, as if touching an invisible picture frame. Tears rolled down her cheeks.

Zoe struggled to recall what had been in that spot.

"Those filthy bastards." Sylvia's voice was little more than a whisper. "They could have my TV. They could have anything else they wanted. But why?" She hiccupped. "Why take Ted's memorial?"

Zoe's throat threatened to close. That's what was missing from the shelf. The display Sylvia had created of her late son's firefighting memorabilia. His badge. A plaque the fire department had made to honor his service. And a triangular wooden frame containing the American flag that had draped his coffin.

Zoe took Sylvia by the shoulders and turned her away from the shelves. "Let's go over to Pete's house. We'll call him from there."

The fight had gone out of the older woman. She lowered her head. "Whatever you say."

Harry and his new "friend" had tottered off, with Barbara promising to show him around. Pete tried to excuse himself. "I have to get back to work." But Nadine kept giving him The Look she'd inherited from their mother.

"Try it over there." His sister pointed at one of the walls in Harry's new room, indicating where she now thought the bookshelf should go.

Never mind that Pete had already moved the thing twice, and that wall was where he'd set the shelf in the first place. However, mentioning the fact would only have raised Nadine's ire, so he dutifully lugged it across the floor. At least it was one of those cheap DIY pieces of crap from the local big box store and didn't weigh much.

As Nadine pondered the aesthetics of the room, Pete's cell phone rang. Zoe's gorgeous face on his incoming call screen was a welcome sight.

"Hey," he said. "How's Sylvia?"

A moment's silence greeted the question before Zoe spoke. "We have a problem."

He sensed the strain in her voice and glanced at Nadine, who was still studying the furniture arrangement and tapping one foot. "I'll be right back," he told his sister and ducked out of the room before she could protest. "What's going on?"

The story Zoe poured out stirred the embers of his tension headache.

"Is Sylvia okay?" He could well imagine her needing an immediate return trip to the ER.

"I offered her some of your good bourbon. She took it."

And Sylvia wasn't much of a drinker. "Have you called 911?"

"No. I called you."

He would have smiled if he wasn't so damned pissed. "I'm still in Brunswick getting Pop settled in." From down the hallway, Pete spotted his father and Barbara chatting with three other gray-haired women. He appeared to be acclimating nicely. "You and Sylvia stay right there. I'll have Kevin get over to her house and look around. I should be back in a half hour or so."

After hanging up, Pete returned to Harry's room and found Nadine waiting. "Let's try it back over there." She pointed at the wall from which Pete had last moved the shelf.

He grabbed his jacket from the back of a chair. "I have to get back to the station."

There was that look again.

"There's been an incident. Someone broke into Sylvia's house and stole a bunch of stuff."

The Look faded to one of concern. "Is she okay?"

"What do you think?"

Nadine nodded. "Of course. You go. I can handle the rest of this."

Which was what Pete had said an hour ago. He approached her and kissed the top of her head. "Call me later."

He ducked out of the room before she changed her mind, punching in Kevin's cell number as he headed for the elevator.

*   *   *

Less than a half hour later, Pete parked behind Kevin's cruiser in front of Sylvia's house. Zoe's pickup sat in front of the township vehicle. She'd phoned Pete fifteen minutes earlier to let him know Sylvia, bolstered by the bourbon, insisted on returning to her house the moment she'd spotted Kevin's car.

The hazard of living only a block and a half away on the same street. Sylvia missed nothing.

Zoe opened the kitchen door when he knocked. He asked her a silent question with his eyes. *How is she?* Zoe responded with a big shrug and a tip of her head toward the older woman, who stood with her back to them at the doorway to her living room.

"Sylvia?" he called.

She didn't move.

"Sylvia."

Still nothing.

Pete crossed the kitchen and caught her arm with the intention of ushering her to the table and a chair. She turned her head away from him, but not before he caught a glimpse of her tear-dampened face. "Hey," he whispered and wrapped his arms around her.

Sylvia—the strong, independent matriarch of the entire township—crumpled against him, sobbing.

He looked at Zoe, meeting her worried gaze.

As quickly as Sylvia had collapsed, she recovered, squirming free. "I'm fine." Her quivering voice belied her words. She sniffled into a tissue she dug from her pocket. "I'm just...really...pissed."

Now she sounded more like the Sylvia Pete knew and loved. "Me too. Now come sit down."

She seemed willing to comply until Kevin appeared in the hallway from the rear of the house and strode toward them, a camera in his hand.

"I've photographed everything." He hesitated before adding, "They made a mess back there."

Sylvia took a step toward the hall, but Pete caught her. "Hold on. Let us do our job before you storm in there and destroy evidence." He looked at Kevin. "Do we need to call in the crime unit?"

"No." Sylvia tried to pull away from him. "I don't want those county clods going through my things. I'll behave. If anyone is going to search through my underwear, I'd rather it be the three of you."

"Three?"

She gestured at Zoe. "Three."

"But there's no b—" Zoe stuttered. "I'm a deputy coroner. Not a crime-scene technician."

Pete filled in the blank. *But there's no body.* "Besides, I have another job for her," he told Sylvia.

"What?" both women said in unison.

To the older one, he said, "Taking you back to my house and keeping you there." He lifted his gaze to Zoe.

She gave him a sheepish shrug and mouthed, "I tried."

"Try harder."

Sylvia attempted to wiggle free of him again. "I'll go. On one condition."

"This is not a negotiation."

"You're damned right it's not. My house. My rules. I want to see what those bastards did to my stuff before you start messing it up more. I won't touch anything. I promise."

It was a reasonable request. "You aren't to step foot in any of the rooms. You can look from the hall, and let us know if you notice anything missing."

"Yes, yes. Now let go."

Pete eased his grip, but continued to hold one arm. Hopefully she would think he was steadying her instead of being ready to stop her. The look she gave him said he wasn't fooling anyone.

The hall was clear. They stopped at the first doorway. Her spare room. The dresser drawers had been pulled out and were empty.

"What did you have in them?" Pete asked.

"Nothing. They were for company to use." Sylvia pointed to the top of a chest of drawers. "I had a small TV up there. It's gone."

"Anything else?"

"Like I said. This room was for company. I didn't keep anything in it."

The next room was the bathroom. In shades of avocado and pink, it was desperately in need of a remodel. The medicine cabinet hung open. Bottles of aspirin and a package of Benadryl lay in the sink along with a couple bottles of nail polish.

"Did you have any prescription meds in there?" Pete asked.

"No. I'm not on anything. I'm healthy as a horse. Or I was until last night."

Pete gave her arm a gentle squeeze. "We're going to get these guys."

"You better." They moved on to the final doorway, and Sylvia choked. "Dear God."

The mattress and box springs had been dislodged and slumped half off, half on the bed frame. Every drawer had been removed from the dresser, the bureau, and both nightstands, their contents strewn on the floor. The closet door gaped open. Shoes had been dumped from their boxes, and several plastic storage bins had been opened and searched. A fireproof box sat in the middle of the mess, its lock broken, papers scattered.

Pete could only imagine what Sylvia was feeling. And after spending the night in the hospital for chest pains. He tried to nudge her away from the door. "Let's go."

"No. You need to know what's missing."

"We can do that later."

Sylvia stood firm. "My jewelry box is gone. I kept my wedding bands in it. And some diamond earrings Ted gave me for Christmas one year. And I had the laptop the kids gave me for my birthday sitting on the nightstand. It's gone." She pointed at the broken fireproof box. "My husband's Army revolver was in there." She huffed an acrid laugh. "I hope they try to use it. The firing pin's missing. But..." She nodded toward the closet. "Ted's hunting rifle was in there, way in the back. I bet they found it."

Pete tightened his arm around her shoulders. "Okay. Now I want you out of here so we can do our work."

"But—"

"No buts. When we catch these guys I don't want our case to be tossed out because you contaminated our crime scene."

She seemed to shrink. "All right."

Back in the kitchen, Zoe was wearing her jacket and held Sylvia's purse and coat. Pete took it and helped Sylvia put it on.

"Go back to my house," Pete said. He looked at Sylvia. "And you get some rest."

For once in her life, she didn't argue.

Zoe sidled closer to him. "I need to keep an eye on Mr. and Mrs. Kroll," she whispered.

Pete rubbed the space between his eyes. "Convince them to go stay with their son until we get these guys off the street."

"They won't go. They're afraid of leaving their house unattended."

Damned stubborn fools. Zoe included. "I'd rather they had to replace their possessions than see them get hurt." Or worse. "Same goes for you."

"No one's going to mess with them when I'm there."

They'd been having this same argument for two days, and he wasn't making a single dent in her resolve. He growled. "Fine. Go."

Zoe kept her voice low. "But Sylvia really shouldn't be alone. In spite of her insistence that she's okay, they found something during her stress test. She has orders to make an appointment with a cardiologist. I'm afraid..." Zoe shot a look over his shoulder at the ransacked living room and then brought her gaze back to his, leaving the rest unspoken.

She was afraid Sylvia might have a full-fledged heart attack.

"What are you two talking about?" Sylvia stood at the door, boots on, coat buttoned.

"Nothing," Pete said. He leaned down, bringing his face next to Zoe's. Sylvia would think he was kissing Zoe goodbye. Instead, he whispered, "I'll get someone else over there as soon as I can."

She brushed her cheek against his, eliciting a deep-seated urge to lift her off her feet and carry her away to someplace quiet and private. When she drew away, her smile told him she was also having less-than-professional thoughts at the moment. "I'll call the farm and make sure everything's okay over there. Then I'll wait until backup arrives."

Pete watched the women slip out, slamming the door behind them. He turned and found Kevin grinning at him. A stern glare wiped the smirk from the officer's face. "You can go home too."

"I thought I'd help you dust for fingerprints."

"You've already been on duty..." Pete checked his watch. "...almost twelve hours. Go home."

Kevin deflated.

Pete walked over to him and clapped him on the back. "Get some sleep. I need you fresh for tonight."

Bolstered, Kevin nodded and headed to the door.

Once Kevin had gone, Pete stood in the middle of Sylvia's living room and surveyed the voids on the entertainment center. As angry as he was about the robbery, the knowledge that these bastards had sent Sylvia to the hospital—and could have done much worse had she been home for their return visit—sent him into a rage. One he needed to control if he was going to nail these punks.

And he was definitely going to nail these punks.

Pete tugged his phone from his pocket and pulled up his contact list.

TWELVE

The Alberta Clipper blasted in earlier than forecast. Nate Williams, Vance Township's weekend officer, had shown up to keep an eye on Sylvia. Nate had once played professional football, or so went the rumor, so his intimidating presence should keep the troublesome patient in line. Maybe. Grateful to be momentarily relieved of her duties, Zoe sped back to the farm through the snow squalls. A phone call assured her that Mr. and Mrs. Kroll were fine, so she continued out the farm lane, past the house to the barn. The wind had the horses kicking up their heels, but the Siren's call of grain rattling in a bucket overcame their playfulness and lured them into their stalls.

With her charges bedded down and the barn doors closed against the winter storm, Zoe climbed back into her truck, her cheeks tingling. When she cleared the top of the little hill and the house came back into view, she spotted Patsy's pickup parked in the backyard. Not in the normal spot higher on the hillside, but right next to the house where Alexander had parked yesterday to drop off his father.

Zoe, however, left her Chevy where she usually did, pulled her hood over her head, and picked her way down the path to the deck, cautious of the slippery footing. As Zoe stomped the snow from her boots, Mrs. Kroll opened the sliding glass door. "Don't worry about that, dear. Come in out of the cold."

The old couple kept the house warmer than Zoe was used to, but at the moment, she wasn't complaining. "Thanks." She shucked off her jacket and bent down to unlace her boots.

"You have company," Mrs. Kroll announced brightly.

Patsy was hardly company.

Zoe removed her thawing footwear and set them beside Patsy's on the rug next to the door.

Mr. Kroll occupied his favorite recliner. Patsy leaned over a portable electric heater that Zoe had never seen before, adjusting one of the settings. For a moment, Zoe didn't notice the person seated and partially obscured by Patsy and the heater.

Mrs. Kroll stepped into the middle of the room, spreading her arms with a ta-da flourish. "Surprise!"

Patsy straightened and stepped aside. A blonde woman in a winter-white pantsuit perched in the chair next to the heater.

Zoe blinked. "Mom?"

Kimberly Chambers Jackson made no move to rise. "Hello, Zoe." Her tone was chillier than the Arctic blast outside.

Zoe looked at Patsy for some clue about what was going on, but her Mona Lisa smile provided nothing.

Zoe stuttered, her questions colliding inside her brain, her self-editor keeping her from asking the big one—what the hell are you doing here? Instead, she said, "I didn't expect to see you."

"Why would you?" Kimberly picked at something on her sleeve. "You never write. You never call."

"I did." Zoe winced at the shrillness of her own voice. She bit down on her lower lip to keep from saying the rest. *You told me to never call you again.*

Kimberly's expression soured further. "And that man you've been seeing doesn't return my calls either."

"Pete?"

"Or have you screwed up that relationship too?"

"Kimberly," Patsy said sharply. "Be nice. Remember why you're here."

Zoe crossed her arms. If her mother wasn't going to at least give the pretense of congeniality, why should she? Besides, her stepfather, who had always been the peacekeeper, wasn't around to intercede. "Why are you here, Mother?"

Kimberly shot a look at Patsy. Zoe translated. *Because you made me come.* Patsy made a stern face back at her, eliciting an exasperated growl. Kimberly cleared her throat. "I understand you have a situation with your horse."

"A situation?" Zoe sneaked a glance at Mr. Kroll, who watched with a look of pity on his face. Did he feel bad for her because Kimberly was her mother? Or because he felt guilty about the situation to which she referred?

Kimberly waved a hand at the Krolls. "They're evicting you, right?"

Zoe had forgotten just how insensitive her mother could be. "No." Zoe's voice wavered. "Not really."

Kimberly turned to Patsy. "You said they were kicking out all your horses."

"They're selling the farm, and the buyers want the horses out," Patsy said.

Kimberly rolled her eyes. "Same thing." She sat forward, fixing her gaze on Zoe. "I know we didn't part company on the best of terms last summer."

That was an understatement.

"And I want to make amends."

Amends? That was the word Patsy had used a couple days ago.

"I've decided to give you the family farm."

Zoe realized her mouth was hanging open. Surely her mother couldn't mean..."What family farm?"

Kimberly cocked her head and gave her a look that made Zoe expect her to say duh. "The Miller place up on Ridge Road."

She did mean...

Memories from last summer flashed through Zoe's consciousness. An approaching storm. A barn.

A dead body hanging from the rafters.

"I thought you'd at least show some gratitude," Kimberly said.

"I don't know what to say."

"'Thank you' would be nice."

A place of her own. A farm. Acreage.

A rundown house. Fences in poor repair.

Memories of a man with a noose around his neck.

"Thank you," Zoe said without much enthusiasm.

Apparently it was enough for Kimberly. She beamed, smugly satisfied with her own generosity. "Good. That's settled. We'll drive out there tomorrow morning to look at the old homestead."

"Why not do it now?" Patsy said.

Kimberly leaned forward, extending her hands toward the heater, palms facing it. "Because it's too damned cold. We'll wait until it warms up tomorrow."

Zoe's mother clearly hadn't seen the local forecast. "I don't think it's gonna get any warmer until the weekend."

Kimberly gave her a dismissive wave. "Of course it'll be warmer tomorrow." As if the power of her will would make it so. She looked at Patsy. "And then you can drive me to the airport for my flight home."

"I'm done back there." Pete lugged his evidence-collection kit into Sylvia's living room to find Baronick lifting a fingerprint from the entertainment center. The sight of its shelves, now smudged with fingerprint powder, made Pete cringe. "Sylvia's going to kill me."

"Why? For letting me inside her house?"

Baronick had a point. Sylvia had never warmed to the county detective. "That too. But at least I didn't let you into her bedroom." Pete had processed the back rooms himself, leaving Baronick to the living room and kitchen.

The detective added the fingerprint card to the others he'd collected and peeled off his gloves. "I'm done too." He glanced out the window and swore. "And I'm heading back to Brunswick before I get stranded. Nothing personal, but I don't want to end up snowbound out here in Mayberry."

Until now, Pete had been too busy to notice the weather. Snow blew sideways. At least an inch had collected on the trees, shrubs, and cars since he'd last looked outside.

"I'll add Sylvia's stuff to the list of stolen items." Baronick slipped into his long black coat. "My men are monitoring all the local online buying sites and social media pages as well as the bigger ones like eBay. Firefighter memorabilia is hot right now." He grinned. "Firefighter? Hot? Get it?"

Pete was too irritated to even bother with a groan. "Check the pawn shops around the county. And the gun shops. Watch out for that Army pistol and Ted's rifle." Sylvia had been right about the burglars taking it.

"Already on it."

"I'll stop at the one in Phillipsburg. I still need to talk to Janie

Baker. She hasn't gotten back to me with an inventory of what's missing from her grandmother's house." Plus he needed to have a chat with her about Marcus. He didn't want to put it off until Oriole's viewing later.

"Keep me posted." Baronick gathered his evidence and his gear and headed for the door. "Hopefully the bad weather will keep these punks at home tonight."

"Amen to that."

Pete's intention to chat with Janie hadn't gone as planned. No one was home when he dropped by. He tried the phone number she'd given him, only to have a machine answer. He explained he wanted to speak with her, but she hadn't called back.

He managed to catch Bub McDermott, proprietor of Phillipsburg's sole pawn shop, as the balding and paunchy wheeler-and-dealer prepared to lock up. Bub tapped the large-faced watch he wore on his wrist. "It's after quittin' time already, Chief."

"I'll only need a minute." Pete handed him the printout of Sylvia's stolen property. "Has anyone been in here today trying to sell any of this stuff?"

Bub squinted and scanned the sheet. "Nuh-uh." He lifted his gaze to Pete. "I'm guessin' this been stolen, you bein' the one to ask and all."

"You guess right."

"I don't deal in no stolen merchandise. You know that."

"Right." Pete ventured a glance at the now darkened display cases and wondered what he might actually find there should he feel like aggravating old Bub. "Just so you know, the Army pistol is missing the firing pin."

Bub grunted. "Ain't worth too much then, huh?"

"Sentimental value to the owner." Pete tapped the paper. "Especially the firefighter memorabilia."

Bub pressed his lower lip into his upper one until his mouth looked like an inverted U. "Collectors go nuts for that stuff, that's for sure. Some of it goes at auction for big bucks. And I do mean big. But I don't deal in no stolen merchandise."

"So you've said. If someone out there doesn't know you're a fine upstanding citizen, they might try to pawn their loot here though. I'd appreciate a call, should that happen."

The shop owner grunted again. "Anything in it for me?"

"My undying gratitude. For starters."

He snorted. "I guess it don't hurt to have Vance Township's Chief of Police owin' me a favor." Bub folded the paper and tucked it in the pocket of his faded flannel shirt. "I'll call you."

Pete's next stop was the funeral home. Phillipsburg's street lights illuminated the heavy snow showers as he parked in the lot along with four other vehicles. Either the weather had kept people away or, at ninety-two, Oriole had outlived most of her friends and family, leaving few to pay their last respects.

The wind slammed the car's door against Pete's leg as he stepped out. At least the temperature hadn't plunged into the teens as forecasted.

Yet.

He tugged his hat down and his collar up and headed across the street to the front door.

As indicated by the nearly empty parking lot, a mere half-dozen mourners gathered inside. Only one, Mr. Troutman, stood near the casket. A sullen Marcus Baker, hands shoved deep in the pockets of a pair of dress trousers—new ones, if Pete was any judge—gazed out one of the windows.

"Chief Adams." Janie approached with a tired smile. "How nice of you to come."

He took the hand she extended to him. It was warm. Or his were freezing. "Didn't you get the message I left on your voicemail?"

She looked puzzled for a moment. "Oh. The number I gave you was my home phone, and I haven't been there all day." She dug a tissue from her pocket and pressed it to her nose. "I'm sorry. I should've given you the one for my cell."

"No problem. I wanted to talk to you about the case, but now isn't the right time."

She gestured to the small group chatting among themselves. "Now's fine. It's not like I have a lot of guests to entertain."

Pete hesitated. Somehow discussing the home invasion at the victim's viewing seemed crass.

Janie must have sensed his concerns. "Really. It's okay." She nodded toward a pair of easy chairs in the back of the room. "How about we sit over there."

Trout had turned away from the casket, and Pete noticed the old man watching them as they settled into the seats. Marcus had also taken notice, although he attempted to cover his interest, taking furtive glances their way.

Pete pulled out his notebook and a pen. "Have you had a chance to make a list of what was missing from your grandmother's house?"

Janie lowered her gaze to the tissue she clutched in her lap. "I'm ashamed to say, I haven't. I started to, but then I came across a box of old photos and...well, two hours later I was still going through them."

"I understand. I know it's hard, but I really need that list in case they try to sell any of her things."

"Yes, of course. I'll go over there after the funeral tomorrow."

Pete winced. He hated being the heartless son of a bitch, forcing the grieving granddaughter to revisit the crime scene. He wanted to say "Saturday or Sunday would be fine," but each additional day weakened their chance of recovering Oriole's stolen treasures. "Thank you. I'm sorry to add to your burden right now."

Janie dabbed her nose with the tissue. "It's okay."

Pete caught Marcus staring at them. The boy quickly turned back to the window. Speaking of adding to her burden. "I'm afraid there's something else I need to talk to you about."

"Oh?"

"Did Marcus mention the incident at the high school yesterday?"

Her eyes widened and she shot a look at her son, who had his back to them. "What incident?" she asked, her voice hard.

"I'll take that as a no." Pete told her about the fight and Marcus' unwillingness to talk about it. "My colleague from the county police spoke with the other boy, who maintained the fight was totally unprovoked."

Janie never took her eyes from her son as she listened. "Are you going to arrest him?"

"I'd rather not."

She brought her gaze back to Pete. Her lips parted in a silent, surprised "oh."

"You've been through enough this week. I don't want to haul your son off to jail on top of it all. But he's headed down a bad path."

"I know." She worried the tissue in her hands. "I've tried talking to him, but he gets angry and storms out when I press too hard. The only person who seemed able to get through to him was—" Her voice broke.

Pete completed the sentence for her, "Your grandmother."

"Yes." Janie pressed the tissue to her mouth and wept. After a moment she sniffed back her tears and sat up straighter. "Tell me what I need to do, Chief. He needs a male role model in his life, but there isn't one. Would it be best...for him...to let him spend a night or two in jail? You know. Tough love?"

Pete looked over at the boy, no longer sneaking glances at them. Instead the kid appeared to want to jump out the window into the cold darkness rather than face his mother. Or Pete.

Thirteen years old. Locked up. "No," Pete said. "I don't think jail's the best thing for him."

"What then?"

He pondered the problem. "Let me work on it."

THIRTEEN

The smell hit Zoe the moment she stepped into the funeral home. The odors of autopsy always sent her bolting for the restroom, but the aroma of funeral flowers sucker-punched her every bit as hard. Memories hurled her back to being eight years old. A closed casket. Her mother sobbing.

For a moment, Zoe considered fleeing out into the cold night air and the blizzard. The weather had been like this a year ago when Ted died too. Same funeral home.

Same floral stench.

On the verge of hyperventilating, she clutched the door latch, the metal cold even through her gloves.

"Can I help you?"

She turned to find the funeral-home director, a gentleman in a dark suit, wearing a perpetual sympathetic smile on his face. "Ah..."

"Are you here for Mrs. Andrews?" he asked.

Oriole. Yes. Janie. Focus. Zoe swallowed. "Yes, I am."

He directed her into a room to her left. "May I take your coat?"

"No. Thank you. I'll only be a minute." She'd seen Pete's car in the parking lot, so she probably would be longer than a minute. But she needed her coat. She pulled it tighter around her to hide her shivering. Not from the cold. From her nerves.

She made it as far as the doorway and eyed the remembrance book on a stand at the entrance. Only a few names had been scrawled.

Exhaling, she stepped into the room and stole a glance at the casket. No one was near it. Janie's son gazed out a window, his back to the room. A small group of older folks perched together in one of the rows of folding chairs, talking quietly.

Pete and Janie sat in a rear corner leaning toward each other, speaking in low tones.

Mr. Troutman stood in the middle of the room, gripping the back of a chair. He looked uncertain. Lost. Zoe had come to pay her respects, to give Janie a hug, and to see Pete. But they were occupied, and Zoe didn't want to interrupt, so she headed toward the one soul in the room who seemed to need a friend.

Mr. Troutman was watching Pete and Janie and didn't notice Zoe's approach. He flinched when she touched his arm.

"I'm sorry. I didn't mean to startle you," she said.

Flustered, the old man smiled and covered her hand with his. "That's quite all right. I'm a bit out of sorts lately."

"I understand."

He studied her. "You're the Chambers girl, right? Zoe?"

"That's me."

He gestured toward the coffin. "Have you seen Oriole yet?"

The icy memories of her father's closed casket and Ted Bassi's open one clamped down on her again. "No." She knew what was coming next. Mr. Troutman would offer to escort her over there and stand with her. She'd be forced to gaze at Oriole's preserved face as he shared stories or maybe comment on how good she looked.

Instead, he gave Zoe a nudge toward the coffin. "You should do that. I'd go with you, but I've been on my feet all day, and my legs are tired. I think I'd better sit."

"I'll sit with you." Zoe realized she'd sounded too eager and winced.

"No, no. You go. I'll be fine."

The trepidation returned. Pete was still deep in conversation with Janie. He hadn't noticed Zoe's presence yet. With no reasonable excuse to avoid the inevitable, she forced a smile. "Okay."

Steeling herself, she approached the coffin. Oriole did indeed look better than the last time Zoe had seen her, which wasn't saying much. Zoe swallowed hard. She never understood this ghoulish business of standing around a corpse. The essence of the person was long gone. Sylvia once told her it was "for the family." But Zoe had been "the family," and the whole ordeal felt more like torture than closure.

"Hey."

Zoe spun to find Pete behind her. "I didn't think you knew I was here."

He leaned toward her and whispered into her ear, "I spotted you the moment you entered the room."

A surge of warmth chased the chill.

"Why aren't you guarding the Krolls?"

"Alexander stopped in for a visit, so I went by to check on Sylvia."

"How is she?"

"She wants to go back to her house. Says my cats are causing her allergies to flare up."

Pete grinned. "She said the same thing to me too. But how about her heart?"

"She wouldn't let me take her blood pressure. And as cranky as she was, I don't think she's in pain. She behaves better when she's not feeling well."

"You've noticed that too, huh?"

Zoe glanced toward Oriole. "Pete, do you mind if we..."

"Do you think she's eavesdropping on us?"

Zoe shot a look at him.

He chuckled and then grew serious. "Do you want to leave?"

Yes. "Not yet. I still want to pay my respects to Janie. But I need to speak with you first."

Pete guided her to a pair of empty chairs next to the entrance, as if he understood she might need to make a quick escape.

Mr. Troutman, she noticed, wasn't where she'd left him. Nor was he resting his tired legs. Instead he had moved closer to the casket. Janie stood next to Marcus at the window.

Pete took Zoe's hand. "What did you want to talk to me about?"

She met his crystal blue eyes, yearned to lean against him and press her face against his neck. "I miss you." Not what she'd intended to say, but it was the truth. "I've gotten used to seeing you all the time."

He smiled. "That's what I like to hear. You know I consider my house to be your home too."

Which reminded her of what she needed to tell him, souring the moment. "My mother's in town."

The change in gears took him aback. "Your mother?" His gaze shifted and then he closed his eyes and growled. "Dammit."

"What?"

"Mrs. Jackson." His face contorted as if he was in pain. "I should have known."

"What are you talking about?"

"I had a message yesterday morning from a Mrs. Jackson. I couldn't place the name, and before I had a chance to think about it, we got busy with the case. I completely forgot to call her back."

Kimberly's words rang in Zoe's head. *That man you've been seeing doesn't return my calls either.* "That's what she meant."

"What?"

"Never mind. You'll never guess why she's here." Zoe told him about Kimberly's grand plan to make amends.

He listened in silence and remained quiet after Zoe had finished. She could tell he was rolling the news around inside that cop brain of his. After what seemed like an eternity, he asked, "Are you going to accept it?"

The question startled her. She'd never considered not accepting it. Somehow, though, that didn't seem like the right thing to say. "I guess so. Shouldn't I?"

He lifted his gaze to meet hers. Those icy eyes shifted into poker mode, but not before she caught a glimpse of something else. Despair. He didn't want her to move out of his house. "It's your decision," he said flatly. "But when was the last time you were over at that farm?"

She didn't have to think about it. "You know the answer to that." He'd been there too, investigating the previous owner's death.

"And when was the last time you were inside the house?"

"I don't think I've ever been in it."

"Uh-huh." He gave her hand a squeeze. "Just don't sign any papers until you check it out and talk to an attorney."

Voices drifted in from the atrium drawing Zoe's attention. The reporter who'd been snooping around Sylvia's place last night appeared in the doorway. While the woman still carried the large leather bag, tonight she wore makeup. Zoe was right. She was a knock-out. Plus she wore a dark skirt, showing a flash of leg below the hem of her coat.

Lauren Sanders spotted Pete and Zoe immediately. Zoe could almost see the light bulb switch on in the woman's eyes as she made the connection between them.

"Chief Adams. Ms. Chambers." Lauren sauntered over to them. "I wasn't expecting to see the two of you here."

Pete stood. "I could say the same about you. I hope you aren't planning to question Ms. Baker tonight."

"Of course not." Lauren raised an eyebrow, and a teasing grin played across her lips. "Are you?"

Zoe climbed to her feet, looking back and forth between Pete and the reporter. He'd struck his best protector-of-the-universe stance. Even in his civvies, the man had a commanding presence that stirred Zoe's heart. But the appreciative smile on Lauren's face stirred something else entirely.

Zoe cleared her throat. "I'm gonna go speak to Janie."

Pete broke free of the gaze he'd locked with the reporter, but he maintained his professional law-enforcement mode. "All right. I'll talk to you tomorrow."

Zoe hesitantly moved away from them. Glancing back, she spotted Lauren Sanders' fingers brush Pete's arm.

No doubt about it. The woman was definitely flirting with him.

Friday morning didn't start well. While Pete's insomnia wasn't an issue for once, he awakened before his alarm as one of Zoe's cats walked across his face. Twice. Sylvia had complained about her allergies so much last night, he agreed to keep the felines in the bedroom with him. They apparently disapproved. Or they weren't happy with Zoe's absence.

He couldn't blame them on that count.

Sylvia sat at his kitchen table with a cup of coffee and a dour look on her face. "I'm going home," she announced, her voice nasal.

Pete had known Sylvia long enough to realize she'd made up her mind. Still, he had to try. "I don't like the idea of you being alone at your place after what happened."

"They've already robbed me blind. There's no reason for them to come back."

"That's not what I mean, and you know it."

She huffed. "I'll call you every hour and check in. But I can't breathe with those damn cats around."

They settled on her checking in every half hour. However, she couldn't leave until Pete shoveled a path through several inches of fresh snow to his Vance Township Police SUV.

By the time he drove her the block and a half to her house, did more shoveling, and got her settled at home, he was on the verge of being late for his shift.

Topping off the morning, he pulled into the station to find Baronick's unmarked sedan in the snow-covered parking lot.

The detective leaned a shoulder against the front office's doorjamb and chatted with Kevin and Nancy while cradling a mug of coffee. "You look like hell."

The mug, Pete noticed, was one of his. "You could at least have brought Starbucks."

"It would have been cold by the time I got here."

"We have a microwave." Pete looked at his secretary, who appeared mildly amused by the exchange. "Messages?"

She handed him a short stack of pink slips. "Nothing earth shattering. The snow's kept everyone inside and behaving themselves."

He pointed at Kevin and crooked his finger before heading down the hall to his office, scanning the messages as he went. A complaint about a township road not being treated quickly enough. Another complaint about the township road truck being too noisy while plowing in the early morning hours. A man over on Ridge Road wanted Pete to have a talk with his neighbors about their barking dogs. Pete knew the neighbors and the dogs. The hounds were generally well behaved but did go bonkers when a deer wandered across the backyard.

The final slip, dated a half hour previous, stated simply, "Call Lauren Sanders. You have her number."

Indeed he did. In more ways than one.

At least there weren't any reports of the utility-worker impersonators wreaking havoc.

A fresh pot of coffee—minus the cup Baronick had poured—sat in the corner of Pete's office. He silently blessed Nancy and picked up his favorite mug. It needed to be washed, but he decided one more cup before it saw suds wouldn't kill him.

With a steaming mug of caffeine in hand, he took a seat. Kevin claimed the one across from him. Baronick dragged one of the chairs on wheels from the conference room and edged in next to the night-shift officer. The detective flopped into the chair and rocked back, stopping short of propping his feet on the desk.

Ordinarily, Pete would have protested the detective's presence, but this morning he wanted to talk to him anyway.

"Anything I need to know?" Pete directed the question to both men.

Kevin reported on a number of minor traffic collisions, courtesy of slippery roads. None of them required an ambulance ride to the ER. "I kept an eye out for the damaged white van while I was patrolling." He shook his head. "Nada."

"I've contacted all the body shops in Monongahela and surrounding counties," Baronick said. "If they take it someplace reputable for repairs, we'll hear about it."

Pete grunted. "'Reputable' being the keyword."

"Or they could just drive it as is," Kevin said.

"Maybe." Baronick took a long hit from the mug. "But there are hundreds of white panel vans on the road. Considerably fewer have passenger-side front-end damage. If they want to be inconspicuous, they'll fix it."

"Either the repairs or the snow seems to have kept them off the road last night." Pete caught and held Baronick's gaze. "Let's get out there and find them. Today."

"Do you want me to stay on duty?" Kevin asked.

"No. Go home. You put in enough overtime covering for me yesterday."

Once Kevin had gone, Pete turned to Baronick. "Are you going to tell me why you're here?"

The detective feigned a pout. "Aren't you happy to see me?"

"No." Pete wasn't about to admit otherwise.

"I'm hurt." But Baronick rocked forward and rested his forearms on the desk, still cupping the mug in his hands. "I agree we need to nail these guys. Mrs. Bassi was damned lucky she wasn't home when they returned."

Pete wasn't so sure Sylvia would concur. "Ideas?"

"I'm going to update our social media posts encouraging residents to be proactive. I think I'll call another press briefing for later this morning too. These guys didn't just crawl into a hole. Someone out there knows something."

Which reminded Pete of why he wanted to talk to the detective. "Lauren Sanders."

Baronick scowled. "Who?"

"She's a reporter for a new local paper."

"Oh, right. *The Phillipsburg Enterprise*. We have a pool going on how long before it folds. My money's on six months. Most of the guys are betting on less than three though."

"But you think this area will support a local newspaper for the long haul." Pete made no effort to contain his sarcasm.

Baronick grinned. "I'm not betting on the paper. I'm betting on that reporter you just mentioned. Lauren Sanders. I don't see her going down without a fight."

"How well do you know her?"

"Personally? I don't. But she's been at every press briefing I've held recently. The woman's the proverbial dog with a bone."

"If the dog happens to be a pit bull."

Baronick's smile faded. "You don't like her." He chuffed a laugh. "What am I saying? Of course you don't. You hate all reporters."

"I gather you do like her."

The detective pondered the question a moment before answering. "I admire tenacity."

"Is she tenacious? Or fixated on this particular case?" Pete slid the message from Sanders across the desk toward Baronick. "She's been here twice. She's left more messages than I care to count—"

"Because you're so good at returning her phone calls."

Pete glared at the detective. "She showed up at the funeral home last night."

This last bit of information seemed to catch Baronick off guard. "She what?"

Pete remained silent, watching the detective mull it over.

"She could have become friendly with Mrs. Andrews' family."

Pete continued his silence.

"But that negates even the appearance of impartiality."

"So Lauren Sanders is either the most insensitive reporter I've ever met," Pete said, "or she's way more invested in this particular story than she's letting on."

FOURTEEN

Kimberly's Florida tan had paled on the drive to the old farm. The snow-covered back roads made for an adventurous trip even in Patsy's four-wheel-drive Tundra. The blast of Arctic air, which hit them the moment the three women stepped out of the pickup, painted a tinge of pink on Zoe's mother's cheeks.

Kimberly let fly a stream of curses that would make a drunken sailor proud. "It was supposed to be warmer this morning."

"No, it wasn't," Zoe said, too soft for her mother to hear. Arguing was never productive where the two of them were concerned, and while it would be heated, it wouldn't help thaw the current situation.

At least the frozen landscape provided a buffer to Zoe's memories of the place. No wagonload of hay. No flies buzzing around a corpse hanging from the barn rafters. The massive maple in the front yard stood stark and naked rather than providing shade to a crew of nauseated farm workers.

The death of James Engle, the previous owner, wasn't the first to have taken place on the property. Decades before, Kimberly's bachelor uncles, Denver and Vernon Miller, had been murdered here, back when they owned it.

Good thing Zoe didn't believe in curses.

She took a step away from the truck's cab and sunk into snow well above her ankles. The wind sliced through her jeans and long johns, chilling her legs. She wished she had on her quilt-lined coveralls.

But Kimberly was wearing them. Having arrived in Pennsylvania ill prepared for January, she'd feigned bravado earlier at the Krolls' house, insisting her idea of a winter coat would be more than sufficient. Zoe, Patsy, and Mrs. Kroll took one look at the stylish leather jacket before combining efforts to provide Kimberly with cold-weather gear.

By the time they set out, she was attired in a pair of Patsy's barn boots, Mrs. Kroll's fur-lined gloves, Zoe's bibbed coveralls, and one of Mr. Kroll's old but warm coats as well as his hat with the ear flaps. Kimberly left the house complaining, but now, standing in front of the dilapidated barn with the thermometer reading twelve degrees—not counting wind chill—she huddled into her borrowed clothing like a turtle retreating into its shell.

Zoe shoved her hands deep into her pockets and squinted against the bitter wind. The house's porch sagged worse than she remembered, but the structure appeared sound enough. She could remodel it little by little over time. New windows. Shore up the porch. Strip that horrible red asbestos siding. Was there clapboard beneath it?

The house had potential. A little fixer-upper.

As she recalled, the barn was in better shape. The massive doors were closed now, and she took a step toward them.

Kimberly, however, trudged toward the house. "Let's get out of this cold."

Zoe looked to Patsy for some support, and while she shot a longing glance toward the barn, she shrugged at Zoe and followed Kimberly.

Zoe glared after them. At least she knew where Patsy's loyalty lay.

The closer they got to the porch, the more rickety it appeared. Several of the floorboards were rotted through, leaving gaping holes. Kimberly stepped onto it and stopped, looking down.

Zoe suspected her mother would have made some snide comments about the place had she not been "making amends" by giving it to her daughter.

Kimberly picked her way to the door, a key ring clutched in her gloved hand. Patsy stepped onto the porch behind her, treading carefully. Zoe feared the weight of all three of them would be more than the old lumber could tolerate, so she stayed where she was.

The screen door screeched when Kimberly opened it. "What the hell?"

Patsy looked over Kimberly's shoulder. "What's wrong?"

"It's padlocked."

Zoe stomped her feet to warm up. "Don't you have the keys?"

Kimberly fumbled through the keys on the ring, trying each one and coming up empty. "No." She let the screen door bang shut and picked her way back across the porch, brushing past Zoe. "There's another door around the corner."

Zoe and Patsy shuffled through the snow behind Kimberly. She was right. The side of the house looked like it had been the front at some point. Zoe searched the yard for signs that a driveway or even a sidewalk had once led to this door, but the snow and a patch of brambles covered any evidence of what might have been. Then again, only strangers had ever used the "front" door of the Krolls' old farmhouse. Farmers tended to use the entrance closest to the barn.

Kimberly climbed onto the concrete stoop with a grunt—an additional step would have been nice, but was nonexistent—and planted her fists against her hips. "This one's padlocked too." She made a half-hearted effort of trying all the keys. None worked. Pointing at Zoe, she said, "Go around to the back. There's an entrance to the basement. See if it's open and then come back and let us know."

Of course. Why should Kimberly waste her energy plodding through the snow when Zoe was at her beck and call?

Another look at Patsy elicited another helpless shrug.

At least the effort might keep the circulation going in Zoe's legs. She stumped through the drifts, rounded the corner, and spotted the sloping wooden bulkhead against the foundation. As she made her way closer, she could see the hasp was flipped open. No padlock here. Zoe almost turned to call back to her mother and Patsy, but thought about the similar set-up on the old farmhouse that had burnt. Zoe shuffled the rest of the way to the weathered doors, grabbed the pitted metal handle, and yanked.

It didn't budge. She kicked snow away from the bottom edge, but knew it wasn't the problem. As predicted, a second effort proved equally fruitless.

She retraced the same path she'd already broken to find her mother hugging herself against the cold and rocking from foot to foot impatiently. "The basement doors are latched from the inside," Zoe reported.

Grumbling, Kimberly dug in her purse and came up with a cell phone. "I'll call the attorney who's been handling all this."

Punching in the number required Kimberly remove one glove.

Her grumbling ratcheted up a notch.

Moments passed as Zoe gathered a receptionist had placed her mother on hold. Meanwhile the wind continued to pierce her jeans, numbing her legs.

"This is Kimberly Jackson," she finally announced into the phone. "We're at my farm right now, and you failed to give me the keys to the padlocks."

There was a long silence.

"The padlocks," Kimberly repeated, enunciating each syllable as if communicating with someone who didn't understand the language.

Another silence.

"There most certainly are. On both doors." Kimberly met Zoe's gaze and rolled her eyes in exasperation. "I don't care if they aren't supposed to be there."

More silence.

"Fine." Kimberly jabbed at the phone, and Zoe suspected she'd much rather have had an old-fashioned landline to slam down. "This is just great. My attorney says no one put padlocks on the doors." She reached out to Patsy, who took the hint and offered a hand, helping her down. Without a thank you, Kimberly turned and tromped away.

Patsy started after her. Zoe gazed at the door. Something wasn't right. She clambered onto the concrete stoop and examined the lock. The hasp and the padlock shined like new. No rust. No pitting.

"What are you doing?" Patsy had paused at the corner of the house and was watching her.

Zoe scowled and shook her head. "I'm not sure." She hopped down into the shin-deep snow and shuffled past her cousin.

Kimberly stood next to the pickup. "Let's get out of here."

"In a minute," Zoe called. She stepped onto the dilapidated porch and tried to ignore the give of the rotted wood beneath her feet as she picked her way across and opened the screen door. The hasp and lock that greeted her matched the other. New.

"Come on." Kimberly's insistent whine sounded like a child who wasn't getting her way.

Zoe made it to safe ground without falling through the porch decking. "Let her in the truck and crank up the heater," Zoe told Patsy. "Then meet me at the barn."

Kimberly's complaining carried over the wind, but Zoe ignored it. Someone had recently installed those padlocks. Her mother was the owner of record, and the attorney knew nothing about them. That meant if Zoe took a pry bar to them, she wouldn't be breaking the law. She hoped there were some tools left in the barn. If not a pry bar, something equally effective at forcible entry.

Except the barn doors also wore a new hasp and lock. "Crap."

"What?"

Zoe glanced over her shoulder at Patsy. Behind them, the big pickup roared to life. If it weren't for the snow coating the windshield, Zoe felt certain she'd see her mother shooting looks that would kill at her.

"I gave Kimberly the keys and told her to warm it up," Patsy said. "Which of course means she could easily drive away and leave us here."

The comment startled Zoe. Not because she didn't think her mother would do it. But because she didn't think her mother would abandon Patsy. Or that Patsy would think such a thing.

Her cousin must have read her mind. "Yeah, Kimberly's used to getting her way and doesn't play well with others when she doesn't."

"And she doesn't drive you crazy?"

Patsy grinned apologetically. "She's family. I've heard they're supposed to drive you crazy."

"I don't know about that, but if they are, she's an expert."

"You should cut her some slack."

Zoe bristled. "Like she cuts me slack?"

Patsy's exhale fogged the air between them. When it cleared, her eyes gleamed. "Kimberly's hard on you because you're her daughter, and she loves you."

Zoe wanted to gag.

"You two have a history. You've been related all your life. I envy that, family conflict and all. I've never had family before, remember?"

Zoe's annoyance dissipated like the condensation cloud of her exhalation. "I'm sorry."

Patsy waved the apology away. "Forget it." She nodded toward the barn door. "What are you doing?"

"Breaking into 'my' house," Zoe said. "Or so I planned, but someone locked the barn too." She looked around and spotted a wooden handle sticking out of the snow. Hoping it was attached to a shovel or a sledgehammer, she high-stepped through the snow and wrapped her fingers around the wood. It didn't budge. At all. Buried in the frozen ground until spring thaw. "There has to be something around here we can use to bust in."

"I'll look over here." Patsy headed around the far side of the barn.

Zoe shuffled along the side between the barn and the house, scraping the snow away with her boot in hopes of finding a discarded hammer or anything that might work.

The pickup truck door slammed. She didn't look, but expected Kimberly to march over and grab her by the ear, insisting they go somewhere warm.

Instead, Kimberly called out to her, "Zoe."

When Zoe turned, she discovered her mother standing there, holding up a small ax. "Would this help?"

"Where did you find that?"

Kimberly thumbed toward the pickup. "Behind the seat."

Patsy returned from her scavenger hunt empty-handed.

Zoe looked at her. "You keep an ax in your truck?"

"Oh, yeah. I forgot."

Zoe snatched the implement from her mother and plowed back to the barn door.

Kimberly gestured at the house. "Why bother with the barn? Just break into the house."

"Because I'd rather replace a few boards than pay for a new entry door."

Kimberly looked oblivious. "Huh?"

"The ax is gonna make a mess. There might be a screwdriver or something less destructive inside that I can use to get into the house."

Kimberly muttered something about the house needing a lot more than just new doors, but Zoe ignored her.

She swung the ax, burying it into the wood next to the hasp.

Patsy planted her gloved fists on her hips. "You could have tried to pry the lock open with that."

True. But Zoe's fingers were freezing and fast approaching numb. Finessing an ax blade between the wood and the metal seemed like too much effort at the moment, and the blade was too wide to use on the lock. Three good whacks was all it took to cut through the plank. She grabbed the splintered piece and ripped it the rest of the way off.

Zoe and Patsy scraped the snow from the base of the door to let it swing open wide enough for the women to slip inside.

Zoe had expected to find hay stacked to the rafters since the last time she'd been there, the neighboring farmer had been bringing in a new crop. Instead, the barn was empty.

Almost.

"What's that doing here?" Kimberly demanded.

Parked in the middle of the cavernous space sat a white panel van, its passenger-side headlight shattered, the grill and front fender showing evidence of a collision.

Zoe looked around, anticipating a band of thieves to jump out of the darkened corners. But the only movement was a faint puff of wind-driven snow finding its way in through a space between the wall boards. The only sound, the wailing howl of the wind.

Kimberly started toward the van, but Zoe caught her arm. "Don't get any closer."

Her mother jutted her jaw. "It's parked in my barn. I can do whatever I want."

"Not this time." Zoe dug out her phone. "Right now this is a crime scene."

Again.

The Toyota Tundra's doors opened as Pete pulled up behind it, and Zoe and Patsy bailed out. A third person remained inside the idling pickup. He glanced in the window as he passed. Kimberly Jackson glared at him from under a hat that looked like it belonged on a lumberjack. Not her usual style.

Zoe led the way toward the barn. "It's in here."

He did a quick survey of the farmyard as he followed her. The only tire tracks into the place were the Tundra's. Footprints trailed from the truck to the house and around to the far side. But even those were in the process of being buffed out by the wind and filled in by the blowing snow. He suspected the van Zoe had told him about on the phone had been parked there since before last night's snowfall.

Drifts made fully opening the barn door impossible without some shoveling. Zoe started to squeeze through, but Pete caught her arm. "I'm going first."

"We've already been inside. There's no one else here."

He gave her a look, and she backed down, stepping out of his way. He noticed the hole hacked in the door.

"I did that," she said. "I told you they had it padlocked. The house too."

The narrow opening was a tight fit for Zoe and a nearly impossible one for Pete. Taking the time to chisel out the frozen earth or rip the door apart might have been the wiser move. His duty belt snagged on the ragged edge of the door. He managed to free the stuck case holding one of his Glock's spare magazines and wedged his way inside.

The barn had been emptied of all hay and equipment. Snow blew through gaps in the siding, revealing just a few of the repairs Zoe would face if she accepted her mother's "gift." The damaged white van was not part of the package.

"Can we come in?" Zoe asked. "It's nasty out here."

"How close did you get to the van?"

"We didn't. As soon as I saw it, I called you and then shooed everyone back to Patsy's truck to wait."

Good girl.

Other than the van, there was nowhere for anyone to hide, except for a small enclosed room in the far corner of the barn. Feed or tool storage perhaps. "Give me a minute," he told her. He stayed along the walls, not wanting to risk destroying any footprints or trace evidence near the vehicle.

The plank door to the small room stood open. One hand on his sidearm, he cautiously peeked inside. The air reeked of moldy grain, but the room, like the rest of the barn, had been stripped bare. Relaxing, he retraced his steps. "Come on," he called to Zoe, who was peering in at him. "But stay by the door."

She slid inside, Patsy close on her heels.

He dug the department's point-and-shoot digital camera from his coat pocket and snapped a wide-angle photo of the van before he started his approach. He took more pictures of the barn floor as he got closer. There weren't any obvious footprints or clumps of mud that might have been left from boot treads. He took a few tighter shots of the damaged grill and fender. A glance through the passenger window revealed an empty cab.

Pete finished with a couple more photos before tucking the camera in his pocket. Once again ready to unholster his sidearm, he released the catch on the sliding side door with his left hand and yanked.

The door glided open. No one jumped out at him. In fact, the interior of the van was as empty as the barn.

"What's in it?" Zoe called.

"Nothing." He took a few more photos and left the rest for the crime-scene techs, who were on their way from Brunswick. He returned to the women, noticing that Zoe was uncharacteristically underdressed for the weather. "Did you check inside the house?"

"Couldn't," she said through chattering teeth. "I was looking for a pry bar or something to break in with when we found the van. That's as far as I got."

"Your mother's still owner of record, right?"

"Yeah."

"And she's okay with us gaining entry?"

"Absolutely. She talked to her attorney and he said he had nothing to do with the locks, so she's pissed." Zoe grinned. "Someone's been eating her porridge."

That's all he needed to know. "I have bolt cutters in my trunk. You two wait in the pickup."

FIFTEEN

Zoe knew why Pete had ordered them back to the Tundra. He feared Oriole Andrews' killers might be inside the house. But curiosity overpowered Kimberly's thin Floridian blood. When Zoe told her Pete was about to cut the locks, she leapt out of the truck, brushed past Zoe, and followed him and his bolt cutters.

"Wait," Zoe called to no avail. She jogged after her mother, who proved to be amazingly fast in shin-deep snow and borrowed boots.

Wearing his patented take-charge expression, Pete blocked Kimberly. "I told you to wait in the pickup."

Zoe couldn't see her mother's face but had a pretty good idea these two would have quite the standoff where stubborn determination was concerned.

"It's my property. You can't enter without my say-so."

Pete caught Zoe's gaze and a silent conversation passed between them. *You said she was okay with me cutting the locks.*

Zoe held up her hands in surrender. *It's Mother.*

Pete's mouth twitched. He turned his gaze back to Kimberly. "You're going to make me get a warrant?"

"No. I'll give my permission to search the place, but not while I'm sitting idly by in the truck."

Zoe put a hand on Kimberly's shoulder. "Mother—"

She shrugged her off. "Not negotiable."

Patsy stepped forward. "Kimberly, the bad guys might be inside."

"Get serious. You think they went inside and latched the padlocks from the outside?"

Zoe met Pete's gaze again. Her mother had a point.

Pete glanced at the house, still ten feet away, then narrowed his eyes at Kimberly. "All right. But you stay right here until I make sure it's clear."

Kimberly lifted her triumphant chin. "That will be fine. You may cut the locks."

"Thank you," he said through clenched teeth and stomped toward the rotted porch.

Patsy nudged Kimberly. "You do realize if there are bad guys inside, they could easily shoot us through the windows from here."

Kimberly gave her a patronizing glare. "There's no one inside. Unless they locked someone in there from the outside."

Patsy nudged her again. "Or unless they've been coming and going through the basement doors on the other side of the house. Zoe did say it was locked from the inside. They could still be in there."

Kimberly's imperial façade gave way. Apparently she hadn't considered this.

Zoe hid a smile behind her glove. Patsy once again proved to be the only person who knew how to deal with Kimberly Jackson.

"I'm cold," she announced. "You girls make sure he doesn't do any unnecessary damage to my house."

Not Zoe's house.

As Kimberly retreated to the warmth and safety of the pickup, Patsy looked at Zoe and twisted her mouth into an annoyed frown. "I better stay with her, or this time she very well may decide she prefers the warmth of her hotel room and leave us stranded."

The locks proved no match for the bolt cutter, and Pete disappeared into the house. Zoe had hoped once her mother backed off, Pete would invite Zoe inside. She knew to stay out of his way and not contaminate a crime scene. The icy wind continued to slice through her jeans as if they were tissue paper. Her cheeks and feet stung. Pulling her hat down and her collar up provided little relief as a blustery gust sandblasted her face with snow that was more ice pellets than flakes.

After several excruciatingly long minutes, Pete appeared in the doorway and waved her in.

Zoe stepped into a cold stark kitchen. Whoever had installed the new locks hadn't bothered to turn on the furnace. At least the house provided shelter from the wind.

But not much. The faded curtains rippled in the breeze seeping through the windows.

New ones would definitely have to top her remodeling list.

"Stay here." Pete's jaw was clenched, and Zoe suspected it wasn't from the cold. "I've cleared the first floor, but I still need to check the second floor and the basement."

He strode out of the room, and from the *clump-clump* of his hollow footsteps on the bare wood floor, she could tell he was headed upstairs.

The kitchen needed work. The cabinets were nothing more than varnished plywood. All appliances had been removed, leaving only gaps in their place. The ancient linoleum was so filthy she wasn't sure if there was a pattern beneath the grime.

Add new cabinetry and flooring to the list. Right after a refrigerator and stove.

She peered through the doorway into the next room and gasped.

Unlike the naked kitchen, the adjoining room was crammed with televisions, computers, monitors, and other assorted electronic gizmos sitting on cardboard boxes.

"I told you to stay put."

Pete had appeared in a second doorway to the kitchen. Only then did Zoe realize she'd moved from her original spot. At least she hadn't set foot into the room used to warehouse stolen merchandise. "Sorry."

His stern glare softened. "They didn't put anything upstairs. Yet. Only these two rooms." He gestured to the room she was looking into and the one behind him. "I'm going down to the basement. Do not move out of the kitchen."

She threw him a salute and he shot a faux angry look her way before disappearing again.

He'd told her not to leave the kitchen—not simply "do not move"—so she crossed to the second doorway. This room's layout was the mirror image of the other except it had a staircase against one wall. Hinges hung along the edge of an opening to what Zoe assumed were the steps to the basement. No door.

Something else to add to her remodeling list.

While there weren't any televisions in this room, there were boxes, some open revealing assorted stuff including a large silver punch bowl, some closed with other stolen items—laptops, jewelry boxes, cameras—perched on top. There were even a couple sets of luggage stashed against the far wall.

These guys had been way busier than she'd thought.

Footsteps clomped up the basement stairs, and Pete appeared in the doorless opening. "Nothing down there." But the growl in his voice told her there was more.

"That's good," she said. "Isn't it?"

He shooed her back into the middle of the empty kitchen. "Part of what's not down there should be."

He'd lost her. "Huh?"

Pete fixed her with a look she'd seen before. Usually right before an argument. "They've torn out all the copper pipes. You have no plumbing."

"Oh." She did a slow three-sixty, taking in the house her mother was "giving" her to "make amends." No appliances. Crappy windows. Ancient flooring. Missing doors. And now, missing plumbing. Her little fixer-upper had rapidly deteriorated into a money pit. In addition to being a crime scene.

"You're not keeping it."

Zoe spun to face him again. "Of course I am." The words slipped from her lips before she had a chance to consider whether he was right.

The muscle in Pete's jaw throbbed. "Do you know how much work this dump needs? Where are you going to find the money?"

She wished she had an answer to throw back at him, but the only honest responses were *yes* and *I have no idea*. Instead she planted her gloved fists on her hips and said, "I'll figure something out."

His expression darkened. "Zoe." He sounded as if he wanted to add *tsk-tsk* to her name. "Don't be a fool. You already have a place to stay. Tell your mother thanks but no thanks."

True. She had someplace to stay, but not a place of her own. And there was another reason Pete couldn't sway her. "No. I'm keeping it. The house might be a wreck right now, but I need the barn. I need a place to keep my horse."

Pete spent the rest of the morning and the early part of the afternoon working with Wayne Baronick and the county crime-scene techs on processing the farmhouse.

Zoe's farmhouse. Unless he could talk some sense into her.

He'd seen the devastated look on her face when he told her about the stolen copper pipes. She knew damned well the place was uninhabitable in its current condition, and she had to know how much time, money, and sweat was needed to edge it even close to livable.

He'd also seen the mule-headed look on her face as he'd sent her, her mother, and Patsy away. The pipe dream of having her own farm excited her. The reality would eventually break her heart.

He felt like a heel for secretly being glad Zoe wouldn't be moving out of his house any time soon. The only smart thing she could do would be to turn down her mother's grand gesture.

Maybe Kimberly already knew about the farm's condition and was unloading the dump on Zoe intentionally. He wouldn't put it past her. Kimberly Jackson would never win Mother of the Year.

By one o'clock, County had towed the damaged van off to their garage. Pete left Baronick to oversee the rest of the evidence collection as well as the confiscation and inventory of the stolen merchandise. He needed to talk to Janie Baker and get a list of what was missing from her grandmother's house.

Pete called Janie from his car, expecting to be put off yet again. She had a valid excuse. The funeral had been this morning. He was surprised and pleased to learn she'd already started on the task and invited him to meet her at Oriole's house.

As he parked behind Janie's car, he spotted Trout on the front porch. Janie stood in the doorway, arms folded, and they appeared to be engaged in a heated discussion. However, before Pete could get out of his vehicle, the argument ended, and the old man shuffled across the yard, toward his house, head bowed, hands shoved deep into his coat pockets.

Seeing Trout again reminded Pete of the key. He'd neglected to return it to Janie, and since he'd left the thing in his desk drawer back at the station, wasn't going to return it today either.

"Hello, Chief." Janie held the door for Pete and then closed it behind him. Her short mousy hair looked like it had been smashed under a hat, and dark circles smudged with mascara, which hadn't survived the funeral service, underlined her bloodshot eyes.

Pete removed his hat, careful not to dump snow on the floor, and wiped his feet on a well-worn throw rug. "I'm sorry to bother you today, but we've had a break in the case, and I really need that list of missing items."

Her eyes widened. "A break? You've caught the guys?"

"Not exactly. We've found their hideout, the van, and some of the stolen goods. They weren't there at the time." For which he was deeply grateful. He didn't want to think about Zoe stumbling into the hornets' nest had the hornets been home.

Janie blew out a relieved sigh. "Oh. Well, that's something at least."

"Don't worry. We'll get them."

She attempted a tired smile and failed. "I'm sure you will."

Pete glanced back at the door. "I see Mr. Troutman was here."

The creases around Janie's mouth puckered. "I don't suppose you could talk to him again and tell him to leave me alone. And to stay away from this house. He acts like he's entitled to come and go as he pleases."

"He was..." Pete searched for an adequate word "...fond of your grandmother. I think he spent quite a bit of time here."

Janie didn't appear swayed.

Footsteps from the room to the right drew Pete's attention. His hand instinctively moved to his sidearm.

"Mom?" Marcus appeared in the doorway and paused. "Oh." The kid didn't sound thrilled to see Pete. "I heard voices but thought it was still Mr. Troutman."

"Mr. Troutman went home," Janie said.

Marcus kept his sullen gaze on his mother. "I went through Gram's china cabinet like you told me to. I can't tell if there's anything missing."

"Thanks, son." To Pete, she said, "I didn't expect there would be. Gram didn't have any fancy china or silverware." She moved to a small table next to the front door and picked up a scrap of paper with scribbling on the back. "I did notice a few missing items though."

Pete pulled his reading glasses from his pocket as she handed the note to him.

"Gram kept some cash in a dresser upstairs. It's gone."

Three items had been scrawled. The first was a row of dollar signs. "How much?"

"I don't know exactly, but she never kept more than a hundred dollars or so handy."

He glanced up from the second notation. "What kind of jewelry?"

"Nothing really valuable. Just a couple necklaces. And a brooch. Oh, and a ring."

From the corner of his eye, Pete noticed Marcus shove his hands in his jeans pockets and lower his head. "Can you give me a description of them?" Pete asked Janie.

Her brow furrowed. "The necklaces were gold. One had a blue pendant. The brooch was a circle and had some stones in it. I'm pretty sure they weren't real diamonds. The ring was real gold though. Vintage, you know?"

"Do you have any photographs? Maybe something with your grandmother wearing them?"

"I'm not sure. I have that box of old photos at home. I'll look through them again."

"Good." Pete frowned at the final item on the list and hoped she had more details on it than she had on the jewelry. "What about this gun?"

Marcus's head snapped up.

Pete wasn't the only one who noticed. "Marcus, go out to the kitchen and finish clearing out the fridge," Janie said.

Pete had seen the contemptuous look the boy gave his mother before. It was the same smoldering glare he'd used on the kid he beat up at that school.

"Marcus, do as I say," Janie said, her tone sharper this time.

He held his mother's gaze for a moment longer before vanishing into the rear of the house.

Janie gave Pete an apologetic smile. "He didn't know Gram kept a gun."

Pete hoped Janie was right about that. "What kind of gun?"

"I don't know much about them. It was kinda small." She held up her hands in an awkward attempt to illustrate the size.

"Was it a revolver or a semi-automatic?"

She gave him a blank look.

"Did it have a cylinder? For the bullets."

Her gaze shifted for a moment. "Oh. I know what you mean. Yes, it had a roller thingie that held the bullets." She gave him a weak grin, pleased with herself for being able to answer his question. "Gram's had it for years. Kept it in a box on the top shelf of her bedroom closet. For protection." Janie seemed to realize what she'd said, and her shoulders sagged. "I guess it didn't do a lot of good."

They rarely do, Pete thought. He held up the paper. "Is that all?"

"I think so. If I discover anything else is missing, I'll let you know."

Pete tucked the note and his glasses into a pocket and thanked her. He glanced into the room where Marcus had disappeared, hoping to have another talk with him, but the boy was nowhere to be seen.

"Please, Chief. Talk to Mr. Troutman again. It's hard enough dealing with losing Gram without him constantly hanging around."

"I think he's just lonely."

"I'm sure he is, but I have too much to do to keep an old man company."

Pete thought of Harry and made a mental note to call him later. Maybe even stop in at Golden Oaks. "I understand. I'll speak with him. By the way, I have a spare key to this house back at the station. I'll drop it off one day. Or you can stop in and pick it up if you want."

"You mean the one I left with that young Officer Metzger? He already returned it to me."

"No. This is another spare."

She frowned. "How did you get another spare key?"

"Your grandmother gave it to Mr. Troutman at some point. I confiscated it."

Janie's frown deepened.

Pete reached out to give her shoulder a comforting pat. "They were friends. He checked up on her."

"Yeah, well, just like her gun, Trout didn't do a whole helluva lot of good either."

SIXTEEN

Cleaning stalls had always been therapeutic for Zoe. While most folks seemed to find the earthy aroma of horse manure offensive, she thought of it as sweet perfume. Today, though, the mounds of "road apples" were frozen rock-hard, as was the sawdust bedding. Mucking the stalls involved more chiseling than scooping.

Even so, she appreciated the strenuous labor. Sweating allowed her to work out her aggression toward her mother, who had bitched and moaned the entire drive back to the Krolls' farm.

Not to mention Zoe's frustration with the state of her mother's "gift." Kimberly's "making amends" was likely to break Zoe's meager bank account. Pete was right. She should turn it down.

But where else could she stable her horse? Keeping Windstar on her own property meant no boarding fees. Sure, there would be some initial unavoidable expenses to repair the fences and the barn, but she could recoup it by bringing in boarders. Perhaps even some of these same horses she'd come to know and love while managing Mr. and Mrs. Kroll's farm.

By the time she'd finished cleaning the last stall, she felt more hopeful. She had a plan. Fix up her barn first. Put the house with its missing doors, plumbing, and appliances on the back burner. Pete wanted her to stay with him. So be it.

For now.

She sliced through the twine on a bale of hay. As she gathered an armload of the stuff, the man-sized door in the end of the barn closest to the farmhouse swung open and a female voice drifted in. "Hello?"

Zoe set the hay down and squinted at the silhouetted figure in the doorway. "Yes?"

The woman stepped inside. "I stopped by to speak with Mrs.

Kroll, but there's no one at the house. I've learned with farmers to always check the barn."

With a jolt, Zoe realized her visitor was Lauren Sanders. Mr. Kroll had a doctor's appointment, but that was none of the reporter's business. "Is there something I can do for you?" Zoe made no effort to mask the chill in her voice.

Lauren approached slowly. "Ms. Chambers." She extended a hand. "Yes, as a matter of fact, I'd like to speak with you too."

The feeling wasn't mutual. Zoe eyed the reporter's gloves—too thin for the brutal cold, but still more functional than fashionable—and shook the offered hand. "I don't know what I can tell you."

"I heard the Senior Killers' hideout was discovered and your mother is the owner of the property. I hoped I could ask you a few questions."

"Senior Killers?"

"It's the name the media is using for these criminals. I'm not the one who came up with it."

Zoe wanted to point out that only one person had died. Giving these guys a name made them sound like serial killers. However, she figured her argument would be lost on the reporter.

Lauren reached into her ever-present tote bag and pulled out a notebook. "Do you mind?"

"As a matter of fact, I do. I'm busy."

Lauren looked around at the empty stalls. "I'm envious, you know. I've always loved horses. Dreamed of living on a farm. I took riding lessons for a while when I was a kid, but my younger brother was deathly allergic and would have horrible reactions from my clothes when I'd come in the house. So my mother made me quit."

The melancholy in the woman's voice struck a chord. Zoe tried to imagine a life without horses. While Kimberly was never the most supportive mother, at least she never blocked Zoe's equine passion.

"I'd be happy to help," Lauren said. "Maybe earn a few minutes of your time?"

The woman wasn't dressed for barn work, but if she was willing to get her dark wool coat covered in hay for the sake of an interview, who was Zoe to stop her? Besides, Zoe never turned down help. "Sure." She scooped up an armload and strode away. "Two flakes per stall."

"Flakes?"

Zoe froze. Had Lauren's sob story been fiction, geared at playing on Zoe's sympathy? Or had the riding lessons not included any of the mundane tasks of horse ownership?

Zoe set the bundle down in front of a stall, grabbed a compacted section roughly four or five inches thick, and held it up. "When a hay bale is cut open, it separates into segments. About this much is what we consider a flake, more or less."

"Oh." Lauren looked at the bale a moment before shoving her notebook back in her tote. She gathered an armload of hay and crossed to the stalls on the far side of the barn.

At least she hadn't tagged along behind Zoe.

The reporter may not have known the terminology, but she did a competent job of distributing the hay. Zoe kept an eye on her for a few stalls, decided she'd grasped the concept, and left her on her own. A few minutes later, they met at the final stall. As predicted, Lauren's wool coat was covered in dried grasses. She even had a few pieces of hay stuck in her hair.

If nothing else, Zoe had the smug satisfaction of dirtying up the woman. "Now you look like a farmer."

Lauren gave a short laugh. A cloud of fog circled her head. "That was fun. Can I help with the grain and water?"

"No. I'll wait until I bring the horses in for the night to fill the water buckets. If I do it now, the buckets'll freeze. And the rattle of grain brings the horses running better than calling them."

"So you'll do that later. I get it." Lauren gazed toward the doors open to the pasture. "I never got to do any real work where I took lessons. They let me brush the horses, but that was all."

A good explanation for not knowing what a flake was. And Lauren had lent a hand, so Zoe figured she owed her a few answers as payment. "You said you had some questions."

Together, they strolled toward Lauren's tote bag. "Yes. I'd like to speak with your mother as well. Where's she staying?"

"She's not. She's either at the airport waiting for her flight, or she's already in the air headed back to Florida."

"Oh." Lauren paused in her stride. "I was under the impression that she'd just arrived."

"It was a short visit." Zoe heard the bitterness in her own voice. She swallowed, determined to keep her rocky relationship with Kimberly private. "My mother doesn't like Pennsylvania's winters."

Lauren retrieved her notebook and pen. "Why were you out at the old Engle farm this morning?"

Of course most of the area residents knew it as the "Engle farm." Zoe's ancestors, the Millers, hadn't owned the place in ages. Around here, a change in ownership took decades to be acknowledged by the locals. Even once she took possession of the property and made it her own, her neighbors would still call it the Engle farm.

"Excuse me?" Lauren jarred her out of her reverie.

Zoe blinked. "Huh?"

"What were you and your mother doing out there this morning?"

"Oh." She debated how much to divulge to the reporter. While she didn't feel her family business was anyone else's concern, the transfer of ownership would be a matter of public record soon enough. She explained how the Krolls' place was being sold and how her mother had no need for the old farm and had offered to transfer it to her.

"That was nice." Lauren jotted something in her notebook. "But that still doesn't explain why you went over there this morning."

"My mother wanted to check it out while she was here."

"Why?"

The question took Zoe aback. "Pardon me?"

"Why would she want to look at property she already owned? Couldn't she simply have turned over the keys to you? If there were papers to sign, you could have met anywhere to do that."

Was the reporter implying that Kimberly had some part in the stolen goods stashed at the farm? Or that Zoe did? "She hadn't seen the place in years. It'd been out of the family for decades. The previous owner, James Engle, passed away last summer and left it to my mother in his will."

"Speaking of the previous owner, he died under some rather gruesome circumstances, didn't he? And right there on that farm, if I understand correctly."

The mental image of the old farmer hanging from the barn rafters jarred Zoe back to the awful emergency call she and Earl had responded to last June. If Lauren Sanders wanted to write some kind of exposé about the farm's long criminal history when Zoe hoped to eventually live there, the reporter was going to have to do it without her help.

"I'm done." Zoe started toward the feed room. Lauren could watch her lock up as a final lesson in horse care.

"Wait," the reporter called after Zoe.

She didn't stop.

"Wait. Please."

Zoe didn't turn around, but the muffled sound of footsteps across the dirt floor told her the reporter was following her.

"I'm sorry."

Zoe spun to face her and waited.

"Sometimes awkward questions are a hazard of my job."

"Past events at the Engle farm," Zoe said, carefully measuring her words, "are a matter of public record."

Lauren appeared ready to debate the issue, but instead pressed her mouth shut and nodded. "You're right. And that wasn't what I wanted to talk to you about anyway."

Zoe crossed her arms and decided to give the reporter one last shot. "What exactly do you want to talk about?"

"This case. The robberies. The stolen goods. The men who are taking advantage of our senior citizens and who murdered Mrs. Andrews." Lauren appeared sincere enough.

"I don't know what I can tell you that the police haven't already released."

"You're a deputy coroner, right?"

"Yeah."

"Then you have inside information on the murder investigation."

Not really.

"And you and your mother discovered the van used in the crimes. Right?" The reporter paused, waiting for Zoe's reply.

Zoe recognized the trick Lauren was trying to use on her. Pete had told her about one of his interrogation techniques. Just be quiet. Suspects hated silence and often would start to babble, spilling more than if Pete had asked questions. She smiled to herself. Living with a cop had its advantages.

Lauren finally must have decided Zoe wasn't going to volunteer anything. "Can you give me an idea of what kind of evidence you found?"

"Sorry. I know better than to contaminate a crime scene. I backed off and let the police do their jobs."

The answer didn't appease Lauren. Zoe sensed the woman was trying to read her. After a moment, the reporter exhaled, her breath again hanging in the bitterly cold air. "Look. I know you have no reason to trust me. But this is more than just news to me. Lives are at stake. I want to find out who's doing this as much to stop them from hurting more elderly people as to get a front-page byline."

Zoe still wasn't sure she believed Lauren's story about her love of horses. She was even less sure about the sincerity of this admission. Lauren was either a reporter with a heart of gold...or a master manipulator.

"Can we go someplace warm?" the reporter asked, a pleading note in her voice. "Sit down and talk? I promise to keep the farm's history out of it. But I've been talking to victims from all over Monongahela County, including Janie Baker. I know you two are friends. I've gotten close with her too."

Which could explain the reporter's presence at the funeral home last night.

"Between the two of us, we might be able to put together what we know to solve Mrs. Andrews' murder and stop these criminals from hurting anyone else."

Manipulation or not, Lauren had a point. Mr. and Mrs. Kroll wouldn't be back for a while yet, and Zoe still had a couple of hours before she had to be on duty. "All right. You go on ahead to the house. I'll finish up and meet you there in a few minutes."

Lauren smiled. Not the controlled one, Zoe had seen before, but an earnest one. Or at least it seemed earnest. "Excellent." Lauren stuffed her notebook and pen back in her tote, hooked it over her shoulder, and strode toward the door. Then she paused and looked back at Zoe. "Do you want me to wait and give you a lift?"

"No, thanks." Zoe didn't know how many more times she'd get to take this particular walk. She wasn't going to pass up the opportunity even if it was frigid.

Lauren flashed another smile and slipped outside.

The idea of cooperating with the woman set Zoe's nerves on edge, but if together they could put an end to this crime spree, it might be worth it.

Pete swung by the station to check in with Nancy and make a few phone calls. The first was to Baronick to update him on the gun, jewelry, and cash Janie had reported stolen from her grandmother's house. The detective reported they were still inventorying the property seized at the Engle farm.

"I left a unit to keep an eye on the place for when these assholes come back for their goodies," Baronick told him.

They made arrangements to meet in the morning. There would be no weekend off for Pete. Not until they busted these guys.

His second call was supposed to be to the Sanders woman. He couldn't put her off indefinitely. But as he pondered a good excuse to avoid her, his cell phone rang.

"This is Debra at Golden Oaks Assisted Living," said the voice on the other end.

His heart threatened to burst out of his chest.

"There's no emergency..." she continued.

He refrained from saying, *then why the hell are you calling?*

"...but your father insisted I phone you for him. He wants to speak with you."

Pete was about to tell Debra from Golden Oaks he'd stop in tomorrow afternoon, but Harry's voice on the phone stopped him. "Son? Is that you?"

"Yeah, Pop. What's up?"

There were some shuffling noises on the line before Harry replied in a conspiratorial whisper, "I seem to have myself in a jam."

"What do you mean? What kind of jam?"

Harry's voice lowered even more. "I've managed to get lost. I'm at some sort of hotel. I don't know how I got here, and your sister isn't around. I'm afraid something's happened to her."

Pete closed his eyes and rubbed the bridge of his nose. "You're fine, Pop. Nadine's fine too. You're..." He hesitated to tell his father he was in a nursing home. "You're on vacation." A lie, but Harry wouldn't remember it in another five minutes anyway.

"Vacation?" He wasn't whispering anymore. "Since when?"

"I'll stop in to see you tomorrow."

"What? No. Wait." More shuffling sounds, and Harry's voice once again dropped. "Look, there's something strange going on around here."

"Are you okay, Pop?" Stories of nursing-home abuse jumped into Pete's brain. "Is anyone mistreating you?"

"No. Heavens no. I mean...as far as hotels go, this one's pretty nice."

Relieved, Pete asked, "Are you getting enough to eat?"

"Yeah. I think so. But you're not listening to me. I'm telling you there's weird shit going on in this place."

"What kind of weird shit?"

Harry's whisper turned frantic. "I think someone here is covering up a murder."

SEVENTEEN

Pete's headache intensified. "Who's been murdered, Pop?"

"I don't know." Harry's frantic whisper sounded desperate. "I saw them taking a body out of here a while ago. Everyone's being very hush hush about it. I know a coverup when I see one."

Pete wanted to point out that it was a nursing home. People died there. And of course the staff wouldn't want to upset the other residents by making a big deal out of it. But mentioning any of this to Harry might distress him more than the idea of homicide. "Tell you what. I'll stop by tomorrow afternoon and look into it."

Harry's voice rose from the secretive whisper to a near shout. "Tomorrow? They'll have destroyed all the evidence by tomorrow."

Pete smiled in spite of himself. His father had never been in law enforcement, but loved a good cop show on TV, and he'd always been vocal in his pride of Pete's chosen profession. Now Pete feared his old man might become the Columbo of Golden Oaks. "You're not exactly in my jurisdiction, Pop. I'll call a friend in the department there and have him investigate."

Pete could almost hear Harry mulling this over. "All right," he finally said. "But you're still coming in tomorrow, right?"

"I'll be there."

After Pete hung up, he keyed in his sister's number. Her voicemail answered.

"It's me," he said after the beep. "Pop just had his nurse call. He's...confused." Pete thought about telling her he still wasn't sure putting their father in an assisted-living facility was such a great idea. But a mental image of a haggard Nadine leapt into his mind, and he reconsidered. "You should go see him. Or call him." Unsure of what else to say, he ended the call, dropped the phone on his desk, and massaged his aching forehead.

His cell immediately rang again. Now what? He flipped it face up to see what had become a familiar number. Lauren Sanders. Dammit. He knew he needed to speak with her. But not now. He tapped "ignore."

Nancy appeared in his doorway. "Chief?"

"Yes?"

"A call just came through county dispatch of a vehicle reported stolen this afternoon from Abbott Electric and Heating."

The pucker of her mouth told Pete there was more. "And?"

"The vehicle is a white Ford panel van."

Zoe stepped out into the blowing snow and pulled her hat down as far as she could and still see. It may have been cold in the barn, but at least the structure provided shelter from the wind. Maybe she should have accepted Lauren's offer of a ride.

As if Zoe's thoughts had conjured her up, Lauren's car appeared at the top of the hill, reverse lights on as it backed toward the barn. Fast. Zoe stepped off the farm lane into the shin-deep snow. For a moment she thought the reporter had lost her mind and was trying to run her down. But the brake lights came on as the car stopped short.

The driver's window powered open and Lauren poked her head out. "Didn't the police confiscate the van from the Engle farm?"

"Yes."

"Do the Krolls have any kind of repair or service men scheduled for today?"

Zoe didn't like the direction these questions were going. "No. Why?"

"Because there's a white van parked next to the house."

She charged around to the passenger side, reached for the handle, and hesitated. She didn't know, like, or trust this woman. What if this was some kind of trick?

But they'd just spent nearly a half hour in the barn and were supposed to sit alone in the house to talk. If Lauren intended to do her harm, there were better opportunities.

Zoe climbed in the chilly car and pointed ahead. "Stop before you top the hill."

Lauren shifted into drive and eased forward. "Why?"

"Because I don't want them to know we're coming." Zoe dug through her coat pockets for her phone. "Crap."

"What's wrong?"

"I was gonna call Pete, but I left my phone in the house."

Lauren plucked hers from the center console. "Here. His number is stored in my contacts."

Zoe glared at her askance. "I know it, thanks." After the second ring, she got his voicemail. "Crap," she repeated, but realized he must have seen Lauren's number on his caller ID and refused to answer. For a brief moment, she smiled.

Lauren braked when the roof of the house came into view. "How's this?"

"Perfect." Zoe handed over the phone. "He didn't pick up. Call 911." She climbed out.

"What do you think you're doing?"

"I'm gonna slip down the hillside keeping out of sight. I can get closer to the house that way. Maybe get a license number on the van."

Lauren cut the ignition and climbed out too. "Oh no, you don't. I'm going with you."

"You'd be more help staying here and calling the police."

"I can walk and call at the same time."

Zoe glared at the reporter. "You just want to get your story."

"Hell yeah." Lauren grinned. "But if I save your ass in the process, what do you care?"

"My ass doesn't need saving," Zoe muttered. However, Lauren did not seem the type to be swayed once her mind was made up. "Stay behind me."

Zoe crept forward on the lane until she had a good view of the house, still roughly fifty yards away. As Lauren had said, an unmarked white panel van, very much like the one from her barn, sat parked next to the deck. The same spot Alexander had parked to deliver his father from the hospital. The same spot Patsy had parked so Kimberly wouldn't have to mess up her boots in the snow.

And the perfect spot to load stolen goods.

Zoe glanced at Lauren, who stood at her shoulder, taking in the same scene. "I told you to call 911."

"Oh. Right." She pulled off one glove and poked at her phone.

Zoe stepped off the plowed farm lane and plunged down the hill through the deep drifting snow. Clumps of the cold, wet stuff dropped into her boots. She ignored the chill and plowed downward, slipping and sliding. The rolling lay of the land and a thick stand of pines shielded her from the view of the house. Adrenaline and exertion warmed her. By the time she pulled up, sweat trickled down her back.

Something—someone—slammed into her from behind. She staggered, catching her balance before face-planting, and spun, ready to throw a punch.

But it was Lauren, who'd followed and stumbled into her. "Sorry."

Zoe growled, wishing the woman would have stayed at the car in spite of the breaking story. "Did you call 911?"

"I have it keyed in, but you took off and I didn't want to lose you."

Zoe looked up the hill to the car, still in plain sight. "You wouldn't have lost me." Yet. But from here to the house? Probably.

"Now what?"

Zoe jabbed a finger toward the phone in Lauren's hand. "Make the call."

Lauren hit a button and pressed the cell to her ear.

Leaving the reporter to give their location to the EOC operator, Zoe shouldered her way into the thicket of pines edging the side yard. Whiskery wet needles clawed at her as she wrestled her way through. One branch swept her knit skull cap from her head as another dumped its load of snow down her neck. Shivering, she retrieved her hat and swore. The effort of plowing down the hill may have warmed her, but the ice and snow in her shirt chilled her to the core.

Still entwined in the pines' pungent embrace, she paused, catching her breath. Ahead of her was the rear corner of the house. Before the fire, she would have been looking at her half of the old farmhouse. Now she was greeted with the sight of a never-used door without a step or a porch. She had a clear view of the rear of the van, but was still too far away to make out the license number.

Once she stepped free of the pines, there would be no cover between her and the house. Venetian blinds in the windows were open, but the room at this end—if Zoe's memory served, Mrs. Kroll's laundry room—was dark. The burglars had no reason to be in there.

She inhaled. And waded across the open yard. Snow hindered her. Slowed her. Threatened to grab her boot and hold on.

She reached the corner of the house, her heart pounding. She turned, pressed her back against the siding. Listened. Watched for movement.

Wondered what the hell she was doing there.

The wind had died down to a cold breeze. The only sound was the whisper of the breeze through the pines. No thumps or scrapes from inside. There was no movement in the trees through which she'd just passed. Lauren had finally cooperated and stayed behind.

No movement around the van or the back deck either.

Zoe had a plan of sorts to get this far, and she'd made it. But—as Lauren had asked her minutes ago—now what? How long before Pete arrived? How long would it take for the burglars to clean out the Krolls' stuff? She squinted toward the van and still couldn't quite make out the license number.

She needed to get closer.

Keeping her back against the house, she slid toward the deck at the far end of it. Reaching the next window—Mrs. Kroll's sewing room—Zoe risked a quick peek through the blinds.

Was there movement? Or did she imagine a shadow passing the interior doorway? She ducked under the window, straightening again on the other side. At last she was close enough to read the van's license now. She dug in her pockets. No phone. No notepad. Not even a slip of paper. And definitely no pen. She'd have to memorize the number.

She read it. Repeated it silently. Several times. Behind her, snow crunched. Lauren, no doubt, had caught up. Good. The reporter could call it in. Zoe started to turn. In her peripheral vision, she caught a flash of movement. A blast of pain.

And all went black.

Abbott Electric and Heating was actually owned by one George Winston. His grandfather had named the family business Abbott so it would show up at the beginning of the phone book listings. In this computer age of information, Pete wondered if it mattered anymore.

Winston owned a small fleet of white vans. Those still parked behind the business had the company name and logo blazoned across their sides.

"I just bought three new Ford commercial vans," Winston told Pete. "Well, used. But new to me. Was supposed to have the logos painted on 'em next week." He held up a pair of magnetic signs. "Until then, I've been runnin' 'em with these. Found 'em on the ground next to where the stolen van had been parked."

Pete pointed his pen at a security camera fixed to a pole on the edge of the lot. "I'll need to check the footage from that."

"Be my guest, but I doubt you'll see much. It's set up to catch anyone breaking in the rear door to the building." Winston growled low in his throat. "I've been too damned cheap to add another camera to watch my vehicles."

Pete suspected that would change in the near future. "Do you have the stolen van's license and VIN?"

"Sure. Come inside and I'll get 'em for you."

From the looks of the office, added security wasn't the only thing Winston hadn't invested in. The floor, desk, and file cabinets could easily have been the same ones his grandfather had used when he started Abbott Electric and Heating in the 1940s. A computer was a more recent, but far from new, addition.

Winston pulled a file from the second drawer of the cabinet and thumbed through the papers inside. "Here we go." He slipped a sheet out and handed the title to Pete. "I can make a copy of that for you if it would help."

Pete jotted down the license number. "It would. Thanks."

The business owner retrieved the paper. "Copier's out front. I'll get the security tape for you while I'm at it. It'll just be a minute."

Pete's mobile radio squawked as Winston left the room. "Any available unit in the area of Vance Township," the county dispatcher said. "Report of an armed robbery in progress. Be advised, injuries reported. EMS is en route." The address she rattled off was all too familiar.

Pete keyed his mic. "County, this is Vance Township Unit Thirty responding. ETA, five minutes."

"Ten-four, Unit Thirty."

"County, do you have an ID on the injured party?"

"Negative, Unit Thirty."

George Winston must have overheard the exchange. He reappeared in the doorway. "I can drop that stuff off at your office as soon as I close up for the day."

Pete called his thanks over his shoulder as he punched through the back door. Crossing the parking lot to his SUV, he dug out his phone and speed-dialed Zoe. "Come on. Pick up." By the time he started the Explorer, the call had gone to voicemail. "Dammit." He noticed the missed call from the reporter's number. She hadn't left a message. Ordinarily, he wouldn't have given it a second thought, but the timing of the call set his gut on edge.

Zoe, where the hell are you?

EIGHTEEN

Pete pressed the Explorer as fast as he dared on Route 15. Wind-driven snow encroached on the plowed pavement, clinging to patches of black ice, and threatened to spin the SUV out of control.

Something about the missed call continued to nag him. He pulled the number up again and attempted to return it, but only got an impersonal voicemail recording. He hung up in disgust as he sped down the last straight stretch. The Krolls' new modular home perched on the uphill side of the road. He braked as he passed it and swung into a left turn he'd become well acquainted with when Zoe lived at the farm.

The lane was more snow-packed than plowed, glazed with ice from vehicles driving over it. Pete jammed the gas pedal toward the floorboards. The Explorer's heavy winter treads dug in at places, spun and whined at others as the SUV slipped and shuddered. The lane climbed the hillside, dog-legging around to bring him up behind the house. The first thing he spotted was Zoe's pickup parked in its usual spot. If she was there, why wasn't she answering her phone?

He took in the rest of the scene. Fresh tire tracks through the snow leading off the lane, into the yard. Someone in a dark coat was kneeling at the rear of the house. That someone saw him and waved frantically.

Pete veered into the snow, churning a new path. He maneuvered around the line of pines bordering the farmyard. Closer now, he realized there wasn't one person down in the white stuff, but two. The second one wasn't moving.

He jammed on the brake. The SUV ground to a stop, and he leapt from his vehicle.

"Chief Adams," Lauren Sanders cried out, her voice strained and damp.

She said something more, but he didn't catch it. A familiar mop of short blonde hair...a flash of crimson...sent his heart plummeting. All he could hear was the echo of stillness inside his head and his chest.

Zoe.

As quickly as the world imploded on him, reality and duty slammed him back. Sights and sounds detonated around him. Distant sirens. Brutal cold. Zoe motionless and bleeding in Lauren Sanders' arms.

He tore off his gloves, dropped to his knees beside them, and elbowed Sanders out the way, too roughly perhaps. "What the hell happened?" He gathered a limp Zoe and tugged off her hat, searching for the source of the blood.

The reporter started babbling, talking too fast to make sense. Pete caught the words "white van" and "clubbed" among the gibberish.

He found a deep gash on the left side of Zoe's head, buried in her hair. Digging a handkerchief from his pocket, he fixed Sanders with a hard glare. "Slow down. Tell me what happened. You're a reporter. Get ahold of yourself and report."

She swallowed hard. Gave a quick nod. And inhaled. As the sirens grew closer, she told him about finding the white van. About Zoe trying to sneak down the hill to get the license number. About how Sanders had stayed concealed by the pines in order to place a call to 911. "I was talking to the operator when I saw a man dressed all in black slip out the door back there." Sanders gestured toward the corner of the house. "He had something in his hand. A club or something. Zoe didn't see him. He sneaked up behind her and when she turned around, he swung."

Pete pressed the handkerchief against the gash and held pressure. "You saw him sneaking up on her?"

"Yes."

"Why didn't you yell?"

The reporter's wide eyes glistened. Her lips parted. The lower one trembled. "I don't know. I should have."

"But you didn't."

She closed her mouth and lowered her face. "No. I didn't."

He bit back his anger, a large part of which was aimed inward.

He'd feared this. Foreseen this. Why hadn't he put his foot down and stopped Zoe from getting involved? "At what point did you place that call to me?"

She stuttered a moment. "I-I didn't. Zoe left her phone in the house, so I loaned her mine."

Why hadn't he answered the damned phone? He fought to gain control of his panic and his guilt. "Then what happened?"

"I must have screamed. He heard me, I think, because he looked my way." She tipped her head toward the pines.

Footprints—Zoe's, Pete presumed—led from the area Sanders indicated.

"I thought he was coming after me next, so I ran up the hill to where my car's parked. I didn't stop or look back until I got there. That's when I realized he wasn't chasing me at all. In fact, the van took off."

She pointed in the direction of the tire marks Pete had noticed coming in. As he looked up, an ambulance turned off Route 15, heading up the lane and around toward them.

Beneath the layers of winter outerwear, Zoe moved. Her lips parted in a groan.

He called her name, soft and pleading. "Zoe. It's me. Pete. Wake up, sweetheart. Let me see those baby blues." She had to be all right.

She had to.

She stirred. Her eyelids fluttered open. Those baby blues had never looked so beautiful.

And dazed.

She looked at him. Or through him. She blinked and shifted her eyes toward Sanders. "Rose? Don't forget to feed the cats."

Then Zoe took a deep breath. Exhaled. And relaxed, her eyes drifting shut.

"Zoe?" For one long horrible moment, he thought she was gone. He pressed his numb-with-cold fingers into the groove on her neck. Nothing. Fighting down the panic, he realized he was pressing too hard. Plus he'd lost most of the feeling in his hands. He softened his touch. And found it. Her carotid pulse. Strong. Steady.

Thank God.

"Who the hell is Rose?" Sanders asked, her voice shrill.

"Her best friend."

Behind him, the Monongahela County EMS ambulance rolled up, tires crunching in the snow. A county police car made the turn off Route 15. A pair of the day-crew paramedics approached. One of them inhaled sharply. "Oh my God. It's Zoe."

Reluctantly, Pete turned her care over to her colleagues. He stepped out of their way, but hovered close enough to jump to her side if she stirred again.

The reporter covered her mouth with one trembling fist as she watched the medics.

Pete hated feeling helpless. Since he couldn't do a damned thing for Zoe, he shifted his focus to catching the son of a bitch who had done this to her.

"Ms. Sanders," he said.

The reporter didn't respond.

He repeated her name, louder.

Her wide-eyed gaze swung to him. Not the pit bull with a bone anymore.

"I need you to think hard. Tell me anything you can remember about the man who did this."

She shook her head. "He was dressed all in black. And when he turned toward me, he had his face covered. All but his eyes. And I was too far away to see those."

"Was there just the one man?"

"That's all I saw."

"What about the van?" He was pretty sure it was the one George Winston had just reported stolen, but an eyewitness confirmation wouldn't hurt.

Sanders kept shaking her head. "It was white. No markings. No windows along the side. Tinted windows in the back. It was too far away to read a license number. That's why she was trying to get closer."

Pete glanced over at Zoe, whom they'd transferred onto a backboard. Most likely, she'd been hurt for no reason. If it was indeed the same van stolen from Winston's lot, Pete already had the license number. He thought again of the missed call. "I tried to call you back. Why didn't you pick up?"

Sanders patted her coat pockets. "Oh." She looked around. "I must have dropped my phone after I called 911."

The paramedics lifted Zoe and the backboard onto a stretcher.

The Monongahela County uniform trudged up to them, and Pete spotted a Pennsylvania State Police unit making its way up the lane.

The county officer introduced himself, and Pete shook his hand. "This is Lauren Sanders. She witnessed the whole thing. Get her statement." He shifted his gaze to the reporter. "Did you see which way the van went?"

"South."

Away from Dillard. Toward Brunswick. "Thanks. Tell the officer here everything you told me and anything else you might remember." Swinging back to the county uniform, he added, "Try to find her cell phone. She says she lost it after calling for help."

"On it, Chief."

He waded toward the rear of the ambulance where they were loading Zoe. "How is she?"

"Still unresponsive, but her vitals are good." The paramedic, whose face was familiar, but whose name escaped Pete, gave him an encouraging smile that they probably taught in EMS school.

"I'll follow you to the ER."

"I'll tell her when she comes to."

When. Not if. Pete wanted to believe this guy more than he'd ever wanted to believe anyone.

The paramedic climbed in. His partner slammed the doors and headed around to the cab. Pete dug out his own cell phone as he plowed through the snow back to his SUV. Once inside, he fired up the engine, cranked the heat, and punched in Seth's number.

"I need you on duty now," Pete said when his officer answered. "Can you make it?"

There was a moment's hesitation. Or maybe Pete imagined it. "Sure thing, Chief. What's going on?"

He dropped the shifter into drive. "Zoe's been hurt. I'm following the ambulance to the hospital. I need you to put a BOLO out on a white Ford panel van stolen from Abbott Electric and Heating." He dug his notebook out of his pocket and flipped it open to relay the license number. "Last seen heading south on Route 15 from the Krolls' farm."

After another pause, Seth's voice took on a tone Pete was well acquainted with—the this-is-now-personal tone. "Same guys?"

"Same guys."

"Got it. Hey, Chief?"

"Yeah?"

"Take care of Zoe, okay?"

Pete waved at the State Trooper as their vehicles passed, one coming, one going, but didn't stop to chat. "Roger that."

Sounds registered first. A low roar punctuated by piercing beeps and whistles. The roar rose an octave. More like a gaggle of geese along a lake. But the beeps and whistles remained. Black softened to gray. And then the light and pain slammed into Zoe's awareness.

"Hey." Pete hovered over her, his image blurred as if she'd gotten moisturizer in her eyes.

She blinked, trying to clear her vision. "What happened? Where am I?" She'd been at the Krolls' place, picking her way through the snow. Why? Oh, yeah. The van. She squeezed her eyes shut, but that sent a stabbing hot pain through her head.

"You're in the ER." Pete's voice sounded odd. Mushy.

She opened her eyes again. Still blurry. "I can see that." She'd spent enough time bringing patients through the ER to recognize the treatment cubicles of Brunswick Hospital's Emergency Department. "How'd I get here?"

"You don't remember?"

"Remember what?"

"The ambulance ride? The guys said you were chatting away with them on the way in here."

She tried to think, which wasn't as easy as one might believe. Ambulance? She shook her head. The pain threatened to carve her brain in half. Bad idea. Very bad idea. She raised a hand to touch a gauze bandage instead of her curls. "They shaved my hair?"

Pete laughed, warm and soothing. "No, my love. Just one patch of it. You took a nasty blow to the head. I think the doctor said thirty stitches."

"Stitches?" That explained the pain, but little else. "Where was I when all this was going on?"

"What's the last thing you remember?"

Zoe struggled to get her brain to clear. "The van." Panic cleared the fog a bit. "Pete, the van's at the farm. You have to get over there. They're robbing Mr. and Mrs. Kroll."

Pete shushed her. Why was he shushing her? He needed to go catch those guys before the Krolls returned home.

"Easy," Pete told her in that same soft tone. "I know all about the van."

He did?

"I was there."

He was? "You caught them?"

"No. They'd gone by the time I arrived. But Seth and the entire county and state police forces are out looking for them."

"Knock knock," called a nearby voice.

Pete turned away from her. "Come in."

The curtain surrounding them swished open, and Dr. Fuller strode in, a comforting smile on his face. "Hello again," he said brightly.

Again?

"What's the diagnosis?" Pete asked him.

"X-rays show no signs of a fracture and the CT scans came back clear." Dr. Fuller crossed his arms. "However, considering all the other indicators, I think it's safe to say she's suffered a concussion."

"Gee." Pete's voice dripped with his patented sarcasm. "You think?"

The doctor chuckled and turned to Zoe. "You ready to get out of here?"

"Hell yes." She pushed up to sitting, but the pain in her head ratcheted up a notch, and her vision blurred even more. She lay back. Gingerly. "Ow."

"Keep her quiet for a few days," Dr. Fuller said to Pete. "Make a follow-up appointment with her personal physician next week. And get her back in here if she loses consciousness again."

"I can't keep quiet." Although the idea sounded pretty good at the moment. "I'm on duty tonight."

Pete squeezed her hand. "They already know you won't be in."

After a flurry of activity, which didn't help Zoe's headache in the least, she found herself in the passenger seat of Pete's township SUV, headed home. On her lap, a stack of discharge papers she'd signed without reading.

She'd been surprised to discover it was dark out when they wheeled her to the emergency entrance. The clock on Pete's dashboard read almost eight thirty. It had been close to two when she'd been at the barn.

"I lost half a day."

"Yep."

"Did you say I was talking to the guys in the ambulance?"

"Yep."

"I don't remember any of it."

Pete kept his gaze on the road, but she caught a glimpse of his cock-eyed grin in profile. "They said you were a chatterbox. They also said very little of it made sense." He glanced at her. "Do you remember calling Lauren Sanders 'Rose'?"

"What?" Zoe tried to piece together the jigsaw puzzle of her memory. The reporter had been at the barn. Drove her back to the house. Zoe had left her phoning for help.

"When you came to before the ambulance arrived. You called her Rose and asked her to feed the cats."

That old adage about "it only hurts when I laugh" was only partly true. It hurt all the time, but laughing made it worse. Zoe closed her eyes. Pete had filled in some of the gaps while they waited for the paperwork springing her from the ER. But he might as well have been telling her about someone else.

"What do you remember?" He glanced at her again. "The guy who hit you. Sanders said she was too far away to identify him. Did you get a look at him?"

Had she? Zoe searched the black hole that was her memory of the last few hours. "I have no idea."

Pete fell silent, leaving her to replay what little she did remember over in her mind. His mention of Lauren Sanders niggled at her. Not because of jealousy this time.

The reporter had been there with her. Had driven her to the top of the hill. Zoe had ordered her to stay behind and call 911. But Sanders had followed.

Zoe fingered the bandage on her head. For a moment, the brain fog lifted, leaving one question clear in her mind even if the answer was not.

Where was the reporter when Zoe had been struck?

NINETEEN

"How's Zoe?"

Wayne Baronick had brought Starbucks for everyone, a rare gesture from the detective, and an indicator of his genuine concern.

"Concussed," Pete replied. "I picked up Sylvia and deposited her at my house. She thinks she's keeping an eye on Zoe, and Zoe thinks she's keeping an eye on Sylvia."

Baronick snickered. "Smart."

Saturday morning Pete normally would have been off duty, but there was nothing "normal" about the current situation. He did at least wear his civvies to the station. He, Baronick, and Nate Williamson, Pete's weekend officer, sat around the conference table with their not-quite-hot cups of coffee.

"Updates," Pete said.

Baronick swiveled in his chair to look at the whiteboard. "The sons of bitches wiped the Krolls out. Stole everything of any value plus some cash. All nice stuff too."

"New," Pete commented. They'd lost everything in the fire and had to start from scratch. "Have you spoken with them?"

"Not personally. One of my uniforms took their statements. At least they have insurance."

Pete made a mental note to stop over there and make sure the old couple was okay. With their poor health, he hated to think what the added stress might do to them. "If there's a bright side, at least they don't have to worry about these guys coming back."

"There's nothing left to steal."

"Exactly." Pete tapped his notebook, open on the table in front of him. "What about the stolen merchandise found at the Engle farm?"

Baronick rocked back in the chair. "There was a lot of electronic equipment. We're in the process of matching it to all the theft reports. No cash or firearms were recovered though."

"Not surprising," Nate said. "They'd keep the cash or spend it."

Baronick scanned the sheet of stolen items. "And they may have already sold the firearms."

"Or traded guns for drugs," Pete said. This was the sort of thing he'd hoped he'd left behind when he moved away from the city. "What about jewelry?"

Baronick flipped a page. "Some of it was recovered. We're still sorting through the odd pieces, but you can tell Sylvia we have her rings and earrings. The jewelry box itself is a little worse for wear, but the stuff inside all seems to be there."

"What about Oriole Andrews' pieces?"

Baronick ran a finger down the list. "Too early to know. The granddaughter's descriptions were pretty vague. We're still mixing and matching a lot of things." He paused and tapped the paper. "Oh. And Sylvia's son's firefighting memorabilia has all been recovered."

"Good." She'd be relieved. "Nate, I want you to pay another visit to the pawn shop in Phillipsburg to check on the firearms." Pete didn't trust Bub McDermott to call the moment someone brought stolen goods into his store—in spite of what he'd promised.

Baronick set the papers on the table. "We're revisiting the gun and pawn shops in Brunswick and the rest of the county too. And to take the recovered items off their lists. I've also updated the BOLO on the van." He eyed Pete. "Your turn. Anything new overnight?"

He closed his notebook. "No. Seth and Kevin spent the bulk of their shifts looking for that damn van, but these guys must have found a new hole to hide in."

"Any new activity around the Engle place?"

"They drove by several times. Nothing." Pete turned to Nate. "I'm going to head there for a closer look. I want you to keep an eye on it too."

Nate looked skeptical. "Do you honestly think they'll go back there?"

"Probably not, but criminals have been known to be stupid." Pete tucked the pen and his notepad in his pocket. "After I check out the farm, I'll pay a visit to the Krolls." If this sent either of them back to the hospital, Zoe would be inconsolable.

"I hate to mention this," Baronick said, "but you're not on duty today."

As if that mattered. "I appreciate your concern, but there's no down time until we catch these bastards. Besides, after I talk to the Krolls, I'm going to Brunswick to see my father."

Baronick grinned. "How's Superman Harry doing?"

Not so super. "He has Alzheimer's. How do you think he's doing?" Pete winced at the sharpness of his tone. "Actually, he's faring pretty well. I think he has a girlfriend."

Nate snorted.

Baronick erupted in full-fledged laughter. "Like son, like father."

Possibly more than the detective realized, but Pete wasn't about to mention Harry's phone call or his suspicions about murder at Golden Oaks.

Zoe rested her elbows on Pete's kitchen table, supporting her chin in the palms of her hands, her fingers shielding her closed eyes. She wasn't sure which symptom was worse—the mother of all headaches or the brain fog.

Sylvia thunked a glass of water in front of her. Zoe peered between her fingers at the droplets sloshed on the table.

Sylvia extended a closed fist toward her. "Here. Take these."

Zoe held out an open palm, and the older woman deposited a pair of tablets into it. "What's this?" Zoe asked, although as badly as her head throbbed, she'd have downed anything that might dull the ache.

"Acetaminophen." Sylvia flapped a paper at her. One of the ones the hospital had sent home with her. "No aspirin or ibuprofen."

"I hope they're extra strength." Zoe downed the pills followed by half the water.

Sylvia tapped the table with one finger. "Drink it all."

"Yes, Mom." Zoe's sarcasm was softened by the knowledge that Sylvia was being way more attentive than Kimberly would have been.

Sylvia lowered into the chair catty-corner from Zoe's. "He's conning us, you know."

The world around her was out of focus, and the coat rack next to the kitchen door appeared to be swaying ever-so-slightly. Zoe slugged the rest of the water and closed her eyes again. "Who's conning us? Dr. Fuller?"

"No. Pete."

Zoe ventured peeking out with one eye. "What do you mean?"

"He brought me over here to watch you. I'll bet he told you to keep an eye on me."

As a matter of fact...

Zoe's expression must have confirmed Sylvia's suspicion. "I knew it. He's off gallivanting around and expects us to babysit each other."

"He's trying to keep us out of trouble."

"He doesn't want us underfoot." Sylvia leaned forward, her forearms resting on the table, her fingers interlaced. "Since we're stuck here, let's take advantage of the situation. If we put our heads together, we might come up with something."

Zoe closed both eyes. "Don't mention my head. It wants to fall off right now, and I don't think I'd stop it if it meant the pain would go away."

"The distraction might make you feel better. Now, what do you remember about yesterday afternoon?"

"I already told Pete. Nothing. I didn't see who did it. Or at least I don't remember seeing them." But thinking about creeping around the Krolls' house brought back her other concern. The one she hadn't mentioned to Pete.

Sylvia patted Zoe's arm. "I can tell you're thinking about something. What is it?"

"Lauren Sanders."

Sylvia pondered the name a moment before brightening. "The reporter."

"That's the one."

"What about her?"

Zoe scrubbed her face with her palms and leaned back, letting her hands rest in her lap. She told Sylvia about the reporter's presence at the barn and later at the house.

"You think this Sanders person had something to do with it?"

"Probably not." Zoe heard the doubt in her own voice. "Maybe."

Sylvia heaved herself out of the chair and started to pace. "She was at my place, right?"

"After the break in. She's a reporter, you know."

"A reporter after a big scoop."

Something else occurred to Zoe. "It was kinda strange..."

"What?"

"She showed up at the funeral home for Oriole's visitation." Zoe remembered the sight of Lauren with Pete and the suspicion she had about the reporter's interest in him being more than professional. But she brushed it aside. "I thought it was odd, a reporter waltzing in like that. She said she'd become friends with Janie, but..."

Sylvia sniffed indignantly. "After a scoop, I'm telling you. Some of those news people don't know when to stop."

The clothes rack in the corner started swaying again. She fought to steady it.

"You know what I think?"

Zoe fixed her gaze on Sylvia, who also swayed, but maybe she really was. "I have no idea."

"I think this Lauren Sanders is in cahoots with these guys. I think she's helping set up the robberies so she can chase a big story. And..." Sylvia planted her hands on the table, leaning toward Zoe. "...I think maybe she's the one who whacked you on the head."

"I hate to admit it, but I've had that same thought myself." She pushed up from her seat and clung to the table a moment until she was sure the floor wasn't about to rush up and slam her in the face.

"What are you doing?" Sylvia asked.

Zoe straightened. Inhaled. And headed for the swaying coat rack. She took down her parka and Sylvia's coat. "Let's go."

"You're not going anywhere."

"Yes, we are. Do you honestly wanna let Pete get away with thinking we'd just be good little girls and play nice together?"

Sylvia scowled at the idea. "Where do you want to go?"

"To the Krolls' farm. I'm worried about them. And maybe being there'll jog my memory."

A smirk crept across Sylvia's face. She took her coat from Zoe. "I'll drive."

* * *

Pete found nothing had changed at the Engle farm. Zoe's farm, unless he could talk some sense into her.

The crime-scene tape hadn't been tampered with. The barn remained empty since the wrecked van had been towed to county impound. The sons of bitches must have found another place to stash their loot.

Pete phoned Nate and ordered him to make a sweep of other vacant properties in the township.

"I stopped at the pawn shop," Nate told him. "Bub McDermott insists it had been over a week since anyone had brought him any firearms to sell."

"Do you believe him?"

Pete could almost hear Nate's grin. "The dude's scared shitless of me. Yeah, I believe him."

Pete chuckled. Nate was often mistaken for an NFL linebacker. He never forced the intimidation factor, but nor did he downplay it. "Good. Keep me posted."

Next stop, the Krolls'.

As Pete's SUV chugged up the farm lane, tires spinning and grabbing hold on the icy surface, he spotted Sylvia's small Escort halfway up the hill, nosed into the snow. Stuck. He swore. What was she doing there? Had she left Zoe alone?

Mrs. Kroll wasn't as perky as she'd been the last time he'd seen her. She ushered him into the living room where her husband, Sylvia, and Zoe sat with cups of coffee.

He shot a glance at both of them. "I should have known."

"We're still babysitting each other," Sylvia said. "That was your plan, right?"

True, but he hadn't intended for them to realize it. "You were supposed to stay inside. I think doctor's orders included resting for both of you."

Zoe made a point of putting her feet up on an ottoman. "We are resting."

"Can I get you some coffee?" Mrs. Kroll asked. "The thieves took my Keurig that Alexander got us for Christmas. But they left the cheap coffee maker I had stashed in the cupboard."

"No, thank you. I'm good."

Mr. Kroll waved a hand at her. "Oh, get the man a cup anyway, Bernice." Pete started to protest as the older woman tottered to the kitchen, but Mr. Kroll stopped him. "You don't have to drink it if you don't want, but it keeps her busy. She's been a wreck since yesterday. Worse when she just sits and frets."

Pete surveyed the room. Wires hung from the wall where the television had been. A stand beneath it sat bare. No DVD player. "I understand a county detective took your statement and listed everything that was stolen?"

"Yeah. Could've been a lot worse, I suppose. We have full replacement on our insurance. And they didn't damage the house at all." Mr. Kroll growled. "We're moving at the end of the month, so no use buying new stuff until we get settled. Would just have to pack it up again. But it's hard on my wife."

"Might be worth replacing some of it before you go," Zoe said. "Just for her."

Mr. Kroll tipped his head side to side, as if weighing the options. "Maybe. Depends on how fast the insurance company mails us a check. At least we feel safe those scumbags won't bother with us again as long as there's nothing for them to steal."

In spite of Pete having said basically the same thing earlier, the comment soured his stomach. "I intend to have them in custody by the time your check comes." He glanced at Zoe, still wearing a bandage on her head. As if murdering a defenseless old woman and almost giving Sylvia a heart attack wasn't enough, now they'd made it as personal as it could get.

Mrs. Kroll shuffled back into the living room and handed Pete a mug. "You take it black, right?"

He smiled at her. "Good memory."

She took a seat next to her husband. "Sometimes."

The comment made Pete think of his father. He winced as he sipped the coffee, and not because it was hot. "Speaking of memory, I don't suppose you've remembered anything else about the day they came to your door."

Mrs. Kroll pursed her lips and shook her head.

"Any distinguishing marks you may have neglected or forgot to mention before?"

"No."

"How about his speech? Did he have an accent or an especially deep voice?"

"No. Nothing noticeable. I'm sorry."

"Don't be." He looked at Zoe. A silent "what about you."

She responded with a shrug and headshake, followed by a pained grimace.

Still feeling the effects of her concussion.

"You have my number if you do think of anything." Pete took another sip. "I'll be going now."

"Where to?" Sylvia asked.

Not only was she babysitting Zoe, however poorly, she was also keeping tabs on him. "I promised Pop I'd drop by."

Sylvia's eyes brightened. "Wonderful." She slapped the arm rests and stood. "We'll go with you."

Zoe shot Sylvia a puzzled look. Pete imagined her thinking, "We will?"

He narrowed his eyes at Sylvia. "Your car's stuck, isn't it?" It wasn't really a question.

She scowled, a child busted with her hand in the proverbial cookie jar. "It's not stuck. I couldn't make it any farther up the hill is all."

"Uh-huh. Right."

"Sarcasm does not become you, Pete Adams." She gathered her purse and motioned to Zoe. "Come on. We'll make sure Harry's new digs are acceptable."

Zoe climbed to her feet, wobbling a bit. Pete reached for her, but she held onto the chair a moment. "I'm okay."

"Thank you so much for the coffee, Bernice. Marvin." Sylvia marched past Pete toward the door, thumping his arm as she went. "And when we get back, you can get my car out of that snow drift."

TWENTY

With Sylvia and Zoe in tow, Pete found his father in the activities room. Other residents sat—some in upholstered chairs, some in wheelchairs— playing a word-association game. Harry, however, stood near the bank of windows, staring out at the snowy hillside beyond.

Pete placed a hand on his father's shoulder. "Hey, Pop."

Harry flinched and turned. "Son? What are you doing here? Not that it isn't good to see you."

What was he doing here? Harry had called him. Pete should have known better than to expect him to remember. "I came to see you." He gestured toward Zoe and Sylvia. "I brought some friends."

"Well, isn't that nice. Any friends of my boy are friends of mine." He extended a hand to Zoe. "I'm Harry. And you are?"

Pete plastered on a fake smile. At least Zoe always dealt with Harry's memory loss better than Pete ever had.

True to form, she introduced herself as if she and Harry had never met.

His brow furrowed as he looked at her, fixated on her bandage. "Did you hurt yourself?"

Zoe touched the gauze. "I bumped my head is all. It's nothing to worry about."

"Oh, good." Harry turned to Sylvia, who also introduced herself.

He winked at Pete. "You're in the company of two lovely ladies, son."

"Yes, I am." He noticed they were garnering the attention of a number of the other residents, distracting them from their game. "How about we go to your room to talk. In private."

"Uh-oh. That sounds om—omin—oh, damn. What's that word?"

"Ominous?" Zoe said.

"Yes. That's it. Ominous." Harry looked toward the double door. "Only problem is...I don't know where my room is."

Pete offered him an arm. "I do."

Harry brushed him off, instead offering both of his to Zoe and Sylvia. "Ladies?"

Pete led the way down the hall, his father being his charming self, a woman on each arm, trailing behind.

After reintroducing Harry to his room—"Are you sure this is mine? I don't remember it"—Pete dragged in a couple of extra chairs from the hallway, and everyone found a seat.

Sylvia reached over and took Harry's hand. "So are they treating you well here?"

Pete could tell his father was searching the corners of his befuddled mind. "I guess so."

"Pop, do you remember calling me yesterday?"

That befuddled look again. "Of course I do."

Of course he didn't. Just as well. Dropping the whole "murder" thing suited Pete just fine.

"What did he call you about?" Sylvia asked.

Pete shot her a look. *Don't help.* "It was nothing."

"Well, clearly it was at the time." Her jaw tightened as she repeated, "What did he call you about?"

"I'll tell you later," Pete said, his own jaw as clenched as hers.

Harry watched them, his eyes widening by the moment. "Is everything okay? It's not Nadine, is it? Is something wrong with Nadine?"

"No, Pop. Nadine is fine."

But Harry wasn't appeased. "Don't you go keeping shit from me. If something's happened to your sister, I want to know."

Pete glared at Sylvia. *See what you've done?* "Honest, Pop. Nadine is fine. I would never keep anything like that from you."

Harry fell silent, but worry still shone in his faded eyes. Sylvia and Zoe both stared expectantly at Pete.

"Dammit," he muttered. "He had his nurse call me yesterday and told me he thought someone had been murdered here."

"I did?"

"You did."

The entire conversation—and Harry's half-ass train of thought— derailed as a knock came on the open door. The elegant woman on the walker, the one who had so beguiled Harry the other day, stood there. "Oh. I'm sorry. I didn't realize you had company."

Grateful for the interruption, Pete leapt to his feet and moved to her side. "That's quite all right. Please come in."

"I wouldn't dream of intruding on family time." She smiled and Pete once again imagined she had been a real knockout in her younger days. She offered him her hand. "My name's Barbara Naiman. I live right across the hall." After a quick round of introductions, she motioned in the direction of her room. "My grandsons are visiting me as well. I wanted to tell Harry to stop over and meet them." As if an afterthought, she added, "You can all come over too."

Pete eyed Sylvia and hoped this time she caught his unspoken command to keep quiet. "That's sweet of you, but as you said, we wouldn't dream of intruding on your family time. We won't be much longer and then I'll drop my father off at your door."

"That would be lovely. Thanks so much."

Barbara maneuvered a slow but graceful turn with her walker and tottered off to her room. Pete glanced at his father. The old man appeared smitten.

"She's quite attractive," Sylvia said.

Harry kept his gaze on the doorway. "Yes, she is."

Pete nudged him, glad for a better topic. "I think she likes you, Pop."

Harry shot a fierce scowl at him. "Mind your manners, son. Barbara is a lady and any relationship between us is none of your business."

But Pete could tell the bluster masked Harry's embarrassment. Pete chuckled. "We should go so you can meet Barbara's family."

Harry shooed Zoe and Sylvia out of the room ahead of them, saying, "Ladies first."

Pete walked with his father to the doorway to Barbara's room. Inside, she sat holding hands and laughing with the same two young men Pete had seen with her days earlier. It struck him how life had come full circle. Instead of a young man meeting his girlfriend's parents, Harry was about to meet his girlfriend's grandsons. "Here we are, Pop."

But he caught Pete's arm, drawing back from the room rather than going in.

Pete chuckled. Apparently, meeting the family never became any less terrifying. "It's okay. They'll adore you. You have the Adams' charm, remember?"

"No, no," he whispered, pulling Pete closer, "it's not that. Son, you need to do your cop thing and check this place out. There's some weird shit going on around here."

The same thing Harry had said on the phone.

Pete eyed him. "Oh?"

Harry lowered his voice further. "People are dying. And not because they're just old. Someone here is a murderer."

Zoe called dibs on the front seat for the drive home. She'd never experienced motion sickness before, but the drive to Brunswick in the rear of Pete's Ford Edge had aggravated her headache. The front was definitely better.

Sylvia hadn't let go of the topic of Harry's earlier phone call, and Pete grudgingly shared his father's suspicions, calling them "foolishness."

"How can you be sure?" Sylvia demanded. "A residence like that? It would be the perfect setup. Did you see the pearls that woman, Barbara, was wearing? A person has to be well off to live in that kind of place. I can see someone killing them for their money."

"Harry's not exactly well off," Pete reminded her. "Neither am I or Nadine."

Sylvia didn't let up until Pete vowed to run a background check on Golden Oaks and its employees.

Even with her brain fog, Zoe couldn't imagine where he'd find the time. She suspected he'd only made the promise to shut Sylvia up.

Twenty minutes later, they were back at the Krolls' farm, standing around the snowbound Escort. Pete lugged a tow chain from his cargo compartment and grumbled as he crawled under the small car to hook it up. From there, it was an easy feat to drag Sylvia's vehicle out of the drift with his SUV.

"Go home and rest," he ordered both of them before driving away.

Zoe stuffed her hands in her pockets as the cold chilled her cheeks. She fixed the older woman with a determined gaze.

Sylvia looked skeptical. "Why do I get the feeling we aren't going home to rest?"

"Are you feeling okay?" Zoe asked, gripped by a moment of guilt. She wasn't the only one who was supposed to be taking it easy.

"I'm fine, dear. But how about you?"

Her vision had cleared a bit even if her brain hadn't. And the headache had subsided to a dull throb. "Actually, I'm feeling better. Let's go check on Janie Baker. I wanna see how she's holding up. Besides, it's on the way home."

As long as Zoe had known Janie, she'd never been inside her house. Located on the same hillside in Dillard as Oriole's, but two streets over, the structure appeared tiny compared to Janie's grandmother's place. One story, square, with ancient aluminum siding that looked more dingy gray than white, the house seemed better suited to be a storage shed than a home.

When Janie answered their knock at the door, her appearance startled Zoe. Her face was as sallow and drawn as someone more than twice her age.

Janie took one look at Zoe and seemed equally as startled. "So what I heard was true. You got hurt by the same men who..."

The unspoken words, *who killed my grandmother*, hung between them.

Zoe fingered her bandaged head. "Afraid so."

"Are you okay?"

Sylvia stepped in. "Of course she's okay. Everyone knows she's hardheaded."

Grateful for the levity, Zoe gave a guilty-as-charged shrug.

Janie ushered them in to a tiny living room. A small sofa, one easy chair, a boxy TV, and a couple of end tables with lamps were all the space could accommodate. "I was just looking through Gram's photos." She gestured toward an old candy box filled with black and whites on the couch. "Sit down. I'll bring you both some coffee." She shambled out of the room.

Sylvia claimed the chair. Zoe picked up the box, sat, and placed it in her lap.

"Poor Janie." Sylvia tsk-tsked. "She's never had a spare dollar to her name. Yet she raised that boy of hers by herself and took such good care of Oriole."

Zoe shuffled through the pictures, glad her vision had cleared. "Yeah. But even in school, she never had anything remotely designer. The other kids used to tease her about getting her clothes at the secondhand store in town."

"The 'other' kids. Not you."

Startled, Zoe met her gaze. "No. I always liked Janie. I loaned her an outfit once to go out on a date. I don't remember if the evening went well, but she looked great."

Sylvia grunted. "One thing's for certain. She never could have afforded to put Oriole in a place like Golden Oaks."

Zoe thought of the lush vegetable garden and the bag of produce the older woman had shoved on her and Earl not so long ago. "Oriole didn't need to be in a place like that. She did well on her own."

"Not so well. She died because she was home alone."

The wistfulness in Sylvia's tone and eyes made Zoe wonder if she was thinking about her own future. Oriole had died because she was alone. Sylvia had ended up in the ER because of the same thugs. "Anyone can fall victim to violence." Zoe tapped the gauze encircling her head. "Being over a certain age and independent doesn't necessarily mean you're doomed."

"Maybe not. But it makes you easy prey for these predators." Sylvia gave a short laugh. "Or uneasy prey might be more accurate."

Janie returned with a pair of mugs. Her hands trembled as Sylvia and Zoe each accepted a cup. "I didn't know how you take your coffee." Janie dug into her cardigan's pocket and pulled out a handful of sugar packets.

Sylvia waved away the offered sweetener. "Black is fine."

Zoe accepted a few of the packets, wondering if Janie had lifted them from a restaurant.

"I can bring you some cream if you want," Janie said.

"I'm good," Zoe told her. "Sit down."

Janie slipped the rest of the sugar into her pocket and came up with a cellophane-wrapped plastic spoon, which she handed to Zoe.

Definitely lifted from a fast-food place.

Janie lowered onto the couch next to Zoe and pointed at the photo in her hand. Sepia toned from age, the picture showed a much younger Oriole with a dashing man in uniform. "That's my grandpa."

"He was very handsome." Zoe handed it to Sylvia, who agreed.

"He died when I was little. Gram always said my mom favored him. Me too, I guess."

Something in the hallway to the rear of the house thumped, and Marcus appeared. He kept his head low and glanced at Zoe then Sylvia before looking at his mother. "The guys are going sled riding up on the hill. Can I go?" His defiant tone hinted at a deep resentment at having to ask permission.

"May I," Janie corrected. "And I've taught you better manners than this. Say hello to our company."

Shoulders hunched, the boy nodded at them, mumbling what must have been a greeting of sorts. His gaze came back to his mother. "Well? May I?"

"Who all's gonna be there?"

He rattled off some names.

Janie looked toward the window. "Okay. But bundle up. It's cold. And stay out of trouble. Please."

With a grunt, Marcus disappeared again.

"Kids," Sylvia said.

Janie rolled her eyes. "Tell me about it. He's a good boy, but he needs a male role model." She shrugged. "And I can't provide one."

Zoe set her coffee on the table next to her and kept sifting through the photos, handing each to Sylvia. Most were old and faded with images of Dillard back in the days when it was a thriving coal-mining town. A few were newer and in color. She came across one, a posed portrait of Oriole, that looked recent. "Wow." Zoe held it up to Sylvia. "I never saw her all dressed up like that."

Sylvia squinted, tipping her head up and down, apparently trying to find the right focus through her bifocals. "Maybe she was going to church. Some folks still dress up for it, you know."

Janie held out a hand, and Zoe turned the photo over to her.

"Huh. I don't remember seeing this one before. It does look recent, doesn't it?"

Zoe rested a finger on the photo. "Beautiful necklace."

The photo quivered in Janie's unsteady grasp. "Yes. It is."

"Family heirloom?" Sylvia asked.

Janie opened her mouth. Closed it again. Maybe it was Zoe's brain fog, but she swore Janie seemed angry. "To be honest, I've never seen it before either."

TWENTY-ONE

Janie gazed at the photo for several long moments before returning it to the box on Zoe's lap without further comment. "I guess you never know what you'll find going through someone's things. She was my grandmother and it still feels...I don't know...intrusive."

Zoe thought about the comment as she held another bundle of old black and white pictures. Maybe Janie didn't appreciate them going through Oriole's mementos. She placed the stack back in the candy box and set it on the sofa between them.

Sylvia cleared her throat. "I suppose we shouldn't keep you, dear."

Janie didn't contradict her.

Zoe took a swallow of coffee. If they were going to leave, wouldn't it be rude to leave a full cup? But the still-hot brew burned her tongue.

"We just wanted to stop in and make sure you're holding up," Sylvia told Janie.

There was another reason for the visit too, but Zoe couldn't remember. Crap. She didn't like this concussion brain fog stuff. Poor Harry. He lived with worse than this every day.

"I really should get Zoe home though," Sylvia continued. "The doctors ordered her to rest."

Janie placed a hand on Zoe's knee. "I'm so sorry. Here you are taking the time to check on me when you should be home in bed."

Sylvia wiggled to the edge of the chair and pushed up out of it. "There is one thing we wanted to ask while we were here. How well do you know that reporter? The new one. Lauren Sanders."

That was it—the other reason for their visit.

Janie shifted on the couch, as if she was about to rise, but didn't. "Not well. Not really. She's been by here a number of times. At first it was all about Gram. Trying to get her story, you know? But lately she's just been looking in on me." Janie managed a weak smile. "Like the two of you. Being friendly."

Zoe managed another sip of the hot coffee. "That's why she was at the funeral home?"

"I suppose. It was kind of nice. I don't have a lot of friends. Never had the time or money to go out to lunch before."

Poor Janie. Still the quiet mouse she'd been in high school. "Once things settle down, you and I will have to change all that. In fact, let's set a lunch date now." Zoe instinctively touched her hip pocket where she kept her phone, only to find it empty. For a moment, she panicked, wondering where she'd lost it. Then she remembered. She'd left it in the Krolls' house when she went to the barn. Her phone had been among the items the thugs had stolen.

Janie must have misinterpreted Zoe's scowl. "That's okay. I know you're busy."

"It's not that." Zoe explained about the phone. "I'll be in touch as soon as I get it back. In the meantime, guess you should call Pete if you need to reach me for anything."

Sylvia took the cup from her and picked up her own still half-full one from the end table. "I'll take these to the kitchen for you and then we'll get out of your hair."

"Don't be silly." Janie stood and reached for the cups. "You're guests. I'll take them. Besides." She gave a dull laugh. "I don't want you to see my messy kitchen." She headed into the other room. "And yes, I do need to get back over to Gram's and do some more packing. She had so much stuff."

A few minutes later, Sylvia and Zoe sat in her Escort, letting the car warm back up and waiting for the fogged windshield to clear.

"We didn't learn a whole helluva lot," the older woman muttered.

"She didn't deny that she and Lauren were friends."

"But why is the reporter woman being friendly? That's what I want to know."

Zoe reached over and clicked the defrosters down a notch from high. "When did you become such a cynic?"

Sylvia gripped the steering wheel, glaring straight ahead. "Since those bastards violated my home and stole my dead son's stuff." She shifted in the driver's seat to catch Zoe's gaze. "What do you make of that photo?"

"Which one?"

"The new one. Oriole dressed to the nines. And that necklace. Didn't you notice Janie's reaction to it?"

"Yeah. Kinda." The headache had returned, and Zoe closed her eyes. "I think I know what that's all about though."

"What?"

"Do you know Mr. Troutman?"

"That old fart who lives a few houses up from Oriole? Everyone knows Trout. He's another one that doesn't have two nickels to rub together."

"I think he was sweet on Oriole. Maybe they were dating."

"Dating?" Sylvia barked a short and sarcastic laugh.

"He was very concerned when we came to take Oriole away that night. It was...sweet."

Sylvia appeared to mull it over. "I suppose it's possible. They'd both been alone a long time. And they're neighbors and all." She dropped the shifter into gear and touched the gas. "I'll tell you one thing though. The necklace in the picture? That was no gift from Trout. That was worth a pretty penny. He could barely have afforded to buy her something from a dollar store."

Saturday afternoon at the Vance Township Police Department was blissfully quiet. Nate was out on patrol. Nancy only worked weekdays.

Pete had the entire station to himself. Taking full advantage, he fixed a cup of fresh coffee and settled in at his desk to do some digging.

Was there something suspicious going on at Golden Oaks?

Besides Harry romancing the woman across the hall. Pete grinned at the thought.

If he was doing a serious investigation into the facility, he'd need a subpoena for their financial and employment records. No self-respecting judge would issue one on the flimsy accusations of an old man with Alzheimer's. Residents' medical records would be better, but infinitely more difficult to obtain.

Instead, Pete pulled up the facility's website. He'd seen it before. This time he searched until he found a list of reviews. Most were four and five star. There were a few with much lower ratings. He clicked on those. However, the comments had nothing to do with suspicious deaths. Instead they complained about high prices and slow response time when a resident needed help.

He compared those with the higher-rated comments and found a number stating the exact opposite. "Excellent care for the price" and "Wonderful caring staff."

Pete closed the page and tried the social media sites with basically the same results. His final effort took more time—scanning the county newspaper's obituaries over the last few months. There were a handful listing variations of "died at Golden Oaks," and they were all folks in their eighties or nineties, and one gal who'd lived to 104 and "passed away peacefully surrounded by her family." God love her.

None of the obits suggested anything out of the ordinary.

Then again, anything beyond the standard "old age" would have resulted in the patient being transported to the hospital.

Which gave him an idea, but before he could act on it, his cell phone rang. He didn't recognize the number. "This is Chief Adams."

The voice on the other end, however, had become very familiar. "Chief, this is Lauren Sanders. I was hoping we could talk."

He'd put her off long enough. Too long. If he'd taken her call yesterday, Zoe wouldn't have ended up with a concussion. And an even better idea occurred to him. "When?"

"How about now?"

Pete checked his watch. Still hours until the Saturday night poker game, and he'd already done his part and bought the beer. "I'm at my office. How soon can you get here?"

"I am here." The bells on the front door jangled.

He rose, circled his desk, and leaned out into the hallway. Sanders waved from the front of the station. He ended the call and motioned for her to come on back.

She settled into the guest chair. "How's Zoe?"

Pete gestured at the coffee pot and Sanders shook her head. "Resting comfortably at home." At least he hoped she was. He took his seat behind the desk.

"Good. I was worried." Sanders dug through her bag. "Did you guys happen to find my cell phone?"

"No. Sorry."

Her shoulders sagged. "Oh well. I suppose it'll show up when the snow melts, and it's probably ruined anyhow."

"I didn't recognize the number you just used."

She held up a small flip phone. "Bought a cheap one at the grocery store just in case my good one hadn't been recovered. I guess I might as well suck it up and buy a replacement."

"I guess." Pete leaned back in his chair and fingered his upper lip. This was the chattiest she'd been since he'd met her.

She came up with her notepad and skimmed to a blank page. Scribbled something. "What's new with the Senior Killers case?"

Pete choked. "The what?"

"I didn't come up with the name."

"Well, I'd appreciate it if you didn't encourage the use of nicknames in the media. It just feeds these guys' egos."

She appeared to weigh the request. "Okay, but I can't stop anyone else from using it. Now. What's new?"

"Not sure what I can add to what you already know. You were there yesterday."

"What about overnight?"

"They've been lying low."

Sanders cocked her head and gave him an exasperated look. "I meant overnight developments."

A little give-and-take might be in order. He slid open a desk drawer. "We've been keeping an eye on the Engle farm, but there's been no sign of new activity there." He went on to tell her about the stolen white van as he pulled out two sheets of paper, one of which he placed in front of her. "That's all the information on the van they're using now."

Sanders' eyes widened as she read. "So you have the license number after all."

He thought of Zoe's attempt to get that information and didn't reply.

Sanders nodded toward the other paper. "What's that?"

He slid it across to her. "The list of items stolen from the Krolls."

She acted as if he'd bought her roses. "Thank you." Her smile turned to a scowl. "You're being unusually cooperative."

Pete came forward and rested his forearms on the desk. "I need your help."

"Oh?"

"What do you know about Golden Oaks Assisted Living?"

She tried to cover her puzzlement and failed. "Nothing. Should I?"

"I'm not sure." Nor was he sure how much he wanted to tell her about Harry. "One of the patients...residents there thinks some of the deaths at the facility might be questionable."

Sanders' gaze drilled into him. She didn't reply for a moment, then said, "It's an old folks' home. And one of the old folks thinks someone's killing the other old folks?"

"That's about it."

She laughed, short and disbelieving. "You've gotta be kidding."

"Wish I was."

"This resident making the accusation...is she of sound mind?"

Pete chose not to correct the gender. "Not necessarily."

"Then why in heaven's name are you looking into it?"

"I'm not," he lied. Sort of. "I'm asking you to look into it."

Sanders stared at him as if he wasn't of sound mind either.

"You'd be doing me a favor."

Sanders leaned back in the chair and gazed into space. "And if I do find something?"

"Let me know, and I'll take it from there."

She fixed him with a cold glare.

"And you'll get the scoop and an inside story."

"And your full cooperation?"

"Absolutely."

She came forward again, jabbing her pen into his desk perilously close to his hand. "I mean on the Senior Killers case."

From the look in the reporter's eyes, there would be no negotiation on this point. Pete was making a deal with the devil just to appease his father's paranoia.

Pete unfolded his hands and extended one to her. "Deal."

Sanders grasped it and smiled triumphantly.

Sylvia fussed around in Pete's kitchen while Zoe set up her laptop at the table. The brightness of the screen intensified her headache and blurry vision, but she had no idea how to tone it down. Or if dimming it was even possible.

Merlin, one of Zoe's two orange tabbies, leapt into her lap, demanding attention.

Sylvia set two plates, each containing a monster-sized sandwich of lunchmeat, cheese, lettuce, pickles, and mayo on wheat, next to the computer. She sneezed. "Damn cat."

Zoe deposited Merlin on the floor with a gentle "shoo." He gave her a green-eyed glare and sauntered to his food dish.

Dabbing at her nose with a tissue, Sylvia pulled a chair around from the other side and took a seat shoulder to shoulder with Zoe. "Eat. You'll feel better with some food in your stomach."

Zoe shot a look at her. "But will you? Are you okay?"

Sylvia pointed at the cat and mumbled something into the tissue.

"We could have gone to your house."

"I'll be fine."

Zoe knew the break-in weighed heavily on the older woman. She might want to be home, but the vacant spots on the shelves served as constant reminders of strangers rummaging through her things. "I can lock Merlin and Jade in the bedroom."

"It won't help." Sylvia tucked the tissue into her sleeve and picked up her sandwich.

Zoe brought her focus back to her computer, pulled up Google, and typed in "Lauren Sanders."

Sylvia took a bite and pointed at the images that popped up. "That's not her."

"Different Lauren Sanders." Zoe scrolled down past several references to a Detroit TV news personality until she came to another reporter with the name. "There she is."

Once they'd found the correct one, the links about her were numerous. Zoe started at the top and clicked.

Sylvia leaned in, reading over Zoe's shoulder. "Are you sure that's the right one?"

The article was from a Philadelphia paper and dealt with the downfall of a major drug ring. The byline and the small headshot next to it were definitely their Lauren Sanders. "Yep."

More links took them to different issues of the same paper. Some were major crime stories, front page, above the fold. Others were multi-part features, delving deeper into stories of human trafficking, elder abuse, and gangs.

"Are you sure that's the same Lauren Sanders?" Sylvia asked again.

"Yes, I'm sure. Look." Zoe clicked a link that brought up the reporter's bio and an enlarged version of the headshot. A few years younger, but clearly the woman who had helped in the barn yesterday.

Sylvia set down her sandwich, wiped her hands on a paper napkin, and angled the laptop to face her. "You eat. I'll read."

As if Zoe couldn't manage both. Then again, the glare from the screen was definitely aggravating her headache. "Okay." She slid the computer even closer to Sylvia and placed her plate in the warm spot left behind.

"According to this, she studied journalism at Northwestern University, graduating near the top of her class. She worked at several top newspapers in Boston and New York earlier in her career before settling in Philly."

"How old is that bio?" Zoe asked around a bite of baloney and Muenster.

Sylvia squinted at the screen. "This one is from five years ago."

"Try to find out when and why she left."

After a half hour of searching and clicking links, as well as sliding the laptop back and forth between them, they managed to ascertain that Sanders' final article with the Philadelphia paper covered a deep-reaching police corruption case. Then nothing. No more bylines. And no explanation for her disappearance. If she'd been fired, they'd kept it under wraps.

Sylvia rose and stacked the empty plates. "It's like she vanished from the earth two years ago."

Zoe scrolled down a little further and found a more recent post. "No. Not from the earth. Just from Philly."

"Oh?"

"Here's something dated last month. A piece she did in the *Enterprise* about the Christmas party at the Kid's Center."

"From police corruption to kids' parties. How far the mighty have fallen." Sylvia turned to face Zoe. "How long has the *Enterprise* been in business? Couldn't have been more than a couple months."

Zoe typed *Phillipsburg Enterprise* into the search bar and skimmed through the results. "Looks like the first issue came out the first week in December."

Sylvia nodded thoughtfully and turned back to the sink.

While Sylvia washed dishes, Zoe continued her online probe, searching for Lauren Sanders on various social media sites. One pulled up at least a dozen accounts for the name, none of which seemed a likely match. Another only showed the wrong Lauren Sanders. And another offered nothing at all.

Sylvia was right. It seemed the reporter dropped off the globe two years ago only to reappear last month.

Zoe's headache had eased, either from the food or from the distraction. Her brain was still fogged, but not enough to stop her from wondering what had brought down a journalistic superstar. And why would someone with her credentials be working at the fledgling *Phillipsburg Enterprise*?

TWENTY-TWO

It was Seth's turn to host the weekly Saturday night poker circle. Pete provided the transportation for Zoe and Sylvia, although he wondered how long they'd be able to stay. Zoe still looked and acted dazed, but in spite of his suggestion that she skip the game, she insisted on going. When he called her hardheaded, she grinned and said she'd heard that somewhere before.

At least he could keep an eye on her.

Seth rented the bottom floor of a two-story company house, walking distance from the police station. Back in the early 1900s, Dillard Coal Company had built rows of the cookie-cutter homes for its workers and their families. Over the last century, some had been razed. Others remodeled beyond recognition. But a handful of the blockish structures remained. Seth's place was one of them. Some might consider the buildings ugly. Pete saw them as historic. Charming.

The interior, however, had seen remodel after remodel. Walls torn down. New ones dividing large rooms into smaller ones. And doors everywhere. If Pete had owned the place, he'd have gutted it and started from scratch.

Seth seemed content with his bachelor pad apartment though. His kitchen counter overflowed with the food and beverages brought by the poker players. Pizza, chips, jugs of pop, and a case of beer.

Zoe's partner, Earl, arrived a few minutes later. He shook Pete's hand and eyed Zoe. "You will go to any lengths to cut out of work, won't you?"

She touched the bandage on her head. "Yep. I got spoiled being off with my knee. Thought I'd try something different this time."

Pete chuckled. At least the concussion hadn't diminished her sense of humor.

The final member of their group, Bruce Yancy, the burly former township fire chief, shuffled in lugging a case of water. Everyone except Sylvia filled paper plates, grabbed their beverage of choice, and settled around Seth's dining room table.

Pete eyed Sylvia. "You're not eating?"

"Not hungry." She rubbed her stomach. "The sandwich I had for lunch gave me indigestion." She shot a look at Zoe. "And her cats still have me wheezing."

"You both could've gone to your house."

Zoe leaned toward him, bumping his shoulder with hers. "She didn't want to."

"Ah." He got it. "Say no more."

Yancy sat across from Zoe and gestured at the bandage. "You should be home resting, young lady."

She swept a hand around the table, pointing at each of them. "Two cops, the county's best paramedic, a mother hen, and my favorite fireman. Do you seriously think I'd be safer anywhere else?"

Earl gave a low whistle. "She's calling me the county's best paramedic? Her head injury must be worse than we thought."

Seth nudged Yancy. "Besides, if she's not thinking straight, we might actually win some of her money tonight."

The good-natured banter settled down for a couple of hands. Pete quickly decided Seth was right about Zoe's diminished poker skills. At least no one at the table was greedy enough to take total advantage of her bad bets.

As Sylvia won the pot for the third hand, she set her gaze on Pete. "Have you found out anything about Lauren Sanders?"

Had Sylvia learned of the deal he'd made with the reporter? He kept his poker face in play. "Didn't realize I was supposed to be investigating her."

Sylvia glowered at him. "Uh-huh." She waggled a finger between her and Zoe. "Well, we did some digging and uncovered some interesting stuff."

"Oh?"

"Who's Lauren Sanders?" Yancy asked.

Pete gathered the cards for his turn to deal. "A reporter with the new newspaper in town."

The retired fire chief snorted. "Do they honestly think they can make a go of it?"

"Apparently." Pete lifted his gaze to Zoe. "What'd you learn?"

She and Sylvia took turns telling him about Sanders' history with the big-city papers.

"Sounds like she was a media rock star," Seth said.

"Yeah." Zoe restacked her poker chips. "And then she just vanished until she showed up here last month."

Pete shuffled the deck, replaying his earlier conversations with Sanders through his mind. Her being a big-deal, big-city reporter made sense. He'd always felt she was in a different sphere from the other news-media types he dealt with. But what the hell was she doing around here? Phillipsburg wasn't merely a step down. It was a plunge to shame the most daring skydiver.

"Hey." Yancy snapped his fingers at Pete. "You gonna let Zoe cut the deck or are you gonna shuffle it until all the ink's rubbed off?"

Jarred from his thoughts, he set the cards in front of Zoe, who waved him off. He kept an eye on her as he dealt. Other than the bandage on her head, most people wouldn't know anything had happened to her. But he noticed little things beyond her usual poker "tells."

"Are you sure you're all right?" he asked her, keeping his voice low.

She hesitated, and he knew she was debating an answer he'd believe. "I'm okay. Not great, but okay." She punctuated the affirmation with a less-than-convincing grin.

Okay-but-not-great described the hand he'd dealt himself. Earl and Yancy either had terrific cards or were set to bluff their way to the pot. Zoe made no effort to fake it and folded rather than call. She excused herself and headed to the counter piled with food.

Once everyone had discarded the duds and Pete had filled their requests, he checked his hand and decided to leave the duel to the others. He pushed back his chair and joined Zoe at the pizza boxes.

"We didn't get a chance to talk earlier," he said, again keeping his voice low. "But I have a favor to ask you."

She chewed, covering her mouth as she said, "Oh?"

"Could you talk to that emergency-room doctor—"

"Dr. Fuller?"

"Yeah. Could you find out if he's noticed any ER patients arriving from Golden Oaks who might have suspicious injuries or illnesses?"

Zoe swallowed and set down the slice of pepperoni pizza. "You're worried Harry might be on to something?"

"No. Not really. Maybe."

She looked at him expectantly.

"After you and Sylvia left his room this morning, he did mention his suspicions again."

Zoe grinned. "You mean that old fart was faking not remembering?"

"Who knows."

"Sure, I can talk to Dr. Fuller."

Pete hesitated asking his next question. "And could you maybe ask Franklin Marshall too?"

Zoe picked up the pizza slice and eyed it, as if planning her next assault. "Already did."

"What?"

"Before you even moved Harry in, I asked Franklin about the place."

Pete had known he was in love with this woman for months. Years maybe, although he hadn't admitted it even to himself at the time. But at that moment, he fell even deeper in love with her. "You did? What'd he say?"

"He said he'd never had reason to investigate any death that occurred there."

Pete hadn't realized the weight that had been pressing down on him until Zoe's words lifted it. He'd have kissed her, but his phone rang.

There was a momentary silence when he answered. Then a low voice said, "I need to talk to Zoe Chambers."

"Who's calling?" Another silence stretched so long Pete thought the caller may have hung up. "Hello?"

"I was told I could reach Zoe Chambers at this number." Something about the voice sounded familiar.

"You can. But I'd like to be able to tell her who's calling."

"This is Marcus Baker."

That's why the voice sounded familiar. "Just a minute." Pete handed the phone over to Zoe. "It's for you. Janie's boy."

She gave him a puzzled look and took the phone. "Hello?" Her expression morphed from perplexed to concerned as she turned and slipped away.

Pete grabbed a paper plate and a slab of pizza for himself before returning to his seat. As he'd predicted, Sylvia and Seth folded, leaving Earl and Yancy to battle it out. Earl finally called Yancy's last raise, and the retired fire chief plunked down a full house, kings over nines. Earl muttered a few choice curses, slapping his cards face down on the table.

Yancy smugly raked in his winnings as Zoe returned and tapped Pete on the shoulder. "I need to talk to you."

He didn't like her tone.

He excused himself and followed her into Seth's living room. "Why was Marcus calling you? And on my phone?"

"Because mine was stolen in the burglary." Zoe handed the phone back to him. "I'd told Janie to call your number if she needed me. I'm one of the emergency numbers she gave Marcus for when she's not around, so she must've given him your number too. Anyway, he said his mom went shopping in Brunswick, so he and his buddies went out for a walk."

Pete had visions of another fight. "What happened?"

"They were over on Oriole's street, and he noticed lights on in the house."

"In Oriole's house?"

"Yeah."

"Did he notice any cars parked around it?"

Zoe winced. "I didn't think to ask. Sorry. But he didn't mention any."

Pete handed her his phone again as he grabbed his coat from the pile on one of Seth's chairs. "Tell Marcus to go home. Do not go into Oriole's house alone."

Zoe waved away the phone. "I already did."

Pete pressed a kiss to the swath of gauze on Zoe's forehead. "That's my girl. You stay here. It's probably nothing, and I'll be back in a few minutes."

* * *

The station was on the way, so Pete pulled into the lot and ran inside to snag the key Trout had given him from his desk drawer.

By the time he parked in front of Oriole's house, the lights had been extinguished. There was no sign of an intruder, no cars parked near the place.

He grabbed his flashlight and stepped out into the cold, grateful that the air wasn't as biting as it had been earlier. He aimed the beam at the partially snow-covered walk. No fresh tracks.

Until he drew closer to the house.

Smudged boot prints trailed both to and from the front door. About ten feet from the door, the tracks veered off the sidewalk and crossed the yard, headed up the hill.

Toward Trout's home.

Pete knelt to study the prints. He couldn't tell for sure without a boot to match to them, but the size seemed consistent with what he remembered of the old man's shoes. What the hell was Trout up to now?

Pete pulled out his cell phone and snapped a photo.

Pocketing the phone, he approached the front door, the key in his gloved hand. He debated the issue of using the key without the granddaughter's express permission. But the kid had called about a possible intruder. Pete doubted Janie Baker would take him to task for making sure her grandmother's property was secured.

He shined the flashlight on the doorknob. No sign of forced entry. He closed his fingers around it and twisted, just in case someone had left it unlocked. But there was no give. He inserted the key. Or tried to. It didn't want to fit into the slot. Must be one of those cheap copies they make at the hardware stores. After wiggling and angling the thing in different directions, it finally slipped all the way into the lock.

But when he tried to turn it, the key refused to budge. It wasn't merely stiff from an imperfect cut job. It wasn't the right key. Closer inspection revealed no indication of the lock having been changed recently either.

Pete straightened and gazed up the hill in the direction the fresh boot prints led. *Dammit, Trout. What are you up to now?*

Two minutes later, Pete parked his SUV in front of the one-story clapboard residence of Alfred Troutman. Unlike Oriole's house, lights glowed through curtains, which even from the outside appeared disheveled. Pete trained his flashlight at the path to the front stoop and the perfect boot print left in the skiff of snow. He retrieved his phone and pulled up the photo he'd just taken. To his eye, the tread looked like a match.

He trudged to the rickety screen door and knocked.

The curtains on the front window swayed slightly. Pete heard footsteps inside, but no one came to the door. He waited. Knocked again. After another minute or more, the footsteps returned, growing louder. The door latch clicked, and Trout swung it open.

The old man stood there in a bathrobe pulled snug at his throat. Pete glanced down. Although Trout's feet were clad in slippers, he was wearing trousers rather than pajamas, and the bottoms of his pants were darker. Damp. From hiking through the snow.

"Chief Adams? Is something wrong?" Trout's eyes had that wide, blank, puzzled look Pete had seen more and more on Harry's face.

Except Pete had serious suspicions about Trout's lack of cognition. "I'm not sure. Do you mind if I come in? I'd like to talk to you, and there's no sense letting all your heat escape through an open door."

Trout shot a look toward something on the floor, but brought his bewildered gaze back to Pete. "Don't mind at all." He stepped back.

As Pete entered, he checked out what Trout had glanced at. Boots, dripping on some sheets of newspaper next to the door.

Trout didn't invite him any further into the house, but closed the door and pulled his robe tighter.

Pete contained a smile. He'd seen women do the same thing in an attempt to cover themselves up in his presence. Somehow, he didn't think Trout was being demure.

"What can I do for you, Chief?"

"I had a report about a possible intruder down at Ms. Andrews' house. Don't suppose you've seen anyone lurking around?"

Trout made a production of appearing thoughtful. "No. I've been inside all night. Watching TV."

The television screen was dark. Pete could have walked over to it and felt for heat, but there was no need. "Really? I thought you kept a pretty close eye on the comings and goings down there."

"I did. I do. But if there was someone down there this evening, I missed it."

Pete folded his arms and fixed the old man with a stern stare. "Because you've been in all evening. Watching TV."

"That's right."

"I thought it might have been you down there again."

"No." Trout dragged the word out as if that made it true.

"That's funny. You see, there're footprints down there leading up here. The same tracks are out on your sidewalk." Pete held up his phone. "I took pictures of them." He tipped his head toward the boots sitting in a puddle on the newspaper. "I bet if I looked at the tread on those, it'd match."

"Oh, no." He dragged it out again. His forehead wore deep concerned creases.

"Your pant legs are wet."

Trout looked down and muttered something Pete couldn't make out.

Pete reached over and gave the collar of the old man's robe a gentle tug, revealing a quilted flannel shirt beneath. "It's kind of warm in here for clothes like that. For taking an evening stroll, though..."

Trout stepped back, snatching the fabric from Pete and wrapping it around him. "Leave me alone."

Pete tsk-tsked. "You know Oriole's granddaughter doesn't want you snooping around down there."

Trout traded bewilderment for childish belligerence. "I wasn't doing anything."

Pete dug the key from his pocket and held it up. "You gave me the wrong one. This doesn't fit the lock down there."

"Did I?"

"Yes, you did."

Trout burrowed deeper into his robe, his shoulders hunched. "I must have been mixed up. I don't remember stuff as well as I used to."

"Uh-huh." But the old geezer's look of befuddlement was back, and Pete couldn't help seeing Harry in those confused eyes. "Just give me the real key to Oriole's house."

Trout dug into his trouser pocket and came up with his key ring. Much like the last time, he struggled to remove one of them and dropped it into Pete's waiting palm.

"Now, Trout, I'm going back down there, and if this key doesn't work, you and I are going to have some trouble."

The old man pouted. "It'll work."

Pete started to turn toward the door, but another question came to mind. "You know that last time I caught you down there, I did a walk-through afterwards."

Trout didn't comment.

"The forensic unit had been there and made a real mess of things. Rummaged through Oriole's things. Left the drawers askew. But I found some of them had been straightened up. Janie claims she didn't do it. You know what I think?"

Still no comment.

"I think you did it."

Trout looked down at his stocking feet and mumbled something.

"Want to tell me what you were looking for?"

"I wasn't looking for anything," he replied quickly. Too quickly. "I was just straightening up the mess. Oriole wouldn't have liked the way you people left her things, all jumbled like that."

"Uh-huh." Pete wasn't at all sure he bought anything Trout said. "Why do you keep going down there?"

He contemplated the question for a minute, still hanging his head. "I dunno. I miss Oriole. I miss my girl. I just like to sit down there and...remember. You know?"

Any desire to further chastise the old man melted away. Pete rested a hand on Trout's shoulder. He wanted to say something soothing, but words seemed inadequate. "Yeah," he said and headed for the door.

TWENTY-THREE

"I'm out." Zoe set her cards face down in front of her. Another lousy hand and her brain was too fuzzy to even consider bluffing.

Earl scowled at her. "You're really off your game tonight."

"Duh." She pointed at her head. "Concussion."

Yancy snorted. "How long are you gonna milk that excuse?"

But Zoe caught the look of concern in the old fire chief's eyes.

"As long as I can." She attempted a grin, but suspected it didn't really come across.

"Hey, I've had concussions before," Seth said. "I played football in high school." He turned toward Sylvia. "But what's your excuse? I've beat your hand four times tonight. That never happens."

"My house got robbed this week. Isn't that excuse sufficient?"

The exchange stirred Zoe from her mental fog enough to take a closer look at the older woman. Sylvia still hadn't eaten. Her brow was furrowed. And was she sweating? Seth's old house was drafty enough that everyone knew to wear sweatshirts or sweaters. In spite of layers of clothes, Zoe still felt the chill. "Are you all right?"

Sylvia made a face. "I think that lunchmeat in Pete's refrigerator must have been bad."

"Maybe." Except Zoe'd had a sandwich from the same stuff and it hadn't bothered her. She pushed her chair back and stood, reaching a hand toward Sylvia. "Come with me."

"I'm playing poker."

Zoe tipped her head to look at Sylvia's cards. A potential straight, but they both knew the odds of filling it. Zoe took them from her and tossed them onto the table.

"Hey."

"You should thank me." Zoe grasped Sylvia's arm and gave a

gentle tug. "Let's go into the living room."

"Why?"

"Stop arguing and just do it."

Grumbling, the older woman complied. Zoe noticed her wince as she stood.

"I'm out too," Earl said. He threw in his hand and climbed to his feet. Catching Zoe's arm, he whispered in her ear, "I have my gear in my car. I'll get it."

Zoe loved her partner. "Thanks."

A couple of minutes later, Sylvia sat on the couch complaining as Zoe held her wrist, checking her pulse. Earl had returned with a small duffle from which he produced a blood-pressure cuff and stethoscope. Zoe kept her gaze on him as he pumped up the cuff and slowly released the air.

Sylvia's pulse was much too fast. Beads of perspiration glistened on her forehead. Zoe mentally pummeled herself for not putting it together sooner. If she hadn't been so darned fuzzy-brained...

Earl draped his stethoscope around his neck and fixed Zoe with a stern stare. "I'm calling the ambulance."

"What?" Sylvia hugged her arm that still had the BP cuff on it. "No. I'm fine. I just need some antacids."

Zoe nodded at Earl, who stood and dug his phone from his pocket. She took Sylvia's hand. "You need to go the hospital."

Pete approached the front door of Oriole's house, the second key Trout had given him clenched in his gloved hand. If the key worked, he'd do a quick walk-through and make sure nothing had been tampered with. Maybe get an idea of what the old man had been doing in there. Then he'd call the granddaughter and update her. Then back to Zoe and the poker game.

If it didn't fit, he and Trout were going to have a serious chat, possibly down at the station.

This key, unlike the first one, slid effortlessly into the lock. He turned it and the latch clicked. Good. At least there was a limit to the old man's shenanigans. Pete closed his fingers around the knob and swung the door open.

From his coat pocket, his phone vibrated. He stepped inside and closed the door behind him before answering.

"Chief, it's Nate." Nothing ever ruffled the weekend officer, but his voice sounded as tense as Pete had ever heard. "I'm tailing a white panel van on Route 15 traveling south near the old junkyard."

"Can you see the license number?"

"Yeah. It's not a match, but..."

"But what?"

"I was thinking. If I'd stolen a van from a business where that sort of thing was kept on record, the first thing I'd do is swap the plates with another vehicle. So I ran them. They came back for a '98 Dodge Ram."

Pete's heart rate kicked up a gear.

"I'm going to pull him over."

"No." Pete thought of what had happened to Zoe when she'd gone up against these guys. "Not without backup." He yanked the door open and stepped back out into the cold. "I'm only three miles away. Radio county for backup. Don't take any chances." He locked the door and pocketed the key. "Do you think they know you're back there?"

"He's keeping below the speed limit. I'd have to say yes."

"I'm on my way. Keep me posted."

Pete hung up and jogged to his car. He turned it around, but hadn't reached the bottom of the hill before his cell rang again.

"He's making a run for it." Nate's voice sounded even more tense, and the scream of sirens blasted through the phone.

Pete flipped on his own siren and emergency lights. "Keep with him as long as you can do so safely." He mashed the gas pedal and careened, fishtailing, onto Route 15.

"Roger that."

He was about to hit the red button ending the call when Nate's shout burst from the speaker.

"Nate? What's going on?"

Was that tires screeching? Or was Pete imagining it? What he did not imagine was Nate yelling, "Son of a—"

And then the call went dead.

*   *   *

Sylvia made a face as she chewed a couple of aspirin at Zoe's insistence. Zoe and Earl had convinced her to lie down on the couch. The poker game ended the moment Seth and Yancy overheard the word "ambulance."

Sylvia had quit blaming the pressure in her chest on heartburn or bad lunchmeat. Fear replaced denial in her eyes.

Zoe held Sylvia's hand in both of hers and gave it a gentle squeeze. "You're gonna be fine." Zoe only hoped the older woman didn't realize she was keeping track of her pulse in addition to offering comfort.

"You have the county's best team of paramedics here," Earl said with a wink. "Of course you're going to be fine."

If Sylvia tried to smile, it looked more like a wince. "You need to call Pete."

"I will," Zoe said. "Once the ambulance gets here."

"I think I hear it now." Seth grabbed his jacket and headed for the door. "I'll go direct them in."

Sylvia gripped Zoe's hand. "If anything happens to me—"

Zoe cut her off. "Nothing's going to happen to you."

"If," Sylvia said, her eyes glistening. "If anything happens, you call Rose."

A lump lodged in Zoe's throat at the thought of having to dump even more bad news on her best friend. "You know I will."

"Be advised," Nate's voice crackled over the police radio, "the suspect vehicle has crashed."

Pete was still a minute or so away. Hearing his officer's voice eased his mind. "Vance Thirty-five, this is Vance Thirty. What's your status?"

"Suspect vehicle has crashed," Nate repeated.

Pete refrained from barking *I know that* through the mic. Police radio transmissions were easily accessible to the public, calling for a more professional demeanor.

"Suspects have not exited the vehicle," Nate added. "Requesting fire and EMS response."

"Roger that, Thirty-five." Pete flipped to a different frequency to place the request. He still didn't know if Nate was the one needing medical help. The officer wasn't likely to broadcast to the listening public that he'd been hurt.

By the time the EOC confirmed fire and EMS were on their way, Pete spotted the red glow of taillights and the red and blue strobes of Nate's car cutting through the night sky. A dozen or so vehicles idled, unable to get through. Pete swung into the empty northbound lane and roared past them.

Nate's cruiser sat diagonally across the road. His headlights and spotlight set the white van aglow as it teetered precariously off the edge of the road. Pete wasn't sure what kept it from rolling on down into the pasture below. He parked his SUV next to Nate, who hunkered behind his open car door, weapon drawn. Distant sirens pierced the air. More help was on the way.

Pete took up his position, shielded by his own car's open door. "Are you all right?" he called to his officer.

"Yeah. When I was on the phone with you, he lost control and ran off the road. I dropped the phone when I grabbed the steering wheel with both hands to keep from wrecking too. Sorry."

"Forget it." Pete was just relieved he hadn't been hurt in the line of duty.

"I've ordered them to step out of the vehicle, but they haven't made any kind of move. And I haven't seen any weapons."

Which didn't mean there weren't any.

Pete grabbed his mic and switched to the PA system. "This is the police. Step out of the vehicle and keep your hands where we can see them."

Nothing happened. He wondered if the occupants might have climbed out on the downhill side, away from their line of vision, and slipped off into the night.

Three marked county police units roared up from the opposite direction, pulling around the stopped traffic to aim their vehicles and their spotlights on the listing van.

Pete caught a glimpse of movement from it. The driver's side door opened a few inches. Pete tensed, raising his sidearm.

"Don't shoot," came a terrified voice. One hand reached out of the van, palm open, fingers spread. "We're unarmed. Please don't shoot."

The door opened a little farther, but appeared to be hung up on something. A second hand appeared, also empty. A male figure dressed in black struggled to squeeze through the opening.

Pete, Nate, and the three county officers eased toward the van, keeping their weapons trained on the man. And keeping vigilant for the second man. Hell, for all Pete knew, there might be a third one.

"Turn around," Pete ordered. "Slowly."

Hands still raised, the man did as told.

Pete continued to direct him to keep turning until he'd turned all the way around and was again facing the van. There were no weapons in sight, but the punk was wearing a bulky winter coat. Hell, he could have a rifle under there.

"Get down on your knees," Pete barked. "Hands on top of your head. And cross your ankles."

The man in black complied, dropping to his knees in the snow.

"Who else is in the van?" Pete asked.

"Just my brother." The man sounded like he was sobbing. "He's in the passenger seat. He's hurt. Please help him."

Pete pointed at one of the county officers. "Search him and cuff him." Then he signaled to the others to circle the van from the front. He thumped Nate's back. "You're with me."

They headed to the rear of the van. Pete kept his sidearm and flashlight trained on the back doors as Nate grasped the latch. Pete gave a nod. And Nate yanked it open.

The cargo compartment held a trio of televisions, a computer, and some other electronics—large and small—plus a pair of hunting rifles and a couple shotguns, all piled against the downhill side of the vehicle. These guys had been busy tonight. Toward the front, he could make out movement from the passenger seat. Not threatening. Just shifting.

"The door's stuck," one of the county officers shouted to them from outside the passenger side.

Pete shone his flashlight around the corner in their direction and discovered why the van hadn't rolled or slid farther down the hillside. The vehicle rested against an old fence post and a small tree, which also jammed the door.

The county officer shined his light through the window. "He has both hands on the dash. Looks like he cracked his head on the windshield. There's a lot of blood."

Pete thought of Zoe, bleeding in the snow, and couldn't dredge up any sympathy even if he'd wanted to. "I'm going in through the rear. Keep him covered."

He holstered his Glock, climbed into the cargo compartment, and picked his way along the sloping floor, around the stolen property. Nate followed. The second man, also attired head to toe in black, kept his hands planted on the dash. Through the windshield, Pete spotted a fire engine on the road above them. Fire and rescue would be able to cut the guy out. George Winston wasn't going to be happy with the condition of his van once this was over.

"Keep your hands where they are," Pete ordered and patted him down as best he could while reaching around from behind. "Do you have any firearms on you or in the vehicle?"

"Not on me." The man's voice quivered. "There're some rifles and shotguns back there."

The ones Pete had already seen. "Where are you hurt?"

"My head. I hit it on the window when we ran off the road."

"Anywhere else?"

"No, sir."

Sir? As far as murdering, thieving con artists went, this one topped the list of polite criminals. Pete shined the light in the guy's face. He squinted. Even though the injury was on the side away from Pete, he could still see the blood. And something about the guy seemed familiar. "Where's your ID?"

"Left hip pocket."

Pete reached for it and the man shifted onto his right hip. Pete pulled out the wallet.

"I think I'm bleeding to death."

"No, you're not." Pete flipped the wallet open and pulled out a Pennsylvania driver's license. "Dennis Naiman?"

"Yes, sir."

"Chief?" Nate called from the rear of the van. "The fire department has arrived."

"Good. Let's get him out of here."

TWENTY-FOUR

Zoe stood at the open sliding glass door to the Emergency Department cubicle, alternately gazing down the hallway and keeping an eye on Sylvia.

The nurses and techs had already drawn blood and taken an EKG. Zoe knew the information on the monitor above the bed wasn't good.

"Where's Earl?" Sylvia asked.

Zoe turned her back on the hallway. "In the waiting room."

He'd driven Zoe to the hospital, but in spite of having seen more than his share of exposed-chested female patients, he'd felt awkward with Sylvia being the patient this time. "I'll be out here if you need me," he'd said.

"I'm being a pain in the ass." Sylvia hooked a finger in the oxygen cannula, freeing it from her nostrils. "You two should go home. Earl has kids and a wife he needs to tend to."

Zoe strode to the bedside, took the tubing from Sylvia, and gently resituated it where it was supposed to be. "We're not going anywhere." Zoe considered quipping that they were sticking around to give her a ride home, but she suspected the older woman knew darned well she wasn't going anywhere.

Soft footsteps in the hall drew Zoe's attention. She turned in time to see Dr. Fuller headed their way. While his expression was unreadable, Zoe took the absence of his easy smile as a bad omen.

He entered the cubicle and whisked the curtain closed. "How are you feeling?" he asked Sylvia.

"You tell me."

He crossed his arms, shot a glance at Zoe, and then focused on his patient. "I've compared the EKG we just took to the one from

Wednesday. I'm afraid there have been some changes."

"For the better?" Sylvia offered a hopeful but weak smile.

Her attempt at humor fell flat. Dr. Fuller didn't return the smile. "I want to send you up to the cath lab."

"You mean next week?"

"I mean now."

Sylvia's face paled in spite of the oxygen. "It's that bad?"

"I don't think it's wise to put this off. If we go in and find a blockage, we have a team available to go in right away and do what needs to be done."

As the doctor proceeded to explain the procedure and its possible findings and complications, a light tap on the glass drew Zoe's attention toward the hall. She slipped out through the drawn curtain to find an anxious Earl.

"How's she doing?" he whispered.

"They're sending her upstairs for a heart cath as soon as Dr. Fuller can talk her into it."

Earl's worried scowl deepened. "I was afraid of that."

"You should go home. I'll stay here and have Pete come get me."

"You sure?" Earl rested a hand on her shoulder and squeezed. "How are you feeling?"

"Much better," Zoe lied. "And yes. I'm sure. Go."

"Call me when there's news."

She shot him a thumbs up. Once he'd walked away, she ducked back inside.

Dr. Fuller had finished his well-practiced spiel and took Sylvia's hand. "Do you have any questions?"

Her damp eyes and quivering lip suggested she had quite a few, but she said, "No."

He caught Zoe's gaze. "How about you?"

"I don't think so."

He gave them his patented comforting smile and patted Sylvia's hand. "Don't worry. We'll get you fixed up and back home before you know it."

After he left, Sylvia looked at Zoe. "Are you heading out?"

"And leave you here? No way."

"But Earl—"

"I sent him home. Once they take you for the procedure, I'll call Pete. But I'm not leaving until you're done and settled in your room."

"That might take all night."

Zoe was sure it would. She grinned and shrugged. "I have nowhere else to be."

Sylvia's expression told Zoe she wasn't buying it. But the scowl quickly faded. "Have you called Rose yet?"

"I'll do that right after I call Pete."

"It's late."

"Not out there." Zoe had become proficient at calculating the two-hour time difference between Pennsylvania and New Mexico.

A nurse bustled into the cubicle and eyed Zoe. "Do you mind stepping out for a minute? I need to prep the patient."

"No problem." She slipped into the hallway, leaned against the wall, and closed her eyes. Her head was throbbing. Her vision was still blurred. And the idea of Sylvia—stubborn, independent, powerhouse Sylvia—being incapacitated made Zoe's heart ache even more than the concussion messed with her head.

All because of those thugs who'd broken into Sylvia's house, the Krolls' house, and Oriole Andrews' house.

Zoe spotted Dr. Fuller writing on a clipboard at the nurses' station and remembered a promise she'd made. She pushed off from the wall and walked toward him.

He looked up at her approach. "Is everything all right?"

"Oh. Yeah. The nurse kicked me out for a minute. But I wanted to ask you about something else if you have a minute."

He set down the pen and faced her. "What do you need?"

"Do you know anything about Golden Oaks Assisted Living?"

"Like what in particular?"

She pondered the best way to pose the question. "Have you treated any patients from there?"

"Sure. Any time one of their residents falls and strikes their head, they have to send them here."

She already knew that much. "Have there been any cases that seemed...suspicious?"

"How do you mean?"

She wished she knew. "You remember Pete Adams? You met him

when Sylvia was in here on Wednesday."

"The police chief? Yes."

"His father just moved in there and, well, he has Alzheimer's and he keeps telling Pete that there's something weird going on." When the doctor didn't respond, Zoe added, "He says people are being murdered."

For several moments, Dr. Fuller didn't react. Then a smile tugged at his lips. "You said he has Alzheimer's?"

"Yeah."

"And his son's a cop."

"Yeah."

He raised an eyebrow at her.

"I know, I know. Pete does too. But it's his father, and if there's even a chance there's anything hinky going on over there—"

The doctor lifted a hand to silence her. "I get it. Tell Pete he can rest assured there is nothing 'hinky' going on at Golden Oaks. I've dealt with them for years and the staff is well-trained and compassionate. Any of their residents who have come through my ER have legitimate illnesses or injuries, consistent with being elderly and not as mobile as they once were."

"What about residents who..." She searched for a polite way to say it. "What about residents who don't survive?"

"You mean questionable deaths?"

"Yeah."

He shook his head. "If I had any concerns, I would have voiced them. And I've spoken with enough of their residents who still have their wits about them to feel comfortable in saying they're being treated well and are in a safe environment."

Zoe relaxed. "Thanks."

The doctor tipped his head toward her, fixing her with a serious gaze. "However, if you or Chief Adams see anything or anyone that makes you apprehensive, let me know. I'll gladly take a closer look."

Pete left Nate to supervise the firefighters as they extricated the injured suspect. After trudging up the embankment, Pete headed for the county's squad car where the van's driver occupied the backseat, his wrists cuffed behind him. The black ski mask had been removed, revealing dark hair wildly askew. The officer who'd taken him into custody stood at the open door keeping watch over his prisoner.

"What do you have on him?" Pete asked.

"Name's Douglas Naiman, age twenty-five. According to his driver's license, his home address is on Franklin Street in Brunswick. I'm running him for priors."

"Good." Pete leaned down for a better look at the kid. If he didn't know better, he'd have sworn the punk was about to burst into tears. "You have the right to remain silent," Pete said and continued to Mirandize him. "Do you understand?"

"Yes, sir."

"Where'd you get the loot tonight?"

Douglas leaned forward, trying to look around Pete. "How's my brother? Is he hurt bad?"

"He's being tended to. Now tell me about the stolen merchandise in the back of the van."

The kid ran his tongue over his lips. "It's not stolen. We're moving some stuff for a friend."

"Wearing black ski masks."

"It's cold out." He made it sound more like a question than an answer.

"Driving a stolen van."

"It's stolen?" The kid tried—and failed—to look appalled. "I didn't know."

"Why'd you run from the police officer?"

"I didn't," he stuttered. "I realized we were late."

"For what?"

By now the kid was visibly trembling, either from the cold or, as Pete suspected, from the exertion of lying. "I don't want to say anything else until I talk to my brother."

"Your brother's going to the hospital."

Douglas' eyes widened. "How bad's he hurt?"

"The paramedics are taking care of him. The sooner you answer my questions, the sooner I can let you see him." Pete didn't mention that the reunion would happen during their arraignment.

The kid appeared to weigh his options. And apparently didn't like them. "I think I better talk to a lawyer before I say anything else."

Pete swore to himself. He turned to the officer standing guard. "Go ahead and take him in."

"Yes, sir," the officer said as Pete's phone vibrated in his pocket.

Sylvia's name and number came up on the caller ID. Had something happened to Zoe? He strode away from the car as he answered. "Sylvia? What's going on?"

But it was Zoe's voice on the phone. "Sylvia's in the hospital."

Not what he'd expected to hear. "Why? What happened?"

He listened as Zoe explained about the chest pains and the trip to the ER. "They just took her up for the heart cath."

Pete closed his eyes, picturing a terrified Sylvia. "Is Earl still there with you?"

"No. I sent him home. It's gonna be a long night. I was hoping you could come and wait with me."

Pete scanned the scene behind him. Police, ambulance, and fire vehicles. Emergency lights sweeping across the snow clogged the road, blocking traffic in both directions. "I'll be there, but it's going to take a while."

"What's going on? Are you still at Oriole's house?"

"Not exactly. But we've caught our burglary and homicide suspects."

"Really? How?"

He gave her a quick rundown of the evening's events.

"Are you sure it's them?"

"Caught them in the stolen van with more stolen merchandise in the rear."

Zoe's sigh traveled through the airwaves to his ear. "Thank God."

Pete noticed movement down at the van. The firefighters had extricated the trapped and bloodied brother, and two paramedics were helping him up the embankment. The punk appeared unhurt except for the gash on his head. "Hold on a second," Pete told Zoe and muted his phone. He met the paramedics and their patient at the rear of the ambulance as one of the medics opened the doors. "Are you transporting him to Brunswick?"

"Yep. He needs stitches."

Pete signaled to another of the county officers. "Cuff him and ride in with him. I'll meet you at the hospital."

"Yes, sir."

Pete unmuted his phone. "Zoe?"

"I'm still here."

"I'll be there in a half hour."

Pete's cell phone rang as he stepped out of his vehicle at the Emergency Room entrance. He recognized Lauren Sanders' temporary number and almost let it go to voicemail.

Almost.

"I understand you've made an arrest," the reporter said when he answered.

Where the hell did she get her information? Or was she clairvoyant? "I'm a little busy right now."

"We have a deal."

"Yes, we do, and as soon as I have any information to share, I'll call you." He hit the red button on his phone, cutting off her tirade. When his phone rang a second time with the same number showing up on the screen, he swiped "ignore."

Five minutes later, Pete left a county uniform standing guard at the cubicle with the injured brother and went in search of Zoe. He tracked her down in a small waiting room on the cardiac floor. Standing in the doorway, he watched her a moment. God, she looked exhausted. She stretched out in an uncomfortable-looking chair upholstered in some sort of ugly stain-resistant fabric. Her ankles were crossed and she rested her head against the wall behind her. She had her eyes closed, but he doubted she was asleep. On the chair next to her, a clear plastic bag held what he assumed were Sylvia's clothes.

Zoe opened her eyes at his approach and gave him a tired smile. "Hey."

"Hey, yourself."

She pushed up into a more standard seated position and combed her fingers through the mop of blonde curls spilling over her bandage.

He took the empty chair beside her and put an arm around her shoulders. "Any word on Sylvia?"

"Nothing yet." Zoe shot an anxious glance at the waiting-room doors. "I'd think we should hear something soon." She turned her baby blues on him. "What about your prisoners?"

"One's in custody at the county lockup. The other's downstairs getting his head stitched. Then he'll join his brother."

"They're brothers?"

"Keeping it all in the family, I guess."

"Local?"

"They're from here in Brunswick. Franklin Street."

She scowled. "That's a pretty nice area. Lots of big old Victorian houses."

Pete didn't care about the thugs' upbringing or home environment at the moment. He was more concerned about the dark circles under Zoe's eyes. "You should be at home. Resting."

"I can't leave Sylvia here."

He surveyed the room. There were rows of chairs, all with curved oak arms. Not a sofa to be seen. The one recliner was currently occupied by an elderly woman who looked like she needed to be admitted herself. "I could make them bring in a cot."

Zoe smiled and slumped toward him. She rested her head on his shoulder, one hand on his thigh. A rush of heat surged through him. "I'm fine," she said.

He rubbed her shoulder and rested his cheek against the top of her head. "You sure? How's your head?"

She snuggled her face against his neck. "It hurts. But this is nice. All things considered."

He chuffed a laugh. "It's pretty bad when your idea of a romantic Saturday night is poker followed by cuddling in a hospital waiting room."

He felt more than heard her laugh. Then she grew still. "What are their names?"

"Who?"

She jabbed him gently in the ribs. "The brothers."

"Oh. Them. Last name's Naiman. It seems familiar, but I can't place it."

"Naiman?" Zoe pulled away from him and sat upright. "Wasn't that Barbara's last name?"

TWENTY-FIVE

Zoe leaned against Pete as they watched a nurse settle Sylvia into a bed in the cardiac care unit.

Still groggy from the anesthesia, the patient eyed the array of cords, tubes, and IV lines sprouting from her body. "Three stents?"

"Yes, ma'am," the nurse said as she raised the head of the bed. "Are you comfortable? Can I adjust your pillow?"

Sylvia mumbled something.

The nurse must have understood it to mean the pillow was fine. She showed Sylvia the controls for the bed, the TV, and the call button while an aide poured water from a plastic pitcher into a disposable cup. "Breakfast will be coming in about an hour. Is there anything you need right now?"

"I don't think so."

The nurse pointed to the red button on the panel of the bed's side rail. "If you do, remember, press this." With an all-business smile at Zoe and Pete, she and the aide bustled out of the room.

Sylvia's gaze landed on them. "Three stents?" she said again.

Zoe approached her. "Afraid so. The doctor found three pretty big blockages, but nothing bad enough to require a bypass. You're lucky."

"I don't feel lucky."

Zoe glanced at Pete. He'd left late last night to transport the stitched and bandaged Naiman brother to the county lockup, but he'd returned at some point in the wee hours. She managed to catch a few hours of fitful sleep thanks to Pete's shoulder and the pillows a hospital volunteer brought. He told her he'd slept too, but she didn't believe him. Still, the tousled salt-and-pepper hair and a touch of five-o'clock shadow only made him look sexier than ever.

He moved to her side and slipped his arm around her waist. To

Sylvia, he said, "The doctor told us you're too stubborn to let something like this hold you down."

The truth was the doctor had also used the word "lucky."

"So I'm gonna live?" Sylvia said, her words mushy.

"Oh hell yeah." Pete leaned down and squeezed her hand. "You'll be back at our poker game next Saturday feeling like a new woman."

"Good. I need to win back the money you stole off me tonight."

Zoe thought about correcting her. *Last night.* But didn't. She nudged Pete. "They told us she needs her rest."

"So do you." He turned again to Sylvia. "We'll be back later to see if you're ready to break out of here yet."

"Take your time. I plan to enjoy the room service for a while."

Which let Zoe know how truly awful Sylvia felt.

In the elevator ride down, Pete took her hand and gave it a gentle squeeze. "How about some breakfast before I take you home?"

Zoe glanced at her watch. "The cafeteria doesn't open for twenty minutes yet."

"How about the Park 'n' Dine?"

"I thought you and Wayne were going to interrogate the Naiman brothers this morning."

"We are. But we've been letting them sit and simmer all night. They can wait until I see you're fed and returned home."

Which was the problem. "The offer for breakfast is fine. But I'm not going home."

"Yes, you are."

"No. I'm not. I want to be there when you talk to those creeps."

Pete crossed his arms. "You don't trust me to do my job?"

"You know I do. But I want to see them. Hear what they have to say from their own lips."

"You're supposed to rest."

That "R" word again. "I will. After I watch you and Wayne interrogate them."

Pete shook his head. "Not happening."

Zoe turned to face him and mirrored his crossed-arms pose. "I'm a deputy coroner. They murdered Oriole Andrews. I have every right to be there as part of my investigation."

The elevator stopped one floor shy of their destination, and a dark-haired man in scrubs stepped in. Pete's set jaw told Zoe the debate was far from over.

When the doors glided open a second time, all three of them exited into a hallway leading to the lobby. The man in scrubs ducked through a door marked "Authorized Personnel Only," leaving Zoe and Pete to stroll down the hall alone.

"First," he said, holding up one finger, "you aren't investigating Oriole's homicide. Franklin Marshall is."

"He always takes the good cases," Zoe muttered.

"Second," Pete held up two fingers, "may I remind you, the coroner's investigation involves the actual body and what's on and around it. It does not involve the suspects."

"Yeah, yeah." Zoe shooed away the minor detail with a wave of her hand.

"And third..." Three fingers. "...the Naimans allegedly murdered her. If we knew for certain, there would be no need for an interrogation or the entire legal process. Remember that."

The *allegedly* thing startled Zoe. "You don't think they did it?"

"Oh, I'm pretty damned sure they did. You're missing the point."

Her headache was amping up again. "I get it. Criminal Law 101." The hallway opened into the lobby with its white marble floors and black marble walls. She stopped and turned to him, setting her face in her best you-aren't-changing-my-mind look. "But I am going to watch you question those two. With or without breakfast first."

Before he could resume the argument, she wheeled away from him and marched out the front door.

Breakfast had been largely silent. Pete knew from Zoe's mule-headed scowl that he wasn't going to sway her. He had to admit, her cheeks were back to their healthy pink, her eyes seemed clear, and her appetite was as voracious as ever. If it weren't for the gauze bandage circling her head, no one would suspect anything was wrong.

But he knew.

He considered turning his SUV toward Route 15 and driving her home in spite of her insistence on going with him to the county police station. She wasn't crazy enough to jump out of a moving car.

However, she might just be crazy enough to pack her stuff and move back into the bunk room at the ambulance garage.

Damn stubborn women.

Pete escorted Zoe into the rear entrance of the station. Wayne Baronick leaned against the wall and looked up from the file he was reading.

"Zoe," the detective said, surprise in his voice. He shot a questioning glance at Pete before fixing his gaze on her. "What are you doing here?"

She struck the same no-compromises pose as she had with Pete. "I'm going to observe the interrogation."

Baronick looked at Pete.

Pete shrugged. *You try to argue with her.*

The detective apparently knew better. "Okay then." He tipped his head toward a door. "Our guests are awaiting our arrival."

They moved into another hallway lined with more doors. Pete had been here hundreds of times, but this was Zoe's first trip behind the scenes of the county police station. He noticed her taking it all in.

"How do you want to play this?" Baronick asked. "Douglas has already lawyered up. He refuses to say anything other than demanding to see his brother."

Pete shook his head. "Not going to happen."

"Right. Dennis, the older one, hasn't demanded representation. Yet."

"Has anyone questioned him?"

Baronick grinned. "I've been saving him for the two of us." The detective aimed a thumb at a door marked Interview Room A. "Douglas Naiman and his attorney are in there." Baronick pointed at another door down the hall. Interview Room B. "Dennis is in that one. Do you want to split up? Each of us take one? Or do you want to double up on them?"

"Let's both work on the one who hasn't invoked his rights. Maybe we'll get something from him we can use to entice the other one to open up."

Baronick flashed his too bright smile. "That's exactly what I was thinking." He handed Pete the file.

Pete tucked it under an arm, opened the door to the darkened observation room next to Interview Room B, and gestured to Zoe. "You can watch and listen from here."

She paused as she stepped inside and turned to face him. "I want you to ask him something."

"What?"

"Ask him if he knows Lauren Sanders."

Zoe's eyes revealed a muddle of emotions. Fear. Anger. Determination. "I will," he promised. He glanced at the window into Interview Room B. Their suspect sat hunched over, chewing his nails, his knee bouncing. "I definitely will."

With Zoe stashed safely away, Pete led the way into the cramped interrogation room. Dennis Naiman squirmed upright in his uncomfortable chair, folding his trembling hands on the table in front of him. He might be the older of the brothers, but he was also the more rattled.

Pete eased into the chair across from Naiman and set the closed file on the table between them. Baronick grabbed the remaining chair and dragged it, the legs screeching like nails on a chalkboard, in front of the door, blocking even the intimation of escape. The detective sat and crossed his arms.

"Good morning, Mr. Naiman," Pete said and followed with another reading of the Miranda rights. "Do you understand?"

"Yeah," the kid replied weakly.

"I'm Pete Adams, Vance Township Police." He tipped his head at Baronick. "He's Detective Wayne Baronick, Monongahela County Police."

The kid's gaze darted back and forth, settling on Pete. "I need to see my brother."

"You mean Douglas?"

He nodded spastically.

"No problem. He's busy right now, but as soon as he finishes talking to the other officers, we'll let you see him."

Naiman's eyes widened for a split second. "Oh. Okay." His knee started bouncing again, making the table vibrate.

Pete struck a casual pose. "I think we've met before, haven't we? Over at Golden Oaks. You're Barbara's grandson, right?"

The kid acted as if the air had been sucked out of the room. His lips moved, but no words formed.

"Don't worry. She won't hear any of this from me. That's what's got you worried, isn't it? You're afraid your grandmother will find out."

Naiman exhaled. The knee stilled. "Yeah."

"She's really proud of you, you know."

Tears brimmed in the kid's eyes. "Yeah."

"Tell me about her."

"Doug and me...our folks were killed in a car crash when we were little. Grandma raised us. Put us through school."

"She sounds like a wonderful woman."

"She is. She'd do anything for us." Naiman's voice quivered. "And we'd do anything for her."

"How long has she been at Golden Oaks?"

Naiman slouched. "Fourteen months. She had a stroke. She was in pretty bad shape for a while. We thought we were gonna lose her. But she pulled through. Physical therapy helped, but she still needed more care than we could give her."

"So you placed her at Golden Oaks?"

"It was the nicest place we could find," Naiman said, his tone apologetic and pleading.

"I understand completely." Not a lie. "You want the best for those you care about."

"Yeah." He sounded relieved, grateful that someone "got" it.

Pete almost felt sorry for the guy. Almost. "But that kind of place, that kind of care, gets expensive over time."

Naiman swiped a hand across his damp eyes. "Yeah. It does. We went through what was left of Grandma's savings pretty fast. She'd already spent most of it putting us through college. We put the house on the market, but it hasn't sold. We didn't want to stick her in the county home."

"You started burglarizing houses."

He propped his elbows on the table and buried his face in his hands without replying.

"Dennis? Did you start stealing to help take care of your grandmother?"

"Yes," he whispered.

"You pretended to be utility workers to gain access?"

Naiman lowered his hands. "Yeah."

"How many houses have you robbed?"

The table began vibrating in time with the knee again. "I honestly don't know."

"You've lost count?" Pete forced his jaw to relax. Getting angry— and showing it—would only put the kid on the defensive, and probably prompt him to demand an attorney.

"Yeah."

"You know we found the wrecked van at the farm where you were stashing the stolen goods."

"Yeah."

"Do you have any additional merchandise warehoused anywhere else?"

Naiman gave a palsied shake of his head. "We haven't had a chance to find another place. The only stuff we have is in the new van."

"About that haul we caught you with last night. Where'd you get it?"

Naiman hunched over as if trying to crawl inside himself. "There was a house a couple days ago on Route 15, a mile or two from Dillard."

That would be the Krolls' place. Pete had plenty of questions about that break-in, but let Naiman continue for the moment.

"Then last night there was a place over on Brice Run Road. Between the junkyard and that house where they sell antiques."

"The Walkers?"

He tried to shrug, but with his shoulders already hiked to his ears, the movement was miniscule. "I dunno. We don't usually get their names."

Pete resisted the urge to reach over and rap his head on the table, once for each of his victims, while Pete recited the names to him. "Were they home at the time?"

"No." Naiman squirmed in the chair. "We stopped in earlier today and knew they had dinner plans with their kids tonight."

"And how did you know that?"

He swallowed hard. "Their calendar."

"What?"

"Their calendar," Naiman repeated. "While we're doing our water company thing to see what they've got, we also check out their calendars. Old people don't put their appointments on their phones. They mark them on their calendars. We'd see when they were gonna be out of the house for a doctor's appointment or whatever. And then we'd go back. We hated doing it. But it was the only way. No one was supposed to get hurt. Old folks have insurance. They'd get their stuff replaced with newer stuff."

"No one was supposed to get hurt?" Pete dropped the casual pretense and leaned menacingly across the table. "That didn't work out so well, did it?"

Naiman shivered as if they were seated in a freezer. "We didn't mean to hurt that woman. She surprised us. No one was supposed to be there."

"Which time?"

The question seemed to startle him. He stuttered, "What do you mean?"

"Which woman didn't you mean to hurt? The one you hit in the head and left to freeze to death in the snow? Or the one you shoved down the steps and left to die in her basement?"

Naiman's eyes had grown so wide, white showed around his dark irises. "What?" He choked. "I don't know what you're talking about. What basement? Yeah, Doug hit that woman who was sneaking around the house a couple days ago. But he said he didn't hit her that hard. And—and Doug said he saw someone else there. I'd have called 911 myself for her if I'd thought no one was gonna find her. You mean she's—she's dead?"

"No." Pete reined in his anger and forced his voice to stay calm. Naiman was on the verge of hyperventilating, and Pete needed to keep him talking. "She has a concussion, but that woman is fine."

Naiman's knee stilled as he closed his eyes. "Thank God."

"But Oriole Andrews wasn't so lucky."

His eyes snapped open again. "Who?"

Pete opened the folder, retrieved an autopsy photo showing a very deceased Oriole, and shoved it in front of Naiman. "The old woman you tossed down her basement stairs. What happened? Didn't expect to find her at home?"

He recoiled from the photo. "I don't know what the hell you're talking about. We never—we wouldn't—"

Pete played back the kid's answers in his mind. Doug had been the one who struck Zoe. "You wouldn't," Pete said. "But what about your brother? Maybe he pushed her down the stairs and didn't tell you about it."

"No. Doug wouldn't do—" Naiman stopped, his forehead creased. Cringing, he ventured another look at the photo. "Oriole Andrews. That's the old lady in the house on the hill in Dillard, right?"

"That's her. She wasn't as lucky as the young woman you left in the snow."

"No." Naiman shook his head vehemently. "No. She was alive when we were there." He met Pete's gaze and held it. "Yeah, we cased her place. Did our water-company routine. But we never went back. For one thing, she didn't have anything worth stealing. But mostly because she reminded us of Grandma." He looked over at Baronick and then back at Pete. "You have to believe me. We didn't—we would never hurt an old lady like that. Ever. And we sure as hell wouldn't kill her."

TWENTY-SIX

Zoe's head throbbed and her legs threatened to buckle, but the concussion was only partly to blame. Listening to Dennis Naiman, watching him melt down, had been more than she'd bargained for. When Pete gathered his folder and stood to leave the interrogation room, she collapsed into a chair she'd refused earlier.

The door to the observation room swung open, and Pete and Wayne stepped inside.

Pete took one look at her and knelt next to her. "Are you okay?"

"Just tired." She studied his face. "I believe him. Do you?"

He shot a glance at Wayne before meeting her gaze. "Yeah. I do."

"I'm not convinced the punk isn't a damned good liar," Wayne said. "And I'm sure not ready to drop homicide from the list of charges we're bringing against these assholes."

"You're gonna start looking at other suspects in Oriole's death though," Zoe said. "Aren't you?"

Wayne looked like he'd sucked a lemon. "I guess we have to."

Pete climbed to his feet and faced the detective. "But let's not release that part to the press. Let the public believe we have the killers in custody."

Wayne scowled. "Don't you think that could be dangerous? If the killer's still out there, do we want the elderly to let down their guard?"

"If the killer is still out there, Oriole's homicide may have been personal. Besides, if our killer thinks we have someone in custody for the crime, he'll do two things." Pete held up one finger. "He won't risk reopening the case by harming anyone else." Pete held up a second finger. "He might let his guard down and let something slip."

A predatory smile crept across Wayne's face. "I like it."

Zoe stood and gave Pete's shoulder a gentle jab. "Speaking of the press, you didn't ask Naiman about Lauren Sanders."

"No, I didn't. But he did say his brother saw someone else."

And he'd admitted it had been his brother who hit her. Not Lauren. However, Zoe wasn't appeased. "Of course he did. You were putting the screws to him about leaving me there. He didn't say whether or not he knew her. She might have been the one who warned them about me." Zoe played out a new possible scenario. "She might have called them. You never found her cell phone, did you?"

Pete and Wayne exchanged glances.

"No," Wayne said.

"Convenient." Zoe poked Pete again. "You can't check it to see who she called."

"But," Wayne said, "we do have the Naimans' phones."

Zoe caught a glimpse of a spark in Pete's eye. "You and your county lab guys can pull the call logs from those." His lips parted in a lopsided grin that reminded her of a wolf contemplating its prey. "And while you're doing that, I have an idea that might yield better results."

"Oh?" Zoe said.

"I promised Ms. Sanders a scoop. Maybe it's time I give it to her."

Douglas Naiman's attorney had ordered his client to not answer any questions the police asked. The younger brother was nothing if not obedient where legal counsel was concerned. Pete left Wayne to oversee the booking of the two men on charges including burglary, aggravated assault, and murder. Whether or not the last one stuck remained to be seen.

Pete phoned Lauren Sanders before he left the county jail. She agreed to meet him at the Vance Township Police Station at noon. In spite of Zoe's demands to once again be a fly on the wall, he took her home. "Get some sleep," he told her while planting a kiss on her bandaged forehead.

Clearly the night at the hospital had taken its toll on her. She pouted, but ceased to argue once he tucked her into his recliner with one tabby in her lap, the other stretched out above her head like a furry orange hat.

"There's another thing that really bothers me," she said as he headed for the door.

"What's that?"

"Their grandmother. If this rash of burglaries has been the only thing financing her stay at Golden Oaks, what's gonna happen to her now?"

He wished he had an answer.

At the station, he removed the "Out on Patrol" sign from the door, hung up his coat, and filled the Mr. Coffee with water and Maxwell House. As the contraption gurgled and sputtered, Pete took a seat at his desk and thumbed through his notebook. Whether or not Lauren Sanders had played a part in the thefts—and especially in Zoe's injury—was only one of his concerns. There was also Oriole Andrews' homicide. If the Naiman brothers were as principled about doing no harm as Dennis had purported, someone else had shoved the elderly woman down her basement stairs.

Then again, Dennis admitted his brother had clobbered Zoe. It wasn't out of the range of possibility that he was lying about Oriole. Admit to assault to deflect the suspicion of murder.

The bells on the front door jingled. He glanced at his watch. Two minutes to twelve. If nothing else, the reporter was punctual.

"Chief Adams?" Sanders called out.

He stood and stepped out into the hall. "Back here."

She strode toward him, attired in the same dark wool coat and carrying the same leather satchel as always.

Pete ushered her into his office and reclaimed his seat. She deposited the tote on the floor next to the visitor's chair and shrugged out of the coat, revealing a navy turtleneck sweater and gray wool slacks. No jewelry. Although attractive, she did nothing to draw attention to herself. Pete suspected she could easily disappear in a crowd. Observe without being noticed.

Sanders fixed him with a displeased glare. Apparently, she didn't appreciate him brushing her off. "If you've called me here to ask about Golden Oaks, I haven't had time to look into it yet. I've been too busy trying to get information about the two men in the white van that crashed last night."

"Those men are the reason I called. I can now confirm we've made an arrest in your Senior Killers case."

The glower vanished. "Wonderful." Her pen poised, she asked, "What are their names?"

"Dennis and Douglas Naiman. They're brothers." Pete watched for a reaction.

There wasn't any. "Can you spell that last name please?"

If she did indeed know them, she was one hell of an actress. "N-a-i-m-a-n," he said and then read their ages and home address to her from his own notes.

"How did you capture them?"

"Officer Nate Williams spotted the suspect vehicle driving south on Route 15 last night. When he ran the plates, they came back as belonging to a different vehicle. At that point the suspects attempted to flee and during a brief pursuit, they lost control and went off the road." Pete detailed the injuries and subsequent arrest. He mentioned questioning the older brother, but left out the part about the denial of having killed anyone.

Sanders scribbled page after page of notes, pausing when he stopped. She eyed him. "So they confessed to killing Mrs. Andrews?"

Sanders was sharp. Pete held her gaze. "Dennis Naiman confessed to being at her house. He states Oriole Andrews was alive when they left. Which was true. She died later at the hospital from her injuries."

The reporter jotted another page of notes before fixing him with that laser-sharp stare again. "Is there anything else?"

Pete had anticipated the question. He intentionally winced and shifted in his chair.

She leaned forward. "There is something else. Tell me."

"Yes, there is, but it's not for public knowledge yet." He pretended to struggle with a decision.

Sanders kept her eager eyes on him, waiting.

He glanced toward the door—knowing full well they were alone—and then came forward, resting his arms on his desk and lowering his voice. "Can you keep this off the record for now?"

"Absolutely." She leaned forward as well, her fingertips lightly resting on his wrist. "As long as you promise to let me know the moment I can run with it."

"Deal." He made a production of wrestling one more moment with the decision to blab. "We're pretty sure they didn't act alone."

Her eyes widened for just a second. "Really?"

Pete nodded. "We think there's a third person out there who helped them cover their tracks."

He watched her mull over this tidbit. "Any idea of this third person's identity?" she asked.

Pete freed his arm from her touch and leaned back in his chair. "I've already said too much. You have my word. As soon as I'm at liberty to divulge more, I'll be in touch."

Sanders hesitated, then closed her notebook and deposited it in her bag. "I appreciate you speaking with me, Chief. How much time can you give me to get this story out before you make an official statement?"

"Detective Baronick has a press conference planned for one. Is that enough time?"

She checked her watch. "Perfect."

They stood and shook hands. Pete watched her scurry out and listened for the bells signaling her exit. When he knew he was alone, he once again settled into his chair to mull over what had just happened.

She'd given up nothing when he sprung the suspects' names on her. But the "news" of a third party being involved had definitely taken her by surprise. Did she have any inkling that he believed the third person in question might be her? If she did, what would be her next move?

Pete had been thinking Zoe was way off base in her suspicions about the reporter. Now, he wasn't so sure.

Zoe hung up the phone after updating Rose about Sylvia's condition and thumped the recliner into its upright position. Rose had considered making the trip back to Pennsylvania, but with Sylvia stable and resting comfortably, she elected to take a wait-and-see approach.

The gray January gloom had cleared. Jade and Merlin had bailed on her and now curled in the spots of sunshine pooling on the back of the sofa. The Steelers had a primetime game tonight so the only things on Pete's antenna TV were infomercials.

Zoe stood, pausing to let the room stop spinning, and swore. There wouldn't be many more days in the Krolls' barn, and here she was, wasting a beautiful one. Stuck. Inside. Because of those punks who bashed her upside the head.

The floor stopped swaying, and she shuffled to the window, squinting like a mole used to being underground and blinded by a glimpse of the sun. Melting snow *drip drip drip*ped from the gutters. She made a mental note to tell Pete he better check them for an ice jam or blockage that was keeping the water from making its way to the downspouts.

Which led her to wonder about the conditions at her "new" farm. Gutters. Roof damage. Leaks. More to add to her to-do list. Stuff she should be dealing with right now.

She turned. Too fast. Waited for the walls to stop moving. And headed to the kitchen.

Her mind ran on a loop. Horses. Farms. Mr. and Mrs. Kroll. Were they all right? How was Sylvia doing in the hospital? Harry...even more stuck than she was.

And Barbara. That sweet old woman with the two thugs for grandsons. What was to become of her now that they wouldn't be paying her bills any longer?

Zoe needed to get out of the house. Out into the brisk air and the sunshine. She should go check on Sylvia. And Harry. And the Krolls. And Janie. There was too darned much to be done to be trapped inside. Her pickup was parked in Pete's driveway. Her keys hung on a hook on the wall. But she'd been ordered not to drive, and the way her head was throbbing, it was one of the more sensible orders she'd received.

A rap at the kitchen door jarred Zoe from her fussing and fuming. She peered through the peephole to see Patsy's face distorted by the wide-angle-view glass.

"Hey," Zoe said as she opened the door and motioned her cousin in. "I'm glad you're here."

"I thought you might have cabin fever."

"You have no idea."

Patsy glanced around the room. "Where's Pete?"

"Working. Is everything okay at the barn?"

"Yeah. Except Windstar misses you."

"Ha. As long as he's getting his grain and hay, he doesn't care who gives it to him."

Patsy chuckled. "True."

"Can I get you something? Coffee? Tea?"

Patsy stuffed her hands in her coat pockets. "No, thanks. I came by to bust you outta here."

Zoe would have jumped up and down, but knew her head would pound like a bass drum if she did. "I'll get my coat."

Minutes later, she clicked the seatbelt in Patsy's Toyota Tundra.

"Where to?" Patsy asked.

Zoe ran the list through her head again. She caught Patsy's gaze. "My farm?"

Patsy's expression turned pensive. "I was thinking that too. We should assess what needs to be done to make it horse-ready. We're running out of time." She shifted into gear and pulled onto the potholed street.

A thought struck Zoe, and tightened the fist that had been squeezing her brain. "I hope my mother doesn't change her mind."

"About giving you the farm? Why would she?"

"Because it's Kimberly we're talking about. And me."

Patsy made a face. "You don't give her enough credit."

"And you give her too much. I'd list all the times my mother has let me down, but I wouldn't know where to start."

"From what I've been told, you weren't the easiest teenager to raise either."

"Teenager? True. But she doesn't have much use for her grownup daughter either."

"And when was the last time you tried to have a civil conversation with her?"

Zoe stared out the window at the passing houses. Patsy used to be her friend. *Her* friend. Now she'd clearly set up a tent in Kimberly's camp. Arguing would do no good. Patsy'd been indoctrinated into Kimberly's view of their mother-daughter relationship. "Maybe you should just take me back home."

"What?" Patsy sounded stunned and hurt at the suggestion. "No. Don't be silly." She fell silent but kept driving, turning onto Route 15. A mile or so down the road, she said, "Besides, this thing with the farm isn't just about you and her."

It took a moment for Patsy's meaning to sink in. "In other words, she's giving me the farm to help you out."

Zoe's cousin squirmed. "No. Well, maybe. I told her about the jam we were in with the Krolls selling their place. I never asked her to help either of us. Giving you the Engle farm was her idea. And it's you she's deeding it to. Not me."

Fifteen minutes later, they stood in front of the barn where they'd found the first van. Clouds were moving in again and the temperature hovered near thirty-two degrees. The partially melted snow created a slurry of water and ice. Zoe's concerns about the gutters turned out to be warranted. She hadn't noticed on their previous trip, but the ones on the house sagged in the middle. And the downspout on the barn was completely detached, leaving a constant flow of snowmelt trickling from the gutter into a small pond at the rear corner.

Yes, Kimberly was deeding the family farm—in all its crumbling glory—to her. Not Patsy.

Thanks, Mom.

Patsy picked her way to the fence, grabbled one of the posts, and tried to shake it. "Well, this one is solid."

Zoe gazed across what had been the pasture. "That's one out of how many? A hundred?"

"At least. Feel up to walking the fence line?"

No. "Sure," she said with forced cheeriness.

TWENTY-SEVEN

There were days when Pete regretted his poor relationship with the press. This was one of them. If he had friends in journalism, he could enlist their help in finding out what was going on with Lauren Sanders. And what had gone on with her that drove her out of the big league.

His own internet search unearthed nothing more than what Zoe had shared with him. Law-enforcement sites revealed a couple cases of Sanders being held in contempt of court for refusing to reveal her sources and one civil disobedience charge surrounding a protest march when she was in college. Nothing violent. Nothing any other reporter didn't have in their files.

Pete picked up his phone and keyed in a number he hated to use for help.

Baronick answered with an annoyed, "It's only been a few hours. You don't honestly expect me to have anything yet, do you?"

"Actually, no, but—"

The detective laughed. "Ha. But I do. Just call me Super Cop."

Pete had a retort for him, but decided against using it.

"I cashed in some favors and got the Naimans' phone logs. No calls to Lauren Sanders' number. In fact, most of the calls were to and from their grandmother and Golden Oaks. A couple were to area pawn shops. We'll pay those guys a visit first thing tomorrow morning. However, there are still a few unidentified numbers we're trying to track down."

"Good. But that's not why I'm calling. How's your relationship with the news media?"

"Better than yours. Why?"

"Lauren Sanders didn't always work for small local news outlets." Pete told him about her history, as much of it as he knew. "Then she dropped off the map. I'd like to know why. And what she's been doing since then."

"And you think I can find out?"

"I think with your gift for bullshit, you've cultivated some friendships that could help. You're giving a statement to the press in fifteen minutes or so, right? Maybe you could pull someone aside for a private chat."

The line fell quiet and for a moment, Pete thought the call had been dropped. But Baronick's loud sigh indicated otherwise. "I don't suppose I need to ask why you're interested in this woman's past."

The image of Sanders bent over Zoe's crumpled form in the snow crept to the forefront of Pete's brain. Douglas Naiman may have struck the blow, but Pete wasn't convinced the reporter hadn't somehow been involved. "I want to know just how far she'll go to get the inside track on a story that might put her back in the big leagues."

They'd made it roughly a hundred yards before Zoe had to admit defeat. She clung to a post—thankfully a sturdy one—and closed her eyes.

Patsy had hiked on ahead, but returned, her fists planted on her hips. "Okay, this was a bad idea."

"What? Accepting the farm as a gift?"

"No." Patsy huffed. "Exerting yourself. You're almost as white as the snow. Should I go back and drive my truck out here to get you?"

"Give me a minute. I'll be okay." Zoe looked back at the stretch of fence line they'd just walked. "At least there are more good posts than rotted ones."

Patsy's enthusiasm had dwindled. "Yeah, but the wire's a mess."

"I don't like barbed wire for horses anyway."

"Me either." She gave Zoe a pained smile. "I guess Kimberly's 'gift' really does leave a lot to be desired."

"Gee. You think?" Zoe immediately regretted the sarcasm. Her cousin looked on the verge of tears. "Don't worry, Pats. I'll make it work." She pushed away from the fence post and slapped Patsy's arm. "Come on. I have someplace else you can take me."

* * *

The bells on the station's front door jangled as Pete ended his call with Baronick.

"Hello?" Seth's voice floated back to him. "Anyone here?"

"In my office," Pete called out. A moment later, the young officer, attired in jeans and a bulky bomber jacket, appeared at the doorway. "It's your day off," Pete said.

"Yours too."

"I don't get a day off." When Seth didn't move, Pete gestured toward the chair across from him. "What's on your mind?"

Seth slid into the seat, his hands stuffed in the jacket's pockets, a scowl on his face. "Something's been bugging me. I couldn't quite put my finger on it, but something was off. In my gut. You know?"

"I do."

"I think I finally figured out what it is."

When Seth didn't continue, Pete said, "And?"

"The locks. Mr. and Mrs. Kroll's door was forced open. So was Sylvia's. But there was no sign of forced entry at Mrs. Andrews' house. None."

Pete stroked his upper lip and the slight prickle of his shaved mustache. No forced entry. Dammit. He should have caught that.

Seth said the words as Pete thought them. "It's almost like whoever broke in had a key."

Maybe because they did. "Trout."

"Huh?"

Pete stood and rounded the desk, heading for the door. He slapped the officer's shoulder as he passed. "Good work, Metzger."

"Wait." Seth scrambled to his feet and followed Pete. "You mean Mr. Troutman?"

Pete grabbed his coat from the front office. "The old man had a key to Oriole's house." Pete silently chastised himself for not pressing Trout about it earlier. Instead of a suspect, Pete had viewed him as a befuddled codger. Hell, Pete had looked at Trout and seen Harry.

Every. Time.

Seth slid his hands from his pockets and crossed his arms. Although he'd struck a serious pose, his hunched shoulders revealed uncertainty. "Actually, Chief, I was thinking of someone else."

"Oh?"

"The granddaughter's son. Marcus? Have you taken a good look at him?"

Pete had the thirteen-year-old's history memorized. Petty vandalism. Skipping school. Hanging out with older kids who had bashed mailboxes. And more recently, a handful of fights, including the one at the high school last week. "The kid has anger-management issues," Pete said more to himself than to Seth.

"Yeah." The officer's shoulders relaxed. "He's been in trouble a lot the last year or so. And the level of violence has been escalating. Yesterday, I was out running errands and I spotted him and his mother out in front of their house. He was really laying into her."

"What do you mean? 'Laying into her.'"

"Yelling. The kid was in a rage. I thought he was ready to throw a punch at her, but when I stopped and asked if I could help, she insisted everything was fine. I wanted to talk to him, but he took off."

Pete hated to admit it. Not only had he been wearing blinders where Trout was concerned, but he'd been allowing Marcus to slide as well. The boy needed a father figure in his life, but Pete hadn't seen him as a hard case. Still, that day in the high school gym, Marcus had been unrepentant about the fight. Could his teenaged hormone-driven anger have flared to rage with his great-grandmother? "I'll talk to Marcus first. Then Trout."

A hint of a smile crossed Seth's face, clearly pleased his idea had been accepted as valid.

Pete slapped the "Out on Patrol" sign in the window, set the alarm code, and shooed Seth out before locking the door. "Go home."

"I'd like to come with you."

Pete eyed him. "Nate's on duty if I need backup. Go enjoy what's left of your Sunday."

Seth straightened. "Chief, I was there that night. I helped Zoe and Earl bring Mrs. Andrews out of her basement. I'd like to see this one through."

Of all Pete's officers, Seth was the one he predicted would end up taking over as chief one day. Or maybe he'd move on to the city and a job as a detective. "Okay," Pete said. "Let's go."

* * *

"I'll wait here." Patsy gazed through her pickup's windshield at Golden Oaks, her nose wrinkled.

Zoe unclipped her seatbelt. "You'll freeze." The glorious sunshine had been obliterated by ever-darkening clouds and wet flakes were again drifting through the air. "Are you planning to keep the engine running the entire time I'm in there?"

"Maybe."

"Oh, quit being a wimp. Come on. You know Harry." Harry, of course, would likely not know Patsy, although he'd helped save her life as well as Zoe's last summer.

Patsy turned a tortured gaze on her. "I've never been in one of these places. I hear they're awful."

Zoe opened the passenger door, letting in a gust of icy air. "Actually, this one's really nice. Come on."

Grumbling, Patsy released her seatbelt and climbed out.

Inside, residents gathered in the front room, some in their wheelchairs, others seated in chairs set in a semi-circle around the piano. A trio of teens stood next to it, studying sheet music. Zoe searched the faces for Harry, but he wasn't there. Neither was Barbara.

Zoe caught Patsy's arm and directed her to the staircase.

"This isn't so bad," Patsy said.

"Told you."

Zoe led the way to the second floor and Harry's room. Soft weeping from inside the room across the hall stopped her. Inside, Barbara sat on the edge of her bed, sobbing. Harry sat next to her, patting her hand. Zoe rapped lightly on the doorframe. "Hello?"

They looked up. Harry appeared distressed, but puzzled. Barbara's eyes glistened with tears. She pressed a small white handkerchief to her nose. "Yes?" The older woman's voice quivered.

"Mrs. Naiman? I don't know if you remember me—"

"Oh, yes. You were with Harry's son visiting. Yesterday, I think. Right?"

"Yes." At least one of them remembered.

Harry turned his gaze to Barbara. "My son? Pete? Is he here?"

Zoe had grown used to "meeting" Harry every time she saw him.

She strode to them, extending a hand to him. "Hi, Harry. I'm Zoe. Pete's friend."

He took the hand. "Zoe? I think...we've met before, haven't we?"

"Yes, we have." She smiled. He was having a good day. "I thought I'd stop in to say hello."

Barbara sniffled. "You should go," she told Harry. "You have company."

"I don't want to leave you."

"You don't have to." Zoe pointed at a pair of chairs and asked Barbara, "Do you mind? We could visit with both of you."

"Please."

Zoe waved Patsy in and dragged the chairs over to face the bed.

"I'm sorry to be such a mess." Barbara dabbed at her eyes. "I just found out—" Her voice broke. "I just found out my grandsons have been arrested."

Harry put an arm around her shoulders. "Hush now. I told you. I'll have my boy straighten this whole thing out."

Zoe exchanged glances with Patsy. No way was she going to tell them Pete was the one who'd done the arresting.

Barbara wept quietly for a few moments. Zoe plucked a tissue from a box on the dresser and handed it to her, wishing there was something more she could say or do.

The older woman sniffled into the tissue. "I don't know what I'm going to do now. Those boys, they've been my entire life. They're my sole support. Emotional and financial. If they go to jail, I'll have to leave here. I have no money of my own left to pay the bills. Where will I go?" As if saying the words had drained the last ounce of her energy, she slumped against Harry, sobbing.

He looked at Zoe, helpless. "We have to do something. Can you call Pete for me? Tell him there's been some mistake. He can get this fixed. Can't he?"

She wanted to tell him it would be fine. Wanted to tell Barbara she'd be cared for and wouldn't have to leave this place. But the lies wouldn't leave her lips.

Behind Zoe, someone rapped on the door. She turned.

"Hello," Lauren Sanders said with an exaggerated smile. "Mind if I come in?"

TWENTY-EIGHT

There had been no answer at Janie Baker's house and her car wasn't in the driveway. "We'll stop at Oriole's house," Pete told Seth. "Janie might be cleaning the place out. If we're lucky, Marcus will be helping his mother. At the very least, she might know where we can find him."

As if reading Pete's thoughts, Seth said, "And we can stop at Mr. Troutman's place while we're there."

"You got it."

As Pete pulled onto Andrews Lane, the county dispatcher put out a call to Nate, requesting he see a woman regarding a disturbance just outside of town.

Pete clenched the steering wheel and wrestled the vehicle on the potholed and slick road. "Call him and let him know we're available for backup."

"Roger that." Seth dug out his phone.

Over the rumble of the SUV's heater, Pete could hear Nate's muffled voice respond.

Janie's battered gray Chevy sat in front of her grandmother's house. The flurries had intensified into snow showers, coating the top half of the small car. At this rate, it would soon look like a large snow drift. The clumps of plump flakes limited visibility and the leaden skies gave the impression of dusk rather than early afternoon. Inside the farmhouse, lights blazed from an upstairs room and a downstairs one.

Seth ended the call. "Nate says thanks, but it's just Mrs. Jennings complaining about some kids sled riding on the road. He's got it."

Pete smiled to himself. Kids sled riding on the road was more on par with a normal police call in Vance Township.

He and Seth climbed out of the car. Pete pulled his collar up as he approached the house. Boot prints on the walk had already been obliterated, making it impossible to tell if Janie had company. The air wasn't as brutally cold as it had been last week; however the slightly warmer temperatures opened the floodgates for heavier accumulation.

Janie was slow to respond to his knock at the door. "Chief Adams." She attempted a tired smile that never reached her eyes. "What brings you here?" An old bandanna bound her mousy hair. Dark smudges on her face and the plaid flannel shirt she wore offered a good hint that she was in the middle of cleaning. She didn't step back to invite them in.

"I'm sorry to bother you. May we talk to you for a moment?"

She glanced over Pete's shoulder at Seth. "Oh, of course." She moved out of their way. "I must look a mess. There's so much to do around here." Her hands fluttered, gesturing at everything—and nothing in particular.

Pete stepped inside and made room for his young officer. "We won't keep you. Is your son here?"

"Marcus? No." Worry sparked in her weary eyes. "Why? Is he in trouble again?"

Pete gave her his best professional smile. "I just wanted to ask him a few questions. He might be able to help us with a case we're working on."

"Oh. He's at home. He had some schoolwork that's due tomorrow."

Pete decided against telling the boy's mother that, no, he in fact was not at home studying. "Thanks. We'll stop there if it's okay with you."

Her eyes shifted. "Maybe you should wait until this evening when I get home. I'd be more comfortable if I'm there when you talk to him. He's only thirteen, you know."

"No problem." Pete reached for the door. "I completely understand. I'll stop in later."

She relaxed. "Great. Thanks so much."

He shot a quick look at Seth before coming back to Janie. "Officer Metzger tells me you and Marcus had an argument yesterday. Are you okay?"

She rubbed her arms against a chill—either internal or external. "Oh, I'm fine. It was nothing. He has a temper. You know that. But he just yells and then goes for a walk to cool off."

"Do you mind telling me what the argument was about?"

"I don't even remember. I think he wanted to go to his buddy's house to play video games and I told him no. Something silly like that."

Pete thanked her for her time and promised to stop at her house later. Seth led the way back to the SUV. Pete noticed their footprints had already nearly filled in during the few minutes they'd been inside.

Seth clicked his seatbelt. "She's covering something."

"Yeah." Pete hated to admit it, but his junior officer might very well have seen the case through clearer eyes than he had. "Can't blame a mother for trying to protect her only son. Especially when he's all she has left."

And especially if that son happened to be the real third person in the Naimans' burglary ring.

Zoe looked from Lauren to Barbara and back again. Did they know each other? Zoe suspected the reporter could act well enough to cover any personal connection, but the old woman? Probably not.

Barbara showed no signs of recognition. She gazed at Lauren with sad, blank eyes. "Yes, of course. Come in," the older woman said. "Do you work here? You must be new."

Lauren maintained her thin-lipped smile as she stepped into the room. "No, I don't work here. I'm a reporter with *The Phillipsburg Enterprise* and—"

Zoe intercepted her, blocking her from moving farther into the room. "Outside. Now."

Lauren blinked. "Pardon me?"

Zoe fixed her with as hard a glare as her throbbing head and blurred vision would allow. "I want to talk to you. Out in the hallway."

Lauren stared at her, agape. Zoe could feel Patsy's, Harry's, and Barbara's stares in the silence. After a moment, the reporter shrugged and turned.

Zoe followed her, closing the door to Barbara's room behind them. "So you do know the Naimans."

"Know them? Chief Adams gave me the names of the two men they busted as the Senior Killers. Dennis and Douglas Naiman. I did some digging and learned their grandmother is a resident here. If that's 'knowing them,' then yes. I do."

"And that's all there is to it?"

Lauren's lips pursed in a puzzled scowl. "What are you getting at? Of course that's all there is."

Had Zoe trusted her instincts right now, she'd have believed her. But her instincts had been compromised by the blow to her head. She planted her hands on her hips. "I think you're more acquainted with the Naiman family than you're letting on. Especially the grandsons. I think you're the one who alerted them to me being outside the Krolls' house on Friday. And I think you've been 'reporting' on this case as a way to get the inside track so they wouldn't be caught." Zoe stopped and realized what all she'd said. She hadn't intended to spill that much information.

Lauren stared, her mouth hanging open in shocked surprise. Zoe expected a rebuttal. Instead, Lauren guffawed. Then burst into full-fledged laughter. Within a few moments, the reporter was wiping tears from her eyes. "Oh...my God," she said, gasping for air. "You think...the third person Chief Adams mentioned...you think it's...me?"

This was not the reaction Zoe had expected. And what third person? But she decided to stand her ground. She crossed her arms. "Then what are you doing here at Barbara Naiman's room if you don't know the family?"

The laughter subsided. Lauren dug a tissue from her bag to dab her eyes. She sniffled. "I told you. I'm working on the story."

"By questioning the suspects' elderly grandmother? That's a little crass, isn't it?" Zoe replayed her words through her fuzzy brain. "Then again, you are a reporter." She let venom drip on the title.

Any evidence of amusement in Lauren's expression transformed to rage. "How dare you. You don't know anything about me."

Zoe hadn't anticipated Lauren's reaction to the previous accusation, and this retort took her even more by surprise. "I know that you once had a thriving journalism career in Boston, New York, and Philadelphia. Front pages. Bylines. Major stories. And then you vanished. Or seemed to."

Lauren glared at her. "You've done your homework on me. Why?"

Zoe hesitated. "I told you. I think you were the Naimans' lookout that day at the Krolls' house." No way was she gonna let on that jealousy had anything to do with it. "And because you've been popping up everywhere. Janie Baker's my friend. So is Sylvia Bassi. And the Krolls. Everyone who's been harmed by these con men. And you've been two minutes behind, showing up on their doorsteps. Attending Oriole's funeral."

The reporter locked eyes with Zoe in what felt like a game of who-blinks-first—a game Zoe wasn't about to lose.

And didn't.

Lauren's fierce façade cracked. She looked around and gestured to a pair of faux-antique chairs ten feet down the hall. "You want to know about me? Fine. I'll tell you."

Pete stood on Trout's front stoop, snow swirling in the air around him. There was no response to his knock on the door. No sounds of shuffling or footsteps from inside.

Seth checked his watch. "It's early, but Mr. Troutman usually goes to his daughter's house for Sunday dinner."

Pete looked at his officer. "And how do you know this?"

Seth offered a sheepish grin. "I dated his granddaughter for a while last summer."

Pete almost asked why he was only learning about this now, but reconsidered. His officers didn't need to share their personal lives with him. Nor did he necessarily want them to. But in this case, the connection offered some potential insight into the situation at hand. Pete gazed down the hill toward Oriole's house, barely visible through the snow. "Did Trout ever bring Mrs. Andrews to these family dinners?"

"No. I got the impression Mr. Troutman's daughter didn't approve of her father having a lady friend." Seth shoved his hands deep into his coat pockets. "She didn't approve of her daughter dating a cop either."

"What did she say to give you that impression? About her father having a lady friend, I mean." Daughters dating cops? Pete already knew all about that.

"I overheard them arguing once. They were alone in the kitchen and I didn't want to eavesdrop, so I can't tell you exactly what they said. But the gist was she thought he was disrespecting the memory of her mother by spending time with another woman."

Pete grunted and thought of Harry and Barbara. The idea of his old man having a beautiful woman to keep him company thrilled him. Too bad the woman in this case had a pair of alleged felons paying her bills. "Let's get back in the car. We're not going to stand in the snow waiting for Trout to get home."

Once at the SUV, Pete kicked the bottom edge of the door to knock the clumped snow from his boots before climbing in. He flipped the defrosters onto high and pulled out his phone.

"You're gonna call Mr. Troutman's daughter?" Seth asked.

"Not yet. We may drive over there." Pete glanced at Seth's pained face and grinned. "Or I can drop you off at the station and go by myself."

"No. That's okay. It's my job."

"It's your day off." Besides, Pete wasn't convinced busting an old man in front of his family was the right move at the moment. He keyed in Nate's number.

"What's up, Chief?" his weekend officer answered.

"I need you to keep an eye out for Marcus Baker. You know the kid, right?"

"Yeah, I know him." There was a note of annoyance in Nate's voice.

"Is there a problem?"

"Not really. And I don't need to keep an eye out for him. He's standing right here in front of me. I'm currently debating whether to lock the punk up or take him home to his mama."

"What's he done now?"

"Those kids that were sled riding on the hillside near the Jennings' place? Marcus showed up and started a fight. Busted one boy's nose. Blackened another one's eye. What do you think I should do with him?"

"Hold him right there. I'm on my way."

Lauren sat with her hands folded and her head lowered. At first she didn't speak.

Zoe waited.

Finally the reporter sighed. "You're right. I had a dream career going back east. Big cities. Major papers. I couldn't have asked for more." Lauren paused. "But I did. I was working on a story. I thought it was the biggest of my career. The one that might bring a job offer from CNN." She fell silent, staring into space at a memory that obviously pained her. She shook her head before lifting her gaze to meet Zoe's. "It was a piece about police corruption on a huge scale. I'd started the investigation at the bottom. Worked up the ladder, finding graft at every level."

Zoe thought of the last article she and Sylvia had found in their online search. Police corruption.

"I was introduced to a new source. Someone inside the department, who had information about the graft going all the way to the commissioner's office. My editor warned me to tread lightly, but I was blind to everything except the idea of nailing this guy and moving on to a big-time television career."

Lauren grew quiet again, closing her eyes. Zoe wondered if she was reliving the experience inside her head—or trying to block out the memories.

After several long moments, Lauren swiped a hand across her face. "Without boring you with all the sordid details, my new source had been planted to feed me false information. Once I'd run with the story, he recanted everything. He went so far as to show them proof that the story was a complete fabrication. Not only did I have egg on my face for that part of the investigation, but now every story I'd written was called into question. The paper fired me. Quietly, so as not to call attention to the error of their ways for ever having employed me in the first place. But everyone inside the news industry knew. No one would give me a job. Hell, I couldn't even get hired to clean their restrooms."

Zoe leaned back in the chair. "Why would he do that? Ruin you, I mean."

Lauren huffed a humorless laugh. "He was planted by one of the police lieutenants I'd taken down. If I was proven unreliable, he could make it look like I'd falsely accused him too."

The reporter's hard veneer may have crumbled, but she restrained the tears giving a sheen to her eyes. Zoe studied her. And believed her.

"All right. So what's the deal with you being here?"

"At Golden Oaks?"

"That too. But at this new newspaper in Phillipsburg, working on this case."

"I've spent two years trying to reestablish my credibility. Small pieces. No bylines. I could see I wasn't ever going to get near where I used to be. But I'm a reporter. And dammit, I'm a good one. A small paper is better than none. At least I get to do what I love, and in this case, maybe help save some lives in the process."

"What about the Naimans?"

"You can believe me or not, but I never heard of them before today. I didn't warn them about you. I phoned for help and then I ran for the car because the guy who knocked you out looked in my direction. I thought he saw me and was coming after me. I thought he might have a gun." The reporter leaned toward Zoe, holding her gaze. "I know I should've tried to do more, but I have to be honest. Bravery is not my strong suit. Remind me someday to tell you about the time I got shot in Philadelphia."

"So you're only here to question Barbara about her grandsons?"

Lauren squirmed, and for the first time since they'd sat down, Zoe suspected the reporter was withholding the truth. "Well?"

"Actually, Chief Adams asked me to look into Golden Oaks in exchange for giving me the scoop on the arrests. He told me one of the residents has made some accusations. I learned the Naimans' grandmother lived here, so I figured I could tackle both investigations at once. I came into Brunswick for the latest news conference and swung by here afterwards." She lowered her voice. "I'm undercover. The staff thinks I'm doing a feature on health-care facilities for the elderly."

One of the residents. Pete hadn't mentioned the resident in question was his father. Zoe bit her lip to keep from smiling. "Have you found anything?"

"Not a thing. I've worked on stories about these kinds of places before, and I have to tell you. This is one of the nicest, most well-run senior care homes I've encountered."

Zoe closed her eyes for a moment in relief.

"So," Lauren said, "are we good? You and me?"

Zoe wasn't sure why the reporter cared, and her expression must have revealed her thoughts.

"I'm relatively new in the area. I'm a reporter." Lauren made self-deprecating air quotes around her job title. "So it's doubly hard to make friends. I was serious about my love for horses. I kind of hoped...well, that you'd give me a chance to prove I'm not a jerk."

Zoe eyed her. "You want to prove you're not a jerk? Go easy on Barbara Naiman."

Lauren winced. "You're asking an investigative journalist to give a key resource an easy ride?"

"No. I'm asking a former big-city reporter to give an old woman a break. She's lost more than most of us over this situation with her grandsons."

Lauren contemplated Zoe's request. Then shrugged. "You have a point, I suppose."

"Thanks." Zoe stood. She'd left Patsy with Harry and Barbara long enough. And her cousin hadn't signed on for a full afternoon of nursemaid duties.

Lauren trailed her back to the room, where everyone was just as they'd left them.

Harry looked up as they entered. "Zoe, I'm so glad to see you." He patted Barbara's arm and climbed to his feet. "I need to talk to you," he whispered to Zoe.

The fact that Harry didn't remember he'd seen her only minutes earlier didn't surprise her. That he knew her name did.

He excused himself and took her arm, ushering her back into the hallway. "I need you to talk to Pete."

"Okay." She considered asking about what, but if Harry was as lucid as he appeared, she already knew.

Helpless desperation glistened in his eyes. "This thing with Barbara's grandsons. He can fix it. I know he can."

Zoe couldn't bring herself to destroy Harry's hope. "I'll talk to him."

Harry took her hand, clinging to it as if it was a lifeline. "Please. I realize I haven't known Barbara all that long, but I..." He lowered his face a moment. When he lifted it to meet Zoe's gaze again, he said, "I care about her. A lot."

The sorrow in the old man's pale blue eyes—eyes that matched his son's—ripped a hole in Zoe's heart. She leaned over and kissed his cheek. "I'll do everything I can."

He smiled weakly. "Thank you. My boy's in love with you, you know."

She couldn't help but laugh. "Yeah. I know."

He held onto her hand as they returned to Barbara's room. Lauren sat on the bed beside the older woman.

Patsy was on her feet, clearly determined not to be abandoned again. "You ready to go?"

"Yeah." Zoe said her goodbyes and followed her cousin into the hall.

"Are you going to tell me what that was about?" Patsy asked as they headed for the stairs.

"I'll tell you on the way back to Vance Township." Zoe already had something else on her concussion-hazed mind. "Do you mind making one more stop before dropping me off at home?"

TWENTY-NINE

Without wind to swirl the stuff, the snowfall created a translucent screen, cutting visibility to little more than a hundred yards. Since it was Sunday, the road crews weren't making a big effort either. Pete was grateful for the Explorer's heavy winter treads as he churned up the narrow road, which probably didn't see much snowplow action even on a work day. Only one set of tracks remained visible in the couple inches of white stuff, and those were quickly filling in.

Near the top of the hill, red and blue strobes emanating from Nate's cruiser swept the gray-white landscape. Pete spotted his officer speaking with a half dozen kids, all in the early teen and preteen age range. An assortment of sleds, inner tubes, and toboggans littered the ground around them. Pete also noted one head visible in the backseat of the cruiser.

With Seth at his side, Pete trudged toward the group.

Nate looked up. "Hey, Chief." He nodded at Seth. "Metzger."

Two boys sat on a downed tree, one holding a wad of bloodied tissues to his nose, the other pressed a mittened handful of snow to his eye. Pete wondered what condition Marcus was in. The rest of the kids stood in a semicircle, hands shoved in pockets or arms crossed. All of them had their shoulders hunched and chins tucked toward their chests. Embarrassed? Sullen? Obstinate? Or simply cold? Hard to tell.

"What's going on here?" Pete directed the question at Nate.

The officer's expression was easier to read than the kids'. Annoyance. "The general consensus is that Marcus Baker jumped these two without provocation." Nate aimed his pen at the wounded pair.

"Really?" Pete feigned mild amazement. "No provocation, huh?" He let his gaze settle on each of the kids in turn.

A couple of them looked up at him, but quickly averted their eyes.

The rest didn't make even that much of an effort.

Pete noticed one smaller boy standing slightly away from the group. He wore a pair of wire-rimmed glasses that sat askew on his face. And unlike the morose expressions the others exuded, this kid appeared more scared than inconvenienced.

Nate again gestured at Bloody Nose and Black Eye. "I've called their parents. They're on their way."

"Can the rest of us go now?" one of the older boys asked, his voice a whiny drone.

The rumble of approaching vehicles drew Pete's attention. He spotted a gray pickup grinding its way up the snow-covered road followed by a dark SUV. The parents of the injured boys, most likely. He wanted to speak to them before they collected their darlings. First though, he let his gaze sweep the rest of the kids. "Does anyone have anything they think we should know?"

A wall of silence met his question.

He turned his back to the boys and addressed his officers. "I assume that's the parents." He shifted his eyes toward the pickup. "I want to chat with them before they leave. Nate, take care of reuniting them with their offspring. Seth, take the other boys aside individually and see if anyone wants to share what happened without his buddies thinking he's a snitch. Then let them go." Pete eyed the loner with the bent glasses. "I want to talk to that one. Afterwards, I'll speak with the parents."

They split up to herd the youngsters in different directions. The small kid with the glasses grew wide-eyed when he realized he'd been singled out by the chief of police. "Can I go home?" he said, his adolescent voice cracking.

"In a minute. Do you mind if I ask what happened to your glasses?"

The boy glanced around as if seeking help, but not really expecting any.

"It's okay, son." Pete unzipped his coat and pulled his reading glasses from his shirt pocket. "I have them too. And I'm always sitting on them or getting bumped when I have them on. They're a pain. Right?"

The boy swallowed. Nodded.

"What's your name?"

He hesitated. "Ethan Yancy."

"Yancy?" Pete thought of the township's retired fire chief. "Any relation to Bruce Yancy?"

The boy nodded again. "He's my great uncle."

"He's a good guy. Do you think you might want to be a firefighter when you get older?"

He shrugged. "I don't think I'd be any good at it."

Raised voices drew Pete's attention toward the vehicles. One of the mothers was yelling at Nate and waving a hand toward the squad car. Nate stood firm and emotionless, arms crossed over his massive chest. Pete started to turn back to Ethan, but the sight of Marcus' face in the backseat window stopped him. The Baker boy wasn't looking at the angry woman. He was watching Pete.

Or was he watching the boy with the glasses?

"Ethan," Pete said, facing the youngster, "what happened to your glasses?" He expected the boy to shoot a fearful look toward the person responsible—Marcus.

Instead, Ethan glanced at the boys who were taking their turns with Seth. "Can I go home now?"

Pete rested a hand on the kid's shoulder. "If someone busted your glasses, you can tell me."

"I just wanna go home."

Surrendering, Pete dug out one of his cards and scribbled his cell phone number on it before handing it to the boy. "Your Uncle Bruce and I are good friends. If anyone picks on you, you give me a call. They won't find out you snitched. You have my word."

Ethan gazed at the card for a moment. Shoved it in his pocket. "Can I—"

"Yes, you can go home now."

It was then that the boy turned his head toward the squad car. And Marcus. Instead of looking fearful or even smug, the boy's expression seemed...grateful. Without a word, he grabbed a small red plastic disk, which resembled a garbage can lid, and shuffled off toward the houses on the far hillside.

Pete turned his attention to the unhappy mother, who had at least lowered the volume of her tirade.

The vocal woman turned out to be Broken Nose's mother. While Black Eye's parents seemed more interested in questioning their son about his part in the melee, Broken Nose's mom held firm in her belief that her baby boy had been the victim of an unprovoked attack. "I want that delinquent locked up," she bellowed while jabbing a finger in Marcus' direction.

By the time Pete assured her that Marcus would be held accountable for his actions and sent her and the other parents on their way with their battered sons, Seth had released the remaining boys.

Which left Marcus simmering in the backseat of Nate's car.

"Have you reached his mother?" Pete asked.

Nate removed his hat and slapped it against his thigh, knocking off a thick coating of wet snow. "There's no answer at her residence."

"That's because she's working at her grandmother's house."

"And that number's been disconnected." He put his hat back on, giving it a tug. "I've tried the cell phone number the kid gave me for her. No answer. I left messages on it and on the home phone."

"Try her cell again," Pete said. "Janie may have been running the vacuum and didn't hear the phone ringing."

While Nate worked on reaching her, Pete climbed in behind the wheel and twisted to glare at the boy. "Marcus, I thought we'd agreed to stop meeting like this."

He looked uncomfortable with his wrists handcuffed behind his back. The comment didn't seem to bother him though. He avoided Pete's eyes, choosing to stare out the window.

"You have the right to remain silent." Pete watched for any reaction from the boy as he read him his Miranda rights. Other than looking bored, there was none. "Do you understand? You don't have to answer my questions without an attorney."

"I understand," Marcus muttered. "And I don't want an attorney."

"All right. What did those two guys do to goad you into beating the snot out of them?"

Either the idea of violence—or Pete's colorful phrasing—brought a fleeting smirk to the kid's face. But he still didn't reply.

"Did you bust Ethan Yancy's glasses too?"

That question snagged Marcus's attention.

"When did you start getting your jollies bullying small kids and old women?"

"What?" Marcus snapped. "Ethan didn't tell you I did that."

"No, he didn't. But I figured while you were busy kicking ass, you must have tossed him in for good measure."

"You don't know anything."

"I know you did enough damage to those other two to earn yourself a trip to juvie."

Marcus turned his gaze to the window again. "Whatever."

"You don't deny fighting those two?"

"Why bother? Everyone saw what happened. All of it. But the only part they're gonna tell you is that Marcus Baker beat up a couple of dudes."

"And Ethan?"

"Anyone who tells you I'm the one who done that to Ethan is a lying sack of shit."

Another time, Pete would have scolded the fatherless boy for his language, but they'd gone way beyond that today. He gave Marcus a moment to cool down. "All right. Why'd you beat up the other two?"

"Does it matter?"

Pete wanted to reach into the backseat and snatch the boy by the collar. Scare some sense into him. Nothing else had worked. But he tamped down the impulse and kept his voice calm. "Yes. It matters."

To Pete's surprise, Marcus faced him. "Because of Ethan."

"What about him?"

"I didn't break his glasses. This time or the other times. They did it."

"They?"

"The ones I beat up. They're bullies. They pick on younger kids like Ethan. Push 'em around. Call 'em names. Do...other stuff to 'em. The smaller kids can't, or won't, fight back. So I do it for them." Marcus lifted his chin, a look of proud defiance on his face.

Pete studied him. "And at the school gymnasium last week?"

Marcus didn't blink. "Robert had been messin' with a girl who didn't want to be messed with. She came to me crying about it. So I waited for him and convinced him to leave her alone."

Pete rubbed his forehead and the headache starting to bloom there. "You're telling me you only beat up on bullies."

The kid squirmed. "Yeah. I guess." It sounded more like a question than an answer.

"What about your grandmother? Who did she bully?"

For a moment, Marcus' expression went blank. Then his jaw dropped and he almost choked. "You think I...Hell, no. I would never..." He clamped his mouth shut. Swallowed hard. Then whispered, "I'm not saying nothing more." Tears welled in his eyes.

Pete wasn't sure if they were tears of grief, tears of remorse, or tears of panic. Nor was he at all sure of Marcus's guilt. "Wise choice," Pete said and stepped out of the car where Nate and Seth waited. "Did you reach the boy's mother?"

"Still no answer." Nate held up his phone. "Do you want me to keep trying?"

"No. I want you to take Junior Avenger here to the station and lock him up for now."

"Junior who?"

"Never mind." Pete pointed at Seth. "I'm going to drop you off so you can get your car. Go over to Oriole Andrews' house. Bring Janie to see her son and have her arrange for an attorney."

"Where are you going?" Seth asked.

"I'm going to interrupt a family Sunday dinner."

THIRTY

"You didn't count on wasting your entire day chauffeuring me around," Zoe told Patsy as they turned up the hill toward Oriole's house.

"I don't mind. You needed to get out."

"But 'out' doesn't usually mean driving around in a snowstorm."

Patsy reached up and patted her dashboard. "My trusty Tundra doesn't mind."

"I appreciate it. But if Janie isn't at her grandmother's, you can just dump me at home."

As concerned as Zoe was about the Krolls, Janie with her unsteady hands and ashen face was the friend who had her most concerned.

She hadn't been at her house when Patsy and Zoe stopped there. Neither was Marcus. Zoe had borrowed Patsy's cell phone and tried to call, but no one answered.

As the Toyota pickup climbed the hill, Janie's car became visible through the heavy snowfall, parked in front of Oriole's house.

"Looks like you were right." Patsy pointed. "She's here."

They pulled up behind the car, and Zoe noticed the glow of lights in one of the first-floor windows.

"I'm gonna drop you off and go feed the horses," Patsy said. "I'll be back to get you in about an hour."

"I hate to make you drive around in this weather plus take care of the barn."

Patsy made a face. "Look. You're worried about your friend. You can't reach her by phone. You're not in any shape to do the barn work. It's fine."

Zoe looked toward the house. Patsy was right, of course, but she hated feeling so helpless. "Okay." She opened the door and stepped down, sinking ankle deep in snow. "Be careful on the roads."

Patsy reached toward her, holding out her cell phone. "Here. You might need this."

"No way. You're more likely to need it than I am. Besides, I'm sure Janie has her phone on her. She probably turned off the ringer or something."

Patsy shrugged. "All right. I'll see you in an hour or so."

Zoe slogged toward the house, but paused to watch Patsy's taillights fade into the hazy white veil of snow. Then she trudged the rest of the way. She stopped again on the front stoop, taking a moment to listen to the silence. It was as if Mother Nature had soundproofed the entire township. There was no pitter-pat of raindrops. No traffic noise floating up from Route 15 below. Only blessed tranquility.

Until a shriek from behind the door shattered the stillness.

Trout's daughter, one Betsy Malone, lived in a large brick home surrounded by a planned community of other large brick homes about fifteen miles from Dillard in a neighboring township. Pete noticed several of the yards still displayed Christmas decorations and lights. One sported a deflated jolly old elf and his reindeer, half covered with snow. It looked like a holiday homicide. Dead Santa and Rudolph, sprawled on a residential lawn.

At least the St. Nick slaying happened outside of Pete's jurisdiction.

Two doors down, he matched the numbers on the mailbox with the address he'd jotted down. This was it.

There were no dead inflatables in the yard.

He made his way up the salted sidewalk and rang the bell. A dour-looking woman with perfectly styled and dyed blonde hair opened the door.

"Yes?"

Pete held up his badge and introduced himself. "Is your father Alfred Troutman?"

"Yes?" In spite of it being an answer, she still made it sound like a question.

"Is he here?"

An assortment of emotions paraded across the woman's face, none of them pleasant. "No. He's not."

The wind was starting to pick up, swirling the snow. "Do you mind if I come inside for a moment?"

The request appeared to startle her. "Oh. Of course." She stepped aside to let him enter and then pushed the door closed.

"Are you expecting your father?" Pete removed his hat, careful to contain the dripping snow to the welcome mat. "I was told he usually comes here for Sunday dinner."

Her expression turned sour. "Yes, he usually does. Yes, we were expecting him."

"Were?"

"My husband drove over to pick him up, but he wasn't there. He's not answering his phone either."

Pete thought of the wicked weather—an old man missing in a winter storm. "Excuse me for saying, but you don't appear concerned."

"Concerned?" She choked a laugh. "My father is notorious for doing what he damned well pleases whether I'm 'concerned' or not."

"I just mean, the elderly do sometimes wander off. If he's outside, missing, in this stuff..." Pete shot a glance toward the door. "...I need to get a team out there searching for him."

Betsy dismissed the notion with a wave of her hand. "He's fine."

"And how do you know this?"

"Because he's my father. He puts on a show of being incompetent, but trust me. He can fare better than anyone I know. He takes great joy in messing up my plans. What I want doesn't matter to him. Never has."

Pete had a feeling he'd walked into an episode of *Dr. Phil*. He tried to imagine Nadine being so indifferent about Harry and couldn't. But once again, here he was, comparing his father to Trout. Nevertheless, Pete intended to find the missing man, whether the daughter cared or not. "Thank you for your time." He moved to put his hat back on.

Betsy jabbed his chest with one manicured finger. "Do you know what my father had the nerve to do?"

"No, ma'am." But Pete suspected he was about to find out.

"He pawned my late mother's necklace. The one she'd promised to me."

"He...pawned it?"

"Yes." Her shoulders rose and fell with a haughty breath. "I've been telling him for a while that I wanted it. That Mother told me it was to come to me after she passed. At first he said he couldn't part with her things yet. Which was fine. I'm not heartless."

The jury was still out on that one.

"But I told him I wanted to wear it to a New Year's Eve party and that's when he told me he didn't have it. Can you believe it? He hocked a family heirloom. I told him to get it back. I'd pay whatever he owed. I just want my necklace." She poked Pete again. "When you find him, you tell him to get it back or...or I'll have you arrest him."

There was so much wrong with this woman's rant that Pete had no idea how to respond. "Yes, ma'am," he said. "If I find him." Pete emphasized the "if" to see how the woman reacted.

She didn't.

Back in his car, Pete mulled over the pawned necklace story. Betsy Malone might be a shrew, but what if her father had given her just cause? Pete had come to doubt the legitimacy of Trout's bewilderment. He'd been lurking around Oriole's house. Why? To cover up evidence of his crime?

He'd likely been aware that someone had been plundering naïve senior citizens in the county. He'd also been aware they'd paid Oriole a visit earlier. Was the old man so down on his luck that not only would he pawn his late wife's jewelry, but also steal from the woman he claimed to care about?

Pete swore at himself for not seeing it sooner.

Nate and Seth were tied up reuniting Marcus with his mother, so Pete punched in another number on his phone.

"It's Sunday. Don't you take a day off?" Baronick said, bypassing all standard greetings.

"I need you and your county boys to help me track down Oriole Andrews' killer."

"You still think we don't already have them?"

"The Naimans may be responsible for the rash of recent burglaries and for assault." They weren't getting off the hook for Zoe's concussion. "But I don't believe they shoved Oriole down those stairs."

"All right. So who are we looking for now?"

Pete dropped the shifter into drive. "Alfred Troutman."

The scream had come from Janie. Of that, Zoe was certain. Had Oriole's killer come back to the scene of his crime? Panicked, Zoe's hand went to her pocket where her phone should be. Only it wasn't. She spun toward the road, hoping to catch Patsy. But the Tundra was long gone.

Zoe tried the doorknob. It turned, and the door clicked open. Inhaling, she tamped down her fear and charged in.

Janie, hands extended out to the side, had her back to the entryway, but wheeled toward Zoe. Standing near the dining room table, Trout clutched a small handgun. His eyes were nearly as wide and frantic as Janie's.

Zoe froze, thoughts tumbling through her head. Why hadn't she accepted the phone Patsy had offered? But even if she had, she couldn't very well ask Trout to hold on a minute while she called Pete. "Wha—" Her voice cracked. She swallowed and tried again. "What's going on?"

Janie took a gliding step to one side, keeping her hands raised.

Trout waved the gun at her. "You stop right there."

Janie obeyed, stiffening.

Zoe realized she was holding her breath. She let it out slowly. "Mr. Troutman, whatever's going on here, you don't need that gun."

He gestured at Janie with it. "Yes, I do. She's crazy."

"I'm not the crazy one." Janie said, her voice shrill. "You are."

"Let's just keep calm. Okay?" Zoe took a closer look at Trout, his hand, and the gun in it. Small, but deadly. A revolver. And the old man's finger rested on the trigger. Keeping her voice low, she said, "Mr. Troutman, why don't you put the gun down so we can talk."

He glanced at her, but kept the weapon trained on Janie. "No." His gaze settled on Janie again. "I just want what's mine."

"It's not yours," Janie said, her tone snippy for someone staring into the mouth of a gun. "You gave it to my grandmother."

"Yes, but I need it back now."

Zoe struggled to understand the argument. "The gun?"

"The necklace." Trout tipped his head toward the dining table in the middle of the room, but kept his focus on Janie.

Zoe risked looking away from the gun to the table. She hadn't noticed before, but an off-white tablecloth covered a lumpy mound. Of what, she couldn't tell. But there was definitely more than a necklace under there. "What necklace?"

"It belonged to my late wife," he said. "Had been in her family for generations. Oriole had admired it, so I gave it to her."

"See?" Janie flicked a finger in his direction. "That's what I said. He gave it to Grandma. I'm her sole heir, so it's mine now."

The photo. The one Zoe and Sylvia and found in the box. The newer picture of Oriole wearing that lovely vintage necklace. "That's what this is all about? A necklace?"

Tears gleamed in the old man's eyes. "I wanted Oriole to have it. But my daughter raised a stink over it. Insisted I get it back."

Zoe tried to make sense of what she was hearing. Of what she was seeing. Trout wanted the necklace back. Oriole refused to return it. They'd fought. And she'd ended up in a heap at the bottom of the basement stairs?

"I got tired of Betsy haranguing me so I told her I'd sold it," Trout said with a self-satisfied nod of his head. He ran his free hand across his eyes and sniffed. "But then Oriole died, so I figured I'd get the necklace back and give it to Betsy just to shut her up." He looked at Zoe, but kept the gun on Janie. "I came over afterwards to get it, but it wasn't in her jewelry box."

Janie slid one foot toward the table. Eased in that direction. Slid the other foot under her. Zoe held the old man's gaze, hoping to keep him from noticing, although she had no idea what Janie had in mind.

"I knew she was searching the house too." Trout waved the gun at the spot where Janie had been, unaware that she'd moved. "And I knew if she found the necklace before I did, I'd never get it back. I guess I was right." He turned toward Janie, only then realizing she'd moved. "Hey."

Before he could bring the gun around, Janie lunged for him.

Zoe followed her lead and leapt forward. Grabbed for the gun. The old man yelped. He raised both arms overhead, the revolver still clutched in his hands. Zoe reached up. Latched onto one arm. Janie clung to his other arm. For an old guy, he was strong, but the two women managed to throw him off balance. He staggered and lurched toward Zoe. For a second, she thought he was going to crash down on top of her.

The gun came loose from his grip. Zoe sensed it sail past her head. She sagged from his weight. Wheeled.

Any other day, she probably could have righted herself. But the concussion sent the room spinning. Or maybe she was the one spinning. Either way, she slammed into the floor, pain searing through her hip and elbow.

Trout hit the ground next to her with a grunt. Janie still had her arms around him. The bandanna she'd been wearing flew off, leaving her hair askew.

The gun.

Zoe twisted, ignoring the pain, and spotted the small revolver a few feet away. She scrambled toward it and scooped it up.

"No," Trout moaned. "No, no, no."

She managed to get her knees under her. Hugging the gun to her chest, she rose to kneeling.

"Are you okay?" Janie squatted next to her, resting a hand on her back.

"I think so. You?"

"Yeah. Give me the gun and let me help you up."

Zoe looked over at Trout. Sprawled on the floor groaning, he seemed like the harmless old man she'd always thought he was.

"No," he groaned.

Her head throbbed and her vision blurred. "Here." She held the revolver out to Janie.

"You don't look so good," she said, taking the gun with one hand, offering the other to Zoe.

"Hitting the floor probably wasn't what the doctor meant by taking it easy." With Janie's help, Zoe climbed to her feet, pressing a hand to her spinning head. "I think I need some air. I'll be fine."

She staggered toward the door. The cold would feel good on her face and in her lungs. Behind her, she heard Trout call out again, "No!"

Zoe turned in time to see Janie, standing over the old man. She lifted the gun. Pointed it at him. And squeezed the trigger.

THIRTY-ONE

The snowstorm had let up, now looking more like the inside of a snow globe than a blizzard. Pete hung up his mic after radioing in an official BOLO for Trout and debating his next stop. The old man wasn't at home and wasn't at his daughter's. Where else could he be?

Oriole's. Of course.

The fact that Pete had taken the key from him meant nothing. The old reprobate probably had a duplicate.

The road back to Vance Township was a slippery mess. Pete dug his phone from his jacket pocket to call Seth. He should have arrived at Oriole's house to pick up Janie a half hour or so ago. Before he could punch in the number, the phone rang in his hand, and Seth's name came up on the screen.

"Is Troutman there?" Pete asked.

"I don't know." Seth sounded winded. "I just arrived at Mrs. Andrews' place. A motorist ran off the road, and I stopped to help."

Pete wasn't surprised. "Troutman might—"

"Chief, there was a shot fired."

Now Pete was surprised. "Where?"

"I think from inside the house. I'd just pulled up and was getting out of my vehicle when I heard it."

Slippery roads be damned. Pete flipped on his lights and sirens, jamming the gas pedal to the floor. "Stay in your vehicle. Radio for backup and wait until it arrives. Do you hear me?"

"Roger that, Chief. Uh. Janie Baker's car is parked here."

"Any others?"

"No, sir."

"Good. I'm on my way. I have Janie's number on my phone. I'm going to call and find out what's going on in there. Then I'll call you back."

"Yes, sir."

Driving one handed while dialing a phone was something Pete would have arrested a civilian for doing. Especially with the current road conditions. The quote "do as I say, not as I do" ran through his head as he located Janie Baker's number and pressed send. The phone rang in his ear. And rang. And rang. Not good. Had the old man gunned down his so-called lady friend's granddaughter?

Just when Pete expected the call to go to voicemail, it connected. "Hello?"

Not the voice he'd anticipated. "Zoe?"

The lively ringtone seemed wildly out of place with the other sounds in the room.

Until now, Zoe's concussion hadn't created hallucinations, but the scene before her was too bizarre to be real. Janie, Zoe's childhood friend, had taken justice into her own hands and shot Trout as he lay helpless on the floor. A pool of sticky crimson immediately appeared at the site of the wound—the upper right quadrant of his abdomen. The ear-splitting blast from the revolver sent Zoe's headache pain to a whole new level of excruciating.

As soon as Janie fired the gun, she'd screamed. Slapped her left hand over her mouth.

But kept a tight grip on the revolver with her right.

The moments that followed were a blur, and not only because Zoe's vision was fogged and her ears were ringing. She stood frozen. Torn between her instinct to jump to Trout's aid and the sight of the gun still aimed at him.

"What on earth did you do that for?" Zoe breathed.

The look of shock and terror on Janie's face didn't mesh with what she'd done and, with her finger against the trigger, appeared ready to do again. A high-pitched keen that sounded like an injured cat rose above the dull bass-drum throb behind Zoe's eyes. She realized the cry was coming from Janie.

"Why did you do that?" Zoe asked once more, louder.

Janie didn't answer but continued the piercing wail.

Trout let out a low moan. "Help me."

Zoe's gaze darted from Janie and the gun to the old man.

She had to stop the bleeding.

Zoe swallowed hard and moved toward Trout.

The crying ceased. "No." Janie's voice was pitched higher than usual.

Zoe paused a moment. Then continued to inch toward him. "If I don't treat him, he's going to die. You don't want that on your conscience, do you?"

Janie caught her lower lip in her teeth and started with the high-pitched squeal again.

Which was the moment the ringtone went off.

Not Zoe's phone. Wrong tone, plus hers was still being held as evidence. The sound was coming from Janie's pocket.

"That's your phone." Zoe fought to keep her voice calm and matter-of-fact.

Janie didn't budge. She seemed to have been turned to granite. A mewing statue with a ringing cell phone in her pocket and a very real gun in her hand.

"It could be important." Zoe extended a hand, palm open, to her. "If you don't want to answer, give it to me." What she really wanted was the gun, but she sensed Janie was more likely to give up the phone.

Still no movement.

Trout pressed a hand to his bloody abdomen. "Help me."

The whining stopped long enough for Janie to say, "No."

Zoe wasn't sure if she was replying to the old man's plea or to her request for the phone. She inched closer.

Janie must have noticed the movement. The keening stopped, and she swung around, bringing the gun with her. Zoe stared at the muzzle and stepped back.

The phone continued to ring. Any moment now it would stop. Voicemail would snatch the call that could be Zoe's only hope to get Trout and her out of here. Alive. "Please, Janie. Let me have your phone." A thought popped into her throbbing head. "It might be Marcus."

Janie blinked. Her eyes shifted. But the gun remained steady.

Zoe reached her open palm toward Janie.

She pivoted back toward Trout, leveling the revolver at him once again. He moaned and closed his eyes.

"Janie, don't," Zoe said as forcefully as she dared.

Janie plunged her left hand into her pocket, came up with the ringing phone. "Here." She tossed it to Zoe.

She didn't take the time to check the ID, but quickly hit the green button, hoping it wasn't too late. "Hello?"

"Zoe?"

Hearing Pete's voice on the other end, she exhaled. "Yeah."

"What the hell's going on there?"

She longed to blurt the whole thing out. But how would Janie react? "We need an ambulance," Zoe said quietly.

She heard Pete's sharp intake of breath. "Are you hurt?"

"No. I'm fine."

Janie started with the wailing again.

"Good lord, what is that?" Pete asked.

"Janie."

"Trout shot her? Is he holding the gun on you?"

"No." Zoe lowered her voice as much as she could. "Janie thinks Trout killed Oriole so she shot him. I think she's having some kind of psychotic break, and she still has the gun. I need to convince her to let me stop his bleeding. Send the ambulance." She moved to end the call before Janie decided to squeeze off another shot, but Pete's voice calling her name made her bring the phone back to her ear. "Yeah?"

"Seth is right outside. I'm on my way along with backup."

Tears burned her eyes. She could only pray Trout would be alive when they arrived. "Tell Seth Janie's armed and isn't thinking clearly." She wanted to say she's out of her mind, but didn't dare. "Pete?"

"Yeah?"

"I love you." She thumbed the red button, ending the call.

Janie didn't react to any of the information Zoe had given over the phone. Zoe wondered if she'd even heard any of it. She acted almost catatonic.

Except she still kept the gun trained on Trout.

The old man had stopped moaning. His eyes remained open and focused on the gun. His skin had grown paler while his blood drenched his shirt and pooled on the floor under him.

Zoe slid the phone into her coat pocket and slowly reached her open hand toward her friend again. "Janie, give me the gun."

"No," she said, not taking her eyes off Trout.

"Please. Give me the gun so we can sort this mess out."

"No. It's too late."

"Okay then." Zoe kept her arm extended but swung it to point at the old man. "I'm going over to him. I need to stop the bleeding."

"No."

She took one step toward him anyway. "If I don't stop the bleeding, he's gonna die. You don't want that."

"It doesn't matter."

Zoe took another slow, gliding step. "Of course it matters. You don't wanna be responsible for his death."

"It doesn't matter," Janie said, forcefully this time.

"It matters to me." Another step. Two, maybe three more, and she'd be at his side. "You know me. I'm a paramedic." Another step. "I have to help him. It's who I am." Another. "Please. Janie, let me help him."

Zoe looked from Trout to Janie, hoping to judge whether her friend intended to fire the gun again. Janie met her gaze, sighed, and lowered the revolver.

Zoe spotted a winter coat—probably Trout's—draped over the back of one of the dining room chairs. She snatched it and dropped to her knees beside him. Balled the coat up and pressed it against the wound. "Hey, Mr. Troutman." She gave him a practiced smile. "How're you doing?"

Pain filled his damp eyes. "Not so good."

"Stay with me. Help's on the way." She looked up at Janie. "I need some first-aid supplies. Didn't your grandmother have some in the bathroom?" A few Band-Aids weren't going to help, but if she could get Janie—and that gun—out of the way for minute or two...

"I don't think so." Janie sounded exhausted. She took an unsteady step back, but that was as far as she moved.

Zoe rested her fingers on Trout's wrist. "Could you go look?" She stretched her left arm, freeing her watch from her coat sleeve and eyed the sweep second hand.

Janie didn't budge.

The lonesome pulsating wail of sirens from far off seeped through the old house's walls and into the periphery of Zoe's consciousness. "Please?"

"There's nothing left up there. I took everything home so I could go through it." Janie lifted the gun again. Not aiming it this time, but cradling it in her hands and looking at it as if she'd never seen the thing before.

Trout's pulse was rapid and faint. His skin, pale and clammy. The ambulance would be there in another minute or so, but until the scene was secure, the crew wouldn't enter. "Janie, you need to give me the gun."

"No."

"Look, I understand," Zoe lied. "Trout killed your grandmother."

He made a sound deep in his throat and wrapped his bloody fingers around Zoe's wrist.

She ignored his protest, pressing the coat against his belly to slow the blood loss. "He's been lurking around ever since. And today he confronted you alone here in your grandmother's house. Pulled a gun on you. You had no choice but to defend yourself. No one will hold you accountable. But look at him. He can't hurt you or anyone else anymore." She swallowed, her mouth dry. "Give me the gun so we can all get out of here."

"No," Trout said, his raspy voice weak. "I didn't."

The sirens were louder now. Right out front. Janie's phone in Zoe's pocket rang. That would be Pete. She kept pressure on the wound with one hand, reached toward Janie with the other. "Give. Me. The gun."

Janie continued staring at the revolver, her eyes glistening. She closed her fingers around it and clasped it to her chest. "No."

Trout grasped Zoe's arm. "You've got it wrong." He wheezed. "That's her gun. I took it off her right before you got here." Another ragged inhalation. "I didn't kill Oriole." He released his grip to point at Janie. "She did."

For a long moment, the only sound was the muffled but persistent ringtone from Zoe's pocket. Inside her head was another matter as the old man's words replayed and echoed. She looked from him to her friend, expecting an indignant denial. "Janie?"

Deep creases furrowed her brow as tears streamed down her cheeks. "I never meant for any of it to happen. I was angry, but I didn't mean to kill her."

The space behind Zoe's eyes cooled. The chill seized the muscles in her neck and squeezed.

The phone in her pocket fell silent.

She tried to form words. Questions. But only one managed to reach her lips. "Why?"

Janie's laugh bordered on demented. "Money. Stupid, huh?" The anguish on her face turned to anger. "I gave up everything to care for her. I have no life. No husband. No time or energy to date. I couldn't hold down a real job because I had to be at her beck and call. And I didn't mind. At first. I always knew she kept money stashed in this house. But she wouldn't tell me where. And she wouldn't give me any of it." She shot a glance at the table with the covered mound on top then brought her gaze back to Zoe. "I live in a dump I can't fix up. I can't afford new clothes. I have a son who'll be going to college in a few years. Except he won't, because I can't afford tuition. I begged her to give me some of her money. I earned it. But she insisted she didn't have any." Janie gave the hysterical laugh again and tipped her head toward the table. "I finally found it today. Hidden in that little space where you access the plumbing for the bathtub." She looked at Trout. "Your precious necklace was there too."

He closed his eyes and muttered something Zoe couldn't make out.

The phone started ringing again.

Janie waved the gun toward her. "Shut that damn thing off."

Still keeping one hand applying pressure to Trout's wound, Zoe raised the other as if surrendering. "I will. Don't shoot."

Janie's face relaxed. Instead of again clutching the gun to her chest though, she aimed it at Trout.

Moving slowly, Zoe reached into her pocket to retrieve the phone. She glanced at it. Similar to her own, but slightly different. She hoped Janie would assume she was trying to find the location of the button to turn it off. In a way, she was. She held it up so Janie could watch. Gripped the phone as if powering it down. But angled it to disguise what she was really doing—swiping the answer button.

* * *

"Pick up the damn phone," Pete growled. His previous attempt had gone to voicemail. He stood outside his vehicle, his eyes on the house. Around him, county police were making plans to set up a perimeter. The county SERT team was on its way with their heavy equipment and snipers. Pete needed intel from Zoe and he needed it now.

The ringback tone in his ear stopped, replaced by muffled scraping sounds.

"Zoe?"

"I can't stop the bleeding." It was Zoe's voice, but distant. "Janie, please give me the gun so we can get him some help."

"No." Janie's voice. Even more distant. "It's too late."

"It's not. You didn't mean to kill your grandmother. I know you didn't. We can get help for you too."

What? Did Zoe just say Janie killed Oriole?

He knew immediately what was going on. Zoe had answered the phone, but not to speak with him. To let him eavesdrop on what was transpiring inside the house. He plugged his other ear, straining to hear. But the approaching sirens drowned out the faint conversation. He ducked inside his vehicle and closed the door against the extraneous noises.

"I don't know," Janie was saying when he could hear again. "Maybe I did mean it. I was so angry that night. I pleaded with her to give me some cash. I had bills. Marcus needed new clothes for school. You know what she said? She told me I needed to learn to budget better. Budget! What a joke. You need money coming in to have a budget. More money than what I make doing odd jobs and selling stuff online. But she never wanted me to get a real job. She needed me to take care of her. To drive her to the doctor and to the store."

There was some other noise on the line. Another voice. Male. Too weak for Pete to understand. Trout.

"Hang on, Mr. Troutman." Zoe's voice. "Help is on its way." More background sounds. "Janie, please let me get him out of here."

But Janie apparently ignored Zoe's plea. "I was so fed up with her. With her demands on my time. With her insistence that I just needed to take responsibility and act like a grownup. How the hell was I supposed to act like a grownup when she treated me like a child? No. Not like a child. More like her personal slave. That's what I told her that night. We argued."

The phone fell silent for a moment, and Pete looked at the screen, fearing the call had been dropped. But the screen remained active. Then another sound came through the speaker. The high-pitched whine he'd heard when he called the first time.

After a moment, it stopped. "We were in the hallway by the basement door." Janie's voice again, but more anguished than angry. "I was going through that chest of drawers, hoping to find the stash. Gram caught me. Called me a spoiled, money-hungry brat. Can you imagine? I got so mad, I grabbed her. We struggled. But—I don't remember her falling. I guess I shoved her. Or she tried to pull away from me. I don't know. I just remember a scream. And then she was at the bottom of the steps. Dead. I thought."

"Mr. Troutman? Mr. Troutman?" Zoe's voice had that urgent tone Pete had heard before. The old man was going to die if they didn't act. Now.

Pete muted the phone and stepped out of his vehicle. Baronick had arrived and was huddled with Seth, Nate, and the county officers. Pete caught his attention and waved him over. "Nate. Seth. You too," he called.

"SERT's five minutes out," Baronick said.

Pete glanced toward the house. "We don't have five minutes."

THIRTY-TWO

Zoe felt for a pulse. It was there, but getting fainter and faster by the moment. "Stay with me, Mr. Troutman." His eyes had closed. She looked up at Janie, who had started pacing, the gun no longer aimed, but still firmly clenched in her hand. "You need to put the gun down so we can get help in here." Zoe wasn't coaxing or pleading anymore. That hadn't worked, and the old man was paying the price.

Janie stopped and eyed the weapon as if she didn't realize she still held it.

But she didn't put it down. "No. They're gonna want to send me to the electric chair for killing my grandmother."

Zoe didn't think now was the time to point out that Pennsylvania used lethal injection. "No, they won't. There're extenuating circumstances. A good lawyer will make a case for temporary insanity. But you have to put the gun down. Now."

Janie continued to stare at the revolver in her hands, appearing to consider her options.

From the corner of her eye, Zoe spotted movement in the entryway. Janie didn't seem to notice Pete and Seth steal up to the dining-room door—until a floorboard creaked.

She spun toward them, gun in hand. Pete and Seth both raised their sidearms.

"No," Zoe cried.

Everyone froze as if time stopped for a moment. Pete met Zoe's gaze, and she noticed his eyes shift to take in the situation. She could only imagine what he was seeing and thinking. She had blood up to her elbows. Trout's blood. The old man's color had grown gray, his respirations shallow.

Then Janie moved. She lifted the muzzle of the revolver to under her chin.

"No," Zoe said again. "Janie, don't."

Her face had contorted, tears wetting her cheeks. "I can't go to jail."

Pete glanced at Seth, who kept his gun trained on the woman and eased along the wall, circling behind her. Pete held up his left hand. Slowly holstered his sidearm. "Let's not do anything rash."

Janie's eyes darted from him to Seth. She sidestepped. "Stop. I'll do it. I swear I will."

Zoe's throat constricted. "You don't wanna do this. Think of Marcus."

The mewing began again. "He's all I've ever thought of. He loved Gram. And I took her away from him. I'm a horrible person."

"Not horrible." Pete had both hands raised now. "You've been under duress. You snapped. Everyone will understand. Give me the gun so we can talk about it."

"There's nothing to talk about." Janie's finger tightened on the trigger.

Zoe half rose from her kneeling position next to Trout. "Yes, there is," she said. "You've been a good mom to Marcus. I know it's been rough, but we'll get you help."

Zoe spotted Janie's eye twitch at the mention of her son's name. "Trust me, you don't want Marcus to go through the rest of his life knowing his mom committed suicide. That's too much of a burden to put on a kid his age. He loves you."

Janie locked her gaze onto Zoe, her eyes so filled with tears Zoe wondered how she could see. "I love him too. Be sure you tell him that."

"You tell him," Pete said. "Just put the gun down and we'll let you see him and tell him anything you want."

"Please, Janie," Zoe said. "You don't want the image of you killing yourself to haunt your son the rest of his life, do you?"

Janie appeared to weigh Zoe's words. The tension in her face relaxed. "No. You're right."

For a fleeting moment, Zoe believed Janie had decided to surrender. To not take her own life.

Then Janie tipped her head toward the table. "Make sure Marcus gets the money."

Before Zoe could process the meaning of the words, Janie extended her arm and pointed the muzzle of the gun—at Zoe.

And a gunshot exploded inside the room.

THIRTY-THREE

"Get EMS in here now," Pete bellowed over the radio as he leapt to Zoe's side.

"Hold this." She took his hand and placed it on the blood-soaked jacket she'd been using to slow Trout's blood loss.

"Got it." Pete wanted to ask her if she was okay, but thanks to Seth, there would be time for that later.

She jumped to her feet and rushed to Janie's crumpled form.

Seth's face had lost all trace of color. He kept his gun directed at the young woman he'd just shot until he managed to slide the revolver she'd dropped well out of reach with his foot.

The front door banged open. Baronick, weapon drawn, burst in ahead of two paramedics with their gear. He surveyed the scene before holstering his gun and waving the medics in.

The pair split up, one moving to Zoe's side, the other dropping to his knees next to Pete.

"Are you okay there, Chief?" The medic clipped a pulse oximeter to Trout's finger and strapped a blood-pressure cuff to his arm.

"Yep."

Zoe's back was to Pete, so he couldn't see her expression. Nor could he see much of Janie. What he did see wasn't moving.

Baronick crossed to stand over Pete. "What the hell just happened?"

He explained how Janie threatened to shoot herself. As long as she kept the gun pressed to her own chin, Seth wouldn't shoot. Janie must have decided the only sure way she could get him to end her life would be to threaten someone else. Zoe.

Baronick swore under his breath.

"We need a second ambulance," the medic working with Zoe

called out.

The detective pulled his phone from his pocket. "On it."

The medic taking vitals on Trout raised one finger. "Hold up a minute." He placed the stethoscope on the old man's chest.

Only then did Pete take a good hard look at Trout. His face had lost its ruddy tint, his lips weren't quite blue, but nor were they pink. Most telling, his eyelids had opened, revealing an unfocused gaze.

The medic touched Pete's arm. "You can stop holding pressure." To Baronick, he said, "No need for that second ambulance." Then he gathered his gear and crossed to their other patient.

Pete sat back. The oximeter remained clipped to Trout's finger, registering nothing. Dammit. He'd been right about the old coot all along. He wasn't a killer. Just a harmless old man in love with the neighbor lady. Looking at him now, Pete again saw his pop—and brushed his sleeve across the sudden burst of heat behind his eyes.

Across the room, Zoe and her two colleagues were working frantically on the young woman Pete had dismissed as a suspect. Mousy, invisible Janie Baker. One of the paramedics climbed to his feet and headed for the door, calling for Baronick to give him a hand. Zoe rose up on her knees. Pete recognized the position. And the subsequent smooth up and down of chest compressions.

He got to his feet. Ignored the screaming pain in his knees. With one more glance at Trout's body, he moved to the table and tossed back the linen cloth. He wasn't sure what he'd expected, but the bundles of twenty-dollar bills shoved into a dozen or so gallon plastic bags stunned him. If he'd had to guess, he'd estimate there was at least thirty grand piled there. A velvety hinged box perched on top of the cash. He flipped it open to reveal a necklace. Vintage. Obviously the treasure the old man had been searching for. And for which he'd lost his life.

Pete turned away from the bounty and moved to Seth's side. "Are you okay?"

The young officer never took his gaze from the woman he'd shot. "Not really."

Pete clapped a hand to Seth's shoulder. "You saved Zoe's life."

"Did I?"

Pete understood what he meant without asking. Would Janie

really have pulled the trigger? There was no way to know. With a
suicide by cop, there were always unanswered questions.

And from the looks of it, those questions would remain that way.

A late January thaw raised temperatures to near forty under a dull gray
Saturday sky. Mounds of dirty snow edged roads, and melted slop
pooled in ruts and ditches.

Standing shoulder to shoulder, Zoe and Patsy leaned against the
front of Zoe's pickup and watched a team of professionals install a
four-rail composite fence around the small pasture next to the barn.

Zoe's barn.

"Where did you get the money for this?" Zoe had her suspicions,
but asked anyway.

Patsy didn't take her eyes from the workmen. "I'm not at liberty to
discuss it." She glanced askance at Zoe, a trace of a smile on her face.

"My mother."

Patsy shrugged. "She didn't think you'd accept the money from
her, so she gave it to me to get the repairs started."

With less than a week before they needed to clear out of the
Krolls' barn, Zoe had to admit, her mother had done okay this time.
"Tell her thank you for me."

"Tell her yourself."

Zoe thought about it. After watching Trout and Janie die in front
of her, life seemed more precious. Holding grudges, especially over
money, seemed ludicrous. A phone call might not patch things up, but
it might ease their long-held tension. "I will."

The answer drew Patsy's full, stunned attention. "Good."

They spent a couple of quiet moments watching the fencing crew
dig postholes with a massive auger attached to the back of their tractor.

"I want one of those," Patsy said.

"The auger or the tractor?"

"Both."

Zoe snorted. "I'll ask my mother to buy you one."

Patsy snickered. "By the way, how's Sylvia?"

"Crabby. Her cardiologist ordered her to lose fifty pounds."

"Think she'll do it?"

Zoe remembered the brisk walk around Dillard's streets she'd taken with Sylvia that morning. The woman griped the entire way—except when Zoe had suggested they take a break. "Oh, no," she'd said, "we have another mile to go."

"Yeah." Zoe grinned. "I think she will."

At the slushy rumble of an approaching vehicle behind them, Zoe looked over her shoulder. She'd expected Pete to meet them, but it was Lauren's gray sedan pulling up behind the pickup. She climbed out attired in her same dark wool coat, but wearing what appeared to be new barn boots on her feet.

"Isn't that the reporter from the nursing home?" Patsy asked.

"Lauren Sanders. Yep."

As Lauren approached, Zoe officially introduced the two women and added, "I didn't expect to see you here."

Lauren shook Patsy's hand then gazed out at the pasture, a smile lighting her face. "I wanted to check the place out. And to ask..." She met Zoe's eyes, her smile turning nervous. "...are you planning to board horses?"

Zoe once again thought she knew where this was headed. "I'll have to, just to make ends meet."

"Because I would really like to buy one, and it would be great if I could keep it with someone I trust."

The trust thing caught Zoe off guard. "The only problem is I'm kind of limited right now. Until I can afford to expand, I only have four stalls." She held up four fingers and ticked them off. "My horse. Patsy's Arabian. And two current boarders at the Krolls' place who don't have anywhere else to go and already asked."

Lauren's disappointment was palpable. "Oh."

Patsy bumped Zoe with an elbow, but directed her question to the reporter. "How well can you ride?"

"I took lessons for quite a while. My instructor said I was a natural."

Zoe feigned a critical scowl. "Have you ever fallen off?"

Lauren looked down sheepishly. "Yeah. Once."

"Good."

The reporter lifted her face, her brow furrowed. "Good?"

"Yeah," Patsy said with a grin. "You aren't a real rider until you've hit the ground at least once. The reason I asked...I'm going to Florida for a couple of weeks next month. If you're willing to jump in and pick up my slack with the barn work, I'll let you ride Jazzel."

Zoe had seen kids at Christmas who were less excited.

Lauren clapped her hands. "Yes."

Patsy held up a hand in a stop gesture. "Jazzel can be a handful. You'll need to lunge her first to wear her down." She glanced at Zoe, nonverbally asking for help.

Zoe nodded.

"And only supervised rides," Patsy added, "until we're convinced you can handle her."

"Fine. Great. Yes. Whatever you say."

A white SUV slowed on the road in front of the farm. Pete. He made the turn into the driveway, slowing even more to splash through the water-filled ruts.

"This place has gotten to be the local hot spot," Patsy said.

One of the workmen hollered and waved. Zoe pushed away from the pickup, but Patsy caught her arm. "I'll go. You have company."

A minute or so later, Pete strode up. "Hey, Beautiful." He pressed a quick kiss to Zoe's lips, sending a tingle along her spine.

Remembering her jealousy, she glanced at Lauren, who had looked away. In spite of all that had happened, Zoe still suspected the reporter had a thing for Pete. But the important part was that he only had eyes for Zoe. "Hey, yourself."

He slipped an arm around her waist, and she leaned against him, grateful for his warmth and strength. To Lauren, he said, "I'm glad to see you here. I was going to call you later about Golden Oaks."

The reporter crossed her arms. "Didn't Zoe tell you? I dug as deeply as I could and didn't find anything out of the ordinary. In fact, I might just move in there myself. Your dad is perfectly safe."

Zoe felt Pete tense.

Lauren pressed her lips together, trying not to laugh. "You know, you could have told me the person calling the place into question was your father."

Pete made a couple of false starts at responding and then said, "Yeah, I guess. But that's not what I wanted to talk to you about anyway."

"Oh? What then?"

"Barbara Naiman."

Zoe looked up at Pete. She had no idea what he was talking about, but a glance at Lauren told her the reporter did.

"Oh," Lauren said.

Zoe tugged at Pete's jacket. "What's going on with Barbara?"

He shot a look at Lauren. "Go ahead and tell her. She's going to dig it out of one of us."

Lauren squirmed. "I didn't want anyone to know."

When she didn't say any more, Zoe elbowed Pete. "Someone tell me already."

Pete waited, but Lauren remained silent. "All right, I'll tell her." He looked at Zoe. "Lauren anonymously paid one year in advance for Barbara's stay at Golden Oaks."

Stunned, Zoe met Lauren's sheepish gaze. Wow. She'd had the reporter pegged wrong. All wrong. "How? Why?" Zoe stuttered.

Lauren shrugged. "I live rather modestly. My father made a killing in the stock market years ago and left it all to me when he died. And I felt bad for Barbara." She looked at Pete. "And for your dad. He's quite fond of her, you know."

"Yeah. I know. I owe you," Pete said. "I just came from visiting Pop and he's as content as I've seen him in years. The move and this...'friendship' with Barbara have been the best thing that could happen to him. Thank you."

Lauren beamed. "You and your dad are very welcome."

Pete cleared his throat. "I've heard rumors Barbara isn't the only beneficiary of your generosity."

Zoe looked from him to Lauren and back. Good thing she wasn't jealous anymore. He seemed to know an awful lot about the reporter, none of which he'd shared with her over breakfast that morning.

Lauren turned up her collar to hide a blush. "I'm late for an appointment. Zoe, please thank Patsy for me. I'll be in touch." She turned and picked her way through the slop back to her car.

Once the sedan had turned and was headed to the road, Zoe faced Pete. "Now what about Lauren's generosity?"

He buried his hands in his jacket pockets. "I just found out she's spoken with Children and Youth Services about fostering Marcus

Baker."

Zoe blinked against an unexpected threat of tears as she watched Lauren turn onto the road and speed away. Memories of Janie thundered over her. From the kids in school taunting her with calls of "Plain Jane" to the quiet, submissive caregiver to her grandmother and the worrisome mother to her fatherless boy.

After the shooting, they'd learned that Marcus had suspected his mother was responsible for his grandmother's death. He'd confessed he knew Janie owned the gun she'd claimed had been stolen from Oriole, but he'd kept quiet to protect her.

Marcus finding a home with Lauren Sanders might be the best thing for him. And for Lauren as well.

It troubled Zoe that she couldn't close her eyes without seeing Janie bleeding out and dying. In time that image might fade, leaving her to remember the woman who'd been her friend. But that last memory led her to another. "Did you talk to Seth?" Officially, the young officer who'd saved her life was on desk duty. However, he'd taken a leave of absence after the shooting and hadn't been returning Pete's phone calls.

"I swung by his house on my way here. Woke him up." Pete gazed into the distance, his eyes narrowing. "The kid looks awful. Hasn't shaved. I don't think he's washed his dishes or taken out his trash in a week."

Not the news she'd hoped for.

"Taking a life isn't like they make it out to be on the cop shows."

She stepped closer to Pete, slinging an arm through his and pressing against him. "You're thinking about the boy you shot years ago. Donnie Moreno?"

"No." A sad smile drew Pete's lip up on one side and he met her gaze. "Maybe."

"Do you think it would help if I stopped by to see Seth?"

"I think that would be nice."

"Okay. I'll head there after I drop Patsy off at her house. Maybe I'll even wash Seth's dishes for him."

"Don't spoil him." Pete chuckled. "He'll expect you to keep house for him all the time."

"No way." She nodded toward the rundown house. "As far as

housekeeping goes, I have enough to deal with. Thanks to my mother's 'gift.'"

He slipped his hands from his pockets and slid them around Zoe's waist, pulling her close. "So you're really planning to move out here?"

"Eventually. But there's a lot of work to do first."

"I warned you."

"I can do some of it after I move in."

She felt the grumbled response in his chest more than heard it. "But in the meantime, is it okay if I stay where I am?"

He pressed a kiss to the top of her head. "You know it is."

"And you never know. You might get tired of your place."

Pete tensed. "What?"

Zoe hid her smile against the front of his jacket. "Have you ever considered living on a farm?"

ANNETTE DASHOFY

USA Today bestselling author Annette Dashofy has spent her entire life in rural Pennsylvania surrounded by cattle and horses. When she wasn't roaming the family's farm or playing in the barn, she could be found reading or writing. After high school, she spent five years as an EMT on the local ambulance service, dealing with everything from drunks passing out on the sidewalk to mangled bodies in car accidents. These days, she, her husband, and their spoiled cat, Kensi, live on property that was once part of her grandfather's dairy.

**Books in the Zoe Chambers Mystery Series
by Annette Dashofy**

Henery Press Mystery Books

And finally, before you go...
Here are a few other mysteries
you might enjoy:

SHADOW OF DOUBT

Nancy Cole Silverman

A Carol Childs Mystery (#1)

When a top Hollywood Agent is found poisoned in her home, suspicion quickly turns to one of her two nieces. But Carol Childs, a reporter for a local talk radio station doesn't believe it. The suspect is her neighbor and friend, and also her primary source for insider industry news. When a media frenzy pits one niece against the other—and the body count starts to rise—Carol knows she must save her friend from being tried in courts of public opinion.

But even the most seasoned reporter can be surprised, and when a Hollywood psychic shows warns Carol there will be more deaths, things take an unexpected turn. Suddenly nobody is above suspicion. Carol must challenge both her friendship and the facts, and the only thing she knows for certain is the killer is still out there and the closer she gets to the truth, the more danger she's in.

Available at booksellers nationwide and online

Visit www.henerypress.com for details

FATAL BRUSHSTROKE

Sybil Johnson

An Aurora Anderson Mystery (#1)

A dead body in her garden and a homicide detective on her doorstep...Computer programmer and tole-painting enthusiast Aurora (Rory) Anderson doesn't envision finding either when she steps outside to investigate the frenzied yipping coming from her own back yard. After all, she lives in a quiet California beach community where violent crime is rare and murder even rarer.

Suspicion falls on Rory when the body buried in her flowerbed turns out to be someone she knows—her tole-painting teacher, Hester Bouquet. Just two weeks before, Rory attended one of Hester's weekend seminars, an unpleasant experience she vowed never to repeat. As evidence piles up against Rory, she embarks on a quest to identify the killer and clear her name. Can Rory unearth the truth before she encounters her own brush with death?

Available at booksellers nationwide and online

Visit www.henerypress.com for details

KILLER IMAGE

Wendy Tyson

An Allison Campbell Mystery (#1)

As Philadelphia's premier image consultant, Allison Campbell helps others reinvent themselves, but her most successful transformation was her own after a scandal nearly ruined her. Now she moves in a world of powerful executives, wealthy, eccentric ex-wives and twisted ethics.

When Allison's latest Main Line client, the fifteen-year-old Goth daughter of a White House hopeful, is accused of the ritualistic murder of a local divorce attorney, Allison fights to prove her client's innocence when no one else will. But unraveling the truth brings specters from her own past. And in a place where image is everything, the ability to distinguish what's real from the facade may be the only thing that keeps Allison alive.

Available at booksellers nationwide and online

Visit www.henerypress.com for details

PROTOCOL

Kathleen Valenti

A Maggie O'Malley (#1)

Freshly minted college graduate Maggie O'Malley embarks on a career fueled by professional ambition and a desire to escape the past. As a pharmaceutical researcher, she's determined to save lives from the shelter of her lab. But on her very first day she's pulled into a world of uncertainty. Reminders appear on her phone for meetings she's never scheduled with people she's never met. People who end up dead.

With help from her best friend, Maggie discovers the victims on her phone are connected to each other and her new employer. She soon unearths a treacherous plot that threatens her mission—and her life. Maggie must unlock deadly secrets to stop horrific abuses of power before death comes calling for her.

Available at booksellers nationwide and online

Visit www.henerypress.com for details